To Lindsey

K B Douglas has worked in the retail sector and *Hell Hath No Fury* is his first published work. He is in a settled long-term relationship and spends his time between the New Forest, Exmoor and the Republic of Ireland.

Best Wishes
Keith
x

K B Douglas

HELL HATH NO FURY

AUSTIN MACAULEY PUBLISHERS™
LONDON * CAMBRIDGE * NEW YORK * SHARJAH

Copyright © K B Douglas (2021)

The right of K B Douglas to be identified as author of this work has been asserted by the author in accordance with section 77 and 78 of the Copyright, Designs and Patents Act 1988.

All rights reserved. No part of this publication may be reproduced, stored in a retrieval system, or transmitted in any form or by any means, electronic, mechanical, photocopying, recording, or otherwise, without the prior permission of the publishers.

Any person who commits any unauthorised act in relation to this publication may be liable to criminal prosecution and civil claims for damages.

This is a work of fiction. Names, characters, businesses, places, events, locales, and incidents are either the products of the author's imagination or used in a fictitious manner. Any resemblance to actual persons, living or dead, or actual events is purely coincidental.

A CIP catalogue record for this title is available from the British Library.

ISBN 9781528982375 (Paperback)
ISBN 9781528982382 (Hardback)
ISBN 9781528982399 (ePub e-book)

www.austinmacauley.com

First Published (2021)
Austin Macauley Publishers Ltd
25 Canada Square
Canary Wharf
London
E14 5LQ

My thanks to all at Austin Macauley for their guidance and to Katrina Thompson without whose help this wouldn't have been written.

Chapter One

"Absolutely ridiculous, I've just spent a week with my sister on a health farm getting detoxed. Then I popped into Tesco on my way home for a bottle of wine and a packet of cigarettes and they don't sell packs of ten anymore."

"It's to stop the kids buying them, Mum," Jennifer Walsh said patiently to her mother, Katherine Reynolds.

"That's what the girl in the kiosk said; more or less. She said it's to make people smoke less, surely buying smaller packs would do that. I expect I'll only smoke one or two of them anyway."

"I know I'll risk sounding stupid, Mum, but why get detoxed if you're going to smoke and drink straight away."

"It's my treat, Jen. I bought a pizza as well. The whole week was for Aunty Doreen's benefit. Detoxing is the last thing I need, I haven't smoked since the funeral and a glass of wine is rare enough these days. Anyway, enough of that; I called to see if you'd all like to come over tomorrow evening for tea. There's a few things I need to discuss with you."

"We can't really make it tomorrow, Mum; Danny has arranged to take us all to the pictures. I'm finishing early, Becky is going to lock up and put the keys through our letter box on her way home."

"She's very young to be doing that, isn't she?"

"I'll be there until we close, I'm only leaving her to finish cleaning up. Elaine will be upstairs if she needs anything. We could pop over this evening for a couple of hours if it's important."

"Not a chance, young lady, tonight is my treat to myself after putting up with a neurotic sister for a week and living on salad and carrot juice. I'm having a pizza with some wine for dinner, then I'm going to smoke one of my very expensive cigarettes, drink some more wine and go to bed with a good book. What time does the film start tomorrow?"

"We're going to the five o'clock screening. The twins want a McDonalds before we go in."

"You'll be out by seven, come in on your way home, you can all stay over if you like; I've had two bedrooms decorated while I was away."

"Are you going to start using your own bedroom again?"

"He's been gone nine months, Jen, time to move on."

"I'm pleased, Mum. We can't really do that tomorrow; we'd have to go back home from Bournemouth to pick Snowy up and then come all the way back to your place."

"Nonsense; drop her off on your way over."

"Have you forgiven Danny yet?"

"I was never really cross with him, Jen, I just thought he needed to suffer for a while. Don't tell him that please."

"For such a lovely person, you've a bit of a cruel streak, Mum. Okay, we'll bring Snowy in about half past three, have our treat and come in on the way back. The twins want to see you, they missed you this week."

"I missed them as well, Jen, I don't know where I'd have been without them since Mark died."

Jennifer sensed that her mother was getting upset. "I've got to go; Danny and the terrible two just came in. If they get past the kitchen, the house will smell of wet dog for a week. We'll see you tomorrow afternoon. Love you, Mum."

"Bye, Jen. Love you too, say hi to Danny and the twins. Look forward to seeing you."

After she put the telephone down, Katherine felt a little empty. Her husband, Mark, had died nine months previously after battling cancer for nearly five years. Katherine had refused to let him go to a hospice and had nursed him at home through the last year when it became clear that it was terminal. After he died, she felt that life wasn't worth carrying on without him. Luckily her daughter and her family saw her through the worst of it and for the last few months she'd been a lot more positive.

She got the wine out of the fridge, decided that it was chilled enough and poured herself a small glass. Then she turned to the pile of letters on the kitchen table. Her neighbour had been in while she was away to check the house so all the junk mail had been put in the recycling bag.

After she'd dealt with the day-to-day mail, she opened the first of two large envelopes that she knew would be waiting there on her return. Even though she knew the contents she still felt nervous slitting them open.

The first one was from the solicitors confirming that the last of her late husband's estate had been dealt with. Katherine knew the contents of the will but still spent half an hour going through the details. She winced a little when she saw the fee for the administration and even more when she saw that she'd had to pay some inheritance tax on the legacy to Jennifer.

The second letter was from the local council planning authority confirming a telephone conversation of two days previously. The factory site that they'd run the business from for more than thirty years had been approved for housing. As it was near to local facilities and housing was desperately needed in the village no one at the authority had objected and the site had been approved for re-zoning.

Katherine was in two minds about the huge impact that any decisions she made could have. Mark had opened the factory on a much smaller scale soon after they were married. Gradually, the business built up and they moved to the current site. The factory next door had gone out of business so they'd bought that site for storage and car parking. The announcement was due to be made public the following Wednesday although most people already knew that it was a foregone conclusion.

She knew that forty-two people depended on her keeping the factory open, some of them had worked for Mark and herself since leaving school and were now middle-aged. She was the sole shareholder of the business and freehold site and felt duty bound to stand by her loyal staff.

Until Mark had become ill Katherine had been by his side through all the ups and downs of running a business. They'd borrowed large amounts over the years to buy machinery and the next-door factory, once or twice they'd been close to the point of no return but had bounced back and the business was now hugely successful. As soon as Mark wasn't able to function, two of his senior staff had taken over running the business.

After the funeral Katherine returned to work, mostly to fill her days. Pete Jenkins and Gavin Spence had done a sterling job and had signed several new contracts. They knew the site was being considered for housing and both were concerned about the future.

After sitting at the table for an hour reading the letters and taking in the enormity of things Katherine decided that she needed some treats. She put her pizza in the oven and poured herself a second glass of wine.

While the pizza was cooking, she made a second telephone call to an old friend of Marks who ran a garage in the village and had helped to look after their classic car since they'd inherited it from Marks father.

"Hi, Les, Katherine Reynolds, sorry to trouble you."

"Never any trouble talking to you, Katherine. Everything all right?"

"Probably as right as it ever will be, Les. I've decided to get the work done on the Jaguar and have it back on the road. You did say to call you as soon as I'd made my mind up."

"I'm pleased; I thought you might have wanted to sell it."

"You told me you'd buy it off me, Les."

"Have you seen what they're fetching now, everyone wants classic cars. Maybe if you let it go half-price to an old friend, I'd be in with a chance."

"Can you pick it up please and get it all done in a couple of months?"

"Of course, are the combinations still the same to get in the garage and the key safe?"

"Yes. Just come and get it whenever it's convenient please, Les, and keep me up to speed on how it's going."

"Probably over the weekend and I'll try and get it done by the end of April."

"Thanks, Les, speak to you soon."

David Reynolds, her father-in-law had bought a brand-new E-Type Jaguar in nineteen seventy-two. He'd rarely used it and when he died Mark inherited it. Mark and Les restored it to a brand-new condition and it had been kept in a heated garage and used sparingly. He'd been a member of the Jaguar owners club and the car had won several awards at the shows.

When Mark fell ill and they realised it wouldn't be used he asked his old friend Les Davies to de-commission it so that it could be stored safely. All the fluids were drained, the battery and wheels removed and the car was put up on stands. They'd applied grease and wax everywhere that was vulnerable and covered it in loose sheets. With the temperature of the garage constant Les told them it could be left like that for several years with little damage.

Katherine had decided that she wanted to keep the car and use it for its purpose rather than keep as an investment and for showing.

When she heard the alarm in the kitchen tell her that her pizza was ready, she went through and took it out of the oven.

She went to the family room, switched the television on and poured herself another glass of wine. She managed to eat three-quarters of it and left the rest to have as a cold snack the next day.

After she'd eaten, she checked the television schedules and decided that nothing was worth watching until *Inspector Morse* came on at nine o'clock. She put her a disc of her favourite opera in the player and turned the volume up. The nearest house was far enough away that her passion for opera didn't upset the neighbours. In fact the nearest neighbour Daphne had told her how much she enjoyed it when she was out in the garden and could hear some of it.

The next part of her evening involved going through the conservatory that joined onto the family room and into the large garden. She could hear the overture finish and the first act begin as she opened the pack of cigarettes and had her first one for nearly nine months. After a few puffs she stubbed it out and put the other nineteen in a drawer in the conservatory. Maybe she'd try another one on Saturday but the likelihood was that she'd take them to the factory and leave them in the canteen.

At nine o'clock she sat and watched Morse solve another murder in his own inimitable way. Katherine had seen most of them before but still enjoyed the writing and production. The fact that Morse drove a vintage Jaguar made it worth sitting through two hours for.

At eleven o'clock she put her electric blanket on in the main bedroom and went into the en-suite bathroom for a shower. She'd been sleeping in the spare room for more than two years, firstly because Mark needed the bed to himself while he was ill and after the funeral, she couldn't settle in there with the memories still fresh in her mind. She'd got rid of all the furniture and replaced it with a new pine four-poster bed, dressing table and chest of drawers; while she'd been away the decorator had put new wallpaper up and painted the doors and skirting boards.

As usual, there was a few tears when she got into bed but after reading a few chapters the wine she'd drunk soon sent her off to sleep.

"Where the hell have you been, Rob? Your father has been round here three times tonight looking for you and why the fuck is your phone switched off again?"

Robin Pargeter-Jones took his smartphone out of his pocket and pretended to study it. As soon as he pressed the button on the side, the screen lit up and the message icons flashed.

"Sorry, Mads," he told his wife Madelaine. "It does that on its own sometimes. I'll have to get an upgrade."

He actually knew the reason. As soon as he'd left the office and called into the pub on his way home, he'd switched it off to save being disturbed while he was with his friends. He only usually had two pints during the evening because he was driving but enjoyed a game of snooker and some banter with several regulars that didn't have a wife and children to go home to. He hadn't left until nearly eight-thirty so it was gone nine o'clock when he arrived home. His first move was to get the whisky bottle and a glass from the drinks cabinet.

"Make it a very small one, Rob. Your father is expecting you round there at eight o'clock sharp to take him to the golf course."

"Why can't the lazy old sod drive himself?" Robin moaned "I was looking forward to a drink when I got in and a long lie-in tomorrow morning. Can't you take him?"

"You know full fucking well I can't. I told you I've got to take Claire into Southampton for that interview at nine and then we're going shopping afterwards. Jonathon will be okay while you take the old fool to the course and then you'll have to try and keep him entertained until we get back."

"Where are they anyway?"

"In their rooms; no doubt on Facebook or snapchat telling all their friends how useless their parents are."

"Not fair, Mads," Robin said as he topped his glass up with ginger ale "They don't go without anything."

"Which is just as well because they've no great prospects have they. If Claire gets her place at uni later in the year, she'll be up to her neck in debt till she's about forty. The very best that we can ever hope for is that when your father pops his clogs he leaves it to us. He's been threatening to leave it to your other children."

"Knowing our luck he'll live to be about a hundred and fucking twenty," Robin said gloomily.

Madelaine poured herself a glass of wine. "You'd better take it steady on that," Robin commented "If you're driving Claire to Southampton in the morning."

"It's my second small glass. Cheralyn had to finish early today so by the time I'd fed the old fool, walked the dog and sat down it was gone seven. I thought about keeping you a dinner but of course you'd know that if you'd bothered to answer your phone."

"She's getting unreliable, why did she finish early?"

"I don't fucking know, Rob. Perhaps she got fed up with him groping her. He grabbed my ass when I put his dinner on the table. Then he said it was accidental, silly old sod. I swear I'll slap him if he does it again."

Robin ignored his wife and went through to the kitchen. As usual, the sink was piled with dirty dishes and the fridge was almost empty. He managed to find some bread and made himself a cheese sandwich.

By the time he'd eaten it was nearly ten o'clock. He sat next to Madelaine on the settee and put his arm round her. She shrugged him off straight away.

"Fuck off, Rob," she said angrily "I've got a headache."

"Maybe you should make an appointment at the doctor, Mads. You've had an awful lot of headaches lately."

"Maybe I should, I feel that I'm going to get a lot more as well. Things might improve if you came in from work on time."

"Maybe things would improve if you didn't drink quite as much."

"Maybe I wouldn't drink as much if we didn't have to live in this shitty little house that your father owns. I thought at the very least we'd know about Tuscany by now."

"I'll ring Giovanni on Monday."

Chapter Two

Robin got out of bed at seven-thirty on Saturday morning when he heard the loud rapping on the kitchen door. His wife seemed to be able to sleep through the noise, Robin thought that perhaps she was awake and pretending.

"All right, Dad," he yelled as he went to the door in his dressing gown "No need to wake the whole house."

His father stood at the door dressed in his best golfing clothes. He was seventy-nine years old, stood six feet tall and boasted that he was fitter than most people half his age. A long military career had indoctrinated a creed of early mornings and plenty of exercise.

"Did she tell you that I wanted taking this morning? If you answered your phone, I would have told you myself."

"If by she you mean Madelaine, then yes, Dad; she did tell me that you wanted a lift. Why can't you drive yourself anyway? I was told you wanted to go at eight o'clock."

"By the look of it you were still in bed. I was up at six, had a workout and a bowl of porridge. It's something you should start doing, Rob. Pick me up in twenty-five minutes please."

As soon as he'd finished issuing his instructions, Richard Pargeter-Jones turned and marched down the path. They had a gate linking the two gardens but his father wouldn't use it. Robin heard his footsteps and the clanging of the iron gates at the end of his father's drive.

Robin went back into the kitchen and made two cups of tea. He left his in the kitchen and took the other one to the bedroom for Madelaine. She seemed to be asleep so when he'd dressed, he sat on the bed and shook her.

"Wakey-wakey, Mads, cup of tea on the dressing table. I've got to take The Colonel to his precious golf club. Don't forget you're taking Claire shopping."

"All right, Rob, no need to shout. I'm awake."

"What time will you be back?"

"I'm taking a teenager shopping, could be anytime. Just make sure Jonathon doesn't stay in his room all day please."

As soon as Robin was dressed, he kissed his wife quickly and went downstairs. He sat at the kitchen table for a few minutes drinking his tea and wondering how bad things would get this weekend. The previous Saturday Madelaine had drunk a bottle of wine and decided that she wasn't going to bother shopping for food. Robin had to go to the supermarket to get enough for them to have a Sunday lunch.

At five to eight he cut through the gate into his father's house and knocked on the kitchen door before going in. His father came through straight away.

"Glad you're not late as usual, Rob, we'll have to get my trolley out of the garage on the way."

His father marched out in front of him and opened the garage door. Robin got the golf clubs and pushed them down the drive to the car.

"Why didn't you drive down there yourself, Dad?"

"If you ever listened to what I told you, then you'd know Rob. It's the AGM today. I'm on the course at nine, then it's lunch in the club followed by the meeting. We like to have a few drinks afterwards, I'd be fine to drive but you know how hot the law are these days; they'd get you blowing in the bag for crossing a white line."

"How are you getting home?"

"One of them might drop me off but if not, I'll give you a call. It'll be after four o'clock."

"So I've got to wait in all afternoon in case you ring. Thanks, Dad, that'll be a waste of an afternoon."

"What had you planned then?"

"That's not the point, Dad."

They reached the car and put the golf trolley in the boot. Robin opened the door for his father and then walked round to his side.

"Have you any news for us on this Italian investment Rob? Some of them are getting cold feet. Nothing seems to be happening."

"It's all in hand, Dad, we're waiting on the Italian solicitor."

"Last weekend Eammon Wells and Jack Dawson were talking about pulling out. If they do, we're all out, Rob, you'll have to refund all the deposits. Christ; you haven't used any of it have you?"

The previous November Robin had provisionally agreed to buy a vineyard from a contact in Tuscany. He'd been in the wine trade several years ago, buying crops before they were ready to harvest and importing the wine. He'd rescued Giovanni from bankruptcy and backed him for two seasons until the vineyard was running at a profit. Now Giovanni was retiring he'd offered Robin the chance to buy the vineyard at a favourable price. However, in the banking crisis, Robin had stretched himself too far and the bank had foreclosed on him. He'd lost his house and business and been forced to move into the house next door to his father. Fortunately his father and uncle owned a successful car hire business in Southampton so he was able to work there.

Even at a heavily discounted price Robin needed to raise a million pounds to buy the yard. As a former bankrupt he had no chance of getting the money unless he could put a consortium together. His father and uncle had been talked into investing, a friend from the bar had been left nearly half a million pounds and said he'd invest some of it. His father persuaded seven members of the golf club to invest a hundred thousand pounds each so the syndicate was formed.

The Italian solicitor was being unnecessarily slow and some of the syndicate were getting nervous. Gloomy economic forecasts and the impending departure of Britain from The European Union was creating more tension. Each of the ten members had paid a ten-thousand-pound deposit in January but no progress had been made.

"I'm not a fucking crook, Dad, of course I haven't used any of it. Just tell them to be patient, it'll be the best investment they ever made."

"So you keep telling me. They're all retired Rob, they want security for their funds at their age."

They hardly spoke for the rest of the twenty-minute drive. As soon as they arrived, Richard got out of the car, Robin opened the boot from inside the car and got out to help his father lift his clubs out.

"I can manage," Richard said crossly. "Just make sure you're at home all afternoon please. I'll phone you if I need a lift."

Robin stopped on his way home for a newspaper and on a whim went into Costa for a quick coffee. By the time he got home Madelaine and Claire had left for their shopping trip. His son was still dead to the world and would be until Robin pulled him out of bed.

Even at fifty-eight years old, Katherine still loved not having to get up until she felt like it. She got out of bed at six o'clock on Saturday morning, went downstairs to make tea and took it back to bed with her. She put the local radio on and relaxed for an hour before rising.

After a leisurely breakfast she decided to go to town to visit her daughter and maybe pop into the factory on the off-chance that Pete or Gavin had decided to work. After her wine drinking the evening before she didn't risk driving so she got her bicycle out of the shed and set off at a few minutes after ten o'clock. She got to the shop after an energetic half-hour ride.

"Hi, Mum," Jennifer said cheerily. "I didn't think I'd see you till later. Nothing wrong is there?"

"Of course not, I just needed a few things for tonight and tomorrow and I want to see if there's anyone at the factory."

"You could have phoned, Mum, I'd have brought what you need."

"The ride did me good, Jen. Maybe a coffee would go down well."

The bakery and tea-rooms that Jennifer had opened three years before was quiet "I'm just going out the back with Mum, Becky," Jennifer told the Saturday assistant. "Shout if you need me please."

"She's a real find, Mum," Jennifer said as she made the coffee in the back kitchen. "I'd like to take her on full-time when she leaves school. Her mother wants her to go to college but Becky said she'd much rather come here."

"As long as she's sure this is what she wants. How's the shop been doing this week? You obviously coped without me."

"I missed you, Mum, that's for sure. Elaine helped a few mornings which was nice. The takings were up again and I think we're going to be supplying that hotel from next week. The chef said they were the best quiches they'd ever had."

"Can you cope? They'll need a delivery every day."

"Jason said he'd come in and do the deliveries if we need him. He gets bored now he's retired and he can walk here from his house."

"What about the baking, will you be able to make enough?"

"Stop worrying, Mum, I'll cope just fine. Do you want a Danish with your coffee?"

"Yes, please, Jen."

"Any hints on what you wanted to see me about?"

"I'll tell you tonight, it'll be nice to see the little ones."

"They're thrilled to bits, I told them we're staying over. Josh said can he have chips for lunch on Sunday please."

"He most certainly cannot, Jen," Katherine said. "We're having a Sunday roast."

They made small talk about Katherine's younger sister, Doreen, for a few minutes until Becky called for some help serving in the shop. Katherine finished her coffee and said goodbye to Jennifer on her way out.

Ten minutes later, she arrived at the factory, she always felt proud when she saw what they'd built a cottage industry up to during their forty years together. Luckily her ride hadn't been in vain, Gavin's car was parked outside the small side door. Katherine went in and shouted from the factory floor so she didn't surprise Gavin by appearing in the office suddenly.

"Hi, Kath, nice week?"

"It was certainly different, Gav, I don't think I'll be a regular visitor. Doreen seemed to think it did her some good which was the point of going I suppose."

"We missed you here, not the same without you."

"Nonsense; if you missed anything, it was the cakes I bring from the shop. What brings you here on a Saturday?"

"I very often pop in for an hour or two to make a start on next week's schedule. It's nice here when it's quiet, no machines running or telephones ringing."

"Mark and I used to work at weekends to catch up sometimes," Katherine lamented. "We'd bring Jen with us and set her playpen up on the shop floor."

"You'd either get done for child cruelty or health and safety violations now Kath. Do you want a coffee?"

"Not for me thanks, I just had one with Jen. I wanted a quiet word, Gav. The estate's all sorted now, I'm officially the sole shareholder of all this."

"Have you made any plans for its future, Kath?"

Gavin was obviously concerned about what Katherine intended to do with the business. He'd worked for them since he'd left school at fifteen more than thirty years previously. Mark had taken him on as an apprentice and he'd steadily risen to his current position.

"You've been through a lot with us, Gav, I still remember Mark coming home and telling me he'd taken on a raggedy-arsed kid with a snotty nose and a very difficult father. He told me you'd be his right-hand man one day. So any decision I make involves you and Pete."

"He was a year behind me," Gavin said. "I thought Mark might treat him different because he came from a better home than I did and had stayed on at school to take his O-levels. He didn't though Kath, he always had faith in me."

"I'm fifty-nine soon, Gav, I want this sorted out by the time I hit sixty next year. Mark and I hoped that you and Pete would buy the business off me after he went and carry on as you've been doing. Do you know what his thoughts are and what do you think?"

"We've spoken about it a lot this last few weeks. Pete's better at all the financial stuff than me Kath. I know he'd love to come in with me and buy it but the thought is that we couldn't afford it. Since we signed those new contracts the turnover is way up, I honestly think you'd be better off talking to one of the big engineering firms."

"If I can make it happen, Gav, will you buy it? Don't worry about the finance at the moment, all I need to know is if you two want it? If you do, I'll make it happen."

"The answer is yes, Kath, I know Pete would agree."

"That's all I need to know for now. I'll explain things better next week. I'll be in for a few hours on Monday, the three of us can discuss what'll happen."

Katherine was close to tears as she cycled back towards the town, she called into the supermarket for some supplies and was home by just after two o'clock. As she came down her drive her neighbour Daphne called out to her and came in as she was putting her bike in the garage.

"How was your week of being pampered then Katherine?"

"Not my favourite experience, Daph. Would you like a quick drink?"

They went through the back door into the spacious, modern kitchen. Katherine made a pot of tea and put some small cakes on a plate.

"Thanks for coming in and picking the mail up, Daph; it's nice having someone I can rely on keeping an eye on the place."

As Katherine was talking, she opened the drawer and got the gift that she'd brought back for her neighbour.

"Here's a little something for you to show my appreciation, it's only some essential oils. They say if you bathe in the stuff it'll knock years off your skin; it actually smells better than the food they gave us."

"You didn't need to get that, Katherine, I don't mind popping over each day while you're away. To be honest it takes my mind off things, I haven't been too good lately."

"Anything you want to talk about, Daph?" Katherine asked. Privately she hoped that her neighbour didn't want to discuss her problems with her but felt it good manners to ask.

Daphne drunk her tea, she was obviously thinking whether or not to open up to Katherine. When she put her cup down Katherine saw a tear run down her cheek.

"It's George," she said quietly "I'm sure he's having an affair again. He's been different for the last few weeks."

"I'm so sorry, Daph, what are you going to do about it?"

"Probably nothing; just hope that it dies a death like the last one. It was his secretary last time."

"Who is it this time? Do you know?"

"I don't know; he's been behaving oddly for a couple of weeks. Coming in late from work some nights, he's been getting new clothes and taking care what he looks like."

"I don't know what to say to you, Daph. You know I'm here for you if you want to get things off your chest."

"They say talking about it helps but I'm not one of those women who can show their emotions willy-nilly. I'll have to put up with it until he's ready to tell everything."

Katherine was at a loss for words, she was pleased when her neighbour finished her tea and got up to leave.

"Thanks again for my gift, Katherine, maybe I'll have a long soak later. I'd better let you get on with your day."

Katherine was quite relieved when Daphne went home after less than half an hour. She'd spent nearly all week listening to her sister's tales of woe. Doreen had just split from her third husband after less than a year and was a nervous wreck. She'd started drinking heavily and had just been banned from driving for the second time. The week at the health spa had calmed her down a little and promises of future trips away together if she kept herself on the straight and narrow offered a little hope.

After her efforts on her bicycle, Katherine was peckish so she had the rest of the pizza from the night before with a cup of tea and a bag of crisps.

The rest of her afternoon was spent making the beds up in the spare rooms for her visitors and getting the food ready for supper. She'd received a provisional offer from a property agent for the land in the post that morning. Her intention was to refuse the offer and go with her own plans for the site.

Robin Pargeter-Jones spent the most unproductive Saturday that he could remember for a long time. Jonathon finally surfaced just before lunchtime, drank a bottle of cola, found some cold food and announced that he was spending the rest of the day gaming in his room.

"I'm linking up with Russell and Sammy Dad," he explained. "We arranged it ages ago. Mum said it'd be okay."

Privately Robin thought that even if Madelaine had agreed to the gaming session, she'd have forgotten about it by now. He'd at least made an effort by offering to take his son out for a burger for his lunch. As soon as Jonathon had grabbed his food and drink, he was back in his room for the rest of the day.

His father duly phoned to be collected from the golf club at just after four-thirty. Robin put his head round Jonathon's bedroom door to tell him he'd be back in an hour. His son eventually acknowledged by waving him away impatiently.

As the manager of a luxury car hire business Robin had the privilege of being allowed to use a Mercedes as a company car. He also had an agency card to pay for his fuel. Luckily, they didn't check his mileage as most weekends he siphoned several litres of petrol for Madelaine's hatchback.

He filled up with fuel on the way to the golf club, by the time he got there his father was waiting impatiently outside the clubhouse.

"I called you three-quarters an hour ago Rob. Poor form keeping me waiting about, I may just as well have caught a bus home."

"You called me thirty minutes ago, Dad, I had to fill up on the way over as well. And you know full well that if you tried to get back by bus on a Saturday you wouldn't get home until tomorrow."

They loaded the golf trolley in the boot of the car and set off for the return journey. Robin didn't mention the vineyard syndicate but almost as soon as they cleared the golf club drive his father broached the subject.

"Young Dawson was stirring things up after the AGM. He's called a meeting of the seven investors for Wednesday evening. Do you want to come and talk to them?"

"Too fucking right I do, Dad, where is this meeting?"

"At the golf club, of course, they're playing after lunch, eating in the restaurant and using the committee room at eight sharp."

"Do you intend on going? Will you back me if it comes down to it, Dad?"

"You know full well I'll support you, so will your Uncle John. We may be able to cover one of them pulling out Rob but if more than one back out then it's over."

The rest of the journey was almost silent. His father fell asleep halfway home so Robin retuned the radio to listen to the reports on the local football matches. Most of his friends at the bar were ardent Southampton supporters, several of them went to every home game. They'd be drowning their sorrows rather than celebrating he thought as their team had just lost a home game that they were expected to win.

He noticed that Madelaine had arrived back while they were out, he dropped his father off and went home to face an angry wife.

"They only fucking refused the card payment, Rob. Claire had picked out some of the stuff she needed for her school trip and we couldn't pay for it. I had to go to a cashpoint to find out how much we had in the account; there was only enough to buy about half the things she needed. What the hell is going on?"

"I'm sorry, Mads, there should have been plenty in there. My salary goes in on Tuesday, give me a list of what you need and I'll go over at lunch-time and pick it up."

"Not good enough I'm afraid. How stupid do you think I looked when we had to leave the stuff there and sneak away like fucking paupers?"

"I said I'm sorry, Mads, where's Claire gone?"

"She's staying over at Laura's tonight. I thought that you were going to spend some time with Jonathon. He's been on his console all day again."

Robin decided to withdraw and went through to the kitchen, there were three cans of lager in the fridge; he drank the first one straight away and took one into the lounge. Madelaine was opening a bottle of wine and had just switched the television on.

"Do you want some dinner, Mads?"

"If that's an indirect way of asking me to cook for you, then you can piss off, Rob. Claire and I had some lunch out; that was when I still thought we had some money. There's some ready meals in the freezer if you want something."

Robin microwaved a cottage pie and drank the last can of lager. Madelaine was on her second glass when he joined her.

Chapter Three

Jennifer dropped a very lively three-year-old golden retriever at her mother's on the way to Bournemouth. Katherine had a short chat to Danny and the twins through the car window, they were running late so after a quick chat they said their goodbyes and drove off.

Katherine took Snowy for a long walk before it got too dark, Mark and she had dogs for most of their married life and she was determined to get one as soon as she'd settled her immediate business. The walk did her more good than the week at the health spa and Snowy didn't stop wagging her tail the whole time. As soon as they got back Katherine made herself a hot drink and gave Snowy some chocolate treats.

Although she knew they were going to McDonalds before the film Katherine got some food ready in case any of them needed anything when they came back. At just after seven o'clock she put the outside lights on and set the food out in the family room. She heard the car doors slam at just after half-past seven, less than a minute later two very excited children burst through the door.

"Dippy and Dopey, did you enjoy the film?"

"Who's Dippy and who's Dopey Nanny?" Jessica asked.

"It doesn't really matter," Katherine said. "Did you enjoy the film?"

"Daddy fell asleep," Jessica said. "He was snoring Nanny."

"I loved the film, Nanny, I want to go again next week."

"You can't go every week, Josh, it wouldn't be a treat if you did. How was your food?"

"It was a McDonalds, Mum," Jennifer said as she came in. "How do you think it was?"

"As long as they enjoyed it, where's Danny?"

"Bringing our stuff in. We're only here for the night but it's like we're going on holiday. No doubt these two will want to go to the play park tomorrow so we've brought their play clothes as well as their overnight things."

As she was talking her husband and the twins father Danny came through the door carrying a large canvas bag.

"Hi, Katherine. How's things?"

"All right thanks. Put that at the bottom of the stairs and I'll get you all a drink. Do you want anything to eat?"

"The twins don't that's for sure. They had everything on the menu at McDonalds. Maybe we could have a bit of supper later, Mum."

"Okay, I'll make coffee. Would Dippy and Dopey like a hot chocolate?"

"Can we have marshmallows and sprinkles, Nanny?"

"What's the magic word, Josh?" Katherine said strictly.

"Abracadabra," both of them yelled in unison and then ran around Katherine's legs giggling.

"Sorry, Katherine," Danny said. "Uncle Billy taught them that one. They've been wanting to catch you out on it all day."

Katherine couldn't help laughing at the twin's antics as she put a saucepan full of milk on the cooker to heat up. While it was warming up, she made a pot of coffee. They carried their drinks through to the family room and settled in the comfortable chairs.

"Presents first," Katherine said. "One each for my favourite twins." She handed a box to each of them. As soon as they opened the boxes their faces lit up.

"We've got onesies," Jessica squealed. "Thanks, Nanny."

"Let's put them on," Joshua suggested. Both of them took their clothes off and climbed into their onesies.

"I tried to get one the same in your size, Danny," Katherine joked. "You'll have to make do with this." She handed him a box of after shave and deodorant from the health spa. She gave Jennifer a box of essential oils the same as the one she'd given her neighbour.

"Thanks, Mum," Jennifer said sincerely. "Where did you get the onesies? They don't sell them at the health spa."

"I saw them in Bournemouth a few weeks ago, Jen, take a photo of them wearing them."

Jennifer finally got the twins to stand still and took a picture with the camera on her telephone.

"New phone?"

"My contract was out so I got an upgrade. The camera is amazing. Time you got up to date, Mum, you've had your phone since before we were married."

"The one I've got does me very nicely, thanks. Can you print me a copy of that picture please?"

"If you had a decent phone, I could just send you the image. I'll do one tomorrow and give it to you on Monday. I assume you're coming in to help."

"Back to normal next week, Jen. I'll be in by four-thirty."

"How the hell you two function that early in the morning beats me," Danny said ruefully.

The twins didn't want to go to bed but they were struggling to stay awake so just before nine o'clock Jennifer took them upstairs to the bedroom next to Katherine's.

"You've had it decorated, Mum, it looks great."

"I'm having the other two done when I'm away in the autumn. Then they can have a room each when they stay."

Ten minutes later, the twins had cleaned their teeth and were ready for bed. Both of them wanted to keep their onesies on even though the radiator had been on in the bedroom.

"They'll be okay in them for tonight, Mum," Jennifer said. "I'll come up later and if they're too hot I'll get them out of them."

"Come and look at my room," Katherine said.

"It's really nice, Mum," Jennifer said. "I love the new furniture, you always wanted a four-poster bed."

"I had to change everything in here and I'm still not sure about using it. I slept in here last night but I'd had a drink."

"Did you get rid of all Dad's stuff?"

"Only the clothes, mostly to charity shops, apart from his disgusting overalls. They went straight into the bin. The rest of it's in his study."

The room Mark had called his study was an extension on the back of the huge garage. He'd sometimes spend the day in the garage working on the Jaguar or one of his motorbikes. The study had a fridge and kettle as well as a set of bookshelves and a big old-fashioned desk. The drawers were full of car and bike magazines. Katherine didn't intend having the room emptied while she was living there.

"Keep sleeping in here, Mum," Jennifer said. "You're doing great."

They went downstairs and helped themselves to food from the table. Katherine had put a selection of cold meats, cheese, pickles and home-made bread ready for supper.

"Open a bottle of white wine please, Danny," Katherine said. "None of us will be driving until tomorrow afternoon."

"Don't keep us waiting too much longer Katherine," Danny said. "You told us you had something to tell us."

"You've not met a man have you, Mum," Jennifer said. "We wouldn't mind."

Katherine gave her daughter a dirty look. "If I did meet someone which is highly unlikely, it certainly wouldn't make any difference whether or not you approved. I need to tell you about some decisions I've made now that your father's estate has been settled. Some of it concerns you two."

"Did he leave me his Honda Katherine?" Danny quipped.

"If you rode that, you'd either kill yourself or get locked up for speeding," Katherine said drily.

"Be serious and listen, Danny," Jennifer told her husband. "Sorry, Mum."

"You're not really getting anything that you wouldn't have got eventually," Katherine told them "Your father and me talked it through when we knew he couldn't survive the cancer. We've signed your house, the shop and two flats over to you. All you need to do is pop into the solicitor and sign the transfers."

Neither of them replied for a moment while they took in the news. Katherine and Mark had bought the shop and flats so that Jennifer could open her business and as a long-term investment. Both flats were rented, one to a friend of Jennifer who also helped in the shop and the other to a couple who had a young child.

Soon after Jennifer and Danny had married Mark and Katherine had bought a house that needed a refurbishment. Jennifer and Danny had lived there on a low rent since they were married. They'd done most of the work themselves, Danny's uncle was a builder and he'd helped when he could.

"That's huge, Mum," a tearful Jennifer said. "What about the rent from the flats?"

"The flats belong to you two so you get the income. This isn't a condition but you should be very comfortably off now. I'd love to see the twins going to Saint Hilda's when they reach secondary level. I know Danny won't agree with it but Mark and I both thought they'd benefit."

"Funnily enough I agree with you, Katherine. I took a bus full of year nine girls down there for a netball match last week and the facilities are amazing."

"They've got a really good music department as well," Katherine said. "The school orchestra were at the church just before Christmas. If your little ones have any talent, they'll make the most of it."

"That deals with you two," Katherine continued "Some other decisions I've made recently. Firstly, I've decided to retire when I reach sixty in just over a year."

"What will you do with yourself, Mum?" Jennifer asked. "I can't see you joining the local women's institute and making jam."

"I've been asked several times to stand as a candidate at the local council elections. While your dad was ill of course I couldn't but it's something I'd like to do. There's also so many places I'd like to see. Doreen and I are going to have a trip abroad every year, Liz wants me to go away with her and I'm also going to try and spend more time at the cottage."

"What about the factory, Mum? Will you still be able to cover for me at the shop now and again?"

"Of course I'll help you out when you need me Love. You'll have Becky soon and if you do start supplying that hotel, you'll need someone else as well."

"Elaine wants more hours, Mum, at least I know I can trust her and Becky."

"I need you to keep this to yourselves until at least next Wednesday please. The factory site has been re-zoned for housing. The county needs at least a thousand new houses over the next ten years; our town has to have its share."

Jennifer and Danny went quiet while they took in the news. "Are you just going to have the factory pulled down then, Mum?"

"Don't make it sound like I'm grabbing the money and running please, Jen," Katherine answered sternly "Pete and Gavin want to buy the business, they can re-locate to a new factory with all the mod-cons. Basically if they take on all the staff contracts and pay for the move they can have the business for nothing."

"Did Mark know about all this Katherine?" Danny asked.

"Of course he did, this has been in the pipeline for nearly two years. He wanted Pete and Gav to have the business but we couldn't really make any plans until the council made their minds up."

Danny had obviously been thinking for a moment about the financial side of the news.

"That site must be worth millions, Katherine. They could put sixty or seventy houses on there."

"A land agent got in touch with me the week before I went away Danny. He offered me several million if it got re-zoned. I've had an even bigger offer this week but I won't sell it."

"Not following you, Katherine, what are you doing with it?"

"I've spoken to a housing society and they seem to think the site could be developed as affordable housing for local people, some rented, some part owned and possibly some sheltered housing for elderly."

"Surely, they'd still buy the site, Katherine, just for a lot less money."

"I'm retaining the freehold of the land; the properties will be sold on long leases and I'll collect ground rent for each one. It's not as lucrative as selling the land of course but there's an income forever."

"It sounds like you've thought it through, Mum."

"Your father and I came up with the idea ages ago but we couldn't discuss it too much. We need housing for locals. If we hadn't helped you with your house, you'd never have been able to afford to live round here would you."

"That's true enough, Elaine's been trying to get a mortgage but unless she buys a studio flat in a rough part of Southampton, she hasn't got a chance."

"Don't say anything to her until the council announce the plans for the area next week please. It'd be nice if she got a place there."

"I know I shouldn't ask Mum but if you don't get anything out of the business and you're not working will you be able to afford all these exotic trips?"

"If I only got a fiver a week from each property, I'd be getting several hundred pounds a week, Jen. There's pension plans of Marks that will keep paying out and some of mine hit maturity when I'm sixty. I'd say I could still put food on the table."

Danny helped himself to some more cold meat and bread.

"If it's food like this, Katherine, we'll be visiting you a lot more. I'd forgotten what your food tastes like."

"You do very well for food, Danny. If anything Jen makes better food than I do."

"Maybe for the shop, Katherine. I have to do most of the cooking at home now."

"Most of the cooking involves making sandwiches for the twins at tea-time and throwing a ready meal in the microwave for himself, Mum," Jennifer explained "I spend nine or ten hours a day at work, I'm fucked if I'll start again when I get home."

"I hope you're not using language like that in front of your children."

"Sorry, Mum, it slipped out. Bed-time, Dan, are you coming up now?"

"Start without me, Jen, I'll just finish my food and wine."

Jennifer hugged her mother and went upstairs, they heard the water running in the main bathroom Danny was a little unsure what to say to his mother-in-law now that they were by themselves.

"Am I forgiven then, Katherine? Who told you what it stood for?"

"You're on probation young man. Jacqui told me. I said you'd called me a MILF and what you told me it stood for and she told me what it actually meant."

Danny looked a little sheepish "I didn't know you were stood behind me Katherine. Anyway you should have taken it as a compliment; you're one gorgeous woman."

Katherine had taken it as a compliment but wasn't going to admit it "We'll say no more about it young man."

"What you and Mark did with his will is brilliant, Katherine, we're set for life. We won't let you down. Was there inheritance tax on what we were left?"

"Hardly any," Katherine fibbed "That's all taken care of. Your responsibility is to ensure those twins get the best start in life."

"With my salary as head of year and the way Jen's shop is doing, we were okay; now we can afford to send the kids to Saint Hilda's when they're eleven."

"I thought you'd have wanted them at the comprehensive."

"They'd have done all right there but they'll do much better at Saint Hilda's. It's amazing there Katherine, they've got a full-size pool next to the performing arts centre. Four of last year's netball team have been picked for the county and they reckon at least two of them could go on to play for England."

Katherine poured them both a second glass of wine and helped herself to a little more food.

"I hear you weren't too impressed with the health spa," Danny said.

"Doreen got something out of it, that's what matters. We're hoping to have a proper holiday later in the year but I expect she'll have met another man by then. She was texting someone in the evenings this week."

Danny thought that he'd better not broach the subject of Katherine meeting someone else. He drank his wine and got up from the chair.

"I'm going up, Katherine."

Much to his surprise Katherine stood up and gave him a hug. "Goodnight, Danny, thanks for looking after Jen and the twins."

Danny went up and joined his wife in the bedroom at the far end of the house, she was still wide awake when he came in. "I thought I'd give you ten minutes with Mum, was she okay with you?"

"She's fine with me, Jen. How about that legacy then? I reckon that makes us millionaires."

"I hadn't thought of that, we'll surely have plenty of spare money, no rent or mortgage and the income from the flats."

"Like your mum said, Jen, we've got to make sure the twins get the advantage of it."

"I know that, Dan, maybe you could think of a way we could celebrate the news."

"I thought you told me we couldn't do it here."

"That was when Mum was in the next room, she's back in her old room now. Not too much screaming and yelling out though."

"That goes for you as well, you do more yelling than me."

"We'll just have to go slowly then, none of your wham-bam stuff please. If the twins wake up, you'll have to see to them."

"What if I go to their room and your mother grabs me and drags me into her room?"

"Keep the noise down and don't wake me up when she lets you go."

"Would you mind if she did meet someone else?"

"I'd love it if she did, she looks twenty years younger and she deserves to be happy. Aunt Doreen is on two or three dating sites. Mum ought to join one, she'll never meet anyone round here."

"I can't see her doing that. She's too good for most guys."

"Careful, mister, she might have forgiven you but I'm not sure I have yet. You wouldn't be the first one to run off with his mother-in-law."

"You won't get rid of me that easily. You know how the story goes; if you want to see what your wife will turn out like have a look at her mum. So I get a younger version of her for now and if you turn out like her, I've won all ways up."

"You'd better get on with winning, Dan, or I'll be fast asleep."

Katherine finished her drink, had half an hour with her book and was in bed before eleven o'clock. She looked in on the twins on her way to her bedroom and saw that Jennifer had got them out of their onesies. Both of them were fast asleep, she stood there watching them for a few minutes before going to her room. She decided to have her shower in the morning so she put her electric blanket on high for a few minutes while she cleaned her teeth and undressed.

Her second night back in her old room seemed a lot easier but she couldn't settle straight away so she switched the lamp on and read for a while. Ten minutes later she was yawning so she settled down and was asleep within five minutes.

She woke up early on Sunday morning and went downstairs in her dressing gown to make tea. It was a cold March morning but she could see the sun trying to break through. She sat in the conservatory with her tea and on a whim took a cigarette out of the packet and lit it. The first few puffs made her legs wobbly and the next few started her coughing so she stubbed it out after smoking a quarter of it. She decided to take the remaining eighteen to the factory the next day.

Jennifer came through shortly afterwards. "You've been smoking, Mum," she said disdainfully. "Leave the door open and make sure the twins don't know you smoke."

"I'm hardly a smoker, Jen, I've already decided that after having a few puffs yesterday and a few just now that I'll get rid of the rest of them. I'm going for a shower as soon as I've drunk my tea."

"Do you want some help with lunch?"

"I'd rather do it myself, I miss cooking. It's hardly worth doing it for one."

"I'm going to make a jug of coffee and take Danny a cup, do you want one?"

"No, thanks, Jen, are the twins still asleep?"

Jennifer went back to the kitchen, let Snowy out and made coffee. Katherine put her head round the door.

"I'm going to shower and dress, shall I wake the twins?"

"Give them ten minutes while we have coffee, all hell breaks out when they get up on a Sunday."

Half an hour later Katherine realised what Jennifer meant. Jessica and Joshua had put their onesies back on and were doing an imitation of characters from the film they'd seen.

Katherine was preparing a joint of beef for lunch while the twins played. "Daddy said you're doing chips, Nanny."

"You know very well it's against the law to eat chips on a Sunday Josh. You had them last night I expect. It's either a roast dinner or bread and water."

"We're leaving our onesies on all day, Nanny, we love them."

"You won't be able to go to the play park then," Katherine said patiently. "And I don't think they'd let you in church looking like that."

After breakfast, Katherine put the joint in and prepared some vegetables while Jennifer helped the twins shower and dress. They were ready to go out at ten o'clock.

"I'd better stay behind and look after Snowy," Danny said hopefully.

Katherine gave him a look that didn't really need explaining.

"You need to get up earlier and think of decent excuses Danny, the vicar encourages people to bring their dogs to church. The walk will do us all good and we can do the play park on the way back."

It was a mile and a half walk to church. Katherine had a quick chat to the vicar after the service, the twins were getting restless so she made her excuses and they went to the play park on the way back to the house.

"Are you going to keep going every week, Mum?"

"Don't worry, Jen, I won't get religious. I find it a comfort, they were all so kind after Mark died. I'll keep going every time I can, if I'm away or busy then I can skip it."

"I know you didn't approve at first Mum but you've got to admit he's sorted himself out since the little ones arrived."

Danny had been trying to make a living as a guitarist in a local group when they'd met. Some weeks he'd been reduced to busking in the town centre for small change. Mark and Katherine liked him but wanted better for their only daughter. As soon as they were engaged, Danny had taken a year-long course to qualify as a teacher. He had a degree so as soon as he was qualified, he had no trouble getting a teaching position, luckily it was at the comprehensive school locally. He'd been promoted to head of year just after the twins had arrived and was being thought of as a future headmaster.

"I'm so pleased your father saw how successful he is, Jen. He used to sit in bed some evenings and talk about you and your family. He was so proud at how you'd turned out."

"I was pretty horrible," Jennifer said with a smile "I just hope Jess doesn't give me the sort of bother I caused you and Dad."

She could see that her mother was getting nostalgic so she yelled to Danny that they needed to get back to the house and ten minutes later they set off for the short walk home.

As soon as they got through the front gate, Danny let Snowy off the lead, she ran down the drive with the twins chasing her.

"Nanny, there's a man here," Jessica called out.

Jennifer quickened her pace, when they got to the house, they saw that it was Les Davies, he was pulling the Jaguar up onto the back of his flat-bed breakdown truck.

"He's picking up the E-Type," Katherine explained. She walked over just as the winch stopped.

"Sorry to come on Sunday," Les said. "I want to make a start on it this week. I had to put the wheels back on to get it on the truck. The tyres might be all right but it wouldn't hurt to replace them."

"It'll hurt my bank balance," Katherine joked. "Do what you think, Les. Do you want a coffee?"

"I'll get it strapped down and be in shortly thanks. Those twins are big for three-year-olds."

"We're six," Joshua said indignantly.

"It's five years since you came and sorted the car out, Les."

"Mum always said that the older you get the quicker time passes," Les said "I thought she was mad. What's happening to the bikes?"

"I don't know," Katherine sighed. "I'd like to keep them but they may have to go eventually."

"Make sure you see me before you sell them. That Honda is worth twice what Mark paid. Some shyster might try to get them on the cheap."

Katherine joined the others in the kitchen, Jennifer was making coffee for the adults and warm squash for the twins.

"You're not selling it, are you, Katherine?" Danny asked.

"Certainly not. Les is going to get it up and running and I'm going to use it. It shouldn't be sitting round gathering dust."

"Nor should you, Mum."

Les came in ten minutes later, drank his coffee and left promising that he'd get the work done and get the car sorted out so that Katherine could use it when the weather improved.

"I'm not selling the Honda yet," Katherine told them "I spoke to a museum curate who told me they'd be honoured to have it on display. They put a plaque up with the owner's name on it. If I want it back, I just have to give them a few months' notice."

"What about your Ducati, Mum, will you ever ride again?"

"I know if I sold it, I'd regret it," Katherine said ruefully. "I'll see how I feel in the summer. We used to love riding to the bike meet on Poole quayside."

The lunch was ready by one o'clock, Danny carved the meat while Katherine and Jennifer served the vegetables. The twins took turns stirring the gravy and putting the saucepans by the sink.

"You'd better take the rest of the joint with you," Katherine said. "I'll never use it."

As she waved them away, Katherine felt the tears start to well up, she went indoors to get ready for another evening alone.

Chapter Four

Robin had a weekend from hell. Madelaine had got progressively drunk and more abusive as the evening went on. She went to bed at ten o'clock after giving him instructions not to disturb her when he came to bed. He poured himself a large glass of whisky and switched the television over for Match of the Day. He didn't follow the football religiously like some of his friends but always wanted to see the local clubs doing well. For the first season ever Bournemouth, Southampton and Brighton were all in the top division. Two of them had lost and the other one had struggled to achieve a draw with a side that they were expected to beat.

He checked the kitchen to see if Madelaine had bought groceries and found the cupboard nearly empty. Checking the freezer produced the same result. The prospect of a trip to Aldi on Sunday morning didn't cheer him up. At least it meant that he could finish the whisky and replenish his stock straight away. Eventually he fell asleep in front of a boring film and woke up at two o'clock in the morning. He decided not to risk disturbing Madelaine so he stretched out on the settee for another few restless hours sleep.

On Sunday morning, he saw the lights come on in his father's house soon after six o'clock. He made coffee for himself and settled down in front of his computer. On his last visit to Tuscany he'd taken several photographs of the vineyard and buildings to show to potential investors, he looked ruefully at them hoping that he could still keep the dream afloat.

He went upstairs for a shower at eight o'clock and went through to the bedroom for fresh clothes. Madelaine stirred as he dressed.

"You didn't bother coming up then," she said angrily.

In spite of her current moods Robin still loved his wife, he knew that if he could somehow rebuild his wine business and move them to Italy that she'd return to her old self.

"I didn't want to disturb you," he said trying to sound cheerful. "I'll bring you a coffee in a minute."

"We'll need shopping, your father is expecting a meal taken round at one o'clock,"

"And not a moment later," Robin joked in a passable imitation of his father's military bark. "I'll nip to Aldi as soon as they open."

"Don't try and use the card, it's right on its overdraft limit."

"I've got a little cash in the business account, I'll use that."

He didn't tell Madelaine that he'd managed to build up just over two thousand pounds in the account that was in his sole name. He'd got some kickbacks from car dealers the month before when they'd replaced some of the luxury cars at work. Then the dealer that bought the used ones had given him a little bonus for agreeing a lower price. He wanted the money to make sure they could afford the tickets to fly to Italy in May.

Five minutes later, he put a coffee on the dressing table, he heard a quiet snore coming from the bed so he decided to leave her sleeping as long as he could. His daughter Claire arrived home soon after nine o'clock and announced that he was the worst father in the world for not being able to afford to pay for her shopping on Saturday. She calmed down a little when he said it would be taken care of during the week.

"Is Mum up yet?"

"She's having a lay in Sweetheart, I think she's feeling a little under the weather."

"Hardly surprising the amount she drinks. Then she has the fucking nerve to tell me not to drink when I go out with my friends."

"It's not nice hearing language like that from a teenage girl, Claire."

"Where do you think I get it from then Dad? I'll be glad to get to uni in September."

"Perhaps you'd be better off spending the weekend working for your exams than drinking with Jane and Tammy."

Putting on a pout Claire stormed out of the kitchen, Robin heard the bedroom door slam, a few seconds later Madelaine appeared downstairs.

"Have you upset Claire?"

"Probably," Robin sighed. "She'll calm down."

"My coffee was cold, is there any left?"

It wouldn't have been cold if you hadn't gone back to sleep Robin thought but decided not to say anything. "I'll make fresh," he told her. "Won't be long."

He was pleased to leave for the shopping trip at just after nine-thirty. Madelaine didn't want to go with him, when he drove down the road, he thought that if he was stopped by the police he'd probably fail a roadside breath test after his drinking the night before. At least he'd showered and changed so he didn't smell of whisky.

After what seemed an eternity queuing at the checkout, he finally drove out of the supermarket car park at just after eleven o'clock. Costa Coffee wasted another half an hour of his Sunday morning, he didn't get home until nearly noon.

"You realise his fucking lordship is expecting a cooked meal in an hour Rob, do you? I thought you'd be back ages ago."

"Don't panic, Mads, I got some chops and new potatoes for him. I'll grill them, it'll be ready on time."

"What about the rest of us then, did you get a joint?"

"I bought a chicken, we'll eat later. I suppose Jonathon is still in his pit."

"He's gaming with his friends; he told me you'd said it'd be all right. Did you get some wine?"

"There's a couple of bottles in the small bag, try and make it last the week. I'll get his dinner on."

At exactly one minute to one o'clock Robin cut through the side gate and rapped on the kitchen door at his father's house. Richard came through to the kitchen and took the tray off him without saying thank you.

"Where's Cheralyn anyway, Dad? She normally puts up an extra dinner for Sunday."

"Some silly crisis with her family, she had to go there for a couple of days. Don't worry, she'll be back tomorrow."

When he went back home Madelaine had opened a bottle of wine and poured herself a glass. He didn't say anything but she obviously knew what he was thinking.

"It's one glass, Rob, I see you could afford a bottle of whisky."

"My whisky will last me a month," he said bitterly. "And it cost less than your two bottles that you'll most likely get through in a couple of days."

Although he knew that it was unlikely Giovanni would see it, he sent an e-mail to him asking if there'd been any progress by the solicitor. He didn't tell him that his syndicate of investors were getting panicky.

Very few people had his mobile number so he was surprised when it rang at three o'clock. He checked the caller display and saw it was his friend Darren Turnbull.

"Hi, Daz," he said. "Not like you to ring me at the weekend."

"No panic, Rob. We're putting a darts team together for tomorrow night after work. Can I put your name down?"

"Of course you can. Where have you been? Haven't seen you all week."

"I've been texting and chatting to a new woman, Rob, I met up with her twice this week."

"Good old cyber dating is it, mate. You won't learn by your mistakes, will you? How many is that since Amy left you?"

"Four or five I suppose."

"Any prospects with this one?"

"Don't think so. I picked her up at her house, she said hello and then kept on asking how much I paid for the car."

"Sounds like she's after your money, how old is she?"

"Thirty-six I think."

"So she's picked up with a hard-drinking overweight guy who's twelve years older than she is. Best of luck with that one. Are you seeing her again?"

"We went for a meal on Friday, she said she'd love to see where I lived so I've said I'll cook her dinner on Tuesday evening."

"I now it's my cynical side coming out Daz but I'd say she wants to see how much you're worth. You haven't had your card stamped yet, have you?"

"I can't seem to work them out Rob. And the answer is no; we haven't sealed the deal and I'd say it's almost certain we won't."

"It's not for me to say Mate but I'd blow her off for Tuesday. Does she know where you live? Which phone did you use?"

"I used the throw away one Rob, and no; she doesn't know anything much about me."

"If you think she's a scammer, leave well alone. Text her and tell her that you can't make it and then change the SIM card in your phone."

"I had much the same thought to be truthful, mate. I've joined a new agency as well, maybe I'll have better luck with them."

"Hopefully I'll have some news from Italy soon Daz, fucking solicitors out there don't seem to understand we want things sewn up quickly."

"I thought you said it all had to be completed by the end of May. You're cutting it fine, Rob."

"We can still go ahead after that, we'll miss out on this year's crop that's all. Giovanni seems okay with that; I suppose he would be, he'll get the profit from it."

"Just keep me posted, see you tomorrow."

He went to the kitchen and started getting dinner ready, by the look of things Madelaine had no intention of doing any cooking. She surprised him by coming in and starting to peel some potatoes.

"Who were you speaking to just now?"

"Only Darren, he's organised a charity darts match for tomorrow, I may be a bit late in from work."

"Nothing new there then," Madelaine answered. "I don't suppose I've been invited."

"It's a man thing Mads, anyway it's Southampton at six o'clock. I can't come all the way home and then get back there,"

Madelaine knew she was being lied to but didn't press the issue "He's not getting cold feet about Italy, is he?"

"I don't think so, he wants to go there in the summer if we've completed. He's met another of his women off the internet this week."

"It must be his looks and charm."

"Nothing to do with his Porsche and swanky flat, Mads."

"I wish some elderly relative would die and leave us half a million. At least we'd get out of this shithole."

"It's hardly that, at least we've got a free house. If we hadn't come here, we'd have been on a council estate somewhere."

As Madelaine had been brought up on a council estate in London, she didn't say anything and flounced out of the kitchen as soon as she'd done enough potatoes for the four of them. Robin went back on his computer while the dinner was cooking, he checked his inbox several times but Giovanni either hadn't seen his message or hadn't bothered to reply.

They finally managed to drag Jonathon out of his bedroom for his dinner. Claire eventually joined them and sat at the table tapping away on the screen of her tablet.

"Can't you leave that thing alone for a few minutes," Robin asked her. "You've had all day to text your friends?"

"Everyone does it, it's called Social Media Dad. Get with the times."

"It's called being rude, Claire," Robin retorted.

Robin looked at Madelaine for support but she ignored him. The rest of the meal was eaten in total silence, as soon as they'd finished eating the two children went straight back to their bedrooms.

"You could have backed me up, Mads, why the hell do they want to be on those things all day?"

"Because they've nothing better to do I suppose. Maybe it's our fault, Rob."

Chapter Five

Katherine woke at quarter past three on Monday morning, took a look at her clock and although she was wide awake decided to sleep for another half an hour until the alarm woke her. When the buzzer roused her at quarter to four, she felt as if she hadn't been to sleep all night. Five minutes later a cup of tea livened her up, after a very quick wash she was on her way to help Jennifer at the shop.

"Hi, Mum," Jennifer said cheerily as she went through the back door into the kitchen. The bank of ovens was heating the room, Jennifer was rolling pastry on the work table. She handed her mother a cup of tea that she'd just poured for her.

"Thanks, Jen, I'll be awake in a minute. What do you want me doing?"

"The tea rooms in Wimborne need fifty fruit scones and thirty plain, Mum. Can you do those first please?"

"Do you need cheese and cherry ones doing?"

"There's enough in the freezer for today, I've got to line out fifty quiche bases ready for tomorrow."

Katherine made a start on the scones, Jennifer took six trays of bread and rolls out of the prover and put them in the ovens.

Jennifer had inherited some basic cooking skills from her mother and learned the rest of them at catering college. They both knew the routines by heart and worked quietly for an hour and a half. They stopped for a much-needed break at six o'clock, the bread and rolls were cooling, Katherine had put the scones straight in the oven as soon as it was empty and they had a few minutes left on the timer.

"Can you make a start on the sandwiches after we've had a drink please Mum? There's a new order and they're collecting them at half seven."

"Who are they for, love?"

"The engineering shop out on the Blandford road. They used to have one of those mobile sandwich vans call in but she didn't turn up twice last week."

"Is it worth doing?"

"The more I can build up the shop trade the easier it'll get Mum. Wholesale is all right but it has to be delivered and they all want it for next to nothing. That hotel didn't; I quoted them full price for the quiches and they didn't bat an eyelid."

By eight-thirty, the wholesale orders were ready for the van driver and the shop was stocked out. Katherine helped Jennifer clean the kitchen and after a drink she left for the factory. She knew that they could manage without her, she'd hardly been there while Mark was ill at home. The office manager Jacqui Russell had taken over most of the work and the new computer installation had speeded up the accounts work. Although she was looking forward to a new life in just over a year, she still loved being part of the success story.

"Here's some freshly made scones for lunch Guys," she told Gavin and Pete when she arrived. They were going through some drawings for a new design. "Thanks, Katherine," Pete said. "Nice to see you back, we missed you."

Jacqui was already at her desk when Katherine went into the office. She'd worked for them since she finished college and Katherine had watched her blossom from a gangly teenager into a confident twenty-five-year old. Katherine gave her a present from her trip to the health spa.

"Don't broadcast it Jacqui, I couldn't bring everyone something back."

"Thanks, Katherine, I'll keep it to myself."

Katherine noticed a difference in Jacqui that she couldn't quite place. "Is everything all right?" she asked.

"Does Jennifer make wedding cakes?"

"She made one last year, I think they were pleased with it." As Katherine answered the question, she realised what Jacqui was trying to tell her.

"He finally asked you," she said. "I hope you said yes straight away. Tell me all about it."

Jacqui spent the next five minutes telling Katherine about her boyfriend's proposal and showing her the engagement ring. They'd set a provisional date for the following summer.

"I'm so pleased for you," Katherine said sincerely. "Jen will make you the finest cake anyone's ever seen."

She went up to the factory office at eleven o'clock when she knew Pete and Gavin would be there, she gave them both a small bottle of after shave that she'd brought back from her holiday.

"I asked Gav on Saturday Pete and I need to know your thoughts. Mark wanted you two to buy this place and I want the same. What's your thoughts?"

"Gav told me you'd asked, I want the same as him Katherine. If you can make it happen for us, then yes please; make it happen."

Katherine didn't need to ask any more, Pete was almost in tears. He'd started there the year after Gavin and had worked his way up through the departments.

"I've made my decision Boys. I want you two and all the staff gathered up on the shop floor first thing on Wednesday. I'll tell you all at the same time."

Jennifer went home as usual at two o'clock, had a light lunch and shower before laying on her bed for an hour's rest. She was up by four o'clock just in time to see her best friend park the car in front of the garage. Even though they'd been friends since college Liz always knocked on the door and waited to be invited in. Katherine opened the back door just as she walked up the path.

"How was it then?" Liz asked after they'd hugged by the door.

"Doreen enjoyed it," Katherine said diplomatically. "I don't think I'll be going again. What about your weekend?"

Liz and Phillip Powell had been to London for a long weekend. It was an anniversary present that Liz had arranged, they'd travelled up by coach on Friday morning, had a day in London, a theatre trip on Saturday evening and returned home on Sunday afternoon.

"I wish I'd taken you Kath," Liz told her. "He hardly stopped complaining the whole time. Said we should have gone by car, the room was too small, he was cold all-day Saturday and then he fell asleep in the theatre."

"Did it rekindle the flames like you'd hoped?"

"Did it fuck; sorry, Kath. He moaned that the bed was too small and uncomfortable and then proceeded to get drunk and throw up in the toilet. About as unromantic as you can get really."

Although Liz was trying to sound light-hearted Katherine knew that she feared that her marriage was doomed. Since the children had left her husband had drifted away from her.

They sat down at the kitchen table, Katherine gave Liz a gift set from the health spa and Liz gave Katherine a terry towel dressing gown that she'd bought from the hotel. Katherine put coffee that she knew Liz liked in the filter machine.

"I know you haven't had a love life for a long time Kath but you've a good reason. That asshole hasn't touched me for months, he sleeps in the spare room half the time, says it's so I don't get disturbed. Jesus Kath, I could use a disturbance every now and again."

"Jen wants me to go on the internet to find a man. I'd always feel I was being disloyal to Mark, maybe I'll feel differently one day; I'm back in our bedroom now."

"Were you pleased with the painter?"

"Come and have a look, he did one of the others as well. I'm going to ask him to do the other two next time I'm away."

"Nice bed, Kath," Liz commented.

"Why did you automatically notice the bed first Liz?" Katherine giggled. "I thought you might have noticed the chintz wallpaper."

Liz laid on her back and stretched out on the bed. "I could get used to a bed this size, you must be planning on meeting someone Kath or you'd have bought a normal size one."

"I'm not totally ruling it out, Liz, but I'm certainly not ready yet. At least I've slept two nights in here. Come and see the other room."

They went downstairs a few minutes later and sat in the family room. Katherine put a disc on for some soft background music.

"They've started swimming lessons at the country club Kath. I know you said you'd like to take the twins, would you like to come with me on Wednesday night to have a look."

"I'd love to, are they doing children's lessons as well?"

"It's adults on a Wednesday evening and children during the day on Saturday. I'll pick you up about six."

"Are you cooking for Phillip or will you have something to eat with me?"

"He can either get his own or go without. It won't take much for us to split up, Kath."

"I'll do us some lasagne with garlic bread and salad then. I hate eating by myself every night."

Katherine served dinner at just after seven o'clock, eventually Liz went home at nine and after a coffee Katherine went to bed with her book.

"Of course we could always sell up and retire Jen. We're fucking millionaires."

Jennifer had put the twins to bed at eight o'clock, read them a story and gone straight to bed. Danny came in later, he tried to get in without waking her but as soon as he climbed in, she woke up.

"Forget it, mister, you're going to be headmaster and make the school the best in the county and I'm going to have a string of bakeries making the finest food in the world."

Danny snuggled up to Jennifer and started stroking her leg gently, even though she had to be up before four o'clock the following morning she felt the familiar tingles and gently encouraged Danny by guiding his hand upwards.

"Is that honestly how you see our lives panning out, Jen?"

Jennifer didn't really want a philosophical discussion on their future, she had just over five hours until the alarm roused her. She wanted to spend one of them making love with her husband and the other four in a deep restful sleep.

"You want to be head and I want the shop to prosper," she said. "But not at all costs Dan, I'd rather be in a council house struggling to pay the rent with two happy and healthy kids than be wealthy and have a dysfunctional family. Now can we please put the discussions on hold for a while."

Twenty fairly quiet minutes later Danny decided that they were both ready, they disentangled themselves and he climbed on top of her for the last movement and hopefully if they'd timed it right, they could both go to sleep feeling fulfilled.

"Slow it down, stud," she urged. "You know I don't like your wham-bam stuff, nice and easy please."

Before they met, Danny's sexual experiences were usually a quick grope in the back of a van or at the very best a hurried session while his parents were out. As a teenager, Jennifer had suffered through many such experiences with several boys, as soon as she was able to live on her own, she made sure that at the very least whoever she was sleeping with could spend the night.

They managed to organise their climaxes within a few minutes of each other, Jennifer lay on her side, put her hand under her head and was asleep within ten minutes. Danny was a little more restless, he went to the toilet, looked in on the twins and laid next to Jennifer thinking.

Until he'd met Jennifer, he'd been very poor but he'd always been happy with the thought that one day everything would turn out well. By the look of things that day had arrived long before it was expected. Most men would have been overjoyed at the situation but Danny was a natural worrier and was concerned that their new-found wealth would upset the balance of their lives.

He'd had around two hours sleep when he heard Jennifer get out of bed at half-past three the next morning. Their house was only a five-minute walk from the shop, she just threw a few clothes on, walked to work and got ready there.

By the time her mother arrived Jennifer had the dough moulded into loaves and rolls and on trays in the prover, the ovens were heating up and she'd started preparing the ingredients to make fifty quiches.

"Here's your tea, Mum, all four scones and then two trays of cheese biscuits please."

"Liz came around last night," Katherine told her. "We're starting swimming at the country club tomorrow night and they're doing lessons for children on Saturday, can I take the twins?"

"That'd be great, Mum. Danny didn't want to take them so he'll be happy enough for you to do it. He wants to start going to football again so if you bring them here on the way back, he'll be able to go with his stupid mates."

"It won't be every Saturday, I want to start going to the cottage now it's empty again. Maybe if I take them on the days Bournemouth are playing at home."

Seven years previously Katherine had inherited half the proceeds of her mother's estate. Doreen had frittered most of her money away, Katherine had fulfilled a dream by buying herself a cottage on Exmoor. She and Mark had only used it a few times before his illness had taken hold. Rather than leave it empty she'd put it in the hands of a local estate agent and it had been let out until just before Christmas.

"Does it want much work, Mum?"

"Not really, in fact some of it's better than before. As soon as the new boiler goes in next month, I'll start using it."

"Can Danny and I have the odd weekend there Mum?"

"Of course you can, Jen, the twins will love it there. I can do the shop on a Saturday and you can go straight from school on the Friday. You'll be there by seven, have all day Saturday and most of Sunday down there."

"If the twins learn to swim at the club, I'll be able to take them to the beach there."

"Liz said she wants to come with me which'll be nice. Phillip is acting up again. I wouldn't be surprised if they split up this time. They nearly did a couple of years ago."

"I can't stand him, Mum, he gives me the creeps."

"He's not the nicest person in the world is he, Liz took him to London for a treat and he didn't stop moaning the whole time. Maybe I'll book one of those theatre weekends; would you like to come with me, Jen?"

"Best to take Liz Mum, she'd get more out of it than me. Or of course you could always meet a nice man and go with him."

Katherine didn't want to get into the pros and cons of internet dating so she quickly changed the subject back to the business at hand.

"What time is Jason coming? Those quiches need putting in don't they."

"Eight o'clock, the same time he comes in every day. They'll be cool enough to wrap by half-seven."

Jennifer realised that her mother didn't want to discuss any potential future romance and they worked quietly until they broke for a drink.

Chapter Six

Robin spent most of the day on Wednesday rehearsing his presentation to what he thought of as a lynch-mob at the golf club that evening. The first time he'd presented his plans he'd come over as the confident salesman that he used to be before the bank decided that they'd put him out of business.

He was convinced that the figures he had given them were accurate. An investment of one hundred-thousand pounds each would be secure as the vineyard was worth at least half as much again. They could expect at least five per cent net earnings from the time the first crop was harvested, with interest rates at a record low and pension pots suffering they could take advantage of his knowledge and earn a handsome dividend on their investment.

They'd also have the advantage of being able to use the guest cottage at the yard on a time share basis, either by using it themselves or renting it. Privately Robin thought most of them were too set in their ways to bother going there but he knew the guest cottage could be rented every week through the spring, summer and autumn.

One of his problems was that nine of the ten in the syndicate were in their seventies and eighties, only his friend Darren was still at work. Several of them were ex-military types and he knew he'd struggle to persuade them how good the investment was. The first time he'd spoken to them one of them had used the cliché, "If it sounds too good to be true it usually is."

He'd spoken to Darren about the meeting at the darts match, his friend seemed quite laid-back but told him that any more than the hundred-thousand pounds was out of the question. He'd bought a luxury flat in Southampton and a year-old Porsche, mostly in the hope of them attracting a woman to share his life. He'd been on several internet dating sites but the women that he'd met either blew him out on the first date or were more interested in his finances. Privately Robin thought Darren wanted to be in the syndicate in the hope of impressing any woman that he was lucky enough to get at least a second date with.

He'd told his father that he'd be at the golf club by seven o'clock on Wednesday so as soon as he locked up he went for a quick drink to bolster his confidence. He only had one pint, he felt he'd need to have at least one more when he arrived to try and sell the idea again.

As soon as the meeting started, he realised that it was a lost cause. Four of the investors had made their minds up to withdraw their support and after his presentation a fifth joined them. Possibly had one of them pulled out he could have got his father and uncle to cover the shortfall, maybe even a little more from Darren. With half of them pulling out he had to admit defeat and promise that they'd all have their ten-thousand-p o u n d deposit returned within the next few days. One of the two that had instigated the meeting asked that they be paid interest on the money that Robin had been holding. When Robin said that he was considering taking a small percentage to cover administration costs he sat down and kept quiet. The interest rates were so low that the paltry few pounds would only cover Madelaine's wine bill for a few months.

Richard Pargeter-Jones had been in the bar since before five o'clock. He'd been given a lift to the club because he knew Robin would take him home and he could have a few drinks without the risk of being breathalysed.

"Forget about it, Rob, it was a good idea but you'll never be able to raise the capital now. Get hold of that fucking wop solicitor tomorrow and cancel the whole thing. Have you paid him for any of the work?"

"A few hundred Euro," Robin lied. "Can I take half from your money and half from Uncle John?"

"Do we get a choice?"

"Not really, if I could split it between all ten of you it'd be about thirty euro each but your mates at the golf club seemed to want all their money back."

"They're good people, Rob, most of them have worked hard through their lives and are a bit wary of losing their savings."

"So they'd rather see it earn one per cent, Jesus fucking Christ Dad, one of them gave me the ten grand in cash. I bet he's got it tucked under his bed."

"I know we're not religious but that's a horrid expression. Just repay the money, John and I will expect to pay a hundred and fifty each but no more."

"If I can replace the magnificent seven, will you and Uncle John still back me, Darren says he's still up for it."

"Find the seven hundred and we'll discuss it then," Richard said bluntly. "We won't get into bed with a bunch of fucking shysters."

Robin kept his thoughts of the seven old fossils to himself, he didn't want to risk upsetting his father.

"Is Cheralyn all right, Dad?"

"She's only able to work Monday to Friday for now, I'll need you and your wife available at weekends."

Robin decided to keep that piece of news from Madelaine for as long as he could. "Her name's Madelaine, Dad, and an occasional please and thank you wouldn't hurt."

Before they had a chance to continue bickering Robin pulled into his drive and stopped the car. He'd deliberately not stopped in the road, he knew his father wouldn't cut through the side gate but would have to walk round in the rain.

"Don't take your car out until after lunch at the earliest Dad, loads of people get stopped the morning after."

When he got indoors, Madelaine was surprisingly sober and calm. "How did it go then?" she asked.

"We've lost five of the syndicate," Robin admitted. "At least there's no hurry to replace them Mads, we wouldn't be able to complete things before this season anyway."

"You'd better ring Giovanni tomorrow and keep him up to date. If we don't get that move to Tuscany Rob I can't go on like this much longer. Cheralyn popped in to make sure I knew what tablets the old fool has to take every weekend now she's only going to do five days. I suppose you knew about that didn't you?"

"He only just told me Mads and that was after I asked him about Cheralyn, he wouldn't have told me otherwise. Try and put up with him for another couple of months. If you upset him, he may very well pull out himself and if he does then so will Uncle John."

Madelaine didn't say anything, her mannerisms told Robin all he needed to know for the time being. As his wife had just poured herself a large glass of wine, he decided to treat himself to a whisky. He'd only had a sandwich at the bar but he just couldn't get interested in getting himself something to eat.

Katherine had already told Jennifer that she was addressing the factory staff first thing on Wednesday and needed to finish by seven-thirty. She'd also requested a box of one hundred small cakes and pastries to leave on the table for the staff to eat at the meeting. Jennifer asked Elaine to come in at six o'clock to make the sandwiches for the shop.

Katherine finished at seven o'clock, washed and changed and was at the factory ready to speak to the staff at eight. Jacqui had come in early and apart from one person on holiday and one off sick the whole work force waited in anticipation for Katherine to speak to them.

The staff room was too small to gather all the staff at the same time, as the numbers had grown, they'd staggered the tea and lunch breaks into two sittings. Katherine stood on a low platform at the front of the shop floor at eight o'clock and began her well-rehearsed presentation.

"Thank you all for coming, I'm sure you've all got a good idea what this meeting is about. There's cakes and pastries for you all, please don't take more than two each so everybody gets some. Marks estate has now been settled, what I'm going to tell you was discussed with him and the decision was arrived at with his full agreement. The local authority will announce today that in order to comply with The County Councils housing requirements this site will be re-zoned for a large housing development. To replace the brown-field site they intend re-zoning some farm land just outside the town. So this factory will be moving there, hopefully within the next year or so."

Katherine noticed the atmosphere change very slightly as the staff took in the enormity of the revelation. She paused for a drink of water and carried on.

"Mark and I obviously discussed the possibility at length while he was ill at home. My thoughts and his were exactly the same; that while we need housing it should be affordable and for local people. So I've been working closely with a housing society and I'm going to jointly develop the site over the next few years. The intention is to build a block of flats for sheltered housing, this will provide safe accommodation for retired people and will free up about forty properties locally.

"The rest of the development will range from studio flats for single people through to three-bedroom houses for families. Some will be rented and some of them will be on a shared ownership. Hopefully some of you will benefit from the decision. Obviously, the re-location of the factory will affect all of you in some way.

"The two senior staff members Pete and Gavin want to buy the factory and that goes along with Marks wishes. I've spoken briefly to both of them but they're only hearing this for the first time. They'll be responsible for finding the best site, organising the construction and fitting of the new factory and moving all the machinery and supplies. We don't need a site anywhere near as large as this one and the factory will be designed around the new machinery that we've installed recently. Part of the agreement will be that they honour all your contracts and working conditions."

She noticed that some of the staff were getting a little restless so she wound up her speech by thanking them all for their loyalty to her and Mark and promising them that Pete and Gavin would ensure their employment and welfare.

After she'd finished, she stepped down from the platform relieved that it was all over with no slip-ups. Several of them came up to the front of the room and thanked her for what she was doing, for themselves and the local housing.

"I'll make you a coffee Katherine," Jacqui said. "You look done in."

"I was trembling up there, it went all right, didn't it?"

"You were great and it's just what's needed. Maybe I'll qualify as a local when we get married and be able to buy a flat on this site."

"You already qualify, you've lived locally for more than ten years and you've worked here since you left college. I'm sure you'll be near the top of the list Jacqui."

Pete and Gavin came into the office after they'd got the production line up and running.

"I wish you'd told us a bit more Katherine, what does it mean to Gav and me?"

"It means that as long as the two of you sign a long-term lease on a site and build yourselves a factory, you'll own the finest business in the county at very little cost. Honouring the staff contracts is a standard requirement of taking over a business."

"What about all the machinery and fittings from here, we'll need to take most of it with us?"

"The older stuff is still viable Pete but it's only scrap value. You'll have to update some of it. The new stuff as you know is leased, you'll have to take over the contract with the leasing company."

"You still haven't given us a figure for buying the business, Katherine," Gavin said.

"I have, Gav," Katherine said gently. "Build something for the future, you've both got sons that can follow on. Make the new factory something Mark would be proud of. Two points and they're non-negotiable I'm afraid. Firstly the Reynolds name stays, Mark started the business forty years ago and I'm not going to let that be forgotten."

"That goes without saying, what's the other point?"

"Don't forget I know the turnover and profit figures, boys, you'll be even better off with a sleeker modern plant. I want you two to own forty-five per cent of the business each and the other ten per cent owned by some sort of staff co-operative. You can hammer out the details with whoever does the legal work for you."

Pete and Gavin were pleased to agree the terms, Katherine went home at two o'clock feeling relieved.

Chapter Seven

"Apart from my very glamourous friend stealing all the limelight in her sexy one piece that was the best evening I've had for ages. Thanks Kath."

"Thank you, Liz; it was your idea to come."

Katherine had collected her friend at six-thirty and they'd had an enjoyable hour and a half in the pool at the country club. Katherine had let her membership lapse while Mark was ill but they allowed her to re-join as soon as she arrived. She hadn't been swimming for several years but after a few worries she felt confident and was doing several lengths of the pool without resting.

"The instructor fancies you something rotten Kath, his eyes nearly popped out when you came through in that costume."

"If we go again, Liz, I'll get something a bit more appropriate, it was either that or a very skimpy bikini I wore the last time Mark and I went to Greece. I might have been arrested for wearing that in public."

"More fucking likely they'd have had to call the police to pull the instructor off you. How the hell do you look like that at our age, you could pass for twenty years younger."

They'd gone for a drink after the swim and had decided to have a meal in the restaurant at the club. Katherine was sometimes a little reluctant to eat out, she always thought that she could put a better meal out for a fraction of the cost. She'd been pleasantly surprised to have a grilled fish fillet, new potatoes and salad at a reasonable price.

"We must go again, Liz, it did me the world of good."

Katherine had taken Liz home, they were in her lounge with a coffee at just after nine o'clock.

"Let's make it a regular Wednesday thing," Liz suggested "It'd break the week nicely, you don't really get out much at the moment do you."

"To be honest Liz I never really got out much when Mark was fit. There always seemed something more important for us to do. Mark was happy enough in his garage tinkering with the car or one of his bikes."

"That's the first time I've ever heard you criticise Mark, you were happy all those years, weren't you?"

"Blissfully happy, Liz, but I've been doing a lot of thinking lately. I supported Mark and I was content to do so; now he's gone I've got to re-build."

"What are you planning then?"

"Just doing some of the things I want to do. Maybe Mark would have done them with me after we retired but I'll never know. I'm going away with Doreen later in the year."

"Where are you going?"

"We've both been looking through brochures, probably a cruise if we see one we like."

"Would any of these plans include me, Kath?"

Katherine noticed a change in the mood. "If you want them to, then of course they can. What about Phillip?"

Liz didn't answer straight away, she offered Katherine another coffee which was politely declined. Liz got herself a second cup and sat down again.

"He's getting weird, Kath, he's spending more time at the hairdressers than I do and he's letting the back grow long. I'm sure he's planning on a ponytail. Then he told me he's going to some motor race in France with his mates in the summer."

"I've only told Jen so keep it to yourself for now please, I'm retiring when I hit sixty. I want to do all the things I missed out on. So if you're available, then you'll be more than welcome to join me."

"I'd pay my way, Kath, where else do you want to go?"

"La Scala to start with, maybe New York, some cruises, London weekends, plenty of long weekends at the cottage. I'm going there for Easter if the boilers done; come with me if you want to."

"I've only seen pictures of it, I'd love to come, Kath. I think Phillip and me will be parting company this year. I can't go on like this much longer."

Katherine sensed that Liz was close to tears, she sat next to her on the settee and put her arm round her to calm her down.

"You've been married more than twenty-five years, Liz, be very sure it's what you really want."

"I may as well be divorced, even if he needed me to cook his meals and clean the house it'd be something. We don't even sit down for dinner these days. His kids only come to visit if they want something."

Liz had been with several useless boyfriends until finally settling down with a divorced accountant. He had joint custody of his children and didn't want any more. Liz didn't mind too much, they had two energetic children most weekends and the occasional week in the school holidays. Until the two girls had got married Liz was content to act as a second mother to them and they treated her with respect.

"Do they visit much?"

"Angela pops in sometimes but she's busy with her family, I haven't seen anything of Sharon since before Christmas."

"Will you be all right for money if you get divorced?"

"I'd get half this house which would be plenty to buy a smaller place with a bit left over. I'd have to stay at work until I'm sixty-six but I was planning on that anyway."

Liz had given up work as a full-time teacher when she'd settled down with Phillip. She decided to resume her career when she reached fifty but to get a teaching position would entail re-training for a year. However the school had taken her on as a full-time teaching assistant. As soon as she'd started the job Liz realised that she enjoyed the post more than if she were an actual teacher.

"You'd stay on anyway, wouldn't you?"

"Probably. It would have been nice to choose what I did. I'd have to find a man Kath, I don't think I could be on my own, that's the trouble with Phillip; at least up until recently I felt we were together."

"Jen keeps on to me that I should be online looking for men. Doreen keeps finding them on there and getting hurt."

"There's good and bad in it I suppose. If we do split up, I'll be on there as soon as I've settled in my own place."

"Doreen was texting the latest while we were away, they all seem perfect till she gets serious with them."

"How many men has she taken up with that she met online?"

"God knows, Liz, she'll say it's four or five but I'd say it's a lot more than that."

"If you went on there, Kath, what would you say you were looking for?"

"I haven't thought about it, Liz, just someone sensible to start with I suppose."

"Older or younger?"

"He'd have to be about the same age. Certainly not older but not too much younger. A lady Jen knows has a boyfriend that's younger than her son. That'd be weird to say the least."

"Mark was a good-looking guy, how important would that be?"

"As long as he wasn't really repulsive it wouldn't matter too much, I'm not that shallow. Smartly dressed is always nice, and someone who had more in common with me than Mark."

"I thought you two doted on each other."

"We did but we liked different things. I love the opera, Mark didn't mind taking me now and again; he loved loud rock music and I went to shows with him. But after forty years you don't mind making allowances, I couldn't do that with a new man. I can't see it happening, Liz."

"Here's literally the million-dollar question. What about money, you're fucking loaded, Kath; could you go out with someone poorer than you; which by the way would be about ninety-nine per cent of guys."

"I hadn't thought about it. I'd like to think I was sensible enough to know if someone was just after money."

"There was a lady on the local news the other night who'd had to sell up because she fell in love with a scammer online."

"I saw it, stupid woman used her life savings and mortgaged her house to send the money abroad to a man she'd never even met."

"You'd have to be careful if you did meet a guy. You know how Phillip sees everything in pounds and pence, he was trying to figure out how much you're worth."

"I've never hidden it but it's not that important. As long as I've got a roof over my head and enough to eat, I'm happy. I'd give up everything and live in a shed to get Mark back."

Liz realised she'd gone too far and changed the subject back to the swimming instructor and how much she was looking forward to a little tuition the following Wednesday. Katherine left at ten o'clock promising to keep in touch daily.

She'd had coffee with Liz so when she got home, she made herself a hot chocolate and looked back over her very productive day. Five minutes after getting into bed, she was fast asleep until the alarm woke her.

Chapter Eight

"On your head be it, Jen, if she flips her lid, I'm telling her I told you not to do it."

"I thought you promised to love, honour, cherish and obey me, Danny. That means you get half the credit for what goes right and half the shit when I mess up."

"Two hundred fucking quid for three months, they're taking the piss, Jen."

"It's because it's for business and professional people. By paying an upfront fee they keep the scammers away. They don't even give out the other one's details at first. They have to e-mail through the agency unless both of them agree to give out their numbers and e-mail address."

"For a fee like that they should send a chaperone out on the first few dates. I bet you fifty pence she doesn't even get in touch with any of them."

Jennifer spat on her hand and offered it to Danny to take the bet. He did the same. "Fifty pence says she fucking will, mister. When I put a photo of her on their site every guy on the books will be after her."

"That doesn't mean she'll reply, she won't even let you send the photo and profile. Can you get the money back if she doesn't want to go through with it?"

"I very much doubt it."

"What time will she be there?"

"The swimming lesson is from eleven to twelve so it depends if she takes them for a McDonalds on the way home. No doubt they'll talk her into it. So they'll be there about two o'clock, I'll be home soon after, Elaine is locking up for me."

Danny had dropped the twins off for Katherine to take them for their swimming lesson. He went shopping on his way home, Katherine was staying over, her birthday was the following Tuesday but it made more sense to all of them to celebrate it over the weekend.

"Shall I make up the bed in the spare room, Jen?"

Jennifer was quite patient with Danny, for all his faults he was an amazing father and she couldn't have run the shop without his support. He seemed to live in a world of his own which sometimes frustrated her.

"If you listened to what I said, you'd know that I did it last night. I've got to get back out the front and help Becky, be very careful with that cake please."

Jennifer put the birthday cake in a strong box and told Danny to put it on the floor of the car. She held the shop door open for him and lifted the hatchback door of the car.

"If he drops that cake at home, Becky, he'll be sleeping in the car tonight," she joked when she came back in to the shop. Becky knew better than to criticise Danny, he was head of year at the school she was at until she'd finished her exams later in the spring. She also didn't want to upset Jennifer, she still hoped to start working there full-time.

"He'll be fine with it, can I go for a quick coffee please?"

"Sorry, I didn't realise it was that time already. Have a short break now Becks and you can go at one if you like. Elaine will be here soon to help."

Jennifer knew from her teenage years that Saturday meant a lot more to a teenager than all the other days put together. Even if they only went to the next town for a Subway or Costa coffee they felt grown up and confident.

Elaine Jenkins arrived at twelve o'clock to help with the Saturday routine, they had to either sell the stock cheap or throw it away. Apart from the cakes that kept for two or three weeks all the bread, rolls, quiches and pies had to be gone by the time the shop closed. Every Saturday one or two locals that knew the routine came in to see what had been reduced.

Jennifer let Becky go at half-past twelve, she went at two o'clock and left her friend to lock up at closing time. About ten minutes after she got home Katherine arrived with two very excited children hanging on to her hands.

"Were they well behaved, Mum?" she asked trying to sound stern. "I told them if they were naughty, you wouldn't take them again."

"They were very good and they love swimming."

"Nanny took us to McDonalds for a treat because we were good Mummy," Jessica said excitedly. "She said she was proud of us."

"So am I, sweetheart, let's make poor old Nanny a nice cup of tea, she looks exhausted." After they'd had a drink, Jennifer suggested that Danny and the twins took Snowy for a walk. She wanted both of them to stay awake all day so that they were tired and went to bed on time.

"I'll get them their tea at five, Mum, and if you and Danny put them to bed, we can have our dinner as soon as you come down."

"I hope you haven't gone to too much trouble, Jen, I'd have cooked us something."

"Nonsense, it's your birthday treat. We're having a nice day here tomorrow, a long walk in the morning, a roast lunch and a birthday tea later. How does that sound."

"Just about ideal, I can't talk you into a trip to church I suppose."

Jennifer screwed her face up. "I'd rather not, Mum, we'll go with you when we stay there but it's not really our thing."

Jennifer made the twins their tea at five o'clock, they were exhausted soon afterwards.

"Nanny will supervise your bath, put your onesies on and you can have a hot chocolate before bed. Nanny will read for you as well I expect."

By eight o'clock the twins were in bed, they were both fast asleep before Katherine had finished their story, she left the door open with the landing light on in case one of them woke up in the night.

"They'll need separate rooms soon, Jen."

"Next year, Mum, it's just easier right now for them to share. They usually sleep all night."

"They will tonight; poor loves are exhausted."

"Sit down, Mum, I'll bring dinner in."

Katherine sat at the dining table, Danny opened a bottle of German white wine that they knew she was fond of. He went into the kitchen and a few minutes later they came back with several serving dishes on trays.

"Help yourself, Mum, there's plenty to go around."

Jennifer had made chicken Kiev, spiced potato wedges and a selection of fresh vegetables.

"That was lovely Jen, those years at catering college didn't completely go to waste."

"I did the potatoes," Danny said proudly.

"He peeled them and blanched them Mum, he might be the best teacher ever but no way am I letting him loose in my kitchen."

Jennifer and Danny cleared the table, Katherine sat on the chair in the lounge and relaxed, they brought her a coffee five minutes later.

"Your life is almost perfect Mum, you're sixty next year and you look forty, you've enough money that you can do exactly as you please, you've got two wonderful grandchildren and a very talented daughter, a lovely home and a holiday cottage and you're going to be a big part of community life over the next few years."

"Not to mention an E-Type and an RC45," Danny added.

"Do you two think I'm that stupid?" Katherine said. "You're going to keep on telling me wonderful I am and then it'll lead on to how much I need a man in my life to complete it."

"You've been great lately, Mum, we thought you'd never get over losing Dad but you seem to be over the worst. I know you can't replace him but you can't be on your own the rest of your life."

"I'm hardly alone, Jen."

"When you get home tomorrow you'll go indoors and won't see anyone till you get to the shop on Monday. Don't tell me you don't mind because I know full well that you do."

"It's got its good points, Jen, I can watch Morse and listen to the opera; your father liked The Sweeney and Bon Jovi."

"And you compromised for all those years, you might find a man that likes the same things that you do."

"That'd be nice if it happened, Jen."

"Then make it happen, Mum, we got you something for your birthday, don't be cross please."

"I thought you wanted to wait until tomorrow when the little ones are up."

"It's better you have these now Katherine," Danny said. "Then if you blow your top the kids won't have to witness it."

Jennifer gave her mother a box. "I didn't wrap it, Mum, it's the phone I was using. I know it's not the latest but it makes your old one look like an antique."

"I was thinking about an update anyway," Katherine said. "The camera on mine is playing up. Thanks, Jen; why would I be cross with you about it?"

"That's the easy bit, Jen," Danny laughed. "The next one wasn't my idea, Katherine."

Jennifer ignored Danny and carried on talking. "I put a pay as you go SIM card in it, Mum, there's some credit on it and there's a card in the box that you can top-up with."

"You'll have to put all the numbers in it off my old phone sometime please."

"You've only got about six contacts in it, Mum, it won't take long."

"Thanks, Jen."

The conversation stopped briefly, Jennifer went and got an envelope from the desk in the corner.

"There's presents for you to open tomorrow, Mum. We got you this for a surprise, please don't be cross with us."

Katherine opened the envelope, she was almost certain what was in it, she wasn't cross because she knew Jennifer was trying to do what she thought was best.

"A three-month trial subscription to a dating website, I don't really know what to say Jen and Danny."

"It's a high-class site for business and professional people Mum. They guarantee that they'll only introduce you to like-minded local people. They won't give out your number or address until you tell them to. They advise that you only contact each other with e-mails at first and they'll forward them for as long as you like."

Katherine didn't say anything, she took the presentation booklet out of the envelope and glanced through it.

"I know you did it because you care but I'm still not sure that I'm ready for all this."

"You are, Mum," Jennifer persisted. "You just don't know it. Have another drink, we can at least fill in your details and do the questionnaire."

Katherine was too tired to be cross and to keep the peace she let Jennifer fill in the personal details on the forms. Then Jennifer started reading out the questions that would determine who they sent her profile to.

"Right, Mum, We're got the basics, I need to fill in all these sections now please. They advise you to be flexible and keep your requirements sensible."

"I might be very tired and a little tipsy Jen but the sensible thing would be for you to put that form back in the envelope and try to get a refund from the agency."

"I suggested that, Katherine," Danny said. "Apparently we can't get a refund."

Katherine was looking at the form, Jennifer gave Danny a dirty look and silently mouthed the words 'Fucking Creep'.

"Come on Mum, all they'll do is read what you're looking for and send you the details of any men that match the things you've written."

Katherine relented so Jennifer went through the questions one by one.

"What age man would you like to meet?"

Katherine didn't need to think too much. "Fifty-nine."

"I think you need to be a little less specific, Mum, give an age range."

"Certainly not much younger, definitely not much older."

"I'll put from fifty-seven to sixty-two then. Would you exclude anybody because of their ethnic origin?"

"I've never given it any thought, maybe if I was younger and it was for a lifetime partner but I don't think it'd matter now."

"I'll put no then Mum but if they send you the details of a black man, an Asian or a Muslim please think very carefully before you respond to them."

"You sound a little bit racist Jen."

"You might thank me for it one day, I'm only trying to do what's best for you Mum. What about height?"

"I'm five eight, not shorter but not a giant. Put five-nine to six-two."

"Any preferences on whether he's retired or working?"

"Not really, it depends on what they're doing. I certainly don't want someone who's a workaholic but neither a man who wants to sit around all day watching the television."

"I'll just put no, Mum. We've written all your interests down on your details, I'll e-mail the agency first thing in the morning and see what happens. Any contact from them will be on your new phone."

Danny asked if he could put the television on to watch the football, Jennifer looked at her mother first and then asked him if he'd mind using the set in the kitchen. He understood that they wanted some time alone together so he poured another glass of wine for each of them and went through to the back room.

Both of them started talking at the same time, Jennifer paused to let her mother speak first.

"I know you mean well Jen and I don't want to seem ungrateful but I really don't know about all this. It all seems a bit contrived to me."

"How can it be contrived Mum. All we're doing is putting your profile up, if a nice guy responds you can e-mail him, if you hit it off you can take it as slow as you like. If you don't think you'll get on with him you just never arrange to meet him and stop e-mailing."

"And will he stop, I don't want hundreds of e-mails a day, you hear horror stories about these guys, they've got a name for them I think."

"They're called 'Cyber-Stalkers', Mum. I told you; the agency won't give out your details unless you tell them to. If you don't like a guy, just stop messaging him and that's the end of it."

"What do they do then, how does it work?"

"Your photograph and name go up on the site. Guys can request to be sent your profile and if they come in the parameters of what you want, the agency send it to them. If say a forty-year-old short guy asked for your profile the agency wouldn't send it to him."

"And the same goes for me? I get to see all the men and request the profiles of the ones I like; if I fit the bill, they send it to me."

"Pretty much so, I need two pictures please."

"You are not taking pictures of me looking like this young lady. I very much doubt that I'll be requesting any profiles of men on the site but I don't want them to think I'm some old hag."

"You look fine to me, Mum."

"That's because you've drunk as much wine as me and you're half-asleep as well. I'll have a shower and do my hair in the morning before we go out."

Both of them were tired, Jennifer had been up since four o'clock in the morning and Katherine had been busy with the twins since mid-morning.

"I'll make a coffee and let you get to bed then Mum. I could sleep till Monday."

Katherine slept well, the wine helped her and she woke up at six o'clock feeling refreshed. She remembered Jennifer and herself filling in the forms from the dating agency and felt a little foolish. She decided not to upset Jennifer and let her take the photographs but not to respond to any contacts from the agency. Jennifer had put the number and e-mail address of the new telephone on the form so she decided not to use it for anything else and keep her contact list on her old one.

She crept through to the bathroom at seven o'clock, Danny and Jennifer were still asleep but when she went past the twin's room, she heard Jessica call out. She went in to see to her and Joshua woke soon afterwards.

"Mummy and Daddy are still fast asleep, come in with me and we'll see if we can go back to sleep."

Katherine got back into the middle of the double bed and the twins climbed in, one each side of her. Five minutes later the children were asleep, Katherine drifted off shortly afterwards.

"Mum, rise and shine. It's nearly eight o'clock."

Katherine hadn't heard Jennifer come in, she'd put a cup of tea on the bedside table. The twins woke at the same time, Katherine sent them back to their room to get into their onesies and go down for breakfast. She drank her tea and slipped into the shower before joining the others in the kitchen. Jennifer got her a bowl of muesli.

"Breakfast, Mum, and then don't forget I need two photos of you please."

"Not dressed like this, Jen, I'll have to at least put some make up on and maybe a dress."

"You look all right to me, Katherine," Danny said bravely.

"You look fine, Mum."

Katherine ate her muesli and got up from the table.

"When we come back from walking Snowy, I'll put a bit of lipstick on and borrow a dress Jen. But if I don't think I look all right then it'll have to wait."

By the time everyone was ready it was almost nine-thirty. "An hour will be plenty for a walk, I want the joint in the oven by half-ten," Jennifer said. She made sure the twins had their gloves and hats on, it was a sunny spring morning but still cold.

They were back just over an hour later, Danny made them a hot drink while Jennifer seasoned the joint and put it in to roast. Jennifer asked Danny to take the twins into the lounge to watch television for an hour and rest after their walk.

"Do you want me to start peeling the potatoes, Jen?"

"You're not putting it off, Mum, nip upstairs and put my black dress on, there's some new tights in the drawer you can have and my black shoes are in the bottom of the wardrobe. Put a bit of lipstick on, I'll jazz up your hair a bit when you come down."

To make her point, Jennifer got all the vegetables out of the fridge, "I part boiled the potatoes last night and did the veg this morning, Mum, you've two hours spare."

Katherine admitted defeat and did as Jennifer had asked. She came down twenty minutes later in the dress, shoes and tights. Her make-up was subtle, she'd put a little eye shadow on and a pale red lipstick.

"That's my glamorous, Mum, sit down and let me do your hair."

Katherine was proud of her long hair but usually wore it tied back. Jennifer let it hang loose and brushed it before styling it with her straighteners.

"That's the best I can do Mum, one day you'll let me cut and style it properly for you."

They went into the lounge so that Jennifer could use the telephone that she'd given her mother to take the pictures.

"Who are you?" Jessica yelled.

"Where's Nanny gone?" Joshua added.

"Thanks for winding them up, Danny," Jennifer said.

"If Jen is going to look like that, I can't wait for her to get to your age Katherine," Danny commented. "You look stunning."

"Take the pictures, Jennifer, then I'm going to put my trousers and comfy shoes back on. Maybe I'll buy myself a onesie to wear on Sundays."

"You'd get them going in church Mum; stand in front of the side wall, it's a nice plain background."

Five minutes later Jennifer had taken twelve pictures of her mother. They agreed on the best two and Jennifer deleted the other ten.

"I could plug the phone into the computer and tidy them up a bit," Danny offered.

"No thank you," Katherine replied. "I'll have to be tidy enough as I am."

Katherine took a great pride in her appearance but didn't overdo her clothes and make-up unless it was an occasion that she thought she wanted to look her best. As soon as they'd settled on the two pictures, she went and put her day clothes back on and came downstairs.

"I've e-mailed your profile and the photos, Mum. The agency will only send your profile to men that fit your requirements. When they send yours, they automatically send you the profile of the man who's received yours. Then it's up to you and him if you start messaging each other."

"And they definitely won't give out my phone number and e-mail address until I ask them to?"

"No, Mum, and the same in reverse, they won't give you the number of any men unless he says it's all right to."

None of them wanted to do very much after lunch so after a few games Danny went and got the presents for Katherine's birthday. Jennifer and he had got her a book that they knew she'd enjoy. It was a guide to the best holidays worldwide and the major attractions they offered.

"I love it, thank you so much," she told them sincerely.

"Open our presents now Nanny," Joshua squealed.

Katherine could tell without opening the presents that it was two compact discs, the first one was a Lesley Garrett disc that Jennifer knew her mother wanted and the second one was a compilation of West End show favourites.

"I love both my new discs Jess and Josh and I love you two for getting them for me. Thank you both very much, I'll be playing them as soon as I get home tonight."

They had a lazy afternoon indoors, the weather had changed to a light rain. Jennifer didn't like the twins watching too much television so they got some games out that they could all join in with.

At five o'clock Jennifer got them all a Sunday tea, she kept it simple apart from the cake that she'd made at the shop.

"Blow the candles out Nanny," Jessica said excitedly. "Don't forget to make a wish."

Jennifer had only put a few candles on the cake, Katherine made a performance of blowing them out to amuse the twins.

"What did you wish for, Mum?"

"I can't tell anybody or it won't come true, you know that Jen," Katherine said. She knew that all she could wish for was in the room with her and while she blew the candles out she'd quietly wished good health and happiness to all of them.

Katherine couldn't recall being happier for several years, she'd nursed Mark knowing that he was terminally ill and the grieving took longer that perhaps it should have done. The estate being dealt with seemed to have been the closure that she was looking for. Other people needed her to be her old self, Jennifer and the twins were the most important things in her life but she felt that her sister Doreen and her friend Liz would need support. Possibly in a lesser way so would her neighbour Daphne.

She went home after tea, she was exhausted after her weekend but was feeling positive about things. Pete and Gav had been to the bank and arranged the loan to pay for the factory re-location. The bank had agreed to lend the money in stages as and when they needed it so that they could borrow exactly how much they required. Both of them thought that if they had the co-operation of the local authority the move could be achieved at well under the amount the bank had promised to lend them if necessary.

After a ten-minute telephone conversation with Liz Katherine made a cup of hot chocolate and took it up to bed. Although she'd only been back in her room a short time, she was confident enough in there to sit up in bed and look through her travel book for half an hour before she went to sleep.

She felt that she should have been cross that Jennifer and Danny had bought the subscription to the dating agency but she knew deep down that they had her best interests at heart. It might be fun she thought; having men that she'd never met look at her photograph and ask for her details. She wouldn't know how many men had actually applied to be sent her profile because the agency would only send them to the ones they deemed suitable. She'd know how many they'd actually sent by the amount she received. Whether or not she responded was something that she wouldn't know until she had to choose. It was always possible that she'd set the bar too high and wouldn't get any response at all.

"Dad wants a lift back from the garage tomorrow morning please Mads. He's getting some work done on his car ready for the summer."

Robin and Madelaine had been a little happier for a few days, he hadn't told her that he'd repaid the deposits to the syndicate and that unless he could raise seven hundred thousand pounds through the summer their move to Tuscany would be a distant dream.

"What time do I have to get him?"

"He said he'll be round at eleven o'clock, can you follow him there and bring him back to his house please?"

"Jonathon needs some money for a school trip, can you draw some cash, I think he said it's fifty pounds."

Robin had been building up his reserves in case he had a chance to impress some potential investors, he's kept three hundred pounds back from his fathers and uncles deposits and a hundred and fifty from Darren's. He'd only paid the Italian solicitor two hundred Euro so he was two hundred and seventy pounds ahead.

"Are you sure it's a trip, he doesn't want to get a computer game with it does he?"

"It's a day out at The Science Museum in London Rob, all his mates from school are going so don't let him down please."

"I'll get it tomorrow, don't drink any more tonight, Mads; you've got to drive in the morning."

"I'm going for a shower and bed Rob, are you coming straight up?"

"Ten minutes or so."

Robin took her invitation as encouragement that maybe sex would be on the cards for the first time in nearly three weeks.

He was watching the highlights of the third Grand Prix of the season but was already getting bored with the predictable race. The current champion had achieved pole position and was leading the race, barring an unlikely accident the result was a foregone conclusion. He switched the television off and went upstairs soon after Madelaine.

When they'd first met twenty-one years ago, Madelaine was working for the public relations company that he used to hire now and again. He'd split up with his first wife the year before and Madelaine had just moved out of London, she didn't know anybody in Southampton so they became close. After a few meals out he decided to try and take things further, within three months they were living together and they married the following year. Until Claire arrived three years later Madelaine had travelled Europe and occasionally further afield with him on his wine buying ventures. The business flourished for the next ten years, they moved to a large detached house and enjoyed the best of things. His first wife had married a barrister, apart from paying a little each month to help with the boys she didn't expect much.

"Who won?" Madelaine asked when she came out of the bathroom and saw he was getting ready for bed.

"I got a bit bored with it, actually I'd much rather be up here with you than watching a few overpaid guys following each other round."

Madelaine slipped into bed, Robin went into the bathroom, cleaned his teeth and snuggled up beside her a few minutes later. "I do love you, Mads, you know that, don't you."

"I love you too, Rob, that's all that keeps me here now. Tomorrow morning no doubt your father will remind me that his two grown-up grandsons are doing sterling work and my two children are a waste of space. Then he'll tell me how wonderful Ruth was with the boys and how much he wishes they lived nearer."

Robin pulled Madelaine across to his side of the bed and started stroking her breasts through her nightie. He felt himself getting harder but Madelaine didn't seem interested.

"I'm so sorry Rob," she sobbed. "Be patient with me. Let's try and get away, maybe at half-term."

Robin was upset, he blamed himself for their circumstances but couldn't see an easy way to improve things.

Madelaine pushed his hand away, he didn't try and take things any further. "I'll see if I can get tickets to Italy. No promises Mads, don't forget about Dad, we might only be able to go Monday to Friday."

"That won't even be worth thinking about Rob, we need to fly out Friday or Saturday and come back the following Sunday. It's not worth going otherwise."

"Maybe we can get Cheralyn to work both weekends Mads, no promises."

Robin got up before Madelaine on Monday morning, he logged onto a budget airlines website and tried to find four cheap seats to Milan. Because of the new law that children couldn't be taken out of school during term-time and also that he wanted tickets for flights at the weekend the cost of the holiday would have used up nearly all his spare money.

Madelaine seemed to have perked up a little overnight, she kissed him on the cheek as she looked over his shoulder at the screen. "We'd struggle to afford Italy Mads, maybe we can go somewhere else."

"Keep looking, Rob, to be honest anywhere is better than staying here forever. Don't lie to me, how likely is it that you can find five new investors in time?"

By telling her that it was five and not seven Robin had already lied to her but he didn't want to build her hopes up too much. "I'm trying, Mads, with this fucking Brexit thing no one wants to invest in anything overseas. Giovanni said he'll keep the offer open for as long as he can."

Robin dropped Jonathon at school on his way to work, Madelaine had to be at home so that Richard could take his vintage car to the garage. He walked round just before to remind her where to follow him to. Madelaine was dreading having him sit next to her in her small car.

Chapter Nine

"Try not to waste all that money Daz, most of the ten is back in your account. I had to keep a hundred and fifty from each of you to cover the Italian solicitor and the bank fees."

"Is it definitely off, Rob? I was looking forward to a trip to Italy later in the year to try out the product."

"If you're still up for it then I've got you, Dad and Uncle John; that means to get it going again I'd need to raise seven hundred grand in the next few months. To be honest Mate I can't see it happening."

Robin had stopped in the bar for a drink on his way home from work. He'd told Madelaine that he had an appointment but would be home just after seven o'clock.

"I'm still on Rob but I'm not going in for any more than the hundred."

"You haven't got through the rest of that money, have you?"

"I'm not fucking stupid, I've bought the flat and the car and I'm not touching the rest of it. That's my pension plan."

"Until some ditzy blonde comes along and talks you into paying for a boob job."

"Won't happen, I blew off that one the other week and I haven't had any comeback from her. Now I've joined this upmarket site for business and professional folk. So anyone I meet on there is going to be all right for cash."

"Or else they're a better class of con artist."

"It's five hundred quid for a year's membership, they reckon that keeps them away. I could have got three months for two hundred but going by my record that wouldn't be long enough so I stumped up for a year."

"How does it work, Daz?"

"I go through the photos on the site, all you get is a picture, Christian name and age. If I see anyone that catches my eye, I request their full profile. They look at my details and if I fit the bill, they send me her profile and mine to her. If I'm not what she wants they just say I'm unsuitable and that's the end of it."

"Seen anything you fancy yet?"

"The trouble is most of them are a bit old. I've asked for six profiles so far, they've sent me three so I suppose three women will have been sent mine."

"And then you text them, e-mail them or what?"

"You send an e-mail to her through the agency. Then if you think there's any hope you e-mail via the agency for a while, they won't give out any numbers or e-mail addresses until both of you say it's all right."

"What about the three you've got, any good?"

"I've e-mailed two of them, no reply yet but I only sent them a couple of days ago so early days. You seem interested mate; trouble with your loved one?"

"Not right now but the way things are at home you never know. Mads had her heart set on Tuscany, Dad's been getting on her nerves lately, he never took to her."

"Bit tricky then, living next door to him."

"We're at his beck and fucking call. He won't phone us, he marches round and storms in, doesn't even bother knocking."

"Bit awkward if you and Madelaine are at it in the kitchen then."

"Fancy a game of darts, the board's free. Not much chance of that, things are a bit thin in the bedroom department right now."

"Get down the doctors Rob, he'll give you a prescription for some little blue pills."

They had two games of darts before Robin decided to go home at a sensible time.

"I'd better get home Mate. And for your information I've no need for any fucking pills, maybe a few paracetamol for her constant headache or maybe some roofies so she doesn't know what's going on."

"Kick her out, Rob, move a younger one in. I'll see you later in the week."

"Not fair, Kath. Have you got a life-size portrait in the garage that gets old, lumpy and grey while you get younger and slimmer?"

Katherine had to think briefly, then she realised Liz was referring to the Oscar Wilde story *The Picture of Dorian Gray*.

"Just healthy living and pure thoughts, Liz."

"Eric didn't have many pure thoughts, not many others got the same attention that he was paying you. One of us could have drowned for all he knew."

Liz was keen on their swimming instructor at the country club, neither of them knew anything about him apart from his name and that he looked to be between forty and fifty.

"How the fuck do you do it? You buy a new costume that's meant to cover you up a bit and it makes you look even cuter. Has it got pads in the back to give your butt those curves?"

Katherine was feeling good about herself, even Liz swearing wasn't upsetting her as much as it usually did. They'd had a meal at the club after their swimming and gone back to Katherine's house for a coffee.

"I got it in Bournemouth last weekend, it was only a cheapie from TK MAX. I thought it was quite sensible."

"Show me the photos from the agency then, maybe I'll see Eric on there, at least I can dream."

Katherine got the phone from the drawer, switched it on, tapped her password in and accessed the website of the dating agency. After going through the menu the screen was filled with small pictures.

"How the hell are you meant to see what they look like from that?"

"Wait a minute, I'll set it up as a slide show then all you do is pause if any of them catch your eye."

They both watched as the picture changed every ten seconds. Both pictures came on the screen, a head and shoulders shot and a full length. Liz asked Katherine to pause several times as the slide show progressed. It took nearly half an hour to show all the men on the books.

"There's a few on there, have you asked for any profiles?"

Katherine looked at Liz and laughed. "I'm not going to do that Liz. Maybe if a guy asked for my profile, was inside what I put down on the application and e-mailed me I might think about replying."

"If a guy gets sent your profile, then they send you his right?"

"That's how Jen said it worked."

"So if she sent them your profile on Sunday with the pictures of you there ought to have been some response by now surely."

"It'd take longer than that, wouldn't it?"

"We're an instant society, Kath, I expect there were loads of dirty old men playing with themselves Sunday night. Have you checked your inbox?"

"The phone's been in the drawer since I got in from Jen's on Sunday, let's check it now."

Katherine went back to the main menu of the agency and found out that seven men had been sent her profile, therefore she had seven profiles of them.

"Let's see them then, can't you get it up on your computer."

"I told Jen to set up another e-mail address on the phone, I don't want it on my computer, Liz. Jen said all I'd have to do is put a new SIM card in it if I want to back out."

"I wish I'd brought my glasses, let's see what you've got then."

When Katherine opened her inbox, she found seven profiles had been sent from the agency.

"He looks nice," Liz said as the third profile came on the screen. "Read his details, Kath."

"He's a sixty-year-old retired solicitor, he's never been married Liz, that rules him out straight away. I only really want a divorcee or widower."

"It'd be better if he was single, Kath, nothing to compare you to."

"He wouldn't understand how important family is to me. I'm deleting him."

When they reached the seventh one, Liz thought that he seemed suitable and suggested that Katherine e-mailed him.

"Sorry, Liz, there's something I just don't like about him."

"He looks okay to me."

"I don't know what it is, as soon as I saw the picture, I knew I didn't like him. I'm deleting the whole lot, sorry to disappoint you. Jen said to leave them on here so she can see them but I'm only leaving any of them on that I'm a little bit keen on."

"If I was a member, I'd have e-mailed the second one and the last one."

"I very much doubt I'll be responding to any. How's things been with Phillip this week?"

"I thought he was having an affair last week, I rang the office and he wasn't there. He was doing a five-day course on a motorbike, he's getting a fucking Harley-Davidson so he can ride to France with his stupid friends."

"I can't say too much, we loved our bikes and I didn't do my test till I was nearly forty."

"I'm not going anywhere near the fucking thing Kath; he is growing a pony-tail by the way."

"Mid-life crisis is it?"

"That was the sports car and I think he was screwing his receptionist, he says he wasn't but I don't suppose he'd admit it if he was."

"When's he going to France?"

"The middle of June I think. Maybe we could arrange something that weekend, a London theatre trip would be nice, especially with someone who'd appreciate it."

"I'd love that, by coach like you did before?"

"Definitely, the coach leaves on Friday afternoon and gets back just after lunch on Sunday."

"That'd be a lovely weekend, if they fit the new boiler do you still want to come to Exmoor next weekend?"

"I'd wear my woolly knickers and come even if it's not done. I just need to get away."

"If it's not done, we're not going, Liz. I like my home comforts and it's bloody freezing down there; we'd have no hot water for a bath or shower either."

"I could find a nice man down there to keep me warm."

Katherine hoped her friend was joking. "You wouldn't cheat on him would you Liz?"

"A chance'd be a fine thing, he'd cheat on me in a flash."

"I don't know how anyone could be married to someone and sleep with someone else, Liz. If Mark had ever strayed, I'd have known straight away."

"You must have been tempted, you were with him forty years; or was the sex that good that you didn't feel the need."

Katherine hadn't ever discussed her sex life, even with Liz. She still didn't feel comfortable being open about it but she didn't want to offend her oldest friend.

"I've already told you; Mark was the only man I ever slept with, I've nothing to compare him too."

"You must have thought about it," Liz persisted. "Didn't you ever have fantasies about a tall, dark stranger having his way with you?"

"It doesn't work that way with me, right from when I first knew about sex, I promised myself I'd only ever go with a man that I was going to get married to."

"So what if you'd slept with Mark when you were engaged and he dumped you?"

"That wouldn't have mattered, I intended marrying him, I didn't sleep with him for a long time after we started going out. Sure, I'd have been cross but I'd have got over it."

"So what about now, would there have to be wedding bells in the pipeline?"

"Maybe not marriage, certainly a proper relationship."

"So if Eric came on to you next Wednesday, you'd knock him back?"

"One hundred per cent definite. Too young."

"I'd better get gone Kath. You want to get to bed, it's nearly ten o'clock."

Because Liz was collecting her and bringing her home Katherine knew that she could have two or three glasses of wine with her meal. She had two hours sleep in the afternoon so that she wouldn't feel too tired by around eight-thirty.

She made herself a cup of hot chocolate and put the television on for an hour, nothing was on so she put a disc in the player and spent the time scanning through the holiday book that Jennifer and Danny had given her.

Eventually as they did every night, her thoughts turned to her life with Mark. Although she'd never admit it to Liz, she did occasionally have fantasies about abandoning her principles and not only since she'd been on her own. Several times in the early years Mark had worked from early in the morning until late at night, come home and gone straight to bed after dinner and a shower. Katherine was at home looking after Jennifer and although she was happy with her life she felt that things could have been a lot more passionate.

She looked at the clock and realised that it was nearly ten-thirty so she switched the disc player off and went to bed. When Mark was alive, they tried to be ready for bed at the same time but quite often if he'd been working all day and was tired he'd go up early and be asleep by the time she got up there. She always tried not to disturb him, sometimes he'd stir and manage to say goodnight but often he'd manage to sleep right through. Katherine would struggle to go to sleep, she'd lay there until the early hours listening to him breathing gently and almost wishing that he'd wake up and want to make love to her. Sometimes on a Sunday morning she'd be up first and make tea and go back to bed, occasionally when that happened they'd fool around but most weekends Mark would want to get up and work on the car or bike.

Katherine didn't go straight to sleep, she was thinking about the profiles that she'd deleted from the telephone. She'd been attracted to one of the men but didn't like to mention it to Liz. The fourth profile was a retired doctor from Dorchester. He was divorced, put his interests down as gardening, travel and the performing arts and had two grown up children with four grandchildren. He was six foot tall and very distinguished looking.

She'd been completely against joining the agency at first but was secretly hoping that she'd get an e-mail from him. In a way, she thought it'd be easier for her if he didn't make any contact but she spent nearly an hour imagining what she'd say if she replied to him.

She finally drifted off to sleep just after midnight, the radio phone-in that she'd been listening to had been about the advantages of meeting a partner via the internet. More than half the callers had found their partners online.

Chapter Ten

"Why did you delete all the profiles Mum? I'd like to have at least seen them."

"There was only one that I'd have been remotely interested in," Katherine said truthfully. "Maybe if I get an e-mail from him this week I'll reply."

"If any more men ask for your profile and you get sent theirs, please let me at least see them."

Katherine had logged on to the website of the dating agency while she'd been drinking her tea before setting off for work. Nothing had arrived since she'd deleted everything the night before, in a way she was slightly disappointed but she was also relieved.

"Liz and I are going to Exmoor next weekend Jen, I'll do the shift on the Thursday and we'll leave first thing on Friday morning."

"That's nice Mum, what's happening between her and her creepy husband?"

"She seems to think it's headed for a divorce, he's going a bit weird on her."

Katherine got home by just after one o'clock, checked her inbox and found that three of the men had messaged her, no word from the retired doctor. She thought it rude not to reply to the e-mails so she sent the same short message to all of them thanking them for their interest but asking them firmly not to contact her again. Two new profiles had arrived, neither of them caught her eye but she left them on there to show Jennifer on Friday.

Just after she'd finished her lunch her neighbour walked up the drive. Katherine could see that she was upset, after she'd calmed her down Daphne explained that her husband George had told her that the marriage was over. He'd been having an affair for two months and he was leaving the house to live with her. Their children were grown-up and living away, he'd made arrangements for an estate agent to market the house and he hoped the split would be amicable.

"How the hell can it be amicable when he's been screwing her behind my back?" Daphne sobbed.

Katherine didn't really know what to say but spent an hour chatting to Daphne and trying to calm her down. Eventually things seemed easier. "Have some food with me later Daph," Katherine suggested. "Give me a couple of hours to get ready, pop back at about five."

While she was alone Katherine got a meal prepared for them and had a shower. Thoughts of internet dating slipped from her mind while she rehearsed what she was going to say later on. She was surprised when Daphne arrived looking a lot better than before.

"I'm sorry to be so silly Katherine, I feel a little foolish. If he was going to leave, I just wish he'd done it years ago. We've not really been a proper couple since his last affair. We haven't even slept in the same room since the kids left."

"Then it's probably for the best Daphne," Katherine said. "Maybe you can get a fresh start and find happiness."

"I'm going to find it very hard to trust someone else Katherine."

"Will you be all right financially Daphne?" Katherine asked trying to change the subject so that they didn't start discussing her prospects of finding another man.

"We'll sell the house, of course, I wouldn't want to live there really; I want a fresh start. So I should be able to buy a bungalow and have a little over. Maybe I'll do a few more hours at work but I'll be fine."

Katherine served a simple tuna and pasta bake with salad. She poured them both a glass of white wine and the conversation stopped while they started eating.

"This is lovely, Katherine, thank you so much for listening to my silly troubles."

"It's not silly at all, Daphne. I'm glad you're enjoying the food."

The conversation after dinner was difficult, Daphne kept saying how lucky Katherine had been to be with a man she trusted for almost forty years. Katherine was pleased when her home phone rang at just before seven. She went through to the hall and answered it.

"Not a problem was it, Katherine?" Daphne asked.

"It was Les Davies, he's doing the work on the Jaguar. I hope it's nothing too serious. He's coming to see me after I've taken the twins swimming, said he didn't want to tell me over the phone."

Katherine was relieved that Daphne went home at nine-thirty, she hadn't rested all afternoon so she made a hot drink and went to bed.

"Did you bring it like I asked, Mum?" Jennifer asked at the shop in the morning "Any new contacts?"

"I didn't look last night," Katherine admitted. "I went to bed as soon as Daphne left."

"Right; as soon as the first batch comes out, we're stopping for coffee and I'm checking it."

An hour later Jennifer had the bread and rolls in the rack cooling, the coffee made and was opening the inbox on her mother's phone.

"Not fair Jen, I'm changing the password. I can't get into your phone."

Jennifer gave her mother a quick glance. "You don't know how to change the password, Mum, you struggle to use the microwave."

While she drank her coffee Jennifer went through the latest profiles and e-mails.

"When did you last check, Mum?"

"Yesterday, just before Daphne came around. Is there any more on there then?"

"Six more profiles and four e-mails. Have a look."

Katherine went through the profiles with Jennifer, one of them was from a sixty-one-year-old business owner.

"He looks all right Mum, e-mail him."

"I'm sorry, Jen, I just don't feel anything for him. He doesn't say what business he has and he's put his status down as separated. If he e-mails me, I might try and find out a bit more but I'm not going to do anything otherwise."

"You'll have to do something, there's an e-mail from him."

Jennifer read the message out loud. His name was Eric, he owned a dry-cleaning shop, had been living apart from his wife for a year and had one grown-up son.

"I'll have to think about it Love but it'll be no I think. If he's been apart from his wife that long they should have divorced by now. Maybe I'll ask him to contact me after the divorce."

Two of the e-mails were responses to replies that Katherine had sent thanking her for replying and wishing her well. The fourth one was from the retired doctor in Dorchester.

Katherine read the e-mail out loud, they both thought that he sounded pleasant. He'd been divorced five years, his children were grown-up and he lived alone. He wanted to travel in the future and was hoping to meet someone to accompany him.

"E-mail him, Mum, he sounds really nice."

"I'll think about it, Jen, I'm not promising. Now delete those profiles and e-mails please, you can leave the one from Doctor Andrew on there for now. I'm not promising but I may very well e-mail him over the weekend."

"What time are you picking up the twins for swimming?"

"About eleven but I need to get them back early, Les is coming round, he wants to see me about the Jaguar."

"Nothing wrong with it is there?"

"He didn't want to tell me over the phone, I'd really like to use it when the weather gets better. Your father seemed to think it was just for showing but I think it needs using."

"Bring them here after the lessons then, Danny's going to the football with his mates."

"Sorry, sweetheart, I'd have put Les off if I'd known."

"If you go travelling the world with your doctor friend, we won't have you as a babysitter will we."

Katherine didn't mention it again but she was already thinking what to say in the e-mail she was fully intending to send that evening.

She took a quiche from the shop to have for her dinner, there was enough salad left so she didn't need to cook. The e-mail took her more than two hours, every time she wrote a sentence she deleted it and re-wrote it until she was convinced it was word perfect. She wasn't trying to impress the doctor but she didn't want to appear either too nonchalant or too desperate. At nine o'clock she decided it was good enough and sent it.

She was tired after her long day so she was in bed just after ten o'clock. She read for an hour and was asleep before the radio clicked off after an hour. She woke up in the night, went for a glass of water, used the toilet and went back to bed.

On Saturday morning she had a lie-in until seven-thirty, got up and had a leisurely breakfast. Just before she was due to pick up the twins, she checked her inbox. Seven new profiles and five e-mails had arrived. She kept the profiles for Jennifer to see later in the morning.

Four of the e-mails related to the profiles that had arrived, she replied thanking them for their interest but saying politely that she wouldn't be contacting them again. The other e-mail was from the doctor in Dorchester.

His name was Andrew Duffy, by the tone of the script Katherine felt that he was well educated and intelligent. He told her that he was only interested in a long-term relationship and described himself as being honest and trustworthy. He lived alone just outside Dorchester, played golf once or twice a week and had travelled extensively.

His hope was that he could meet a lady around the same age, to be friends with at first but hopefully leading to something long lasting. He invited Katherine to e-mail him with some more details of how she saw her life for the foreseeable future.

Before she went to collect the twins, she wrote and sent a short e-mail explaining that she was busy for most of the day but would e-mail him either that evening or on Sunday morning.

After the very enjoyable trip to the swimming pool Katherine dropped Jess and Josh at the shop and went home for lunch. She was relaxing in the family room when the doorbell rang.

"Hi, Les, you sounded worried when you rang, is everything all right?"

Les looked a little concerned and didn't look directly at Katherine. "You'd better have a look," he said quietly. "I let one of the lads use a new cutting compound on the bodywork, he said he didn't mind working on it in his own time and I trusted him to do it properly."

They walked round the side of the house to the garage where Katherine could see Les had parked the car. As she got closer, she could see Les starting to smile.

"It's amazing, Les, it looks brand new, I thought he'd damaged the paintwork or something. Is it all done?"

"All done, new tyres all round and a new battery. Everything else has been serviced, all the fluids replaced, the brakes stripped and serviced and the bodywork as you can see is done. I got that little tear in the seat repaired and had the carpets steamed."

Katherine sat in the driver's seat and remembered how excited Mark had been when he'd put the car back on the road after a winter working on it.

"Have you done the bill, Les, I'll do a cheque now if you like."

"The tyres and battery are the main expenses, I've done all the mechanics and Mike did the bodywork. The labour won't cost much Katherine. I'll send the bill in the week."

"I'll run you back in a bit, Les, can I get you a coffee?"

Katherine made them a drink, they took them into the garage and sat in Marks study at the back.

"You'll have to do something about the bikes one day Kath, will you ride again?"

"Maybe I'll get you to get my Ducati back on the road for the summer, I might have the odd trip on it. The Honda's going to a museum soon I think; the Bonneville is staying exactly as it is for as long as I'm here."

They chatted for a while about Mark and his love for his bikes and cars. Katherine proudly drove Les back to his garage in her Jaguar.

Robin was having a mixed weekend, he'd argued with Madelaine, it seemed to be a daily occurrence but was worse on Saturday and Sunday when Cheralyn the housekeeper to his father wasn't there.

One piece of good news was an e-mail from his old friend Giovanni in Italy. He still wanted to sell his vineyard but was prepared to wait until after the current crop was harvested and sold. He didn't give Robin a specific date but hinted that if they hadn't completed the transaction by the end of November he'd put it on the open market.

Mark had been truthful to Giovanni about the syndicate pulling out. His old friend was sympathetic, he suggested that if Robin could find enough investors, he'd keep a ten per cent stake for himself. Robin thought that he could get his father and uncle to put in an extra fifty-thousand pounds each, with his friend Darren putting his share in it meant that Robin had half the cost covered.

"Well, that's fine and fucking dandy," a tipsy Madelaine commented when he told her on Saturday afternoon. "Only half a million short, we'll soon get that together."

Robin had told his wife that his father's friends at the golf club had all pulled out and wouldn't be investing.

He'd decided that he didn't want to spend the little cash that he'd built up on a trip at half-term. The air fares and expenses would have taken most of his reserves, he was also mindful of upsetting his father by leaving him alone for too long.

Madelaine had responded fairly predictably by storming into the kitchen and opening a second bottle of wine.

"Right, we're going somewhere from Monday to Friday and if we don't then I'm going somewhere without you and I may not fucking come back," was her reaction. "Bad enough that we have to be at his beck and fucking call every weekend, now he's dictating our holiday."

By seven o'clock on Saturday she'd finished the bottle of wine and gone to bed, Jonathon was staying at his friends and Robin wasn't quite sure where Claire was. He decided to see if his friend Darren was available for a game of darts or snooker.

"I blew off a date with a supermodel for this," Darren joked. "At least let me win the odd frame."

Robin wasn't in the mood for joking but didn't want to upset his oldest friend. "Sorry, mate, I'm not good company tonight."

"Trouble at home?"

"And getting worse," Robin admitted. "I reckon I've got half the vineyard money covered but I honestly can't see where the rest of it's coming from, Mads got pissed and went to bed, the old man is running us fucking ragged at the weekend and I can't remember the last time I got fucking laid."

"Kids all right?" Darren quipped.

"On the rare occasions that they bother to spend any time with us then if they get off Facebook for a few minutes to ask us for something they seem okay."

They had to give up the snooker table to some noisy youngsters and the dartboards were all busy so they found a quiet corner to sit and chat. Robin was nursing his drink, he was on his second pint and losing his driving license would have made things even worse.

"I suppose as you were able to come for a pint the search for a woman isn't going to plan then Daz; five hundred quid down the toilet by the sound of it."

"I've been asking for profiles," Darren explained. "Because they only send them to me if I'm somewhere near what they're looking for I've only had a few sent to me. Most of the women on there are a bit older than the ones on free sites, I've only e-mailed five women since I've been on there, three replied and I got knocked back by all of them."

"Sorry, mate, I know you had high hopes from this one."

"There's new ones signing up all the time, I haven't given up on it."

"How many women are on there then?"

"A couple of hundred I'd say, not thinking of having a little dabble, are you?"

"I've got enough trouble already, Daz."

"How serious is it, mate? Not another divorce on the cards I hope."

"Dad always reckoned Mads was a gold-digger but she's stuck by me since we lost the house. It's not the money now, she knows if we get to Tuscany it'll be hard work for a year or two. She said the other day when she was sober that she reckons there's no hope, that this is as good as her life will get now."

"I don't want to sound horrible but the old guy must be nearly eighty, he'll go on soon enough, you'll be okay then; I didn't have much a year ago."

"He's fitter than you and me, I can't even think about that. What if he has to go in a nursing home, even if he went on now he might not leave it to us, there's my brother in South Africa and his family. He might very well leave a load to Ruth and the boys, no good relying on it Daz."

"Can you find five more investors in time?"

"I've got to try but the banks won't touch me, I think this Brexit thing's putting people of investing abroad as well."

"Surely there's rich punters that lease those posh cars off you, isn't one of them up for it?"

Robin took a gentle sip of his drink wishing that he could safely have another "Most of them have got less than me Daz, why do you think they lease a Mercedes or Beemer?"

"Because they can't afford to buy one?"

"Exactly. I'm off soon, let's have a look at these women on your saddo dating site then, see if we can find you someone."

"Just because you're six-foot-tall, good-looking with the gift of the gab and could pull most women by winking at them doesn't mean we all can, mate."

Robin had always been considered handsome which made it a lot easier for him to attract women. Darren had struggled with his weight for a long time.

Darren finished his drink and looked at his watch. "I'm off home to drown my sorrows in front of my huge telly. Come back for a coffee and I'll put them up on the laptop."

"I mustn't be long or she'll think I'm cheating on her."

"You wouldn't do that would you?"

Robin drained his drink and stood up. "I might not have much Daz but I'd never do that to her, in spite of how she's been lately I still love her."

Darren squeezed himself into his Porsche, Robin followed him to his riverside flat and parked behind him.

"Wow, you've got it done out nice," Robin commented when they got inside.

"I use the second bedroom so the lounge keeps nice and tidy," Darren explained. "I had an interior designer do this room and the main bedroom."

They went into the modern kitchen, Darren made coffee and they took them through to the spare room. As soon as they got in there, Robin realised that Darren didn't spend much time in the lounge. The room smelt of stale cigarette smoke and looked like something out of the before section of a design programme.

"I assume if you bring any women back here you lock the door to this room."

"I like a bit of disorder in my life Rob, sit down and I'll get on to the site."

Within two minutes Darren had accessed the dating agency web site and set up a slide show of the female members. Robin agreed with him that most of them were in their fifties and sixties and too old for his friend.

"I wouldn't mind someone older," Darren said. "I've asked for some of their profiles and haven't received them so I suppose they're after someone their own age."

"Why don't you lie about your age then?"

"No sense to that," Darren explained patiently. "If I said I was sixty odd, they'd only send me the profiles of women that want a guy that age. That's why they reckon you don't get the fucking scammers on this site like you do the others."

"So you've sent all your details in but all the women see is your two pics, your first name and age, have any of them asked for your details?"

"Only three so far, I didn't really fancy any of them."

"How many men on there?"

"About the same I think."

Darren switched the site to the section where the men looking for women were pictured. Robin had a quick count and thought there was at least two hundred male members. They had a quick count of the women and reckoned about a hundred and fifty were on there.

"Christ, Daz, that's about three hundred and fifty folk paying five hundred each, there's money to be made doing this."

"More than that, Rob. There's a shitload of gay and lesbian members as well."

"Say four hundred members paying five hundred each, that's two hundred grand for putting a few pictures on line."

"You'd have to be a bit of a computer genius to put it all together."

"I'm not thinking of setting up a business doing it, mate, I'm just saying there's big money in it. Go back to the women, let's see if we can find one for you."

"I've been right through them, I've asked for the profiles of the ones I like."

Darren set up the female members as a slide show, now and again they paused to have a good look at the pictures.

Darren paused at a picture of an attractive lady. "I asked for her details bur didn't get them, she's fifty-nine so I'm most likely too young for her."

Robin took a good look at the pictures of the lady Darren had taken an interest in. "She's never fifty-nine, that's got to be a ringer. I bet they put fake pictures in to keep guys interested. Of course she might be looking for a toy-boy and you're too old."

"I've never seen someone that age that looks as good as that," Darren agreed.

Robin looked closely at the photos. "I know that woman from somewhere."

"Maybe it is a fake then, Rob, perhaps she's an actress or model earning a bit on the side."

"I can't think where I know her from, Daz, I've seen her somewhere. It'll come to me, if it's a con job we'll complain and see if we can get your five hundred back."

They switched the computer off and went through to the lounge. Darren poured himself a large glass of wine.

"Sure you won't join me?"

Robin had drunk his coffee and would have liked a drink. "Can't risk it, they'll breathalyse you for anything these days. One of our customers was in a little shunt the other week, the law came because the road was blocked. It wasn't this guy's fault; some dopey bitch drove into the back of him. They still nicked him for being just over the limit."

"Stay over then, you can sleep in the pit."

"Mads would never believe it, mate, she'd reckon I'd been with a woman. I'd better get on, I'll see you in the week."

Robin drove home carefully, he'd only drunk two pints during the evening and was confident he'd pass a roadside test but didn't want to take the chance. He went in to find that Madelaine had got out of bed and was sitting in front of the television waiting for him.

Luckily for Robin she seemed to be in an affable mood. "Where did you go?" she asked.

"Just for a game of snooker with Darren at the sports bar in town, then we went back to his place for coffee. He showed me all the women on the internet he's been chasing."

"Sad fucker," Madelaine said. "Why doesn't he go somewhere apart from the sports bar, he'll never meet anyone there."

"It's how it's done these days apparently, Mads. I was reading about it the other day, something like two-thirds of people meet online now."

Robin poured himself a small glass of whisky and sat next to Madelaine on the settee. He was pleasantly surprised when Madelaine moved closer to him and held his hand.

"I know I've been a right bitch lately Rob and I'm sorry. Let's go to bed and see if we can forget about your father and Tuscany for a while."

On Sunday morning, the good mood Madelaine had been in the night before continued, she went to Aldi at ten o'clock and bought fresh food, had a meal ready to take next door at one o'clock and did a little housework. They sat down for a quiet evening, Claire was out and Jonathon was in his room on the games console.

"If you're halfway to raising the money, Rob, there must be a way of getting the rest of it. Doesn't Giovanni know anyone that'd back you? He fucking owes you, he'd have been bankrupt if you hadn't backed him. Then he didn't do anything when we went under."

"He'd hardly got straight himself Mads, that's why he's doing such a good deal for us now. That place is worth much more than a million, I reckon in ten years with proper care we'd be straight again."

"We'd also be handing most of the money to a syndicate don't forget Rob."

"There'd be plenty in it for us Mads. Don't forget most of the growers aren't very business-like, they sell the crop to someone like me to market for them. I wouldn't need to do that, we'd be making serious money, pay the others a dividend and there'd still be plenty for us."

"You've got to find the money somehow, Rob."

"There's fortunes to be made with that internet dating but you'd have to be a bit of a computer wizard to set that up and it'd cost thousands to get it going."

"I still don't see why it's so popular, sitting in front of a computer looking at strangers. Then there's all these mental fucking women that fall in love with guys on death row in America, what's all that about?"

"These serial killers get fan mail from women, maybe that's where Daz is going wrong. If he murdered a few women and got locked up for life they'd be chasing him."

"He's going wrong because he's a lazy fat fucker who drinks too much. He needs to join a fitness club or even play golf. A bit of fresh air and exercise wouldn't hurt him."

"There was a photo of a woman on the site, I know her from somewhere Mads. I just can't place her."

"Not one of your ex-girlfriends is it?"

"She's supposed to be fifty-nine, it's got to be fake; she only looks fortyish."

"Maybe she lies about her age."

Robin realised Madelaine was kidding. "I doubt she'd add twenty odd years, Mads," he agreed. "I reckon it's a fucking scam. I'll remember where I've seen her one of these days. If I prove its fake Darren can complain, I'd reckon he'll get a refund."

Chapter Eleven

"Christ almighty, Kath; you're lucky I'm not a lesbian. I'd be all over you like a rash if I was."

Katherine had collected Liz for their Wednesday treat at the country club. She hadn't decided to use the Jaguar until the last minute but as it was a nice April day she put the roof down and drove over to her friend's house. She put a headscarf on to keep her hair from flying all over her face.

"Why the fuck are you on an internet dating site?" Liz asked. "All you need to do is put that short dress of yours on, get a pair of fuck-me shoes and you could have your pick of men. Make sure my little Eric doesn't see you."

"I'd be safe," Katherine joked. "I think he's gay."

"You could convert gays with this thing Kath, Phillip reckons it's the sexiest car ever. Good job he can't afford one, he reckons you'd have to find a hundred and fifty thousand for a decent one."

"I'd never sell it, or the Bonneville. I'm using this, Mark used to leave it in the garage and only take it out to Jaguar shows. He'd spend more time polishing it than driving it."

"Please tell me we're going to Exmoor in it next week."

"Sorry, Liz, unless you can get a van to follow us with all the things I'm taking and a fuel tanker to be on standby."

"Spoilsport."

Katherine put the roof up and they went into the club, her swimming was getting back to how it was before Mark was taken ill. She could do several lengths non-stop, most of the swimmers were novices and watched her with envy.

They had a meal in the restaurant after the session, Katherine stuck to mineral water as she was driving the Jaguar. Liz had been arguing with her husband most nights and seemed determined that her marriage was doomed to failure.

"We're in separate rooms now Kath," she admitted "It's only a matter of time now. I almost wish he was having an affair."

"Are you sure he isn't?"

"He'd have told me at the weekend, we were yelling at each other for hours."

"Have you told him you're coming to Devon next week?"

"His reply was fucking good job, don't come back. Maybe I won't, Liz. I could rent somewhere for a few months while the house was being sold. In a way I'll be pleased to get out of it now."

"You've been together a long time, Liz, it's a big step."

"I'm young enough for a fresh start. How's your hunt going?"

"It's hardly a hunt. There's only been one I'm remotely interested in; the retired doctor. We've been e-mailing each other. I think I might ask the agency to give him my e-mail address."

"As soon as I get settled, I'm joining that agency. It's nice that a guy only gets your details if he's close to what you're looking for."

"Andrew seems really nice, there's just something I can't quite place about his e-mails."

"What do you mean; weird or creepy or what?"

"Nothing like that, just very formal in some places. Almost like I'm applying for a job and he's interviewing me."

"It should be the other way around."

"He said he'd like us to meet up soon."

"Are you going to?"

"I don't see why not, the agency say that you should only meet during the day at first and somewhere public."

"That makes sense I suppose, wait till after our weekend away though. I don't want you running away with him and spoiling our break."

"I wouldn't do that to you, Liz, we go back too far."

"So apart from the doctor there's no one else caught your eye?"

"There's a few on there that look okay I suppose. To be honest Liz I'll see how things work out with Andrew and leave it at that. My immediate future revolves round Jen and the twins, getting the factory sorted, developing the land and several trips away."

"Any particular order?"

"Jen and her family would always be first."

After they'd finished Katherine took Liz home and went in for a coffee, Phillip was there; he virtually ignored his wife but was pleasantly polite to Katherine.

"Liz said you're getting a Harley-Davidson Phillip."

"They're delivering it next Wednesday Kath. I expect you'll sell the bikes now the estate's settled, won't you?"

"I don't think I'll sell them, maybe the Honda will go to a museum but I'll keep the others."

"What about the factory site, any movement yet?"

"We've got to re-locate first, it'll be quite a while."

Liz deliberately seemed to be ignoring her husband so after a few pleasantries he went to his study.

"Asshole," Liz remarked. "Why didn't he just ask you how much money you're worth. Fucking good job he didn't see the car."

"As soon as people see it, they automatically tell me how much it's worth Liz, I don't care if it's worth a thousand or a million. Marks Honda is worth double what he paid apparently; who cares."

Katherine went home at ten o'clock, she was a little upset at the breakdown of her friend's marriage. She laid in bed for half an hour reading and listening to the radio before settling down.

"Dad wants a lift to the garage tomorrow morning, Mads."

"Can't you drop him off on your way to work?"

"I suggested that but he's got an appointment at the hospital at eleven-thirty and he wants to go straight there. Can you take him at ten o'clock please?"

"Not too much choice by the sound of it, if he starts touching me up I'll leave him by the side of the road."

"He's been a bit better lately, hasn't he?"

"Only because I've been bribing Claire and Jonathon to go round with his food and shopping. I can't wait to get away at half-term."

"Are you still going to visit your mother over Easter?"

"I wanted Claire to come but she's told me she can't, you could come Rob."

Robin liked Madelaine's mother but as Cheralyn was away for Easter he had to stay and look after his father.

"I'd better not, Mads; if Claire forgets to do his dinner, he'll go off on one again."

When Robin got home the next evening, his father came around straight away, he was in one of his moods.

"Your wife was late this morning, Rob, I only just got there on time. I had to park in the hospital car park, I've got a dent in the door; I think someone banged their door against it."

"How bad is it?"

"I spent thousands on that respray last year, it doesn't matter how fucking bad it is. It'll have to go back to the workshop before the show."

Richard had a nineteen sixty-five Mark Two Jaguar. He'd bought it while he was in the army in the nineteen-seventies and had it completely restored in the nineties. Every year he took it to the owners' club annual summer show, he'd won best in show for the last three years.

"That's not till July, Dad, plenty of time."

"Not the fucking point, if she hadn't been late, I would have parked in a better place and it wouldn't have been damaged."

"Where is she anyway?"

"I don't know, probably drunk again. No doubt that's why she was so late this morning."

"She hardly drank last night, she knew she had to take you."

"If I can't get the work done by the show, I'll never forgive her. She didn't even fucking apologise."

As his father was talking about the annual Jaguar show Robin remembered the picture he'd seen on Darren's computer on Saturday. He recalled where he'd seen the lady in the picture.

"Do you remember about eight years ago Dad when I came to the show with you? An E-Type vee twelve won best in show that year. An old-English white convertible."

"Fucking debacle that year, mine was the best by a mile and they put me in third place. I didn't mind too much coming behind Joe Knight and his XK, even though I reckon it was a sympathy vote but that fucking E-Type shouldn't have won Rob."

"I only had a quick look at it Dad, it looked immaculate."

"It was spotless, can't argue with that. But the chap that it belonged to had replaced the radio with a fucking disc player. How can that be classed as original Rob?"

Robin cast his mind back and recalled the mood his father had been on the drive home.

"You had a right go at the judge about it. Do you remember who owned the E-Type, Dad?"

"I remember he had it left to him. Those E-Types were a fucking woman's car Rob, why the hell they put that ridiculous vee twelve engine in it I'll never know? The straight six XK lump is the best engine ever built, the twelve cylinder did about five to the gallon; they only built it for the Yanks."

"I'd like to know his name, Dad."

"I'll look it up when I get home, it'll be in the club magazine for that year. I know he was fucking loaded. He owns a factory out in the forest somewhere, Joe had a chat to him, said he had thirty-odd men working for him."

Richard went back to his house, as soon as she heard him go Madelaine came downstairs, she'd obviously been drinking and was upset.

"He's been over here twice since he came back from the hospital Rob, how the fuck can it be my fault that someone opened their door on his precious car?"

"What time did you go around for him then?"

"You said ten o'clock, I was just going around when Mum rang. I was there by five past ten. I'm not one of his troops Rob, he had to right to talk to me like that."

Robin tried to put his arm round his wife but she pushed him away. "He never liked me from the start, at our wedding he was telling me how good a mother Ruth was and how much he missed her."

"He'll get over it, have you eaten?"

"Not yet."

"I'll put a couple of pizzas in the oven, what about Jonathon and Claire?"

"I may not be Mrs fucking perfect Rob but I know how to feed my children thank you. If you hadn't realised it's nearly half-past eight, they had tea at six."

Robin got the food out of the oven half an hour later; they sat in front of the television with it. Robin watched the news headlines and then flicked through the channels looking for something he liked. Eventually he settled on a film, they sat in silence eating and watching the hero catch the bad guy and walk off with the girl.

"I suppose it's better than watching that so-called reality telly Mads," Robin said. "Wouldn't get a big audience if they filmed us would they?"

"Maybe if I killed the old fool and said he assaulted me, I'd get all the sympathy, do five years in a loony-bin and we'd be free and clear of him."

"He's still my dad, love," Robin laughed. "Mind you it's not the worst idea I've heard."

Although the mood was a little lighter Robin sensed that any small thing would upset Madelaine again. He sat closer to her but she pushed him away. She stood up and got herself a glass of wine. Robin poured himself a glass of whisky and sat down again.

"I recognised a lady on that dating site Darren signed up to, maybe if I can prove it's a fake I can at least get him his money back. I might even get him a bit of compensation, they wouldn't want negative publicity."

"Maybe she's on there looking for a man."

"I know she was married to a wealthy guy, he had thirty or so people working for him, he drove a seventy-two E-Type. I doubt she'd need to go online to find a man."

"It's a bit weird. They say that's how it's done now but I don't think I'd do it."

"You're lucky you've got me then, Mads."

Madelaine went quiet for a moment, for the last few weeks she'd been wondering how her life had spiralled downhill over the last few years. They'd lived in a beautiful five-bedroom detached house, travelled abroad most years and wanted for nothing. Then Robin had overstretched the business loan and the bank had foreclosed on them.

Robin was furious, he'd been in business on his own for more than fifteen years, had several large business loans and had always managed to service the interest payments. He maintained that the bank foreclosed on him because he had enough assets to cover most of the capital that he owed. After the house was sold the loan was almost cleared but the business couldn't carry on.

His father had bought the small house next door to his after his mother died, he had a full-time housekeeper living there.

Robin and his family were living in rented accommodation so when the housekeeper gave her notice his father had said they could live there. Robin was already working for the car leasing company owned by his father and uncle and living in the house seemed to be ideal. Since they'd been living there three more housekeepers had come and gone, the latest one had been there a year and been reliable until recently.

Madelaine had worked at first to help with the finances but she'd suffered from sciatica and had to give her job up. Richard had suggested that she be his housekeeper several times, one of the reasons the others hadn't lasted long was that they felt threatened by him. As an ex-army officer he felt that most people were inferior to him and treated them as such. One of them had to be given money when she left, she'd threatened to report Richard for sexual harassment.

She was dragged out of her quiet moment by the noise of the back-door slamming, Richard had come around with a magazine in his hand. He came through and completely ignored her.

"Found who that E-Type belonged to, fellow called Mark Reynolds."

"Thanks, Dad, can I borrow the magazine please?"

"As long as I get it back, make sure there's no wine spilt on it."

Madelaine had a glass of wine in her hand so she knew the remark was directed at her. She didn't say anything but Robin could sense her mood.

Richard marched out of the room without acknowledging Madelaine or saying goodnight.

Chapter Twelve

"I love it here, Kath, the cottage is beautiful; we can walk to the pub and the beach as well."

"Much more likely to be the pub this weekend, Liz, too cold for swimming in the sea."

Katherine and Liz had left first thing and arrived at the cottage in good time to walk round to the pub for a late lunch. They unpacked when they returned, Katherine had taken several boxes with her.

"Why the supplies Kath?" Liz complained when they'd finished unloading the jeep.

"It's nice to have spare bedding here in case anyone else uses the place," Katherine explained. "I want a couple of changes of clothes here as well. And there's a few bits of food for the stock cupboard."

"We're only here for the weekend, there's enough food to last for weeks."

"If the weather's nice, I might ride the Ducati down here for one of the bank holidays in May. Jen, Danny and the kids are coming as well, most likely at half-term."

"Can she leave the shop?"

"I can do extra hours, Elaine can help as well and Jen can do extra the week before. If you've nothing on you can help, I can pick you up on the way in."

"At four o'clock in the morning, piss off, Kath. Unlike my glamourous friend I need my beauty sleep. If we've finished stocking the place up can we please find that bottle of wine I brought."

"It's in the fridge, I'll get it."

By ten o'clock they'd polished off the first bottle and made good headway on a second.

"I'm beat, Liz, bedtime for me. Do you mind?"

"Of course not, I won't be long behind you. I hardly slept last night. Phillip came in at ten-thirty from his mate's house and we had a set-to."

"What about this time?"

"That's the stupid thing really, my car needs servicing, he usually does it but when I suggested he did it while I was away with you he started fucking moaning."

"That seems a bit petty to have a row about, if he can afford a new Harley he can afford to get your car serviced at the garage if he doesn't want to do it himself."

"He just wanted to start a row about something; not that important. Did you bring that other phone so you can e-mail your doctor friend?"

"No," Katherine said firmly. "I'm having a weekend away with my best friend, he can wait. We've got each other's e-mail details now so we don't have to go through the agency."

"Are you still going to meet up with him Kath?"

"In a week or two, no hurry."

"I'd have wanted to go a bit quicker than that."

Katherine stood up and stretched. "Bedtime I'm afraid, you know where everything is don't you?"

"This might sound silly Kath but would you mind very much if I used the second bed in the big room and shared with you. I won't snore, promise."

"Of course I don't mind," Katherine said. "Scared of the dark, are we?"

"I've been sleeping in our room on my own so long, Kath; it'll just be nice to have someone there."

They took turns in the bathroom, both of them were in bed by ten-thirty, even though she was tired and tipsy Katherine didn't go straight to sleep. They both sat up in their beds chatting.

"What are we doing tomorrow, Kath?"

"A long lie-in, breakfast and then a nice long walk round the beach and village. Neither of us will be fit to drive till Sunday morning."

"Are we going to Barnstable on the bus then?"

"If you want to, then of course we can."

"I miss curling up with a man after sex, Kath, there's nothing quite like it."

"Mark would be asleep within a minute of finishing, I'd lay there just listening to him breathing for ages."

"Phillip never did that, when we first got together, we'd just talk, make plans sometimes."

"What sort of plans?"

"Anything really. We could talk about sex in those days as well. We'd chat about what we'd done and think of something to do the next time."

Katherine was normally uncomfortable talking about sex and her married life with Mark, maybe the wine had loosened her up a little.

"Mark couldn't talk about sex at all, I think maybe he was a bit on the shy side."

"Didn't you chat about what you wanted to do?"

"To be honest, Liz, there was never a lot of variety in what we did, in bed, in the dark with Mark on top."

"At first, Phillip and I mixed it up all the time, one day he came home early, I was at the sink doing veg and he took me from behind while I stood there."

Katherine thought the conversation was getting a little too intimate for her tastes. "I've got to get some sleep, Liz, if you get up before me, you can bring me a nice cup of tea."

"Goodnight, Kath, thanks for being my friend."

"Night, Liz, we'll have a nice long walk tomorrow."

Madelaine collected Jonathon from school and went straight to her mothers in London for the weekend. Claire stormed out soon after she came home from college saying that she may be home later but that Robin shouldn't wait up.

After he'd done himself a ready meal, Robin scrolled through the television channels and couldn't find anything he wanted to watch. He logged on to his computer and wistfully looked at the pictures he'd taken in Tuscany.

He picked up the Jaguar club magazine and leafed through the pages until he found the results of the annual show. There was a large photograph of Mark Reynolds standing next to his E-Type that had won best in show. Robin got a magnifying glass and studied the picture hoping to see his wife in the background but there was no sign of her.

He went back to the toolbar on his computer and got onto the internet. Five minutes later he'd found out that Mark Reynolds had died the year before after a long illness. He'd left a widow, a married daughter and two grandchildren.

He poured a large whisky, he was a little disappointed to find out that Katherine was a widow, he'd hoped that if he found out somehow that she was happily married he'd have some sort of leverage against the agency and possibly get his friend a refund.

Half an hour later he'd dug into the history of the factory and found the story about the re-development of the site. The story said that Katherine was going to sell the business to two of the senior staff.

He managed to find Katherine's address from the telephone directory and went on to Google Earth to get a satellite view of her house, after he'd worked out that it was worth at least a million he moved the map to look at the images of the factory. Even to his untrained eye he realised that the site was huge, he thought that depending on the type of development that was done at least fifty luxury homes could be built on the site. If they went for cheaper properties then maybe they could squeeze in a hundred or more.

Robin poured himself another glass of whisky. He got a jotter from the desk and tried to work out how much Katherine was worth. He didn't know the value of the site but a hundred properties would raise several million pounds; possibly as much as ten million.

He wasn't drunk but after three glasses of whisky was pleasantly relaxed, he turned his attention to the sale of the business. According to the reports they employed forty-two full time staff, with an estimate of four hundred pounds a week for each one that gave her a wage cost of around a million per year. To sustain that sort of wage cost he estimated that the turnover of the factory would need to be at least five million pounds, possibly more. Surely the sale would be at least as much as the annual turnover, if not more.

By the time he went to bed after more drinks he estimated that the lady he'd seen on the dating site was worth a minimum of ten million and possibly nearer twenty.

His father had strangely offered to take him for a round of golf on Sunday morning so Robin got up just before seven o'clock, had a quick shower, a light breakfast and was round at his father's house at exactly eight o'clock.

"Short of playing partners, Dad."

"I thought it was time we had a round of golf that's all, no need to sound ungrateful. You don't play enough these days. We used to play most weekends before you met your new wife."

"You can use her name, Dad, Madelaine; remember."

"I'm old, Rob, not fucking senile. Ruth rang me last night, how the hell you ever let that one go I'll never know."

Robin tried to change the subject. "That E-Type won't be there again this year Dad, the guy that owned it died last year."

"Her boys are a credit to her, Rob, that lazy son of yours seems to spend all the time in his bedroom."

They played the third hole in virtual silence, Robin was thinking that if his father could see in Jonathon's bedroom he could also see into the room that he shared with Madelaine. If she wasn't feeling too well, she'd very often have a lie-down during the day and have a shower when she got up.

He didn't mention Mark Reynolds or the car again, they finished the round at twelve o'clock so Richard took him into the club for an early lunch. Several of the failed syndicate were enjoying a drink before their round.

His father wanted a drink with his lunch so he grudgingly allowed Robin to drive home, when they got to the car park he pointed out the small ding in the passenger door.

"You can hardly see it, Dad, they might not even have realised that they did it."

"They'd have known all right, at least I've time to get it done before the show. He's having the spray shop re-fitted so he won't do it just yet. The show's at the end of July so as long as I get it there a few weeks before it'll get done."

Robin had driven the car several times before and still didn't get any pleasure from it. He preferred a modern car like the Mercedes he used as a company car. They were home at just after three o'clock, Richard announced that he was going for a sleep and would like a meal at seven.

Katherine and Liz left the cottage after lunch on Monday for the drive back, the traffic was heavy and they spent several long delays discussing the trip and making plans for future ventures.

"That might be the nicest trip I've had for a long time," Liz commented. "Did you think any more about our London weekend?"

"I haven't yet," Katherine admitted. "Do you want to do the same as you did with Phillip, catch a coach from home?"

"Better than going by train, the coach takes you straight to the hotel and on Saturday takes you and collects you from the theatre. Shall I get on and book it?"

"As long as you tell me the date straight away so I can keep it clear."

"If you get together with your doctor friend by then I'll be upset, Kath, I'm really looking forward to it."

They were sat in a short queue of traffic just after leaving the motorway at Taunton, Katherine reached across and squeezed her friend's hand.

"After Mark died, you were there every time I needed some support, I know I was a pain but you helped me through a bad time. I'll never forget about that, Liz, and I promise I'll never let you down."

"When Phillip and I part company, can I use the cottage now and again please? I'll pay you rent for it and leave it clean and tidy."

"How long do you think you can go on like this then, surely better to call time on it if you feel it's inevitable."

"I'm giving it until he's been to France with his mates, it's my birthday the weekend after, last year he only remembered at the last minute. He took me shopping and let me choose some clothes, said he couldn't think what to get me, lying fucker. If he lets me down this year, I'm moving out straight away, I can rent a place for a few months."

Katherine was in two minds, she was living in a four-bedroom house by herself and felt guilty that she hadn't told Liz straight away that she could come and stay with her until things got sorted out. The thought of having such a close friend living there temporarily was tempting but Katherine knew that eventually Liz would move out and she'd have to get used to living on her own again.

While Mark was ill Katherine had seen more of him than ever before, when he was fit he was either at work or in the garage working on something. He'd thought about getting a traction engine for his retirement, Katherine didn't mind him having his hobbies but was hoping that if they retired, she'd eventually get to spend more time with him.

She thought that eventually she'd offer Liz a room for as long as she needed one. They'd always been close but this was the first time they'd been away together, they'd walked for miles on Exmoor and along the beaches, had a meal at the local and a day out shopping in Barnstable. Liz was looking forward to the London trip.

"Maybe next time I go there I'll ask Jen if I can borrow Snowy for the weekend," Katherine said. "She'd have loved the beach."

"I thought you said you were getting a dog soon."

"So did I Liz but not right now. There're too many other things I want to do. If Jen doesn't mind me taking some time off have you thought any more about a week away in the summer holidays?"

"I thought you'd be going away with Doreen."

"She doesn't work now so we can go anytime, you'll have to go in the school holiday. Any ideas?"

"Had you thought of anything? I wouldn't like to go anywhere too hot, if it's July or August maybe it'd be better to stay away from Greece or Spain."

"How about Amsterdam? I've always wanted to go there."

"That'd be great, we can fly from Southampton. It's only a short flight, there's so much to do and see there."

"We'll have a look on the computer on Wednesday after the swimming shall we."

"Keep an open mind, Kath, you want to go to Milan don't forget."

"This will sound very silly, Liz, but it's one of the places I'd planned on getting Mark to take me to. I wanted to visit La Scala to see La Traviata with a man I loved on my arm."

"Your doctor might fit the bill."

"Early days, Liz, I haven't even met him yet."

"Put that right this week, e-mail him tomorrow and if he wants you to meet up make an arrangement for later in the week."

Madelaine arrived home on Monday evening in a foul mood. Jonathon had been sulking all weekend because there was no internet access at his grandmother's house. The car had broken down on the way home, luckily the breakdown service had repaired it by the roadside but recommended that she had it repaired permanently at a garage as soon as possible.

"The fucking thing's on its last legs Rob," she complained. "It'd be much more sensible to replace it. The AA man reckons it'll need a complete new exhaust straight away, he's only strapped it up."

"I know a guy that can fix that up, Mads. We can't afford a new one yet."

"It'd make more sense than keeping that heap going. The garage that advertises on the radio is doing a deal, a small deposit and five years interest free credit on year old ones."

"I don't know if our credit rating is high enough to take out a loan that big Mads. Might be worth a look I suppose."

"How's his fucking lordship been this weekend?"

"Okay I suppose, as long as he gets his meals on time, he doesn't moan too much. I had a round of golf with him, I had to throw the last few holes to make sure he won."

"Did you go for a drink with Darren?"

"He's away visiting his folks, I'm meeting him for a quick drink after work tomorrow."

Katherine and Liz were back at six o'clock after a longer trip than they expected, there'd been an accident and they had to take a detour.

"Let me at least do you a meal, Kath," Liz suggested when they finally stopped in her drive.

Katherine was tired after the long drive, she sat in the kitchen with a coffee while Liz got some food from the freezer.

"It's cheap and cheerful I'm afraid, Kath."

"Beans on toast would have done, I'm not used to driving in traffic like that. If I go in the summer I'm riding there."

"I've had the best time I can remember for ages Kath. I'm looking forward to our summer trip already."

While they were eating, they heard a rumbling noise from outside. "Easy fucking rider," Liz remarked. "At least he'll be outside for an hour cleaning the thing. Don't take the piss out of his ponytail, Kath, he's very proud of it. He'll be getting tattoos done next."

Katherine went home at eight-thirty, just as she was going Phillip came in from the garage. Katherine thought his hair looked ridiculous but didn't comment on it.

Liz was almost in tears when she hugged Katherine as she was leaving. "See you Wednesday, don't forget to e-mail your doctor."

Chapter Thirteen

"Who's the man that Elaine was kissing goodbye this morning Jen? Has she got a new boyfriend?"

"Not exactly a boyfriend, Mum, he stays over now and again that's all."

Katherine wasn't quite sure what Jennifer was trying to explain to her "It's called having a friend with benefits, Mum, at uni they called them fuckbuddies. He stays over a couple of nights a month, sometimes he pops in for a quickie after work."

"So he's just using her for sex, that's disgusting."

"If anything, it's the other way around, Elaine said he wanted something a bit more serious, she told me she likes him for what it is but not for anything too heavy."

"That's revolting, how can anyone just sleep with a man with no thoughts of a future?"

Jennifer knew full well how women could have casual sex with a man without commitment either way. Before she went away to university, she'd had several boyfriends, as soon as she left home, she discovered that she enjoyed sex for the sake of it and didn't want a full-time boyfriend. She knew that she had to take her studies seriously and enjoyed the work, a boyfriend would have been too much of a distraction.

"Don't judge her, Mum, plenty of girls go out, get drunk and grab the first guy they see. There was a story on telly last week about a girl that caught a dose while she was on holiday in Ibiza. She'd slept with nine different boys in two weeks."

"Maybe it's me that's got it wrong then Jen and the rest of the world that's normal. I just couldn't sleep with a man that I wasn't in love with."

"Did you e-mail Doctor Andrew, Mum?" Jennifer asked diplomatically trying to change the subject. Her mother obviously knew that Danny hadn't been her first sexual experience but didn't want her to know too much more,

"When I got home last night, there was two messages from him. I replied but it was a bit late to wait for a reply, anyway there was an e-mail from him on there when I got up, we're meeting up on Friday afternoon."

"That's great, Mum, going on a date. Behave yourself, wear something sensible and don't let him go too far."

Katherine looked at Jennifer and they burst out laughing. "I know we were a bit strict with you Jen, it's because we cared about you."

"When Jess gets a boyfriend, I think Danny will chaperone them for the first few months."

"Now you've got your own children can you see how we worried about you?"

"I just keep telling myself not to get paranoid but sometimes I can't help it. They're my world, Mum."

"It's how we cope, Jen, I had to say goodbye to Mark but at least I had you, Danny and the twins. I couldn't have gone on without you lot."

"Where are you and Andrew meeting on Friday?"

"On Poole Quay, we can go for a drink, maybe even a meal if we get on all right. I'm actually quite looking forward to it."

"I was kidding just now, Mum, but I mean this. All he's got is your e-mail address and you can get a new one straight away. Don't tell him too much about yourself, if he knew you were loaded it might change things."

"I don't think he's after me for my money Jen."

"That's not what I meant, Mum, it may just as easily put him off you. Some men feel threatened by a powerful woman."

"I hadn't thought of it that way round."

"Park the jeep in the multi-storey and walk down to the quay, that way he won't see the car. He could probably trace you by the registration number and find out where you live."

"That's drastic, Jen."

"It's common sense, Mum," Jennifer said patiently. "If he's a fraud, he'll be chasing you for your money and if he's genuine he might be put off by it."

"Best to leave buying a car for a few months, Mads."

"Best for who, Rob, that heap of mine won't get through its next test? Did you look at that deal at the garage?"

"It's only a good deal if you want to keep it for years, I worked out that it depreciates faster than you can make the payments for at least two years. So if we move to Italy and try to sell it after a few months we'd have to find a lump sum to pay the finance."

Madelaine sat quietly fuming "How fucking likely is an Italian future now then Rob? You want to raise half a million and you're saying we can't afford a car."

Robin tried to keep his temper "All I'm saying is wait a month or two and see how things work out. If we have to get you a car then we will; please be patient Mads."

"Your father came around earlier, he said can you please pop round after he's had his dinner."

"That's a bit vague, he normally gives an exact time."

"He eats his meal at seven o'clock, give him ten minutes to eat that, another five to get himself a glass of sherry. So if you leave here at nineteen-fourteen hours you should be okay."

"You remember I was telling you about that woman I recognised on the dating site Darren signed up to?"

"The one you thought was faked?"

"I know who it was, Mads, she was married to a guy that upset Dad at the Jaguar show; he won best in show. He died last year so it looks like it might be genuine."

"That's a shame, you won't make your fortune exposing them."

"She's a fifty-nine-year-old widow, I reckon she's worth fucking millions Mads."

"How do you work that out then, is she advertising herself as a wealthy old woman?"

"All the members get is two photos, one head shot and one stood up, their Christian name and age. Darren asked for her full profile but they only send it to people who are somewhere near what she's looking for."

"Why did your mate ask for it then, she's way older than him? Did you tell him she's loaded?"

"I haven't seen him since I found out who she is. Her husband had an E-Type, it won best in show at the Jaguar club, Dad appealed because he said it wasn't original. He died last year, she's inherited a business worth maybe five million, building land worth maybe as much as ten million and a house that must be a million easily."

"You don't know he left it to her Rob, any children?"

"One daughter."

"She could come up with the money then, are you going to try and get hold of her?"

"It'd look a bit suspect, Mads, she's not going to hand over half a million to a total stranger."

"You reckoned when we met you could sell ice to Eskimos Rob, the worst she can do is say no."

"Giovanni said he might be able to put something together out there, mind you if he could do that, he wouldn't need us."

"Have you spoken to anyone apart from the banks that laughed at you and the ten in the syndicate that chickened out?"

"One or two guys that lease cars, they're a waste of space Mads. One guy said it sounds great but he didn't have any spare cash. I've been trying to get hold of some private investors but they won't take a chance on me."

"So this woman is our last chance, get hold of her, Rob?"

"I doubt she'd even see me, Mads. How the fuck would I ever start a sales pitch?"

"You're the salesman, Rob. This is going to be difficult for me to tell you, sit down and pour yourself a drink, we need to talk right now."

Robin went to the cupboard and poured himself a small glass of whisky. He was thinking how ominous Madelaine sounded. "We need to talk," was the exact expression his first wife had used just before she'd left him.

"When I was up staying with Mum, I just felt relaxed for the first time in ages. We got on so well Rob, this is difficult to tell you. Since Dad died, she's been so lonely living there by herself."

Madelaine was starting to shake a little, Robin thought she was going to start crying. He poured her a glass of whisky and handed it to her.

"If we don't get to Italy, I'm going up there to live with her in September Rob. I don't want us to break up but I just can't stand this any longer. When we came here after we lost the house you said it'd only be temporary. I just can't see what else to do."

Robin thought for a few minutes and collected his thoughts. He poured himself another drink and sat next to Madelaine on the settee.

"I do love you, Mads, you know that don't you?"

"I love you, Rob, it's not enough though. Claire is off to uni in Essex at the end of September, I'd be nearer to her if I was in London; Jonathon could either come with me or stay here with you and your dad."

"And if I get the Italian venture going?"

"You know I'd set my heart on Tuscany Rob, we got so close to it. I'd go with you of course. But I know if I stay here with you, I'm going to get worse, I didn't tell you but I went to the doctor last Wednesday. He gave me a prescription for fucking happy pills and told me it was the early stages of clinical depression."

"Have you been taking them?"

"Not yet, he told me I can't drink if I'm on them. So in a few weeks you'll either have an alcoholic or a fucking zombie on your hands."

"What time are you meeting him then?"

"We're meeting at four, that'll give me plenty of time to have a shower and get changed."

Katherine and Liz had been for their regular Wednesday swim at the country club, Liz had dropped Katherine home and gone in for a coffee.

"Did he e-mail you last night or today?"

Katherine looked puzzled "No, not since we arranged the meeting for Friday."

"He's no romantic then, Kath, if he was, he'd have messaged you just to make you feel good."

"We're not teenagers, he said he'll message me Friday lunch time to confirm the time."

"If you were teenagers, you'd be out buying slutty underwear and booking a room. You haven't been to an Anne Summers party, have you?"

Katherine blushed a little "Certainly not, firstly anything like that is several months in the future, if ever. Secondly, I think I'm a little old for slutty underwear, I didn't even wear any when I was young."

"Christ, Kath, you are so fucking stiff-assed; I suppose you must have had sex because you've got a daughter."

"I don't like talking about it, Liz, I know it's silly. When Jen was twelve, I had a word with her about what goes on. She may well have known more about it than me."

"Talk to me about it then for fuck's sake, Kath; if you can't discuss it with me, you'll never get down and dirty with your doctor friend."

"I had a couple of glasses at the club, if I'm going to do this, I need a gin and tonic. I'll just have to cycle to work."

Katherine made her friend another coffee and made herself a drink. She went to the kitchen to get some ice and sat down again. "You start then Liz, ask me something."

"Did you sleep with Mark before you got married?"

"Yes, but not straight away. It was a couple of months and we both knew it was serious."

"And did the earth move straight away?"

Katherine thought back almost forty years "To be honest, Liz, we were both inexperienced and it took a few times before it came together. My turn then; how many men have you slept with?"

"At the risk of sounding like an old slapper it's nine. That's not as bad as it sounds but I'm not proud of it. I've never cheated on anyone Kath. Not that I haven't thought about it lately of course."

"That's not loads but it's eight more than me. You must have been in love with them, weren't you?"

"I don't see why but I suppose so, some of them were real losers, Kath. One or two of them saw me as a conquest. Don't forget it was the seventies, some of my friends of the time would go with anybody that asked."

"Was Phillip one of the losers or one of the ones that saw you as a conquest?"

"Not fair, I'm supposed to be getting you to open up about your sex life and I'm getting the grilling. Phillip was neither, we dated for a few weeks and fell in love. Right, Kath, did you two ever do anything except have sex at night in bed? Be honest now."

"I'm having another drink, can't you stay over and have one with me?"

"He won't even know I'm not there. Go on then, do me one of those gin and tonics with ice."

Katherine made them both a drink and sat down again, she was feeling relaxed and surprisingly was quite enjoying talking to her friend.

"Don't dodge the question, Kath."

"No Liz. We only ever made love in bed. Mark didn't even like doing it if we were staying with family. He thought we'd be overheard."

"Who was in charge of it then?"

"I'm not really sure what you mean, Liz. I suppose it really depended on how we both felt and what sort of day we'd had."

"Come on then, say for example you felt horny and Mark just wanted to go to sleep. Who'd get their own way?"

"I wouldn't feel like that unless Mark started touching me so in that way I suppose he was in charge. If he wanted to go straight to sleep, we'd just snuggle up nice and close. He usually went straight to sleep; he got tired after working all day."

Katherine was getting more embarrassed by the conversation, she got them both a drink. "Last one for both of us. I'll be cycling, you should be fine by the time you leave."

"Thanks, Kath. Jesus Christ, girl, you have missed out on a lot. Didn't you ever just want to grab him and have animal sex on the floor or in the garden?"

"Honestly, Liz, it never crossed my mind."

"You haven't lived, Kath. We'll have to get you trained up a little bit before you get down to business with a guy. My best friend's a born-again virgin."

"If your friend doesn't get to bed soon, she won't be good for anything tomorrow. I've got to be up earlier so I can cycle to work. Do you want to borrow a nightie or something?"

Katherine was hoping that her friend wouldn't want to share her four-poster bed. She hadn't minded sharing the room in Devon but wouldn't have been comfortable having Liz sleeping in her bed.

"Just a toothbrush would be good thanks Kath, I'll pop in home and get changed on the way to work. Which of your three spare bedrooms am I using?"

A relieved Katherine showed Liz the room, found her a new toothbrush and kissed her goodnight. She went to her room, undressed and got into bed. Normally when she'd had a few drinks she slept soundly but she laid there listening to the radio and thinking about her life with Mark.

To the outside world everything must have looked perfect but Katherine had always felt that she'd given up a lot for Mark over the years. She hadn't minded at the time but for the last ten years or so she was getting increasingly frustrated at the lack of variety in her life. Mark and she had obviously had discussions on what life would be after they retired, he seemed to think that life wouldn't be too much different.

Katherine wanted to travel a lot more but if anything they'd travelled less as they got older. Apart from a week in Greece the year when he was in remission from the cancer they hadn't been abroad since they'd taken Jennifer to Disneyland when she was thirteen.

Katherine had hopes of going to New York for her fiftieth birthday but Mark had been reluctant to take two weeks of work and they'd put the trip off. Every time she'd mentioned it he'd made an excuse and they'd delayed it, then he'd been taken ill and trips to America were put to the back of her mind. Now she was determined that one of her first trips with Doreen would be New York, she was determined to see an opera at The Met, visit the department stores that she'd only seen on television and visit all the famous locations.

She was still uncomfortable discussing her sex life with Liz, or anybody else, she always felt that side of her life was between Mark and herself. The sexual side of their marriage had never been very adventurous right from the start. They'd both worked long hours at the factory trying to build up the business, some evenings Mark would work until nine o'clock and come home exhausted.

When they had made love Katherine had always felt a little short-changed. Most times Mark had managed to make her climax, when he didn't, she'd wait until he'd fallen asleep and then gently bring herself there.

She'd read stories of adventurous women that tried all sorts of different positions, dressed in exotic lingerie or used accessories to liven up their sex lives. Even when she'd been at her hairdressers one afternoon, she'd heard another customer discuss her fantasies while she was having her hair done. Katherine told Mark some of the stories hoping that he'd want to try at least a different position sometimes.

Maybe if she and Andrew made things work, she'd try to be a lot more assertive, not just in the bedroom but with all the other things that came with a partnership.

Chapter Fourteen

Katherine left the factory at twelve-thirty on Friday and went straight home. She only had a light lunch, she was hoping that if she got on well with Andrew they'd go for a meal in Poole. Before she showered and changed, she poured herself a very small glass of wine and went into the conservatory. On a whim she decided to try a third cigarette from the packet she'd bought on her way back from the trip with her sister.

The wine and cigarette relaxed her, she was excited and nervous at the same time. Jennifer had tried to calm her down, she'd given her mother specific instructions for the rendezvous that morning at the shop. She'd instructed her to arrive in the multi-storey car park with plenty of time to spare, find a quiet parking spot in the corner and walk down to the quay.

Andrew had asked her to meet by the food kiosks, Jennifer advised her mother to be fashionably late, to walk along the opposite side of the road so that she could see if he was waiting for her and try to be very laid back when she walked up to him. Jennifer also said that she'd phone her mother at six o'clock in case she needed an excuse to get away.

In fact Katherine was driving home with a sense of disappointment when Jennifer rang, she had the hands-free kit in the Jeep so she answered and told her daughter what had happened.

"He was a horrible man, Jen, it shows how easy it is to fool someone. His e-mails seemed so nice."

"What was the matter with him, Mum?"

"I didn't expect to fall in love at first sight, I'm not that naïve; there was no attraction at all though. His clothes were about twenty years behind the times and looked like they hadn't been washed or ironed for months. I didn't let that put me off at first, we decided to go to the tea-rooms for a drink."

"What happened then?"

"He had no manners or style, he went in first and didn't hold the door for me; then he sat down at the table at the back without asking me if it was all right."

"Was it all right?" Jennifer asked patiently.

"Not really, if you're going to Poole Quay for afternoon tea surely you'd want to sit by the window. We ordered tea, he didn't ask me if I wanted anything to eat which I thought was a bit off."

"What did you talk about?"

"It was almost like going for a job interview, I think as soon as I met him, I wanted to get away from him Jen. He upset the waitress a little as well. She was only about sixteen."

"How did he upset her?"

"She got the order wrong, he shouted at her and called her stupid. She had bright pink hair, you know what teenagers are like. She put the order right but he wouldn't stop talking about how awful todays youngsters are. I made an excuse and left, I'm almost home now."

"I'm sorry, Mum, I know you had high hopes. When you come in to get the twins in the morning, we'll have a look through the ones that have arrived this week and see if we can sort out another man for you to message."

"Not a chance young lady, I'm going to phone Liz and see if she wants to come out somewhere tomorrow night. I'm sure we can find somewhere nice to go, maybe a meal and a show in Bournemouth."

"Please don't give up, Mum. There is a nice man out there for you, if you stop now, you'll never meet him."

"I'll see you in the morning, what time is Danny dropping off the little ones?"

"About ten o'clock."

"See you in the morning then, Jen, Love you."

"Bye, Mum, Love you too."

Robin got home on Friday to find Madelaine had been drinking since lunchtime. Jonathon was sitting in the lounge with her, as soon as his father came home, he went to his room to get on his games console.

"Where's Claire?"

"Fuck knows, she came in from college and went straight out. She said she'd be back Sunday."

"Christ, Mads, look at the state of you. Do you want some food?"

"I want to get out of this fucking place Rob, away from your father. I just want us to be back to how we were."

"You haven't taken any of those pills, have you?"

"It's not the worst idea you've had Rob. Maybe best to take the whole fucking lot."

Robin was alarmed, he hadn't realised quite how depressed his wife had got "It wasn't a suggestion, Mads. Let's get you a coffee, maybe a lie-down on the bed for a couple of hours."

He went into a messy kitchen and made a pot of coffee, he really needed a stiff drink but thought he'd better not. She'd finished a bottle of wine but not yet bothered to open another one. At least she managed to drink some coffee, he helped her upstairs, took her top clothes off and tucked her under the duvet. He sat next to the bed holding her hand for a while until she'd fallen into a heavy sleep.

When he went downstairs, he thought better of drinking any whisky, he switched the television on but couldn't settle. He sat there in the silence thinking of how his life had been and what it could be given the opportunity.

He'd married Ruth straight after university, his father had wanted him to follow in his footsteps and join the army but Robin wanted to branch out on his own. The boys came along fairly quickly and everything was good for the first eight years. His wine business had possibly been too successful, he seemed to spend several months a year travelling, Ruth left with the boys to start a new life; he concentrated on what he knew best and the business continued flourishing.

He was able to pay towards the boys but Ruth was with a wealthy man and didn't push him for too much.

His business went well for several more years, he met and married Madelaine and they moved into a large detached house. Claire and Jonathon were well balanced children, Robin still had to travel extensively but everything seemed to be going well.

The banking crisis of two thousand and eight worried him but not excessively, he borrowed heavily at some points of the year but had always managed to cover the interest payments and repay the capital on time. He was a little more stretched than usual two years later when the bank lost faith in him and insisted that his business loan be repaid. He didn't have the capital to pay his debt and as his property was collateral for the loan the bank took possession and shortly afterwards he was forced into bankruptcy.

Robin took things badly and started to drink heavily, eventually they had to move out of their rented house, his father owned the small property next to his house and they moved in there. Richard Pargeter-Jones and his brother John Jones ran a reasonably successful car leasing company in Southampton and they'd given Robin a position there.

He always felt that the bank had given him a raw deal, he knew businesses that didn't own enough assets to cover their loans and were allowed to continue trading. He felt that his house was re-possessed because he had almost enough equity in it to cover his debts.

While he was trading successfully, he'd developed a strong friendship with an Italian vineyard owner. For three seasons he subsidised the vineyard, the crop was very poor for two seasons and Robin would have been justified in walking away, he persisted though and was rewarded over the next few years.

Giovanni Contini, the vineyard owner was a true Italian and had never forgotten the loyalty that Robin had shown. Now that he was planning to retire he'd spoken to Robin about the best way to market the vineyard. Madelaine and the children had been to Tuscany several times so as soon as Robin knew that he could buy the yard at a heavily discounted price he asked Giovanni to be patient and let him try to raise the funds.

Now the months were passing by quickly and he'd lost his backing Robin couldn't see any way to raise the million pounds needed to buy the vineyard. It covered several acres of prime land with a large house, a cottage and the potential for future development. Robin knew that if he had two or three seasons that were a success the value of the yard would be at least half as much again.

By the time he went to bed it was nearly midnight, he undressed and climbed in next to Madelaine; she stirred slightly but didn't wake up. He put his arm on her waist and whispered that he loved her and was sorry for the pain that he'd caused her.

Katherine got home at six-thirty on Friday evening, poured herself a drink and phoned Liz.

"How did your first date go, Kath?"

"I rang to see if we could have an evening out somewhere tomorrow night Liz. I won't be seeing him again, he isn't a very nice man at all. I'll tell you tomorrow if you can come."

"What do you want to do, a meal out maybe?"

"I'd rather see a show or concert, if I can find somewhere, I'll book up online and let you know tomorrow. Any ideas?"

"Just an evening out would be lovely, Kath, let me know later please."

Katherine went online but couldn't find anything at any of the local theatres that caught her eye, she rang Liz again at ten o'clock.

"There's really nothing much on, how about the cinema?"

"That sounds nice, I haven't been for ages."

"I'm dropping the twins back at the shop after lunch, shall I pick you up about three, come here for a meal and we'll go to Bournemouth after we've eaten."

"Lovely, Kath, see you about three tomorrow."

After she'd spoken to her friend Katherine made herself a hot drink, just before she went to bed she checked her phone, several more profiles had arrived but only one of them piqued her interest. She didn't delete them but was determined not to be persuaded to contact any of them. Andrew had e-mailed her thanking her for coming and saying that he'd like to see her again. Katherine replied telling him that although she'd been pleased to meet him that she didn't believe there was any chance of a relationship. Jennifer had told her that it was simple to set up a new e-mail address, if she received unwanted messages, she'd change her contact details.

Before she went to bed, she took some tenderloin pork fillets out of the freezer for Saturday, most people would have eaten out in Bournemouth before the film but Katherine enjoyed cooking, living on her own didn't give her many opportunities to prepare and cook a nice meal.

Robin slept right through the night, he heard Madelaine get up in the morning but drifted back to sleep. Ten minutes later she sat on the edge of the bed and shook him awake.

"Cup of tea sleepyhead, what time did you come up? I didn't hear you."
Robin shook himself awake and took a sip of tea.

"To be fair, Mads, a gorilla could have got in next to you and you wouldn't have noticed. You hit the bottle early last night."

"I don't want to rely on those pills Rob, a drink settles me down a bit."

"Be careful, Mads."

Madelaine went downstairs, Robin drank his tea, dressed and joined her in the kitchen.

"Any plans for today?" he asked her.

She shrugged her shoulders but didn't say anything so Robin assumed that she hadn't made any plans.

"Let's take Jonathon somewhere then," he suggested. "He can't stay on that console all weekend."

"I'll ask him when he gets up. What's going to happen to us, Rob, I don't want to leave but I can't see any other way out."

"I love you, Mads, I don't want you to go."

"I can't cope, Rob, if I stay here, I'll get worse."

"Our only way out is to buy the vineyard off Giovanni but I can't see any way of it happening Mads. Maybe if I ask him, he'll lease it for a couple of years."

"Do you think he will?"

"Not really," Robin admitted. "It's worth a try I suppose."

"Would your father and uncle still help with the finance if we weren't buying it outright?"

"Probably, I can't see Giovanni going any further than he has, he's already letting it go cheap and he said he'll retain a ten per cent share to help us out."

"What about that rich old biddy at the dating agency then? Any thoughts there?"

Robin thought of the photograph he'd seen of Katherine Reynolds, "Old Biddy," didn't really do her justice he thought but didn't say so. "I've had thoughts," he admitted. "I just can't see how I'd go on about asking her to invest half a million in a venture that the banks won't touch."

"You read about women that get conned out of their life savings by men they've never met," Madelaine mused. "You reckon she's worth between ten and twenty million, she could buy that vineyard and not even notice the cost."

"That's why that agency works the way it does I suppose, Mads, it's only that I happened to recognise her. You'd think she'd be able to find herself a man easy enough with her life-style."

"That's why she's gone on the site I suppose," Madelaine said "Wouldn't a man feel threatened by a woman with that much money. Loads of really rich people are lonely because they don't know if someone's only after them for their money."

"At least I'd never have that problem," Robin joked. He immediately regretted saying it, if Madelaine did leave would he ever be able to find someone else? He didn't have much to offer anyone, he wasn't even sure if his father would let him stay in the house if he was on his own.

"I enjoyed that," Liz said on the way home from Bournemouth. "I haven't been to the cinema for ages."

"Mark liked the James Bond films," Katherine said. "He didn't like the new ones though. We saw *Casino Royale* at The Odeon but he didn't enjoy it and we didn't go again."

"We must go again, Kath. Any more thoughts about our trip to London in June?"

"I've had a look, come back home with me and see what you think. Why don't you stay over again, will Phillip mind?"

"He won't fucking notice," Liz said bitterly. "A few months ago he'd have missed me if I hadn't done his dinner, he's not even bothered about that now."

"Do you want anything to eat?" Katherine asked when they got back to her house at just after eleven o'clock.

"I think that feast that you put out earlier will last me till tomorrow," Liz groaned. "How the hell do you ever get food to taste like that?"

"It's all in the preparation Liz. Most English people cook their food and then put all the sauces on afterwards. Those pork fillets were in a marinade all day, the flavour is cooked into it."

"When I do a roast dinner, I just put the joint or the chicken straight in the oven. What should I do then?"

"Go down to the village pub and have a meal there. Do you want a gin and tonic?"

Katherine made them a drink each, they sat in the family room and she booted up her computer. After looking through several tour companies London weekend excursions they settled on a coach trip leaving locally on Friday afternoon, two nights in a hotel and a theatre visit on Saturday evening.

"They don't say if there's any guided tours included on Saturday," Liz said. "When Phillip and I went, we had a coach tour of all the landmarks in the morning. Mind you he didn't stop complaining about the driver."

"It might be nice to have the day free anyway. We can go to a gallery and then find somewhere nice for lunch. I'm really looking forward to it. I'll book it on Monday."

"Do it now online."

Katherine probably could have done the internet booking if she'd put her mind to it but would rather do it over the phone or go into the travel agents on Monday and do it. "Monday will be soon enough, let's go through to the lounge."

"I'm sorry it didn't work out with your doctor last night Kath. Was he as bad as all that?"

"Probably not," Katherine admitted. "I was thinking that if I didn't know Mark and we'd met like that now I wouldn't have wanted much to do with him either."

"That's a surprise, I thought you two were the happiest couple in the world."

"We were happy," Katherine told her friend. "We knew all the little quirks we had and worked round them. But if we'd just met at our age it'd be different."

"Are you going to e-mail any more men on there?"

"I doubt it, there's a profile on there from a man who looks and sounds rather nice. He's a sixty-one-year-old widower from Christchurch. He's a retired teacher, Andrew seemed to have a problem with youngsters; they'll mostly grow out of the silliness like Jen did."

"I wonder sometimes, half the trouble is the parents, some of them are worse than the children."

"The girl who works at the shop wants to do her training there rather than college, her mother wants her to go to college and university."

"What were you like as a teenager then, Kath? Miss goody two-shoes I suppose."

"I knew I didn't want to waste my life, a girl at school got pregnant when she was sixteen. That gave me more sex education than anything. I wanted to fall in love and get married."

"I know you're proud that Mark was the only man you slept with but you must have had other boyfriends before you met him, didn't you?"

"We went out mostly as a crowd, I sort of teamed up with a boy once or twice but not what you'd call a boyfriend. All they wanted to do was impress me by showing off."

"Showing off what?"

"Anything really, how fast they could drive or ride their motor-bike, how much money they had, how much they could drink. All it did was put me off them. Do you want another gin?"

"I'd better only have another one, I'm feeling a bit squiffy. I hardly slept last night again."

Katherine made two more drinks and put a disc on for some background music.

"This is nice, what disc is it?"

"Jess and Josh gave it to me for my birthday, just a selection of show songs."

"I wasn't going to say anything until it's confirmed Kath so keep it to yourself please. I think I've found a flat to rent. The agent is ringing up on Monday, if I get it, I'm leaving Phillip."

"Big step, Liz."

"It's the only step, he hasn't been near me for fucking months. I know I laugh at your sex life but at least you've got the prospect of one now. I can't go the rest of my life without a bit of passion."

"It's not for me to advise you but don't just give yourself away, you're worth more than that. Elaine who lives above the shop has someone known as 'A friend with benefits'; he just comes around and they sleep together with no commitment."

"I'd want more than that," Liz agreed. "One of the teachers at school's got it right I think. She's married to a nice guy but they don't have sex, so she found herself a bi-sexual woman to keep her satisfied."

"She must have had those feelings before."

"That's what I thought but she says not. I couldn't do that Kath. Even you driving your E-Type couldn't turn me that way."

Katherine was relieved to hear that from her friend, she thought the conversation may have taken a very different turn. They'd had a lovely meal, a night out and two very large gin and tonics. She wasn't sure how she'd react to a sexual advance from her oldest friend.

"Nor could I, Liz," she agreed. "I don't mind being on my own. In some ways it's quite nice. And of course there's always the thought that I'll meet the man of my dreams."

"Who is he then Kath? What's Mr Perfect got to be like?"

"Tall, dark and handsome, that goes without saying. Well educated, classy without being a snob, good sense of humour, fairly clean living. Religion wouldn't bother me but I wouldn't want a complete atheist. Someone widowed or divorced about my age, he'd have to have children or he'd never understand how I feel about Jen and the kids."

"How many of those conditions did the doctor fill last night?"

"He was divorced. Hardly surprising too."

"You didn't mention he had to be seriously fucking loaded Kath."

"That wouldn't really matter, as long as money wasn't that important to him."

"Come on then Kath, open up a bit, what happens when you meet this guy, you go out with him a few times and you decide to get down and dirty with him. What do you do, wait for him to ask you politely?"

Katherine blushed a little. "I don't know, just let nature take its course I suppose."

"Christ, Kath, you need to be a bit more up front than that. What happened the first time with Mark then?"

"It seems like yesterday, my parents were away for the weekend, I cooked him a meal and we went up to bed."

"Did the earth move for you?"

"I felt a little short changed," Katherine admitted. "Neither of us were experienced, it wasn't a disaster because we loved each other. It got better over the years, Liz."

"You didn't tell me what you're going to do when you meet the second mister right, Kath. Didn't you ever mix it up a bit with Mark?"

"I'm getting uncomfortable talking about it, Liz. I don't really know what you mean by mix it up."

"You might be just about fucking perfect but if you don't loosen up a bit, I'll tell you exactly what'll happen. You'll get with a guy and if you ever get to sleep with him you'll do exactly what he wants and when he wants to do it."

"We used to try different positions sometimes."

"Wow, that's daring. Did you use your mouths on each other?"

"I need another drink, do you want one?"

"I think I need one."

"Come with me, Liz."

Katherine poured two more glasses of gin and tonic, went to the kitchen and got them some ice and they went into the conservatory.

"I had one yesterday before I got ready to meet Andrew," Katherine said as she got a cigarette out of the packet. "I know it's silly but it does calm me down a bit."

"Phillip smokes little cigars because he thinks it makes him look cool. You're not getting off that easily, girl; did you give him a blow-job and did he go down on you?"

"Not very often," Katherine finally replied. "I didn't mind but Mark thought that if he let me take him in my mouth he'd have to go down on me and he didn't really like doing it."

"You haven't lived yet, to have a guy down there sucking and licking you is about as good as it gets, Kath. I loved blowing Phillip when we first got together. Sometimes he'd be driving and I'd just lean across and get it out. We were on the motorway once and he must have slowed down a bit, a foreign lorry passed us and the driver could see exactly what we were doing."

"I'd do it with a new guy if I thought we were serious."

"Wow; that's very daring. Did Mark ever tie you up?"

Katherine almost choked on her drink. "We never got into that sort of stuff, Liz, do you and Phillip do it then?"

"Not with Phillip but one or two other guys liked it. The first time I was fucking terrified. He laid me on my tummy and tied my hands to the bedstead."

"Did you know he was going to do it?"

"Not at first, he used my stockings. It just got me so fucking horny, I'd almost finished by the time he climbed on top of me. It takes away all your inhibitions, Kath, you can just let go and enjoy the moment. Sometimes he'd tie my hands tight behind my back, I'd kneel in front of him and suck him off."

"I can't imagine me doing any of that."

"What about sexy underwear; stockings and skimpy pants? Have you got any or is it sensible Marks and Spencer stuff?"

"It all looks so uncomfortable, I'd rather wear tights than mess about with stockings and suspender belts."

"Guys like stockings, you can leave them on as well. When he's running his hand up your leg and it touches skin, he knows he's nearly there."

"I think it's time I went to bed Liz, do you need anything?"

Liz smiled coyly. "Nothing that you've got Kath I'm afraid."

Katherine and Liz went upstairs, they kissed goodnight on the landing and went to their rooms.

After she'd cleaned her teeth and undressed, Katherine laid in bed listening to the radio and thinking about what they'd been discussing. She hadn't been entirely truthful about her sex life with Mark. Although she adored him and was fiercely loyal, she'd always felt as if she was being short-changed in the bedroom. Most times when they'd made love, Mark had finished long before her. Usually he'd manage to keep going long enough but quite often he'd just roll off her, kiss her goodnight and be asleep almost straight away. She'd usually stay awake feeling very frustrated and have to finish the job herself.

The way Liz had been talking to her seemed to be a world away from her sexual experiences, she'd actually been quite stimulated by some of the talk.

She tried to imagine herself doing some of the things Liz had described and wearing sexy underwear. She'd read stories of women that enjoyed being tied up but had never imagined herself in that position. Maybe it would take her inhibitions away but she couldn't imagine trusting anyone enough to let him do that.

Mark had very occasionally used his tongue to stimulate her but Katherine knew that he didn't like doing it so unless he volunteered she didn't encourage him. If she took him in her mouth, he'd let her get him hard and then push her away.

She was in two minds about what Liz had told her about the lady at school taking a female lover. She'd always thought that another woman would know what to do and how to satisfy her but had never felt inclined to test the theory.

Katherine was relieved that Liz was sleeping in the spare bedroom that night, she'd felt more stimulated during their conversation than she had through most of her married life.

Eventually, she drifted off to sleep around one o'clock in the morning. She heard Liz get up in the night and use the toilet and for a brief moment hoped that she'd come in to the main bedroom and slip in next to her.

Chapter Fifteen

Katherine took Liz home after lunch on a sunny Sunday afternoon. Phillip was stood in the drive when they arrived at her house, he was wearing a leather waistcoat, smoking a small cigar and had been polishing the chrome on his Harley-Davidson.

"Fucking idiot, he's got a bandana as well. I doubt he'd have the nerve to wear it when I'm around."

"Mark used to have a few opinions about Harley riders," Katherine agreed. "I'd better not mention them to you in case you use them on him."

Liz made them coffee and they sat in the lounge watching Phillip through the window.

"I'm going to get Les to put my Ducati back on the road I think, I miss riding."

"Just don't join up with that fucking loser and his stupid friends, Kath."

After they'd had their drinks Katherine went home to an empty house, this was what she hated most about being on her own. She was indoors by four o'clock, locked the doors and settled in front of the television for a marathon session of *Midsomer Murders*.

Robin had a very quiet weekend at home with Madelaine.

Darren phoned him on Saturday morning to tell him that one of the regular crowd that went to watch Southampton play their home games had dropped out. Darren offered Robin the ticket for the game, for a moment he thought about going but he knew that they'd be going for a drink afterwards and didn't want to take the risk of leaving Madelaine on her own for too long. He'd put her tranquilisers away but couldn't really hide them, if she took them according to the doctors instructions they'd do her some good but Robin was concerned that she'd mix them with alcohol.

They finally managed to drag Jonathon away from his gaming console after lunch and went to Ocean Village for the afternoon. Jonathon decided that he wanted to go to Pizza Hut for his food so they had a pizza there before they went home. Southampton had failed to score yet again and from what the reporter was saying he hadn't missed anything very exciting.

They'd stopped at Aldi on the way home, Robin tried to talk Madelaine into not buying any wine but she insisted on buying two bottles. She promised him that she wouldn't binge drink and said she'd make them last the week.

When they got home his father was waiting by the back door, they'd had the lock changed soon after they'd moved in so that he couldn't get in when they were out. He was furious, no one had brought his dinner round at five o'clock. He'd driven to the local fish and chip shop for his food.

"Sometimes Dad would treat us to fish and chips on a Saturday night," Madelaine commented. "We thought we were so fucking lucky, that old sod thinks it's a hardship."

"I hadn't realised how late it was," Robin said.

They sat in front of the television for the evening, Madelaine didn't touch her wine; not long before bed Robin made them a small whisky and ginger ale each.

Because Madelaine hadn't lost her temper all day the mood was surprisingly light-hearted, they were in bed before eleven o'clock, Madelaine kissed Robin goodnight and turned the other way straight away. Robin reached across and tried to pull her to him but she pushed him away.

They made sure that his father got a meal on time on Sunday at the correct time, after lunch Robin was bored and they argued about petty things, Madelaine had been on the internet looking at cars at the local dealership and set her heart on a nearly new hatchback.

Robin once again tried to put her off by saying that if they moved to Italy, they'd lose a lot of money and tried to persuade her that her car would last a few more months. Madelaine stormed out of the room and lay on the bed sulking. When she came downstairs Robin apologised and said that if they hadn't raised the money for the vineyard by the time her current car needed a test certificate they'd get her a new one.

She finally opened a new bottle of wine and sat sulking in front of the television on Sunday evening.

"How fucking likely is it that we can raise the other half a million then Rob? Be realistic and at least tell me the truth. Have you heard from Giovanni lately?"

"He's still up for keeping a ten per cent stake but he won't lease it to us. He's not convinced about the ten per cent either but he said if it's being split ten ways he'll have a share of the syndicate with us."

"So we've either got to find someone to put half a million pounds up or get another load of wealthy backers. Tell me the truth Rob, how fucking likely is any of it?"

"It was a dream come true, Mads," Robin answered gently. "Getting away from here, we all loved Tuscany and the way of life, I know I could get the yard more profitable than Giovanni and I've got the contacts here to market the product."

"Is it still remotely fucking possible? Maybe we should start buying lottery tickets, Rob."

"From what I can see that's the only way we'll raise the money in time," Robin admitted; he was almost in tears as he spoke. "You stuck by me and came here with me and I've let you down again, sorry, Mads."

"Any thoughts on this rich widow on the dating site Rob. You hear of these women sending their life savings off to guys they meet online, how much did you say she was worth?"

"At least ten million and possibly twenty," Robin mused. "She could buy the place as a little hobby, Mads. All because she married some rich fucking factory owner."

"You don't know that," Madelaine said sharply. "It might have been her money just as easily. Isn't there any way of contacting her? You used to be a hell of a salesman Rob, you sold it to a team of fucking golfers last year."

"I suppose I could give it a try, how the fuck do I talk her into it Mads? She's probably got a team of financial advisors telling her the best way of protecting her assets."

"Better for her to invest in us than have some Nigerian scam her out of it."

"Why Nigerian, Mads, bit racist, isn't it?"

"Any fucking where then, they get sold the contacts for a few pence each, if one in a thousand fall for it they're likely to come out ahead. Can't you just e-mail her and ask her for a few thousand to buy your way out of the army or something? That's how they start the scam, then once they've got their feet under the table they keep on going back."

"Forget it, I'm not some sort of fucking con-man, I don't think I'd even know where to start. Anyway Darren reckons this site is exclusive for professional and business people, they don't even give out e-mail addresses to their own clients until both sides agree to it."

"You could get her e-mail address though, the factory must have a website."

"It'd look fucking iffy, do I tell her that I saw her on a dating site? Then what, ask her for half a million-investment money?"

"She can only say no, Rob, Christ; you give up quick these days."

"This way, Mads, at least I keep a bit of dignity. Don't forget I went bankrupt, she'd get a background check done at the very least. Then she'd likely have me fucking arrested,"

"It's not illegal to ask somebody for investment, Rob."

"Not going to happen. We've got a few more months, maybe something'll come up."

Madelaine poured herself a glass of wine and sat there on the settee quietly thinking.

"How many people are there on that agency site?"

"We had a quick look at the guys, about a hundred and fifty of them and maybe two hundred women, Darren says they've got a gay and lesbian section but we didn't look there."

"So for argument's sake there's a hundred and fifty guys, it's possible you're the only person that knows she's loaded. Did you say your mate asked for her details?"

"I expect he's too young; they only send the profile to the ones that come somewhere near what the lady's looking for."

"Why don't you join then, ask for her profile and e-mail her. How much is it to join?"

"Daz paid five hundred for a year, I think he said you can get three months for two hundred."

"If you took a potential investor out for a decent lunch it'd cost you that Rob. Give it a go, you must have two hundred in the business account surely."

"I already told you, I'm not going to try and con her out of the money."

"I'm not suggesting that you do Rob, give it a go for fucks sake. If you get sent her details you can e-mail her a few times, maybe meet up for a coffee and give her some of the old Rob Jones. It worked on me."

"Back when I was a high roller, Mads."

"So be one again. Just be the old Rob, wine and dine her and sell her the investment."

"So how do you see if going then? I join the agency and ask for her profile to be sent. If they send hers to me they automatically send mine to her. Do I e-mail her right away?"

"If I was looking for a guy and your profile arrived I'd be on the computer straight away before someone else grabbed you. Say you join tomorrow, you'll get her details straight away if they're going to send them. Give it till Wednesday. If she hasn't been chasing you, then we'll write an e-mail between us. Come on Rob, take a chance on it."

Robin was bored anyway so he went online and scrolled through the internet dating agencies until he recognised the name of the one Darren had joined.

"That's the one, Mads, I recognise the advertising bullshit."

"I thought there'd be all sorts of testimonials and pictures on it."

"Part of the sales pitch, they say unless you fit the requirements of the ones you ask about they won't send the details out."

"What's this woman like then? Tell me what you know about her."

"She's a fifty-nine-year-old widow. Her husband owned a successful factory employing forty-odd staff. He had an E-Type Jaguar, apparently his father left it to him. That's it, Mads."

"How pretty is she, you must have seen her in person to recognise the picture on the site."

"Briefly a few years ago," Robin said. He was being a little cagey. "Quite attractive for an older woman."

"Get an application form on the screen. Let's see what they want to know."

They read all the questions that they needed to answer.

"We'll have to try and think of exactly what she's looking for, Rob; otherwise they won't send her details when you ask."

"I'm not happy about this, I'm going to have to tell a pack of lies."

"All salesmen do it, Rob. You said yourself that back in the eighties and nineties you could have made a fortune flogging endowments and pensions. You told me the guys selling them had to bluff and bullshit their way into a client's life. Just keep as near to the truth as you can."

"What the fuck do I write then? Put yourself in her place and tell me what you'd be after."

"She's fifty-nine and loaded, how old was her husband?"

"Fifty-nine when he died, so a little older."

"She won't want an older guy but you might be a bit young. I'd say she'd want someone between fifty-five and sixty. No older than her but she'd be worried about anyone being too much younger. Put yourself down as fifty-eight."

"Lying about your age is meant to be women pretending they're younger, not men saying they're older."

"You'll just have to be a bit careful about what you discuss. Anything before say nineteen seventy-five and you'd have been at school."

"Do I look fifty-eight?"

"If you told someone you were, they'd believe you, as you said no one adds years. They want to know your interests and what sort of relationship you're looking for."

"This lunacy is your idea, tell me what interests I'd have."

"Nothing too specific Rob. You could put classic cars but maybe she only went because her husband did. She might have hated it. Country and coast walking is always good, some sort of performing arts."

"What sort of arts?"

"Keep it vague, if you put down that you love ballet or heavy metal music, you could put her off."

"What do I write then?"

"Just put that you enjoy concerts and shows."

They spent an hour trying to imagine the things that a widow might want in a prospective partner, eventually they'd put a profile together.

"Are you sure, Mads? This is taking it a bit far. It's two hundred quid we can't really afford."

"Put your card details in and join the site Rob. It's better odds than buying lottery tickets."

"Not that much better."

"Maybe if you don't get her details there'll be another one on there with a bit of spare cash."

Katherine only got halfway through the first episode of her murder drama when the doorbell rang. She was grateful for the interruption, she looked through the spyhole and saw it was her neighbour.

"Hi, Daphne, come in."

"Sorry to bother you on a Sunday Katherine, I popped round yesterday but you were out."

"It's nice to see someone, I'd just been thinking about getting something to eat. Have you eaten yet?"

"I'm going out for dinner, Katherine, thank you anyway. I think its good news, I hope so. George and I seem to have made it up. He tells me he's finished with his girlfriend and wants us to stay together."

"I hope you'll be happy," Katherine said sincerely. "You're a special lady Daphne, don't sell yourself short. Most women couldn't find it in their hearts to forgive their husband and have him back."

"He's on his last chance, he knows the next time he'll be out of my life."

They went through to the kitchen, Katherine made them a cup of tea and they sat at the table chatting. Katherine told Daphne about her meeting with Andrew at Poole.

"You're very brave, maybe that's why I've taken George back. I don't think I could get used to someone else."

"I know what you mean Daphne, I only did it to keep the peace with Jen. I don't think I'll be getting with anyone else. I hope George keeps on the straight and narrow now. I can't understand the women these married men sleep with. They must know they're breaking up a marriage."

"She knew, Katherine; George said she boasted about being able to take him away from me."

Chapter Sixteen

"Daphne came around yesterday tea-time, Jen. Her husband decided to split with his girlfriend and stay with her."

"You don't sound thrilled to bits, Mum."

"I'm pleased that they won't be moving but he's very lucky she's forgiving him so easily."

"What if Dad had cheated then; would you have had him back?"

"I don't believe your father would have even looked at another woman. I actually think I might have forgiven him eventually, I don't know for sure. One thing I can't get my head round; why do these women sleep with married men?"

Jennifer had slept with at least one married man while she was at university, she knew full well why she'd slept with him but couldn't tell her mother the truth.

"Maybe he told her it was over with his wife, maybe she was lonely. Unless you know the circumstances Mum you can't really judge."

"I can judge, Jen, it's revolting. I still can't believe Elaine, is her friend a married man?"

"I don't think so, Mum," Jennifer knew that Elaine had two men that she slept with and one of them was married. Luckily she wasn't lying, she didn't know which one her mother had seen.

They broke for their drink when the first batch of bread had come out and the ovens were heating up to bake the sausage rolls and meat pies for the day.

"Right, Mum, it didn't work out with Andrew, let's see if we can find someone better for you. Let me see the phone please."

"It's at home, Jen."

"I'm not letting you off that easy, Mother," Jennifer said in a stern voice "Bring it with you in the morning please or I'll have to come round after work."

Katherine knew that her daughter was getting a little revenge for their strictness when she was young so she took it the right way.

135

"I got a profile from what seemed to be a nice man. He's a retired teacher from Christchurch."

"Single, divorced or widowed."

"He's a widower, his profile says that his wife died two years ago."

"Nice looking?"

"Just a normal looking middle-aged man. He e-mailed me but because I was meeting up with Andrew I put him off. He messaged me again wishing me all the best which I thought was nice and said I'd be welcome to message him anytime."

"You've had all weekend, why haven't you got in touch with him then?"

"If I happen to meet a nice man and we get on well, it'll be for a long time Jen. A few days won't make any difference."

"E-mail him, Mum. Bring the phone in anyway and we can see what else is on there."

"Did I tell you Liz and I are having a London theatre weekend in June. I'm booking it today, we go on the Friday on the coach and get back on the Sunday. Danny will have to take the twins swimming that day."

"I might take them Mum. Elaine and Becky can do the shop for me. This might sound horrid because I know you and Dad were the best parents ever but I'm not putting the business ahead of the twins."

"I agree with you Jen, we probably did spend a bit too much time working and not enough with you."

"I didn't mean it like that, Mum, I just want the best for my little ones while they're little."

Robin came home from work to find Madelaine in tears on Monday evening. Claire and Jonathon were in their rooms and Madelaine was in the lounge. She was sat in the dark with just the light of the television.

"What's the matter, Mads?"

"The usual, Rob. My sciatica is playing up a bit, his fucking lordship was complaining because I didn't iron his golf trousers yesterday, just the same old shit."

"Do you want me to do you some dinner?"

"Have you had anything yet?"

"There's some pizzas in the freezer, I'll put a couple in the oven. Cup of tea?"

"I haven't been drinking but I took one of my pills this morning and another one an hour ago. I'm upset because I'm fucking ashamed of myself for getting like this Rob. I should be strong for you and I'm letting you down."

"No you're not, Mads, I'll be back in a minute."

Robin came back a few minutes later, he'd put two pizzas in the oven and made a pot of tea.

"A bit of news," he said as he sat next to her on the settee. "That profile came from the agency, which means she's got my details as well."

"What does it say then, how close did we get?"

"We actually know most of it, Mads. She's Katherine, fifty-nine and widowed. She wants to meet a man around her own age, she's currently working but wants to retire next year. She puts her interests down as classic cars, cooking, swimming and opera. She hopes to do a lot more travelling in the future. One daughter and twin grandchildren, one of each, that she looks after quite a lot. That's it really, we got it pretty much right didn't we."

"You didn't e-mail her, did you?"

"I'll need you to coach me a little bit, Mads. I'm still not happy spinning her a pack of lies."

"You don't actually need to lie, apart from your age of course. She's not going to ask you that anyway. It's called lying by omission Rob. She's got the basics from your profile, just keep to general stuff for now. Do you know anything about the opera?"

"It's not over till the fat lady sings?"

"You'll have to bone up on a few popular ones, just for the sake of conversation. It won't be any use pretending you know anything about it but as long as you can mention one or two you'll be all right."

"I've heard of a few, I'll get online before I meet her and get a few basics."

"If she likes opera, she'll like musicals, we've been to one or two at The Mayflower, read up on them as well. I'd keep away from talking about classic cars, you don't want to let it slip that you know about her E-Type. You've travelled more than most people so that'll be something to get her interested. You're a pretty good cook when you put your mind to it and you can swim after a fashion."

"So all I'll have to lie about is a wife and children then?"

"By omission, Rob. Tell her you divorced Ruth and when and tell her there was two boys from the marriage that stayed with their mother. She won't ask if you married again so you won't need to lie about me will you."

"I'll have to lie about what I do for a living, on the profile I wrote that I've got a wine importing business."

Robin got the pizzas out of the oven, sliced them up and brought them through. He looked at the wine bottles but left them alone; if Madelaine had been taking her sedatives she shouldn't be drinking alcohol at all.

"You've still got the business Rob, you registered it again when you were discharged from your bankruptcy, okay I know you're not trading but you can tell her about all the trips you've been on and wine you bought, just don't mention when it all happened."

"You seem to be enjoying this, Mads."

"I don't want to leave Rob but I'm fucking going in September when Claire goes to uni. You haven't come up with anything to stop me yet."

"I can't come with you; you know that don't you?"

"I haven't said I expect you to, have I? You hated staying there before we came here."

"Say I meet up with this woman then. How the hell do I get the subject round to her investing half a million in a vineyard?"

"You said these financial consultants used any means they could to sell endowments and pensions. Remember that guy that tried to sell his lordship next door a pension? He wormed his way in by talking about golf."

"And I wormed him back out pretty fucking quickly when I found out."

"That's not the point, Rob, that's how you do things. Shit, you used to sell wine by the container load. You must have stooped to a few tricks sometimes."

"Not really, I had a good product that they wanted, maybe a lunch out and the odd free bottle."

"So what's the difference, I bet you steered the conversation to something they were interested in and tried to impress them didn't you?"

"You were the marketing expert, Mads."

"Half of marketing is fixing on a target, Rob. Plenty of time I was what they call "Eye-candy," if the target was a guy. You're probably the best-looking guy on that website, how many other ladies' profiles did you get?"

"Quite a few, should I have asked for more than just hers? Won't the agency think it strange that I only asked for one?"

"I don't see why it should. How many is quite a few?"

"Eighteen," Robin admitted. "And yes, Mads; I deleted all of them, and the e-mails from some of them. You'd think they'd hold back a bit until they know who they're writing to."

"Bit forward are they?"

"Only a couple of them, most seem quite nice. When do we e-mail this Katherine then?"

"Wait till Wednesday, Rob, it'd be so much better if she contacted you first."

"Anything worth watching on the telly, Mads?"

"Not really, why don't you study up on opera and musicals. You need something to have a conversation about when you meet her."

Robin switched his computer on and accessed You Tube. He spent the evening watching excerpts of various operas from the most popular composers. Some of them he found boring but the occasional excerpt he found quite enjoyable.

He'd been listening to the music on the headphones because Madelaine had a headache. He'd only intended to listen to one or two, he realised when Madelaine got up to get ready for bed that he'd spent over three hours reading and listening about operas and their composers.

"You seemed to be enjoying that," Madelaine said when he came up to bed.

"It's all right, Mads, I couldn't really listen to all that Italian stuff but there's a few sung in English. If I ever get to meet this woman, I'll know a bit about it anyway."

"You don't want to try and make out you're some sort of expert, just say you enjoy the production and pick two or three that you can learn enough about to bullshit your way through."

Talking about trying to sell Katherine the idea of an investment seemed to have calmed Madelaine down a little. Robin tried to pull her over to his side of the bed but she pushed him away. He lay there for a few minutes thinking about the future. If Madelaine carried out her threat and left to live with her mother he'd be devastated, she'd stuck with him through the worst time in his life. When they'd lost the house and his business had crumbled he'd been on the edge of a breakdown and drinking heavily. They'd stayed briefly with Madelaine's mother before finding a house to rent, after six months Richard had offered them the house next to his and they'd moved there.

Robin had tried to re-start his wine importing business but after being made bankrupt and homeless his heart wasn't in it and they'd settled into a very dull lifestyle. Madelaine was never happy there but she tolerated it to support her husband.

When Madelaine had to give up work due to her sciatica things started to go downhill, Richard got more demanding as he got older, he was perfectly capable of looking after himself but insisted on a house-keeper coming in daily to cook and clean for him.

Three of the housekeepers had left, the current one, a forty-five-year-old divorcee called Cheralyn had been coming in for two years but Robin thought her days were numbered. One of his fears was that now Madelaine was home all day he'd insist on her looking after him.

Madelaine was facing away from him so he nestled in behind her and put his hand on her hip. She put her hand on top and squeezed his hand gently.

"I'm sorry, Rob, I really am. I just can't go on like this for much longer. Tuscany offered us a way out and I really thought we were headed there."

"I'll get the money for us, Mads, we'll be there this year."

"Your swimming is amazing, Kath, how the hell do you find the energy to do all those lengths?"

"Don't forget I come on Saturday as well. Jess and Josh are happy enough in the little pool with the teacher, she's a lovely girl called Carly."

"Any more men on the horizon?"

"I e-mailed the teacher I told you about but I don't think it'll go anywhere, Liz. He idolised his wife and I think he just wants someone to take her place in his life."

"Has he got children?"

"They're grown up and he doesn't see much of them. They live quite far away."

"Any other profiles arrived?"

"I didn't check till I got back on Monday, three more and two of them e-mailed me."

"High hopes for any of them?"

"Not the two that wrote but the other one is certainly a looker. As soon as Jen saw his picture, she insisted I e-mailed him."

"Did you?"

"Not yet, maybe if I haven't heard by the weekend and I'm bored and drunk enough. I've got the phone in the Jeep; I'll show him to you after we've eaten."

"Why no E-Type tonight? I was looking forward to that."

"Jen and her lot are going to the cottage for the Mayday bank holiday, I took them some things over there for her to take down."

After they'd finished their meal, they sat in the front of the Jeep in the club car park and Katherine opened the inbox on her phone. As well as the profile of Robin she saw he'd e-mailed her; it had arrived while they were swimming.

"Show me then," Liz insisted.

"He's e-mailed as well, Liz, hang on a minute."

After Katherine had read the e-mail she showed Liz his pictures and profile.

"Wow; he's fucking gorgeous Kath. E-mail him right now, tell him the agency put the wrong picture of you up and that your name is Liz. If you don't want him, girl, I'm having him."

"I'll reply tomorrow, read his e-mail; see what you think."

"He's perfect, Kath, his own wine importing business, likes the arts and says he travels extensively. What's not to like?"

Katherine took Liz home and joined her for a coffee.

"E-mail him as soon as you get home, Kath, otherwise he'll get snapped up before you get your hands on him."

"Let's get a bigger picture of him, can I use your laptop please."

"Can you get it on mine then?"

"All I need to do is get on the web site and put my password in, Jen showed me how to do it; before you ask I can only e-mail him from my own phone."

"I wouldn't dream of it."

Katherine accessed the agency and put her password in, she made sure that Liz didn't see the numbers and letters as she entered them. Even though she knew that her friend wouldn't be able to contact any of them she didn't want her to be on the site looking for men on her behalf.

"Wow," Liz exclaimed. "He's never fifty-eight Kath, he looks ten years younger. Who's that guy that played James Bond a few years ago? He could be his more handsome brother."

"Pierce Brosnan; he is similar I suppose."

"Ask him to keep his Saturdays free and can you book the church and honeymoon, Kath."

"If I write to him, it'll just be the very basics, I'm still not sure about any of this internet dating thing."

"It's perfect for older people like us Kath. Just say for example one of the teachers at school asked me out and we had a torrid love life for a month or two and then broke up. I'd have to see him every day at work. I don't see how you'll ever meet a guy any other way to be truthful. As soon as I'm settled away from Phillip I'm joining an agency."

"I could easily meet a nice man while I'm away travelling with you or Doreen."

"Highly fucking unlikely though. No excuses, Kath, get hold of this Rob and grab him pretty quick."

Katherine was home soon after ten o'clock, she decided not to write an e-mail until the following day. She made herself a hot chocolate, thought about a cigarette and then thought better of it and got a pen and paper out of the desk drawer.

The next hour seemed to pass in a few minutes, she sat there practising what to write when she sent the e-mail. She'd told Jennifer and Liz that she wasn't sure but every time she looked at the picture she knew that she had to try. Her friend had said he looked like Pierce Brosnan who'd played James Bond. Mark was a big fan of the Bond films, they'd seen them at the cinema shortly after release. Katherine had never seen the attraction of the films but the four with the Irishman playing the lead role had piqued her interest more than the others.

She went to bed soon after she'd written what she thought would be a suitable reply to his e-mail. Although she had to be up early to help Jennifer at the shop she didn't go to sleep until gone midnight. The late night radio eventually sent her off to sleep until the alarm buzzed her awake.

Chapter Seventeen

"Did you e-mail your hunky admirer then, Mum?"

"He actually contacted me, there was a message on my phone when I came out of the club last night. I'll send my reply off this afternoon."

"What are you going to tell him?"

"He sent me a really nice e-mail, Jen, just telling me the basics. He said his marriage broke down because he was away travelling, he's still on speaking terms with his ex-wife but she lives a long way away. He still travels a lot but says he wants to settle down in the next few years."

"He wants to stop travelling and you want to do more, you'll have to compromise, Mum."

"He means travelling for his business I expect, Jen."

"What else does he like doing?"

"He's a busy man by the sound of it. My profile says I like the opera, he likes more or less any live music, especially musical theatre but he hasn't been to see one for a few years. He likes beach and country walks, that's nice because I still think I'll be getting a dog next year."

"I assume he drives, did you say he lives in Southampton?"

"He's based there; whatever that means. I suppose if he travels that much maybe he hasn't actually got a proper home round here."

"Be careful he's not just someone after a rich widow then so he can retire in style."

"I'll be very careful, Jen. The agency say they're very proud that they've got a good record of sifting through applications and their members not being scammed."

"The two hundred up front would scare off a lot of them I suppose."

"I suppose it would," Katherine laughed, "At least they'd get a better class of scammers. I haven't received a letter telling me I've won the Nigerian lottery or have a billionaire cousin that can't get his money out of Iraq."

Robin finished early on Thursday, it was a quiet day and his secretary was quite capable of dealing with anything for an hour or two. He went for a haircut and a quick shopping trip to Ocean Village. Madelaine had more or less instructed him to buy some smart casual clothes for his first meeting with Katherine. He'd received an e-mail from her in the afternoon. She seemed keen and had told him quite a few things about herself. He bought a new white shirt and some tan trousers that he knew would match his vintage leather jacket.

After his shopping he met Darren at the sports bar for a drink and a few frames of snooker.

"How's the woman hunt going then Daz?"

"I've been e-mailing a woman from the agency Rob. She's forty-eight, a doctor from Portsmouth. Nice looking, divorced with no kids."

"One immediate problem, you're a Southampton fan, if she follows Portsmouth it'll never work."

"Not going to be an issue Mate, she doesn't follow football. But she seemed to be all right about me going to the games. She plays golf most weeks, I might give that a go if we get on all right."

"Dad plays three or four times a week, I started but I never really enjoyed it."

"How's things at home?"

Robin didn't want anyone else to know that his wife was going to leave in the autumn if their circumstances hadn't improved in the meantime.

"It's not good," he admitted. "Madelaine went to the doctors, she's still suffering from sciatica; he also gave her some anti-depressants."

"My mum used to take them, get her off them as quick as you can Mate, she'll be like a fucking zombie."

"I don't know whether I'd prefer her on those or drinking Daz."

"No news of your Italian adventure getting going I suppose, do I have to find somewhere else to take the lovely Doctor Annabella?"

"Annabella, she's not Italian, is she? If you have to shout out her name when you finish it'll be time to get dressed before you're done."

"I expect it'll be Anna or Bella when we get to know each other. I'm quite hopeful of this one Rob."

Robin had to be careful not to mention Katherine and what he was doing. "I'm not really sure about Tuscany, Daz, I'll give it until November and if I've not found a backer by then, I'd say it's not going to happen."

"If it doesn't happen, I'm thinking of buying a place in Spain, Rob. Can I count on you for a bit of guidance?"

"Are you set on Spain, there's plenty other places?"

"I'll listen to your advice, Rob, at least I know I can trust you."

Robin felt guilty when his friend said that he trusted him, although he wasn't planning to cheat Katherine he still felt ill-at-ease contacting her via the dating agency. To earn her trust he'd have to convince her on two counts. Firstly that he was interested in her and secondly that the yard was a legitimate investment.

He made his excuses at a little after six o'clock and went home. Madelaine, Claire and Jonathon were eating their food in the lounge "There's a meal in the kitchen," Madelaine shouted when she heard him come in "Put it in the microwave for a minute just to make sure it's hot enough."

The children disappeared as soon as they'd finished eating, Rob sat down and ate his dinner in front of the television.

"Katherine Reynolds replied to my e-mail, Mads."

"What did she say then?"

"Just what we expected really, she was widowed last year, she wants to retire next year when she hits sixty, wants to get a dog, a few things about her daughter and grandkids."

"Wait till tomorrow and e-mail her back. Tell her you're on a wine buying trip to France or somewhere."

"I'm amazed that you're up for this, Mads, you actually seem to be getting enthusiastic about me going after her."

"It's our last chance, Rob, you've had long enough to raise the funds."

"I'm still not comfortable with this, Mads. To get her to trust me enough to invest she'll be expecting a full-on relationship. What the fuck do I do, ask for half a million up front?"

"Just wing it, the very worst will be that you'll have a civilised afternoon tea somewhere, shake hands and that's it. Okay, we'd be two hundred pounds down, just think how much it'd cost if you tried to get her to invest the normal way."

"I'd have to put a proper package together, get surveys of the yard done and cost breakdowns. Maybe I'd have to pay for a trip out there for her and accommodation, I guess it'd be a couple of thousand and I don't think she'd go for it."

"Just think of yourself as the top salesman that you know you are Rob. Wine and dine her a bit, say that you want to settle down in Tuscany. Make out you're going bust if you don't get the backing. Just make it up as you go, Rob."

Robin was relieved that at least Madelaine didn't seem to be drinking or taking her tablets. She wanted to watch the television so he booted up his computer and watched several excerpts of popular operas and stage shows.

"You'd better do a bit of catching up on your wine too, Rob. You'd only have to slip up on one thing for her to realise you're not what you say you are."

"I think I know my way round the wine business Mads."

"You did a few years ago, what if you e-mail her tomorrow and tell her you're in France checking out a particular grape and they're not growing it anymore. It's growing time and you'll be able to use that as an excuse for not seeing her very often. You've got to get it fucking right, Rob."

"How soon should I suggest we meet for a coffee?"

"E-mail her tomorrow, tell her you're in France and will be back in a week. Just make sure you check the growing areas in France for crop and weather news."

"Don't be too proud to ask me, Liz, if you need anything at all just say the word."

Liz Powell was on the telephone to Katherine telling her that she'd signed a six month lease on a flat. She was due to collect the key from the agent the following day.

"You'll have your work cut out for you soon keeping your James Bond lookalike happy. Have you heard from him today?"

"He's away, Liz. He said May and June are his busy months. We've got each other's e-mail addresses now so we don't have to message through the agency. Rob said he's back later in the week and would love to meet for coffee."

"Have you booked a room?"

"I won't rise to that, Liz. I said if he messages me on Thursday I'd be able to meet him on Friday afternoon for tea."

"Wowee; that's very adventurous."

Katherine knew Liz was only joking and laughed along with her friend. She'd been e-mailing Robin for two weeks, they seemed to have plenty in common and she was looking forward to the meeting.

"What about the other guy you were messaging then?"

"I think he just wanted a replacement for his dead wife, Liz. He seemed to think he could just find another woman and carry on exactly as he did before. He seems like a lovely man but not for me."

"It leaves the way clear, girl, did you go on the Ann Summers website?"

"A long way off yet. Will you still be coming to the club for our swim tomorrow night?"

"I wouldn't miss my favourite night out. I'm picking the key up in the morning but I won't actually move in until the weekend, maybe even early next week."

"Does Phillip know yet?"

"We sat down and had a chat on Sunday afternoon, he was in a hurry to go off with his fucking stupid mates on their bikes. He didn't seem to care very much to be honest."

"Are you going to go for a divorce or is it a trial separation?"

"I'm not going back, Kath, I'd rather live on my own than be unhappy living with someone. I don't love him anymore."

After their conversation Katherine was in two minds, she always felt sad when she heard of marriage break-ups but her friend had sounded positive on the telephone so hopefully she'd made the right decision. She read the newest e-mail from Robin that had arrived that morning. He'd come back from his trip to Spain but had gone to France two days later. As soon as he'd suggested they meet on his return she'd felt that the time was right. He was due back on Thursday morning and was hoping that they could meet on Friday afternoon.

"Are you sure you want me to go through with this, Mads?"

Madelaine had been having a bad week, the day before she'd argued with Claire about something trivial and had drunk a bottle of wine before Robin got in from work. Her father-in-law was being very difficult with his housekeeper who'd been threatening to leave. Richard had insisted that if Cheralyn did leave that he wouldn't replace her and that he'd be expecting Madelaine to fetch and carry for him.

Robin came in from work on Wednesday evening almost frightened of what he'd find. He was surprised to see that his wife had stayed sober and not taken any medication. She'd also cooked a casserole in the slow cooker.

"It's been two weeks, Rob, you could have asked for a meeting last week. If you leave it too long, she'll think you're not interested."

"Darren said some of them e-mail each other for weeks before they meet. Two weeks is okay, any suggestions where to meet her?"

"Best to leave it up to her, Rob. I expect she'll want to meet for afternoon tea so maybe either in the forest or maybe Bournemouth. Will Sandra be able to cover for you all afternoon?"

"I told her that I'll probably need to finish at two o'clock and asked her if she can lock up for me. That won't be an issue."

"Have you got all the story about France and Spain straight, if she catches you out it'll be over before you even ask her for an investment?"

"What the fuck am I meant to talk about then? Jesus, Mads; I'm bound to mess it up and forget things."

"All you've got to remember is what you used to be Rob. When we first started seeing each other you were the top dog. Be him again, you can talk about your trips. Don't forget she likes the opera, that famous opera house is in Milan. You can tell her you've been to Milan which is true enough."

"Have you seen his lordship today?"

"I heard him shout at Cheralyn, if she goes it'll be even worse here Rob."

"I'm messaging her later, I'll tell her that I'm flying in tomorrow from France and ask her if we can meet on Friday."

"If we get about six hundred thousand for the house, Kath, I might buy a little flat and spend the rest on a car like this."

"That might not be the most sensible thing you'd ever do, I love it but I most certainly wouldn't ever have bought one. Les is getting my Ducati ready for Whitsun, that's just as sexy as this for a fraction of the price."

"It's the rider, not the bike. You wear those tight leathers and look like a fucking movie star when you ride it. Put me in an outfit like that and I'd look like a beached whale."

Katherine had collected Liz for their swimming evening and meal out at the country club.

"Have you heard from the lovely Rob Jones about Friday yet?"

"I'll check the phone when I get home, as far as I know he's coming back to England tomorrow and we're meeting on Friday afternoon."

"Have you decided where you're going?"

"If Rob doesn't mind, I thought we could met at Burley Tearooms. It's lovely there, maybe it won't be too busy until the holidays."

"Are you taking this, he'll be putty in your hands if he sees you turn up in it?"

Katherine laughed at her friend's ideas. "I don't think that would be very sensible, Liz. The jeep is a little less obvious, I can park behind the pub and walk across to the tea rooms. I'm going to take this really slow and carefully."

"Be careful, honey, don't lose this one, certainly not before I meet him."

Chapter Eighteen

On Friday Katherine felt like a nervous teenager going on her first date. She'd arranged to meet Robin at the tea rooms in Burley at four o'clock. It was a beautiful mid-May afternoon, in normal circumstances she'd have had no reservations about using the Jaguar but she didn't want Robin to either be attracted to her for the wrong reason or put off because he felt threatened by being with a wealthy woman.

Since the previous week she'd stopped going to the factory on a Friday, Jennifer had altered the baking schedule so that she didn't need to do as much on Saturday but it meant there was a lot extra on a Friday. By the time they got the work done now on Friday it was almost ten o'clock so Katherine worked right through and then went straight home.

She set her alarm as soon as she got home and snatched an hour's sleep on the sofa in the family room. After a light lunch she spent a relaxing hour in the kitchen garden before going in to get ready.

Ridiculous, she thought to herself as she put her clothes ready and prepared for a shower. She was almost trembling with the thought of spending an hour or so in a tea-rooms with a man. Before she showered and changed, she went back downstairs. She looked at the half empty bottle of wine but decided that it wouldn't be wise to have a drink. She went into the conservatory, found the packet of cigarettes and went into the garden to smoke one.

She'd arranged to meet Robin in Burley at four o'clock so there was no hurry to get ready, after her shower she spent half an hour trying to make her hair look its best.

She went through most of her wardrobe before settling on a long flowing skirt, a cream blouse and nude sandals. Before she dressed, she stood in front of the mirror in her underwear and studied herself. On a whim she changed her bra and pants for some that she thought looked slightly sexier, she didn't know why but she felt more confident wearing them.

She parked the Jeep in the car park behind the pub and sat there until a minute or two to four o'clock. By the time she walked across to the tea rooms she was trembling, in fact when she got to the edge of the road it took all her nerve not to turn round and walk back to her car. Eventually she plucked up the courage and walked into the large car park by the side of the thatched tea rooms.

As soon as she went into the car park, she saw the driver's door of a Mercedes saloon car open, a man stepped out straight away carrying a small bouquet of flowers. He smiled and walked towards her. As they got closer, she saw a very sexy smile on his face.

"Katherine, I presume, it's a delight to meet you at last."

She didn't actually know what to do now, should she run up and kiss him, offer her hand or run back to her car. Robin made it easy as he politely touched her on the shoulder and gave her a gentle kiss on the cheek.

"It's lovely to meet you too, Rob, you didn't need to bring flowers; that is if they're for me."

"They're for you, Katherine, would you like to leave them in the car for now?"

He handed the flowers to Katherine, it was a very subtle bouquet of around ten mixed blooms.

"Thanks, Rob, I'll be proud to take them in with us."

Katherine was conscious of people looking at them as they went through the door into the quaint tea rooms. A waitress showed them to a table by the window, gave them a menu each and said she'd be back to take the order in a few minutes.

They were both a little nervous, Katherine put her flowers on the seat next to her and tried desperately to find something to talk about. Robin broke the short silence.

"I'm sorry it's taken so long for us to meet, Katherine, my schedule is hectic in the spring and early summer. Lately, it seems to be busy throughout the year."

"I suppose it's always springtime somewhere," a nervous Katherine answered. She was desperately trying to think of something to say that wouldn't make her seem like a ditzy teenager who was about to swoon in the presence of her favourite boy band.

"It is a busy time in Europe," Robin answered. "I'm flying to Italy in the next few days. There's a vineyard in Tuscany that's experiencing a few issues."

"I haven't been to Italy," Katherine said wistfully. "One of my ambitions is to see La Traviata at the opera house in Milan."

"La Scala," Robin commented. "I've seen it from the outside, it's very impressive. Would you like something to eat or just a drink?"

He'd obviously seen the pretty waitress approaching the table with her notepad.

"I normally eat fairly healthily, Rob, but I'd actually love a cream tea, if you don't mind of course."

"That sounds like a nice idea," Robin said. He asked the waitress for two cream teas, she wrote down the order, gave Robin a cheeky smile and left them at the table.

"Nice girl," Robin commented.

For the next hour they chatted about life in general, the longer the conversation went on the easier Katherine found the situation. The young waitress left them alone, they called her over for a fresh pot of tea at just after five o'clock.

"Am I keeping you from anything, Katherine?" Robin asked politely. "It's a lovely afternoon and the time seems to be flying."

"I've no plans for tonight, Rob."

"We could get dinner if you like."

What Katherine actually wanted to do was sweep everything off the table and have wild sex with Robin. By the look the waitress gave her when she served the fresh tea, she wasn't the only one with the thought. She thought it would be more prudent to behave herself.

"Maybe dinner next time Rob," she said, "This has been lovely but I don't want to rush things."

As soon as she said it, she regretted it, they'd eaten their food and had a second pot of tea so without a meal the date would soon be at an end.

The waitress came and asked if they needed anything else, Robin said not and asked for their bill. He paid and added a generous tip. Katherine picked her flowers up and they both stood up. She'd taken her jacket off while they were having their tea, Robin helped her on with it and they walked back to his car.

"It's a lovely car, Rob, I like the colour."

"It's not mine, Katherine, I'm rarely settled at the moment so I find it easier to lease one when I'm in England."

There was a difficult silence for a few seconds before Robin gently kissed her on the cheek. It took a lot of willpower for Katherine not to turn her head and kiss him full on the mouth.

"It's been lovely, Katherine, I'd really like to see you again. You don't have to decide right now, message me later or tomorrow and tell me what you think."

Katherine knew exactly what she was thinking but told Robin that she'd be in touch with him soon.

"Where did you park?" he asked. "Shall I walk you back to your car?"

"Don't worry, Rob," she said quickly. "It's only just through the cut and in the car park. Thank you so much for my lovely flowers and tea."

With a lot of willpower Katherine said goodbye to Robin and walked across the road. She was determined not to turn and look but as Robin drove out of the car park her head turned almost automatically. He gave her a wave and blew her a kiss before driving back towards Ringwood. She walked to her car and sat there for a few moments thinking.

She rang the home number of her friend Liz but it went straight to answerphone so she tried her mobile. Liz answered almost straight away.

"Dish the dirt then, Kath, how did it go?"

"Where are you, Liz, can I get a drink with you on my way home?"

"I picked up the keys to the flat Kath, I'm there now. Why don't you pop round, I've got coffee here or we could go for a snack?"

Liz gave Katherine the directions to the flat, she was there by just before seven o'clock.

"It's a nice flat," Katherine said truthfully. "I could live here quite happily."

"I don't think I'll stay that long; I've got it for six months; if we've sold the house, I'll buy a little bungalow somewhere. If not, I think I can rent it for six months at a time. Enough about me, how did you get on with your James Bond lookalike?"

"I've got mixed feelings, Liz, he's gorgeous and I could quite happily spend the rest of my life looking into his beautiful eyes and let him look after me."

"So do it, honey," Liz interrupted. "Why the mixed feelings?"

"I still feel that I'm letting Mark down, silly as it sounds."

"Mark would give you his blessings, Kath. What's he like in real life, what did you talk about?"

"Just life in general really, he's very well-travelled and sophisticated."

"Is he rich?"

"I don't believe he ever mentioned money, I suppose he must be all right for funds. He drives a newish Mercedes but he told me it was leased. He didn't try and impress me which was nice. Some of the e-mails I got from other men were a bit on the pretentious side."

"Have you arranged to meet again? Don't tell me you're not seeing him again, girl, if you give him the elbow, I want him. In fact, we could share him."

"We said we'd message each other, I'll message him when I get in, thank him for a nice time and tell him I'd like to see him again."

"Soon I hope."

"He's flying to Italy after the weekend, apparently he has to visit a vineyard in Tuscany next week."

"Take some time off and go with him."

"Trust me, Liz I could have made a fool of myself without suggesting anything like that. I wanted to ask him if he as e-mailing anyone else but I didn't know how to ask."

"Just ask him straight out, tell him how much you love him and want to marry him and have his babies."

"I won't even bother trying to reply to that. Are you sleeping here tonight?"

"I'd have to go back home and then back here again so probably not tonight. I need some food as well."

"Come back with me then, I'll do us a snack and help you move the rest of your things tomorrow."

"Now I remember why you're my best friend; that sounds lovely. Aren't you taking the twins swimming in the morning?"

"I don't have to get them until eleven, we can get to your house by around nine, bring the stuff here and then go to the club; you can come as well if you like."

"How did it go then, Rob?"

Robin had driven straight home from Burley and was indoors well before seven o'clock.

"More or less as we thought, Mads, she's very nice. You'd never know she was a multi-millionaire. Very unassuming and easy to get on with."

"Did you tell her that you were e-mailing other women from the agency?"

"I thought she'd have asked, no, Mads; I didn't ask but I will next time."

"Have you arranged to see her again? Did you mention Tuscany?"

"I've said I'll message her, I might wait though until I get a message from her. I told her I'm flying to Italy early next week to sort out a few problems at the vineyard."

"Why don't you e-mail her from here, make out you're in Italy and send her pictures of the vineyard. Have you got any on the phone you're using for the agency?"

"I've got some on the new phone, I suppose I could download one or two from the computer to the old phone and send them."

"You've got to try and sell her Tuscany, Rob. Make out everything else that you do is a roaring success but that you're having problems with the vineyard owner in Italy."

"Surely it'd be better if it's the other way round, she's hardly likely to invest if she thinks it's losing money."

"If you tell her how profitable it is, she'll be even more suspicious Rob. She's got to believe that you and her investment can turn the business round. Tell her you can buy the place at a bargain price and have it making fortunes almost straightaway."

"That's for a few weeks' time, Mads, I've got to build up her trust. I've got to tell you it all seems a bit fucking sneaky doing it this way."

"It is fucking sneaky, Rob, no worse than any salesman or woman trying to get a deal done though. Have you eaten?"

"A couple of cream scones."

"There's some sweet and sour chicken in the slow cooker, you can heat some up in the microwave if you want. After you've eaten you need to go online, read up on this La Scala place, maybe you can order a souvenir from Amazon or off E-bay."

"You've really thought this through, Mads."

"Because I love you, Rob, but I can't put up with things the way they are; you know that. Cheralyn isn't going to be there much longer and his fucking lordship will expect us to be running round after him."

"If we move to Italy, he'll have to find someone else."

"This house will be empty, he can do what he did before. Let someone live there rent-free if they look after him."

"Hi, Liz, haven't seen you for a long time. I hope you're not leading my mother astray."

"Nice to see you, Jen. The shop looks terrific, where did you get the two new assistants from?"

The twins had been in the kitchen with Elaine and came through to the shop covered in flour.

"I'm sacking them soon, nothing but trouble."

Katherine came into the shop as the twins came through, after they'd hugged her she had to brush the flour off her black trousers.

"Remember these two, Liz, they used to be two lovely well-behaved children."

"We still are Nanny," Josh said. "Aunty Elaine and Becky got us floury."

"I don't think we can go swimming," Katherine joked. "It'll turn into glue if you get wet."

After a few minutes chatting, they put the twins into the back of the Jeep and took them for their swimming lesson. Katherine and Liz sat in the cafeteria watching them and chatting about Robin.

"You should have e-mailed him last night, Kath, he'll be thinking he's not the man for you."

"I could be playing hard to get."

"Well, don't, Kath, you already know he's the one don't you?"

Katherine thought for a minute, Liz saw that she was smiling and spoke again.

"As soon as we take these two back, we'll go to your house and you can e-mail him Kath. I'll keep on nagging at you all day until you send it."

Katherine had already made her mind up to message Robin after lunch. At the very least she wanted to thank him for treating her to tea at Burley the day before.

Danny was going to the football so they dropped the twins back to the shop and went back to Katherine's for a late lunch. As it was a fine May afternoon they sat outside with some baguettes and lemonade.

"Right, Kath, have you get the phone here or indoors. It's time to start begging Rob to be your man for the rest of your life."

Katherine took the phone out of her pocket and wrote Robin a message. She showed it to Liz before she sent it.

"It's a bit formal, Kath. I'm surprised you didn't put Yours Sincerely Mrs. Katherine Reynolds at the bottom."

Katherine re-read it and altered one or two words. She added some kisses after her name at the bottom.

"How's that then, Liz? Better?"

"It could still be a bit more casual, you haven't suggested when you can meet up again either."

"I don't want to be too pushy. I wonder if he's messaging or meeting up with anyone else."

"You could always ask him."

"Not now, Liz, maybe if we do meet up again, I'll try and find out. Shall I send it then?"

"Get it gone otherwise he'll be thinking he's offended you and go looking elsewhere. When's he off to Italy?"

"He said in the next few days so Monday or Tuesday I suppose."

Katherine sent the e-mail, they didn't expect an immediate reply but left the phone on the table while they finished their lunch. At three o'clock they decided to finish moving Liz's things from her house to her flat.

"I'm cooking you dinner Kath, no excuses. I couldn't have done this by myself."

"What's Phillip had to say about it all?"

"I don't think he cares Kath. I'm joining that agency sometime in the summer and I'm going to meet the perfect man."

"Do you think there's two on there then?" Katherine teased. "Because I may have found one already."

"Check your phone, see if there's a reply yet."

Katherine checked her inbox and was delighted to see a reply. After she'd scanned it quickly, she read it out loud to Liz.

"You've got him, girl, I said you should have gone with him. Now you'll have to wait a few weeks to sleep with him."

Chapter Nineteen

Katherine and Robin messaged each other several times over the next ten days. Robin asked her if they could meet for a meal as soon as he came back from Italy. Katherine didn't have to think for long before agreeing to meet him in Ringwood for dinner. She was planning on riding her Ducati to Exmoor after she'd finished at the shop on Friday so they arranged to meet on Thursday tea-time at a pub on the outskirts of the town.

It was a beautiful early summer afternoon, she looked wistfully at her Ducati and E-Type but decided that she'd better stick to the Jeep for the time being. She'd made sure to get two hours sleep before getting ready for the date. This time she didn't feel nervous and was looking forward to seeing him again.

She tried two or three different outfits before deciding on a lemon dress with a white jacket and shoes. She was going to go bare legged as it was too warm for tights but on a whim she put a suspender belt and pale tan stockings on. Liz had taken her shopping in Bournemouth the weekend before, she'd treated herself to some new outfits for the summer and her friend had talked her into buying several sets of skimpy underwear, suspender belts and stockings.

Mark had never really taken much interest in what she wore, he always told her she looked nice when she dressed up to go out but she felt that he could have been a little more attentive sometimes. She stood in front of the mirror before she put her dress on and thought that for fifty-nine she still looked in good shape.

As soon as she drove into the car park at the pub Robin got out of his Mercedes and walked across to her.

"Nice to see you again, Katherine, you look lovely tonight."

Katherine wasn't quite sure what to say or do for a moment, should she admire what Robin was wearing, throw her arms round him or offer her hand. He made the decision for her by gently putting his arms round her, kissing her on the cheek and mentioning why he was wearing a suit.

"I know it looks a little formal but I've just come from a meeting with a financier, maybe you wouldn't mind if I lost the tie when we get inside."

"It's nice here," Katherine said, "And it doesn't look like it's too busy yet either."

"I haven't been here before, it certainly looks nice. Is the food good? I haven't eaten since breakfast."

"Some of the food is wonderful," Katherine said. "My daughter owns a small business, she supplies quiches, pies and cakes to several local pubs and restaurants. This is one of her best customers in the summertime."

They got to the bar and ordered drinks, the menus were on the table so as soon as they sat down they both scanned the offerings. Robin seemed a little distracted. "Tell me what you want, Katherine, and I'll have the same."

"I'm a little biased," Katherine admitted. "I'm going to have some broccoli and stilton quiche, salad and new potatoes."

"Then I shall have the same."

Robin had taken his jacket and tie off, he was wearing a white shirt that looked like it had been tailored for him. As he walked back, Katherine felt a sense of pride that she was with such a handsome and smartly dressed man.

"I didn't order dessert," he said when he arrived back at the quiet table in the corner "But they have a strawberry flan on the counter that looks exquisite. If we're not too full after our quiche than maybe you'd like some of that with fresh cream topping."

"The strawberry flan will go down well after our main course, Rob," Katherine said. She didn't like to tell him that at five o'clock that morning she'd been cutting up the strawberries and making the flan.

They talked about what they'd been doing since their first meeting. Robin seemed a little quiet to Katherine, she thought perhaps that he was tired or stressed. She told him that she was planning on going to Exmoor the following day for the weekend. She didn't quite know why but she held back the fact that she rode a Ducati and was hoping the weather would be nice enough to ride there.

The conversation went a little quiet when the food arrived, Katherine was pleased to see that the chef had arranged the salad and potatoes beautifully on the large oval plates. Robin tucked into his food, as soon as he tasted the quiche he admired the taste and quality.

"She supplies around twenty hotels, pubs and tearooms now," Katherine told him. "She does pies, quiches, scones and cakes. She also bakes bread, rolls and baguettes for her shop."

"Does she produce everything on the premises?"

"Everything is made fresh daily and, on the premises, she's there by four o'clock in the morning."

"You must be very proud of her; this quiche is amazing."

"She works very hard, Rob. I'm glad you're enjoying the product."

After they'd finished their main course the waitress cleared the plates and asked if they needed a dessert. Katherine said she could manage some flan so Robin ordered two slices with fresh cream. Katherine was tempted to tell him that she'd made the flan but kept quiet.

Katherine had been dubious about meeting a man online but sitting opposite Robin and listening to him tell her about his trip to Italy and his forthcoming trip to France and Spain was the nicest evening that she could remember for many years.

Eventually she plucked up the courage to ask if he'd been seeing anyone else that had responded to his profile. He didn't answer straight away, after a moment he admitted that he'd been e-mailing another widow from Southampton.

"I don't know if I'll be in the position to offer either of you what you're looking for Katherine. My business takes me all over the world and I've been divorced from Ruth for many years. I'll find it hard to adjust to a normal life."

Katherine was disappointed to hear that he was in contact with another lady. She didn't want to rush headlong into a full-blown relationship with a man that she'd only just met but she felt that she needed to try and build something with Robin that would last for many years.

Trying to hide her disappointment Katherine made small talk for a moment but Robin picked up the difference in her mood.

"I'm sorry if you think I'm letting you down Katherine," he said gently. "I've only messaged the other lady a few times and now that we've met up twice my next e-mail to her will be to tell her that I won't be messaging again."

Katherine was relieved but still a little concerned about his comment that he'd find it difficult to be in a relationship with the current lifestyle that he had.

"Why did you join the agency then Rob? Surely your lifestyle lends itself to romance. What could be nicer than flying off to the wine growing areas in the world?"

"It's a bit like being a chocolate tester Katherine. It gets very stressful sometimes. I'm not getting any younger, my boys are grown-up now and I get lonely. I thought that if I met a lady and fell in love that I could change my lifestyle before I retire."

"Do you still think that way, Rob? The way you spoke just now made it sound that you don't."

Robin didn't answer straight away, he seemed to be thinking about his reply. "I'd like to think that perhaps I can change my lifestyle Katherine, it's arrogant to even think that anyone could change theirs to fit in with my difficult schedules."

That sounded a little rehearsed Katherine thought as she finished her drink. Robin offered to go to the bar for some more so she sat at the table alone thinking about what he'd said. She was planning on retiring in a years' time and would welcome the chance to spend time travelling round Europe, maybe South Africa, Australia and California.

There were four women in their twenties or thirties at a table nearer to the bar, as Robin walked back to the table with their drinks Katherine watched them looking at him. One of them said something to another; Katherine saw her cover her mouth with her hand to stifle a laugh.

He seemed a little distracted when he came back and at down, Katherine asked him if everything was all right.

"I'm having a few issues with my father," he said truthfully. "He has a house-keeper who's likely to leave and need replacing and he's a difficult man. The trip to Tuscany could have got a lot better as well. I'm sorry if I seem a little tired and grumpy."

Katherine was a little distracted; she was trying to hold herself back from grabbing Robin and having sex with him on the pub floor. Her friend had described her as a born-again-virgin and that was exactly how she felt. She saw the ladies at the other table glancing across at them and felt proud that she was with Robin but worried that nothing was going to come of the meetings with him.

"Your father must be quite old, is he fit and healthy?"

"He's fit, healthy and very difficult I'm afraid."

"What's the problem in Italy, Rob?"

"It's nothing too serious at the moment, Katherine," he replied. "Hopefully it'll sort itself out over the next few months. Have you any plans for the weekend?"

"I usually only go to help my daughter on a Friday now so I should be finished by late morning. I'm going to North Devon for the weekend."

"How much time do you spend at the factory now?"

When they'd met at Burley, Katherine had told him that her husband owned a factory and that she worked there part-time. She hadn't told him that she now owned the business or anything about the proposed development.

"I really don't need to be there at all," Katherine admitted. "I work three or four hours Monday to Thursday. It's more important to me that Jennifer gets as much help as possible with her business."

"Have you decided what you're doing about the factory?"

Katherine had decided but was still being a little cagey in telling anyone outside her immediate family her decisions.

"Probably a management buy-out but it's early days yet. The estate has only just been settled. The staff must be taken care of, any buy-out has to include their contracts."

They made small talk for an hour before Robin looked at his watch and said that he had to leave. They walked together back to the car park.

"I brought you a little gift from Italy Katherine, it's in the car."

Robin opened his Mercedes and got a small gift bag off the front seat, he handed it to Katherine.

"That's possibly the nicest present I've ever been given Rob, thank you so much. I'll be listening to it on the way home at full volume."

Robin had brought her a compact disc of one of her favourite operas, La Traviatta; it had been recorded live at La Scala in Milan.

"Did you go to Milan?" Katherine asked, "I may be very jealous if you did."

"I didn't go to Milan," he said truthfully. "I thought you might like it."

Although he was an accomplished salesman and the whole relationship with Katherine was being built under false pretences Robin hated lying to her. He'd managed to buy the compact disc online from an Italian vendor.

"It's absolutely perfect, Rob, and I love it."

Both of them were a little nervous about how they should say goodbye, they promised to message each other over the weekend. Robin eventually took charge of the farewell by putting his strong arms round Katherine and pulling her in for a hug. This time he kissed her full on the mouth, he didn't make it last too long but Katherine went slightly weak at the knees while they were so close. After they separated, he looked a little guilty, Katherine wanted him to kiss her again but he stepped back and they said their goodbyes.

Chapter Twenty

"How did it go then, Mum? Dish all the dirt."

"There's no dirt to dish Jen. We had a lovely meal, actually we both had quiche and salad followed by a very nice strawberry flan. He brought me a lovely present from Italy and we said goodnight."

"Did you kiss him goodnight then?"

Katherine blushed a little but Jennifer didn't notice. "Nothing passionate but yes Jennifer; we did have a kiss goodnight."

Jennifer didn't say anything straight away, they were both busy finishing off the work for the Friday morning rush. At half-past-ten they sat down in the kitchen and let Becky look after the shop while they had their coffee.

"I sent off all the forms yesterday Mum. She's officially an apprentice now. Her Mum's okay with it as well, she's earning a decent wage and she'll do better than she would have done at college."

"Perhaps we'd have done better by finding you that sort of training," Katherine mused. "I don't think catering college was the best thing for you."

Jennifer was sitting quite close to her mother, she put her hand on top of Katherine's. "I'm doing all right now, Mum, that's all that matters."

Katherine squeezed her daughter's hand. "I'm proud of you, Jen, so was Mark. Just make sure that little girl out there gets looked after and the best possible start."

"She will, Mum; don't worry. What about the scrummy Rob then?"

"He's very special, Jen, but I'm still not really sure. He's not sure either. I'll message him later from the cottage and try and see how he sees things going."

"Are you still riding down?"

"Absolutely, I'm off home as soon as we've cleared up, a quick change and I'll be away. I can grab a bite to eat at the services and still be there for tea."

"Will you be okay riding that far? You haven't used the bike for years."

"I'm looking forward to it. It's been serviced and I've had a few little rides round the village. I'll text you as soon as I get there."

Katherine was home by eleven o'clock, had a quick wash and put her leathers on. She left before midday, stopped for fuel and lunch on the way and was indoors by four-thirty. She messaged Jennifer and Liz to say that she'd arrived safely and then settled down for a rest for an hour. After she'd made herself some food, she e-mailed Robin.

He replied early in the evening, Katherine was a little confused by what she read. He was flying to Spain on Monday and said that he wanted to see her as soon as he got back but he didn't mention anything about the other lady that he'd been messaging and said nothing about the possibility of a long-term relationship with her.

After she'd showered and eaten, she walked to the beach and sat there until it was nearly dark. She had a glass of wine at the pub near the cottage and got back at just after ten. Her friend Liz telephoned soon afterwards.

"How was your ride down there, girl? Did you squeeze into those leathers?"

"I loved it, Liz, my ass is aching a bit now though."

"What about last night then? Did you rip each other's clothes off and make the earth move?"

Katherine almost told her friend the truth; that ripping his clothes off and having wild sex in the car park was exactly what she'd wanted to do.

"It was lovely, Liz," she answered. "He bought me a CD from Italy. We had a lovely meal in Ringwood."

"Steady up, you'll be having a cuddle next."

Katherine and Liz chatted for twenty minutes or so, Katherine told her friend that Robin seemed a little confused as to whether or not he wanted to take things further.

Liz did what any best friend would and tried to build up her confidence.

"He wants to see you again," she said finally. "All you can do is go with the flow. It'll all be fine. If I haven't seen you meantime, I'll expect you to bring your E-Type on Wednesday."

"I've got a spare helmet, I may bring the Ducati."

"You're not wearing your slutty underwear on it are you. If you have an accident and they see that God knows what they'll think."

"Woolly knickers and thick tights, Liz. See you next week, if it's fine I'll bring the Jaguar."

Robin messaged again to wish her goodnight and twice on Saturday. As it was warm and sunny Katherine made herself some food and rode to Doone Valley for a picnic. She got back in time for a shower and a walk to the beach in the evening.

Sunday looked a little cloudy so she decided to leave in the morning and try to get back in the dry, she was home by just after lunch-time. After giving her bike a quick clean she rang Liz to see if she was at home.

"Come on over, Kath, I'm bored stiff here on my own."

Katherine was at her friends flat by three o'clock, they had coffee and chatted in the lounge.

"Is it all right here on your own now you've settled then, Liz?"

"It's all right in some ways, Kath, I can please myself what I do and when I do it. I just get a bit depressed now and again. The house is on the market, Phillip offered to buy me out but only for about a third of the value."

"Are you going for half each?"

"Do you think I'm being a bitch then? Don't forget I owned my flat before we married and that went into the house."

"I should think it's fair splitting it equally Liz, as long as it's final between you and Phillip. Maybe he'll up his offer."

"He says if I want more it has to be sold, it's over Kath; I'm sure now. I'm going to try internet dating in a week or two."

"Do you fancy a week away in the summer holidays?"

"I'd love it, where would we go?"

"I don't want to go anywhere it'll be too hot, Liz, have a think and we'll choose something we both want."

"Is your sister coming?"

"Let's make it just us two this time Liz. Doreen can be a little difficult at times."

"Can you give me the details of the dating agency, Kath, I'm going to sign up for three months. I don't think I'll be as lucky as you but I can try."

"I'm still not sure about Rob," Katherine sighed. "I already know I want him Liz but I don't think he wants a commitment. Just going out with him every now and again when he decides he wants some company won't be enough I'm afraid."

"Funny that; I'm looking for exactly that. A man to wine and dine me and then give me a good seeing to. Someone who doesn't just want dinner on the table and his shirts ironed."

"Well, you're not having, Rob. I'll just have to make sure he wants me, Liz."

"Did you wear your slutty underwear the other night then?"

"Not the really slinky black stuff, I'm saving that for a special night. I wore a suspender belt and stockings for the first time ever."

"Did Rob like them?"

"He didn't know, at least I don't think he did, maybe he'd have felt the suspenders when he cuddled me in the car park."

"And did you notice anything? Was he pleased to see you?"

"He said I looked nice; I think he was pleased to see me."

"Christ, girl, you are naïve sometimes. Was it a tube of smarties in his pocket or was he pleased to see you?"

Katherine realised what her friend was talking about. "We didn't get that close Liz, maybe in a date or two."

"Third date next time, he'll be expecting a little nibble."

"I thought I'd be able to play a bit hard to get," Katherine admitted. "But I swear to God if he'd wanted me on Thursday, I'd have been hard pushed to say no."

"It's not like you're sixteen, if you want him then go for it."

"It's a big step for me, I need to at least have some hope of something long-term."

"Of course he may well be thinking the other way around, that he won't make a commitment until he's sampled what's on offer."

"Have you messaged your rich widow today?"

"She's gone to Exmoor for the weekend. She's probably got a holiday home down there. I messaged her just after lunch but she hasn't replied yet. I expect she's on her way back."

"You've seen her twice, Rob, have you got anywhere near asking her for an investment?"

"Not anywhere near yet I'm afraid. I've planted the seed, I told her I'm having issues with the yard in Tuscany, when I saw her on Thursday I told her

I've been meeting with a financier. Next time I see her I'll make out I'm only on a flying visit to England to try and raise funds."

"Do you think you can talk her into it Rob? Did you tell her that you were e-mailing another lady?"

"I said I was in contact with a widow in Southampton but that I was going to stop e-mailing her. I'll have to go steady at this Mads, I'm only going to get one shot at it."

"Have you e-mailed Giovanni yet? You said you'd do it this morning."

"I sent it when you were having a lie-down. No answer the last time I looked but I know what he'll say. We've got until the end of November and he'll put it on the open market. He'll sell it fucking quickly too, Mads."

"If you hadn't stuck by him all those years ago he'd have had to sell up and get out. He owes you Rob; if he does sell it maybe he'll give you a cut."

"I don't think he'll see it quite like that, Mads, he's giving us first refusal on the place at a cut price and I reckon that's as far as he'll go. I might try to get the whole lot from Katherine Reynolds and forget about the other three."

"Has she got that kind of money?"

"I bet she's worth twenty million. That site must be worth ten, maybe even more. Plus the factory and the house, if she puts the whole lot up we'll make a fortune in a few years."

Madelaine had been better for the past few weeks, Robin put it down to the fact that he'd given her some hope of actually moving to Italy and running a vineyard. She'd stopped taking the tranquilisers and been drinking a lot less.

Jonathon came into the lounge and sat down. "Can we get Sky telly please, Dad?"

"No," Robin answered, "If we manage to get you off your gaming console for the odd hour or two we don't want you glued to the television."

He stormed out of the room complaining that all his friends had Sky television and that his life was boring.

"Your dear father reckons he needs to go in the army for a few years Rob, says it'll make a man of him."

Robin poured himself a small glass of whisky. "He used to say that about me all the time when I was that age. I wanted to go to university and he wanted me to enlist. Luckily Mum was on my side."

"I don't know how she put up with him all those years."

"He wasn't as bad then. If we move to Italy he can move someone else in here to look after him."

"Don't forget to message your other woman Rob. Tell her you're coming back to England next Friday for a couple of days for meetings with your backers. Take her somewhere really nice, maybe a picnic."

Chapter Twenty-One

"I joined the dating agency, Kath. Your handsome man is still on there, shall I ask for his profile and then he'll get mine. See if he e-mails me?"

"You can ask but he won't get in touch with you Liz, concentrate on finding yourself a nice man. Why don't you throw yourself at your lovely swimming instructor?"

"He's gay, Kath, he doesn't even notice you flashing your boobs at him."

"I do not," Katherine said indignantly. "I haven't got that much to flash and they're a lot more covered up than yours."

"He doesn't look at mine either, are you sure you don't want me to try and honey-trap Rob?"

"Quite sure, thank you. He's flying back to England tomorrow night, we're meeting for tea on Friday. It's a surprise for me because he wasn't due back yet. Apparently he has a meeting on Friday morning with some bankers. Then he's going to Spain on Saturday morning."

"You'll have to find a very quiet spot somewhere for your third date shenanigans."

"There won't be any of those, whatever they are. We're meeting on Bournemouth beach for an early tea."

Katherine had collected her friend and taken her to the country club on Wednesday for their swimming session. After the pool time they were in the restaurant having a meal.

"I've got a few ideas for our summer trip," Katherine told Liz. "Why don't you come in for tea after work tomorrow and see what you think?"

"I just want to get away somewhere for a week."

"It's not very long till we got to London for the weekend. I'm really looking forward to that."

"What have you got planned for Friday then? If you're meeting on Bournemouth beach you could wear your skimpy bikini. If he comes out of the sea in his trunks will you please film it for me?"

"Certainly not. I told him I'm bringing a picnic, he's paid both times we've met so it'll be my treat. Just a nice romantic picnic and a walk along the beach, I'm really looking forward to it."

"It's your third date, honey," Liz insisted. "You ought to be going a bit further than holding hands."

"I still can't quite work him out, he seems to want a relationship but for some reason he's holding back. I keep asking him things about himself but he changes the subject."

"Have you told him everything about you yet?"

"Like what?"

"Like the fact that you're a fucking multi-millionaire, you've got a car worth more than plenty of people's houses, a holiday cottage, you ride a sleek Ducati, used to drive trucks for the factory, you've only had boring sex with one man in your life and your glamorous friend helped you choose some really slutty underwear."

"I've held back on most of that," Katherine admitted. "He knows Mark was my only boyfriend."

"I bet he doesn't know you haven't had a good fuck for years."

Katherine was a little shocked by the bluntness but admitted that she hadn't even slept with her husband for several years.

She lowered her voice so that no one on the tables near to them could hear the conversation.

"I'm terrified of that side of it Liz, what if I'm a let-down if we ever get to bed together? Mark and I were never very adventurous in the bedroom."

Liz laughed at her friend's insecurity. "It'll be fine, Kath, just go with it, girl. You'll have to come out of your shell a bit, maybe he's the same."

"I don't fucking believe him Mads. He wants me to pick his car up from the garage on Friday. I'm supposed to be meeting Katherine. I can't put her off, I told her I'm only in England for the day."

"Go in the Jaguar then, you can park it up and walk to the beach. As long as she doesn't see it you'll be all right."

"I'm going to tell her I'm in trouble with the deal in Tuscany and the only way out is to buy the yard. She thinks I'm only in England for a meeting with my bankers."

"Don't get her too panicky yet that you're going to go bust if you don't raise the money. She's got to believe in you."

"I'll have to go well early and find a spot at least a mile from the beach, I'll find a quiet side road to park up, I can always tell her I came on the train I suppose."

"You'll have to look after the fucking colonel next weekend, I'm going to be at Mum's with Jonathon."

"What's Claire doing?"

"What eighteen-year-olds usually do at the weekend, drinking, probably drugs and sex, maybe she'll do a little work but I very much doubt it."

"I'd like to finish nice and early tomorrow Jen, I'm meeting Rob on the beach for tea and I'd like to do a bit of shopping in the afternoon."

"Yes, Mum, you really need more new clothes."

"I want something to wear to the theatre when we go to London. Just a nice plain dress."

"You bought that black one when you went with Liz a while back."

"I'm not sure about that one, it's a bit short, Jen."

"It looks fine, Mum. You've got lovely legs. I wish I could get away with wearing stuff like that. Have the day off, it'll do you good. Elaine said she'd be able to do the odd early morning; I'll text her at lunch-time. We'll manage fine for the day."

"If you're sure you can manage."

Although it wasn't raining on Friday it wasn't as sunny and warm as it had been all week. Katherine enjoyed her lie-in and spent an enjoyable hour in the garden before getting ready. She decided on a pair of white summer trousers and a loose blouse for the picnic. On her way she called into the shop for the food, Jennifer had put up plenty of food for the two of them, Katherine had put a bottle of very low alcohol wine in a cool box to drink with the food.

She went to several shops before settling on a plain black dress that she thought was perfect for the theatre in London. She'd arranged to meet Robin at four o'clock so she had plenty of time to drive to the beach car park. As she drove past a side road she saw a beautiful Mark Two Jaguar reverse parking. She was sat in a traffic queue, she watched the offside door open and was surprised to see Robin step out and lock the door.

The lights changed and she had to move just as Robin walked round the front of the car to the pavement. Katherine carried on driving and was parked in the seafront car park a few minutes later. She sat in the car listening to a disc until her phone bleeped with a message from Robin that he'd arrived. She got out of the car, got the picnic from the back and they met on the beach path. As soon as he saw her he held his arms open for an embrace, she put the food and drink down on the path and fell comfortably into his arms. He kissed her full on the mouth before they disentangled themselves.

"Let me carry that, Katherine," he said as he picked up the picnic basket. "We'll find a nice quiet spot for our picnic."

They settled in a nice sheltered spot on the sand, Katherine opened the picnic basket and got the wine out. She poured them a glass each and started putting the food on paper plates.

"This looks amazing, I was expecting a cheese sandwich and a can of Coke."

"My daughter put it up at the shop, it's very low alcohol wine; we'd have to drink about two bottles each to fail the breathalyser."

Robin didn't mention that he'd parked around a mile from the beach or that he'd driven a classic car to Bournemouth for the date. They made small talk while they ate. Katherine had included two slices of strawberry flan and a small jar of fresh cream.

"Quite magnificent," Robin said truthfully when they'd finished eating and put the plates back in the basket.

"More wine?" Katherine suggested, Robin nodded so she poured two more glasses. "How was your trip?"

"It's been an eventful week, sorry I forgot your gift." Robin delved into his jacket pocket and brought out a small bottle of Chanel perfume. "I hope you like it."

"I can't imagine that any lady could be given a bottle of Chanel and not be delighted Rob. You don't have to bring me a present every time we meet."

Katherine noticed that he'd changed the subject from his trip so she asked again.

"The trip is just routine visits checking on crops and dealing with growers," Robin answered, "I'm slightly annoyed that I had to fly back but at least this has made it worthwhile."

"Are you leaving again soon?"

"I've a meeting tomorrow morning and I'm flying out in the afternoon. I'm sorry if I'm a little distracted Katherine, I've a problem in Tuscany that is causing me some major worries."

"What's the problem, Rob?" Katherine asked. As she spoke she moved in a little closer and took his hand in hers. She was pleased that he didn't take his hand away.

"It's a financial issue that won't go away quickly. I've ploughed thousands into the yard out there and it seems the owner has defaulted on some loans. If he goes bankrupt it's his own fault but he could drag me down with him."

Katherine didn't know what to say, she squeezed his hand and leant in for a kiss. Robin responded and they spent the next few minutes in silence kissing and holding hands like teenagers.

"I'm sure it'll work out for you, Rob."

"I'm not too hopeful at the moment, Katherine, I've a few more weeks of meetings before I know the outcome. I may need to put a finance package together myself."

"When are you back again, Rob?"

Robin thought for a moment "If all goes to plan I should be back late on Friday. Perhaps we could have an evening out next Saturday, the theatre perhaps, maybe a little supper?"

"I'd love that, Rob, shall I book some tickets for us?"

"If you don't mind, I'll give you the money when I see you. Maybe Bournemouth Pavilion Theatre if there's anything on there?"

"What about The Mayflower at Southampton? I don't mind driving up there."

"I'd prefer Bournemouth," Robin said. "But anywhere that you find something nice for us to see. I'll leave it up to you."

They both seemed to realise that it was getting colder and made preparations to leave.

"Where are you parked?" Katherine asked.

"It's a little bit of a hike there," Robin said. "Let me help you get the things in your car. The walk back to mine will do me good."

Katherine was going to mention that she'd seen him park but as he hadn't said anything about his car she kept quiet. When they'd packed the picnic basket they walked back to her car. She put her hand in his as they strolled to the car, after three meetings she was finally feeling comfortable in his company but still a little concerned about his lack of showing that he wanted a long-term relationship.

Katherine opened the back door of the Jeep, Robin put the picnic basket in and closed the door. They stood facing each other for a moment before he held his arms open for her to fall into. This time the goodbye kiss was delivered with a passion that he hadn't shown before. Katherine was taken aback by the hunger of him. At one point she had to step back slightly to draw breath. He was using his tongue gently as well, exploring the inside of her lips. Finally they parted and she got in the driver's seat.

Chapter Twenty-Two

Katherine went online and found that there was a show at the Tivoli Theatre in Wimborne the following Saturday night. She telephoned the box office and booked two seats at the front of the balcony.

Liz came for lunch on Sunday, it was a beautiful June day, Katherine took her Ducati out for an early morning ride across the forest and got back just before nine o'clock. After her shower and breakfast she prepared the vegetables and seasoned the meat. She had two hours in her garden before putting the joint in the oven.

Liz arrived at one o'clock just as Katherine was taking the joint out of the oven. "It'll be half an hour, Liz, everything's ready, glass of wine?"

"Just a small one to be polite. Give me all the juicy stuff from Friday and then I'll tell you about my love life."

"It was just a lovely afternoon Liz, we had a picnic, a walk on the beach and just sat there chatting on the sand."

"Chatting?"

"There was a little bit of kissing and cuddling."

"Snogging?"

"When we said goodbye there was a certain amount of that," Katherine said, "He must have thought I wouldn't bring enough food, I'm sure he had a banana in his pocket."

"I expect he thought he'd have a little nibble," Liz said with a huge grin. "When are you seeing him again?"

"Saturday night, we're going to The Tivoli at Wimborne."

"Back here afterwards?"

Katherine ignored the obvious inference. "He didn't suggest dinner first but I'm going to give Rita at the tea-rooms a call and see if we can eat there, we may be able to park at her place and walk to the theatre."

"Back here afterwards?"

"He'll have to bring me home of course, it'd be rude if I didn't invite him in for coffee."

"Feeling a bit more comfortable about it now are we?"

"I just want him, Liz, I'm still scared of it but I'll have to try and let go a bit. At least if I don't have to drive I can have a drink, that'll help me relax a bit."

"Has he told you any more about himself or is he still holding back?"

"We're both holding back, Liz, I saw him park his car a long walk from the beach. It was a Mark Two Jaguar, like the one Inspector Morse drives. I had a very quick look on the way home, it's immaculate, about nineteen sixty-four, the number plate is his initials and one digit. Those numbers cost thousands, I tried to buy one as a birthday gift for Mark but I couldn't afford it."

"He might be richer than you then."

"He doesn't really talk about it, he dresses well. He doesn't try and impress me with wealth, I said how nice his Mercedes was and he told me it was leased."

"If he was a bullshitter he wouldn't have told you that, he'd have made out it was his. I expect he's worried about meeting a gold-digger; much the same as you."

"That brings you up to date with my love life, now tell me about yours."

"I'm going out with one tonight, he's from Bournemouth. I'm meeting him at Bailey Bridge in Christchurch."

"Do you know much about him?"

"He's hunky, that'll do for now."

As it was a warm sunny afternoon they sat out on the patio with their lunch. Katherine had roasted a leg of lamb and served it with Jersey new potatoes and vegetables.

"Dessert?" Katherine asked.

"I'm sure you've made something special so it'd be rude to refuse."

Katherine had made a summer pudding with fresh fruit, she served it with ice-cream.

"I hope Oliver doesn't want to buy me dinner later, I'm stuffed."

"Do you know much about him yet?"

"We've been swopping e-mails, he sounds okay. He's a bit old, I put sixty down as the top age and he's sixty. He was a property developer."

"Please don't mention the factory site Liz, I'm still getting offers for it."

"Big bucks?"

"I turned down five million last week. The way I'm doing it there'll be a good income from the land for eternity."

"It must be nice to be able to turn your back on that sort of money. Most wouldn't."

"If I took the money and ran I'd be cheating Mark, we talked about it before he died. This is what he wanted."

Liz went home at half-past four promising to tell Katherine about her date. Katherine read for a while, watched an episode of Morse and was in bed by soon after nine o'clock.

The week seemed to drag on, Katherine was looking forward to Saturday like a child for their birthday. Each day she'd be counting the days until she saw Robin. She'd e-mailed him every day as usual, they'd arranged that he would pick her up at five o'clock to give them time to eat before the theatre. Katherine rang Rita Callaghan, the owner of the tea-rooms that Jennifer supplied. She booked a table for six o'clock and Rita said that they could park the car in a private space at the back. It was only a short walk from there to the theatre.

Katherine and Liz had their evening at the country club on Wednesday. Liz had told Katherine all about Oliver, she didn't think there was any chance of a relationship blossoming.

"He's nice looking Kath but that's about all."

"Surely being filthy rich helps doesn't it?"

"I think property developer might have been stretching it a bit. All he did was buy a place, live there for a year, tart it up and then sell it for a profit."

"Any other prospects?"

"I've e-mailed a few guys but nothing's jumped out at me yet. I'm meeting Oliver for a drink tomorrow after work but only to tell him that there's no hope."

"You'll find someone, my sister Doreen rang yesterday; she's found Mister Perfect again so she says. No doubt it'll be lovely for a few months before it all goes wrong."

"You haven't told me much about Saturday yet."

"I've told you everything, we're eating at the tea-rooms and going to The Tivoli."

"I want the nitty-gritty, Kath. What are you wearing?"

"Just a nice skirt and top, nothing too dressy."

"Wear that short dress we bought."

"I'm fifty-nine, Liz, not nineteen."

"You've got better legs than most teenagers, wear the dress, slutty black underwear, shiny black stockings and fuck-me shoes."

"I haven't got any fuck-me shoes."

"Those black strappy ones will do. So you've wined and dined him, taken him to the theatre and he drives you home. What next?"

"I'm inviting him in for coffee, I told you that."

"Not good enough, what if he says no? As soon as you stop the car you lean over, give him a sloppy kiss and tell him he's coming in. Then get out of the car before he has a chance to say no. As soon as he's indoors you're in charge."

"I'm still terrified, I just don't know what to do Liz."

"Make the coffee quickly and take him in the family room, your lounge is too posh for fooling round in. Snuggle up nice and close on the big sofa, if he doesn't put his hand on your thigh then you put it there for him. Once he gets there he'll be putty in your hands."

Katherine smiled at the thought. "The first time with Mark was awful, we were both terrified. I lay there, he climbed on top and it was all over with in about two minutes."

"Did it get better?"

"It took a while."

"You haven't got a while with your hunky man, girl, I expect he's been round the block a few times. You've got to take charge. He's got his hand on your thigh, if he doesn't start stroking you then push his hand up. I guarantee you that as soon as he reaches the top of your stocking he'll be all yours."

"Should I stand up and invite him upstairs?"

"If you're snuggled up on your big sofa with his hand up your dress, then seize the day, girl. Just do it there and then. All this talk is getting me horny as fuck Kath; I might give Oliver a treat tomorrow as a parting gift."

"Don't you dare," Katherine said. "Find a nice man, you deserve one after Phillip."

"I haven't had sex for months, Kath, I even thought about ringing Patrick, he's an old boyfriend and someone told me he's split from his wife."

"Why did you break up with him?"

"He's a fucking lying cheat. But while I was with him we got down and dirty an awful lot. He was the one that liked tying me to the bed."

"Did you like it as well?"

"It takes away all your inhibitions. Patrick used to think he was in charge but he wasn't. You can really let yourself go. He was the one that tied my hands tight behind my back. I knelt on the floor and give him the blow-job to end all blow-jobs."

"I think I'll put all that on hold for a while, Liz."

Robin had stopped off at the sports bar on his way home from work. He was having a game of snooker with his friend Darren and losing badly.

"Your minds somewhere else, mate, that's another frame to me. Fucking good job we're not playing for money."

"Sorry Daz. How's it going with the lovely lady?"

"We've been out a few times. I think she's lovely Rob but I'm not sure if she thinks the same about me."

"If she hasn't given you the elbow yet then she must think something of you."

"I'm worried about taking it to the next level Rob, what if I don't measure up?"

"Don't worry about it, I'm sure you'll be fine."

"Easy for you to say, mate, you've got it at home on tap waiting for you every night."

Robin took a sip from his drink, he didn't want to have to buy another round. He had enough spare cash for Saturday but Madelaine had insisted on having the exhaust on her car repaired before driving to her mother's for the weekend.

"Not much of that going on right now Daz. She's either doped up on sedatives or been boozing, I keep thinking I'll get home and find she's been on both. I haven't seen any action for fucking months."

"That's bad news, at least I've got the prospects to look forward to. She'll be okay Rob, just see her through it."

"It's got worse the last couple of weeks. She saw a specialist and she's been diagnosed with clinical depression. I can't see how we'll get through it as things are."

"What about Tuscany then? Is she still up for moving there?"

"She says it's the only way we'll be together. Christ, Daz; if I don't get something together, she's leaving in September."

"I'll still back you Rob, you know that."

Robin knew his friend would invest in him but he was hoping to ask Katherine for the whole investment to buy the vineyard. Then he could ask Darren, his father and his uncle to invest their money in further developing the business, possibly even building some holiday cottages.

"You're a good mate, Daz."

Chapter Twenty-Three

Saturday eventually arrived, Katherine had arranged that Danny take the twins swimming to give her all day. Jennifer was coming round at two o'clock to do her hair in a slightly different style. She spent the morning at home, did a little gardening and gave her Ducati a clean.

She was nervous by lunchtime, she made herself some food and sat out on the patio for half an hour. Just before Jennifer was due, she smoked one of her cigarettes, she looked at a bottle of wine but decided against it.

"You've been smoking Mum," Jennifer said as soon as she arrived. "I can smell it on you."

"Just one to calm me down, I'll be showering before I get dressed."

"Have your shower before I do your hair then, otherwise it'll get ruined later."

Katherine showered and washed her hair, she put a robe on and went downstairs. Jennifer sat her in the chair and half an hour later announced that she was finished. Katherine looked in the mirror and was delighted with the results.

"Thanks, Jen, it looks great."

"Do you want me to do your make-up?"

"I'm quite capable thank you."

She'd bought some glossy red lipstick that she didn't really want her daughter seeing. Jennifer asked what she was wearing.

"Nothing fancy, it's only a meal at Rita's and The Tivoli."

"Fourth date, Mum, you never know."

Katherine was relieved when Jennifer went home just before four o'clock, she looked at the wine and cigarettes again but decided against either. She went upstairs and put her skimpy black bra and pants on. The black suspender belt and shiny black stockings followed soon afterwards. Then she sat in front of the mirror and did her make-up. She kept it quite subtle until she put the glossy red lipstick on. Before she put her dress on she paraded in front of the mirror and studied herself.

"Damn I'm still sexy," she said out loud, she was trying to convince herself but she actually felt ridiculous. When she put her dress on she looked again and felt a little more comfortable with the effect. She thought it was slightly too short for her age and that she'd have to be careful getting in and out of the car.

The week before she'd gone online and ordered a pair of stiletto heeled shoes, she tried them on but wasn't confident enough to wear them. She had a pair of Cuban heeled shoes with straps that came slightly up her ankle, she put those on and was delighted that they looked fine with the dress. A black jacket completed the ensemble and she was ready when she heard the car stop outside at just before five o'clock.

She waited for the bell to ring before she answered the door, Robin was stood outside holding a bouquet of flowers.

"Wow, you look stunning, Katherine, I love your hair like that."

He handed her the flowers, she invited him in while she put them in a vase and took them into the family room. Robin was wearing a black leather jacket, smart trousers and an open necked white shirt.

He had a different car this time a two-seater Mercedes sports car, he held the door open for her. Katherine remembered to hold on to the hem of her dress and climb in carefully.

"This is a nice car, Rob," she said as he got in the driver's seat.

"Only for this visit sadly; they didn't have a saloon for me."

She'd given him the postcode for her house to programme into a sat-nav but he seemed to know his way into Wimborne.

"I've booked a table for six o-clock so there's no hurry. What sort of a week have you had?"

"Okay," he said. "Mixed really; what about yours?"

Katherine reached across and took his hand, the car was automatic so he could easily drive one handed. She rested his hand on her leg and covered it with her own.

"I've been looking forward to tonight all week Rob, just the normal really; work, swimming and home."

He looked across and smiled. "I'm glad you've been looking forward to it, let's see if we can make it a night to remember then."

Katherine smiled to herself, a night to remember was exactly what she had planned.

She remembered the first time that Mark and she had tried to have sex, her parents were away for the weekend and they had the house to themselves. She suggested that he told his parents that he was staying with a boy from college but he didn't want to lie to them. He said that he may be late home and that they shouldn't worry. They trusted him and knew that he wouldn't let them down.

They'd been out for an early drink and were back at her house by eight o'clock. Both of them were a bundle of nerves, they'd talked about it and they knew the basics but up to then all they'd done was kiss and cuddle. They undressed and climbed into her single bed, eventually with more than a little guidance from Katherine Mark managed to hit the spot.

About two minutes later, a very disappointed Katherine was thinking was that it? Mark grunted a few times, told Katherine that he loved her and fell asleep. She laid there for two hours before waking him up and sending him home.

By the time they were married it had improved somewhat but Katherine still felt a little short-changed. After Jennifer had arrived their sex life was restricted to occasionally, mostly at the weekends if Mark wasn't too busy working or going to car shows with his father.

They arrived at the tea-rooms at ten to six, Katherine showed Robin where to leave the car and they went straight in, the owner showed them to a nice table in the window and brought them a menu.

"It's nice to see you again Katherine, how's Jennifer and her business doing?"

"Very well thank you Rita. This is my friend Rob."

Rita was a divorcee in her forties, Robin stood and shook hands with her. Katherine noticed that Rita held on to his hand for slightly longer than normal, she looked at Katherine and smiled knowingly.

"This is nice," Robin said as he looked round the tea-rooms, she usually closed at seven o'clock but if there was a show at The Tivoli she stayed open a little later. Five of the ten tables were occupied by diners, Rita was clearing another table so Katherine assumed that she'd been busy.

"She does very well here, especially in the summer, we supply her with scones, cakes and quiches; we have to come daily now."

They both ordered fresh salmon fillets with new potatoes and salad. For dessert they had cheesecake and fresh cream. Robin insisted on paying and gave the waitress a generous tip. Before they left Rita came to their table with a slip of paper.

"This is the code to open the back gate when you come out of the theatre Katherine, just key the numbers in and it unlocks automatically. When you close it, just make sure it's firmly closed."

"Thanks, Rita," Katherine said. "And thank you for a lovely meal."

Rita gave Robin a lingering look as they stood to leave. "She fancies you," Katherine told him.

"Or maybe she fancies you," Robin said. "You look good enough to eat tonight."

There was a small queue in the theatre foyer, they stood there looking at the forthcoming attractions. Katherine was proud to stand there holding hands with her handsome man.

"It's lovely here," Katherine said. "A proper old-fashioned theatre, you can almost smell the atmosphere."

They took their seats at the front of the balcony five minutes before the show started.

"Nice seats Katherine," Robin said. "I'll give you the money for them later." He was hoping that Katherine wouldn't remind him later, he had forty pounds in his wallet and that was about the limits of his funds until his salary went in.

Katherine had no intention of taking the money for the seats, Robin had paid for dinner; she thought that maybe he was the type of man that always had to pay for everything.

"I like the balcony," Katherine said. "Sometimes it's a little far away but not here."

They sat there through the first half of an amateur production of a musical, at the interval Robin bought ice-creams and they stood in the upstairs foyer with them.

"I love these amateur productions, Rob. They put so much effort into them."

"I wish I had half their talent," Robin commented. "I can't hold a note."

Katherine sat spellbound through the second half, live theatre was her ideal way of spending an evening. Mark liked rock music so through their marriage they'd both compromised. She'd stood with him through Status Quo and Bon Jovi and he'd sat quietly through operas and musicals with her. Robin seemed to be enjoying the performance, when they came out for their curtain call he stood and applauded appreciatively.

They walked hand in hand back to the car, it was still warm at ten-thirty in the evening. Katherine entered the code on the gate and it clicked open. While she closed the gate Robin walked round the car and held the door open for her. When she sat down this time, she didn't hold the hem of her dress to make sure Robin got a good look at her long shapely legs and stocking tops.

Katherine was pleased that Robin seemed to have genuinely enjoyed the show, once again on the way home she put his hand on her leg and covered it with her own. They pulled up outside her front door at just after eleven o'clock.

Taking her friends advice she leant across as soon as he pulled up and gave him a very passionate kiss. When she stopped she opened the door for herself and announced that she was making coffee for them both. Robin didn't get out of the car straight away, Katherine was worried that he'd drive off but just as she opened the front door she heard his car door close and the central locking click.

Katherine stood waiting for the coffee machine to finish, she tensed a little when Robin stood directly behind her and put his arms round her waist. He was close enough that she could feel his hardness against her. As soon as she'd poured the coffee, they went through to the family room and sat close together on the large sofa.

"This is a nice room."

"It's more comfortable than the lounge, Rob, we can relax in here."

As she was talking, Katherine snuggled up even close to Robin and put her spare hand on his thigh. As soon as he put his hand on top of it she moved them both back to her leg. Her dress had ridden up a little as they sat down, she didn't want her stocking top showing just yet so she put their hands just below the bottom of her dress.

As soon as they'd both finished their coffee Katherine leaned across for a very passionate kiss, she made sure her tongue brushed against his lips, as she was kissing him she pushed his hand slowly up her thigh and held it there.

"It may be better if I left soon Katherine," Robin said. "I'd hate to take things too far and offend you."

"You'd offend me more if you left, Rob," she replied, as she was talking she pushed his hand a little further up until she felt it touch her bare thigh. He kissed her back even harder and she felt his tongue exploring her mouth. By now she was determined that he was going to take her upstairs, she'd put clean bedding on the double bed in the spare room. Although she felt that she'd moved on from Mark she didn't want to disrespect him by taking another man to the room they'd shared for so many years.

Five minutes of kissing later she didn't think that she could walk upstairs unaided. She hadn't had sex for several years but the familiar feelings were running through her. Finally his hand reached her pants and she felt his fingers gently stroking her.

He was kissing her very passionately at the same time, he took his tongue out of her mouth for a moment.

"You must tell me to stop if you think I'm going too far," he told her. "As I said before, I'd hate to offend you."

"You're very proficient with your tongue, Rob," she said, she was trying to sound sexy but wasn't sure if her voice had the effect she wanted.

Robin broke off from kissing her on the mouth and started kissing her legs, when he reached her stocking tops and he was kissing bare flesh he once again reminded her that he'd stop if she told him to, Katherine kept quiet but she put her hand on the top of his head and encouraged him to explore further. After what seemed an age, he was kissing her through her pants, she parted her legs enough for him to squeeze his head inside her thighs.

"You don't mind me being down here, Katherine," he said. "And as you just said I'm very good with my tongue, tell me to stop anytime don't forget."

Katherine had a very good idea what Robin was about to do and she had no intention of telling him to stop. He was still kissing her through her pants, she wasn't sure that she could hold back much longer. Finally Robin stood up and put his arms under hers, he pulled her up so she was standing in front of him and kissed her hungrily on her mouth.

"Are you sure?" he asked. Katherine didn't reply so he took her silence as an acceptance. He reached up her dress and slid her pants off. Then he took two cushions off the sofa and put them on the floor. He sat on the floor and guided her to where he wanted her standing. Then he laid down with his head on the cushions and told her to kneel over him. He spent a few moments kissing her thighs before reaching the top, he gave her a last chance to tell him to stop; again she knelt there in silence. Finally, his mouth was over her and his tongue was furiously probing and licking her.

Mark had never taken Katherine to orgasm with his tongue, he'd rarely ventured down there but Robin was definitely an expert at pleasing women that way. After less than five minutes, Katherine felt the feelings well up and shortly afterwards she was screaming out in ecstasy.

Robin stood up after Katherine had climbed off him, she threw her arms round him straight away.

"My turn now, mister, only fair that I return the favour."

"Only if you're comfortable with using your mouth, Katherine, some women find it distasteful."

"Shall we go upstairs and lose some clothes, Rob?" Katherine suggested. Robin nodded and she led him by the hand to the spare room. They undressed each other in turn until they were both naked, after standing close for a moment they climbed into the huge double bed.

As soon as they were lying down, Katherine put her head under the bedclothes and moved down the bed. She'd used her mouth on Mark now and again but this time she was looking forward to the experience. She dribbled some saliva on him and ran her lips up and down him before taking him in her mouth.

Robin was stroking her again, suddenly he stopped her movement with his hand and asked her to stop.

"It's a little while since he's seen any action, Katherine," he whispered. "I don't want to go off too soon."

"Close your eyes and think of Angela Merkel."

"Ready for the main course, Mrs Merkel?"

Katherine automatically laid on her back, it was the only position that Mark had ever used. He climbed on top of her, she was wet enough for him to slip comfortably in her.

She'd never climaxed twice in a day before but with Robin inside her and kissing her she felt the feelings start again. He called out and she realised he'd finished but fortunately he kept going long enough and a few moments later she was crying out again and trembling. He stopped moving but stayed there on top of her kissing her hungrily.

Eventually, he rolled off and lay beside her with his arm across her stomach, neither of them spoke until Robin asked if he could use her bathroom. She pointed to the door of the en-suite room and he left her in bed on her own. When he came back and climbed into bed he settled down beside her, she was hoping that he'd spend the night there but hadn't liked to ask him. She was tired after a long day, they chatted briefly about the show and what they'd just done but Katherine fell asleep soon afterwards.

She looked at the clock when she woke in the night for the toilet, Robin was fast asleep on his side facing away from her, it was three o'clock in the morning, she got back into bed and lay there thinking about the best night she could remember for many years. Eventually she went back to sleep until seven o'clock. She wanted the toilet and a drink so she slipped her bra and pants on and went downstairs.

She made herself a cup of tea and sat in the kitchen with it, when she'd drunk it she was going to take one up to Robin but thought that the occasion deserved something a bit special. She got a bottle of sparkling white wine from the cupboard and a bottle of orange juice from the fridge and mixed a jug of Bucks Fizz. She put the jug and two champagne flutes on a tray and took them upstairs. Robin was still asleep, she put the tray on the bedside table and watched his breathing for a few moments. He must have sensed her presence, he shook himself awake and sat up in bed.

"I brought us a drink," she said. "You deserve a treat after your efforts last night." She poured two glasses and handed him one. He sipped at the cocktail and looked at her longingly.

"Not fair," he said. "You covered all the good bits."

"I didn't want you to get too excited," she teased.

She was going to get back into bed but decided to sit on the bed next to him. They both finished their drinks and put the empty glasses on the tray. Katherine stood up and stretched, Robin looked at her in her underwear as if he hadn't seen a woman for a long time. She thought briefly and then instructed him to get out of bed and stand up in front of her.

"I thought you'd be a bit more pleased to see me," she said. Then she took him in her hand and felt him getting harder. She decided that she'd try out her friend's theory about being in control of the situation.

"Do exactly what I say please," she instructed. She got one of her stockings off the floor and handed it to him. Then she turned the other way and put her hands behind her.

"Tie them together please, nice and tight."

Robin looped the stocking round her wrists and pulled them together. "Tighter please, I could easily slip out of that."

He pulled them tighter but she still thought he could go further "Tighter please, my grandson could do better than that."

Robin pulled the stocking as tight as he could, Katherine almost cried out as it bit into her flesh but she actually seemed to be enjoying the pain. She knelt on the floor in front of him and dribbled saliva on him, then she started kissing and licking him. When she was satisfied that he was hard enough she told him to put his hands on her head. She took him in her mouth and started moving, after a while she took her mouth away for a rest. When she was ready she took him in her mouth again and started moving slowly up and down him. He took a step backwards so that he slipped out of her mouth briefly.

"Getting close," he told her. "Do you want me to take it out just before I finish?"

"If I wanted you to do that I'd have told you," she snapped. "Just put your hands on my head and hold them tight please."

This time she moved with a little more urgency until she felt his hands slow her down. A split second after she heard him call out she felt her mouth fill up, she'd never done that to Mark; the first thing she noticed was the warmth in her mouth. She stopped moving and swallowed it as soon as he'd taken himself out of her mouth.

"Bring it back please," she instructed. "I need to clean it all off you." She kissed and licked him and then announced that he was clean enough.

She turned round so that he could untie her but he'd tied her so tightly that he couldn't untie the knot straight away.

"There's some scissors in the bathroom cabinet, Rob, you'll have to cut me free." She was feeling a little foolish as she stood there waiting, her wrists were also hurting with the stocking cutting into her flesh. Robin came back with the scissors and cut the stocking away.

Robin poured her a drink and she sat on the edge of the bed with it, she rubbed the red marks on her wrists, they were burnt slightly where the stocking had rubbed against her.

"That was stunning Katherine, you're quite a surprise."

Katherine had surprised herself but didn't want to tell Robin that she'd never taken a man all the way with her mouth and had never been tied up in the bedroom.

"I thought as I was two one ahead in the climaxes I'd let you catch up," she told him. "I didn't want you leaving feeling cheated."

Robin was feeling guilty but tried not to show it. He hadn't cheated on Madelaine before and he also felt that he was being cruel to Katherine.

"I'd better make you some breakfast, Rob."

She slipped her dressing gown on, Robin put his shirt and trousers on and followed her downstairs.

"I hate to think I'm letting you down, Katherine, but as soon as we've eaten I have to go. I must see my father this morning and I've a meeting later with a possible backer."

"On a Sunday; he must be keen."

"He's a private investor, he knows I'm flying out tomorrow and agreed to meet me today. I think the only way to pull myself out of a possible situation is to actually buy the vineyard in Tuscany. I offered him half a million but he said he won't accept less than a million pounds."

"I suppose it makes some kind of sense but spending that kind of money surely entails a lot of risks, especially if you're using an investor. He'll be expecting a good return on his investment."

"If I get it for a million, it's a bargain, Katherine. With a little work and a decent strategy it could be worth half as much again inside a year. The crop is always high quality and the wine one of the finest from Italy."

"I'm sure you'll do what's best Rob," Katherine was disappointed that he wasn't going to spend long there with her. She'd planned on showing him the E-Type, maybe even taking him for lunch in it. "When will I see you again?"

"I'll message you every day from Italy and I'll try to get back for next weekend. I can't promise I will but if I get the finance sorted out the sale should be a formality."

Katherine cooked scrambled eggs with fresh salmon and toast, Robin said that he preferred tea in the morning; she made a pot, poured two cups and they took it on trays into the family room. The two cushions that Robin had rested his head on the night before were still on the floor, Katherine picked them up, looked at Robin and giggled a little.

"I forgot to tidy up after myself," he commented. "I'll remember next time."

They sat at the dining table with their food and ate quietly, Katherine thought that the comment he'd just made at least indicated that he wanted to come back for more. She wanted him to stay for the day but almost as soon as they'd finished eating he stood to leave.

She followed him to the car, as soon as he opened the doors he turned to Katherine and held his arms open. She fell into his arms for a long embrace. When he kissed her goodbye she felt some tears but blinked them back before he noticed.

After ten minutes of very passionate kissing he finally drove off, Katherine stood in the drive until she saw the back of the car disappear, she went back indoors and cleared the breakfast dishes before going upstairs to finish dressing.

She went into the spare bedroom, stripped the bed linen and put it ready for washing. She put clean linen on and tidied the room. The torn stocking was on the floor, Katherine picked it up and remembered how she'd felt with her hands tied and kneeling on the floor. She took the dirty linen, the tray with the jug and glasses and the stocking downstairs.

The rest of the day went by in a blur, Liz telephoned to ask about the night before. Katherine told her that she didn't want to talk about it over the phone and that she'd tell her when they met for swimming on Wednesday.

She was in her bed by nine-thirty but she didn't sleep well, most of the night she was thinking that she wanted Robin in bed with her. He'd messaged her telling her that he'd met with the financier and was on his way to the airport. He said that he hoped to be back by the following weekend and was looking forward to a repeat performance.

Katherine had decided that if Robin came back she was going to take him to Exmoor for the weekend. She wanted to be with him properly this time, to go walking on the moors, to cook his meals and to share her bed with him again.

Chapter Twenty-Four

Robin was thinking the opposite; that he wanted to see Katherine the following weekend to ask her for an investment, preferably the whole million pounds and then be out of her life. He drove straight home from her house to be faced with an angry father who was demanding to know why no one was there overnight.

Luckily Robin managed to convince his father that he'd just had too much to drink and stayed over at Darren's for the night. As soon as he got home he showered and put all his clothes in the wash. He messaged Katherine telling her more lies than he was comfortable with and then settled down in front of the television for the rest of the day.

Madelaine arrived home early in the evening in a foul mood, she'd been held up in traffic on the motorway and the car had broken down shortly afterwards.

"The breakdown man said it wants scrapping as soon as possible Rob. Fucking thing overheated just after we cleared the traffic jam."

"It'll go on for a couple of months Mads. I'll know next weekend whether or not Katherine Reynolds is likely to come on board with us in Tuscany."

"Have you seen her this weekend?"

"I messaged her just now," Robin said truthfully. His wife seemed to think that lying by omission was legitimate, as long as she didn't ask if they'd slept together he had no intention of telling her. "Next time I see her I'm going to ask her about backing me to buy the vineyard."

"Does she trust you enough do you think?"

"I'll find out, won't I," he snapped.

"If she doesn't back us it's over Rob. I was talking to Cheralyn on Friday, she thinks she'll have to finish soon, I know he thinks I should be his fucking slave but it's not happening."

"What sort of weekend did you have? How's your mother?"

"She hates living on her own Rob, apart from that she's fine."

"Darren has a spare ticket for the cricket next Saturday, I can have it if I drive him up there."

"Where is it, can we afford it?"

"Nottingham," Robin lied. "It'll only cost the petrol and I can charge most of it on the card."

"Will you be back Saturday night or stay up there?"

"It's too far away to drive there and back in the day but Darren knows someone with a flat up there we can use so it won't cost anything."

"When are you seeing your rich widow again?"

"I'm not sure really, maybe I'll just put the proposal to her in an e-mail."

"Do you really think that you can sweet talk a million pound investment out of her Rob? I know it was my idea but it's a hell of a long shot."

"You hear about these wealthy women getting conned out of their lifesavings by guys they've never met. At least what we've got on offer will make her a serious profit."

Katherine was still a little mixed-up Monday morning, she went to work early as usual; Jennifer quizzed her about her date with Robin.

"It was a lovely evening, Jen, Rita did us proud with dinner and let us park the car there, the show was great, quite the nicest evening out for a long time."

"Any afters Mum?"

Katherine blushed, Jennifer was busy taking the first batch of bread out of the oven and didn't notice. She'd had to wear a blouse with extra-long sleeves to cover up the burn marks on her wrists from where Robin had tied her hands with her stocking.

"For me to know and you to wonder about, dear."

"That means yes, Mum, if you and Rob hadn't got down and dirty, you'd have told me."

"How many of each scones do you want again Jen?"

"Don't try and change the subject, a hundred of each fruit and cheese, fifty of each plain and cherry. Did he come in for coffee and a nibble?"

Katherine started cutting out the fruit scones and didn't say anything. Jennifer took the hint and kept quiet.

"Pete and Gavin seem to have secured the new site for the factory," Katherine told Jennifer. "It's got planning permission for a big enough building."

Every time Jennifer tried to quiz her mother about the events of the weekend Katherine changed the subject. By the time they'd got everything finished Jennifer had given up on trying to find out if her mother had slept with her new man.

"You're allowed to have sex, Mum," she said as Katherine left for the factory "It's as natural as breathing and eating, don't be ashamed of something that makes you happy."

When Katherine got home from the factory, she checked her inbox for a message from Robin, he'd only messaged her once on Sunday which had upset her a little. There was a message on her telephone that he'd sent at nine o'clock that morning. He'd arrived in Italy and was trying to negotiate the purchase of the vineyard from the owner.

He wrote a little about the events of Saturday but Katherine was a little disappointed with his reaction. Maybe he was used to sleeping with different women and it hadn't meant as much to him as it had to her was her only thought. She wrote and deleted several replies before sending one that she thought was suitable. She still hadn't told Robin that she loved him, if he came to Exmoor the next weekend she planned on saying it to him in bed.

She didn't want to do any gardening after her shower so on a whim she took her Ducati out for a ride. She stopped to see if Liz had arrived home, just after she pulled up her friend walked round the corner.

"When you take your helmet off and shake your hair loose I wish I was a lesbian Kath. That is so damn sexy."

"Any chance of a coffee Liz?"

"Of course, I want to hear all the juicy bits."

Katherine was wearing a sports bra and cycling shorts under her one-piece bike leathers so when they got indoors she took them off and stood in the kitchen with Liz while she made them a coffee.

"Are you sure you're fifty-nine Kath? You're still so fucking cute."

Katherine didn't really know how to react to the compliment so she didn't say anything. Liz handed her a coffee and noticed the marks on her wrists.

"Jesus, girl; I hope you asked him to tie you up. Tell your best friend all about it then."

Katherine was a bit embarrassed telling Liz about the antics but with a little coaxing the whole story came out.

"On the floor of the family room indeed, you couldn't wait to get him upstairs then."

"It just seemed right, Liz."

"I'll never be able to look at you the same again, tied up and blowing him indeed."

"It was your fault, I'd never have thought of doing that. I've never done it before."

"When's the next performance taking place?"

"Hopefully at the cottage next weekend, he's in Italy on business for the week."

"Our London trip is still on I hope."

"Of course it is, I wouldn't let you down for anyone Liz."

"I know you wouldn't."

Katherine went a little quiet for a moment, her friend asked if everything was all right.

"I think so, Liz. I wanted to tell him I love him but we're both still holding back."

"That's natural at our age, it'll take a long time for me to trust anyone totally."

"I assume you ended things with Oliver. Anyone else on the horizon?"

"I'm e-mailing one or two, I thought it'd be a lot easier than this. I've got a date for Friday night if I want, he's ten years younger than me."

"I'm going to Exmoor on Friday straight after I finish at the shop. I'm either taking my E-Type or the Ducati. Rob hasn't seen either of them yet."

"He hasn't told you about his Jaguar?"

"Not yet, I expect he will when he sees mine."

They chatted about things for an hour, Liz was cooking so she invited Katherine to eat with her. By the time she went home it was just starting to get dark outside. Liz had put her mind at rest about Robin keeping so much from her. They kissed goodnight outside before Katherine put her helmet on.

"I hope those burns have faded a bit before our swim on Wednesday, Kath, they'll all know exactly what they are."

"They're almost gone now, I'll keep putting cream on them. Thanks for listening Liz, see you Wednesday."

"I think Mum got a good seeing to on Saturday night Dan. She had rope burns on her wrists, I reckon she let him tie her to the bed."

Danny didn't know how he was meant to respond so he kept quiet and let Jennifer carry on.

"She wouldn't tell me anything, I don't care what she gets up to but she's so fucking two-faced. When she found out Elaine had a fuckbuddy, she thought she was a right slapper. Now she's sleeping with a guy she's only just met."

"She must think an awful lot of him if she's sleeping with him straight away."

"Before I went off to college, she used to fucking lecture me all the time, I was old enough and sensible but the way she used to nag at me really pissed me off."

"Fancy her being tied to her bed, you'd think she was a bit old for that sort of thing Jen. Maybe we ought to spice things up in the bedroom a bit."

"Fuck off, Danny, you'd get me all tied down and fall asleep, I'd be there till you needed a pee in the night."

"I thought you'd be pleased that your mum has met someone Jen, you were the one that bought her the subscription to the dating agency."

"I am pleased, Dan, I really am. I just wish she wasn't quite so fucking smug when she talks about sex, then she gets down and dirty straight away with the first man she meets."

Robin went for a drink on his way home from work on Monday evening, he met Darren in the sports bar.

"I hate asking you to lie for me Daz but can you do me a big favour Mate. I need an alibi for this Saturday. I've told Mads that you've got me a ticket for Trent Bridge on Saturday and that we're staying overnight."

"Found yourself a little bit of action to replace what you're missing out on at home, Rob?"

"I can live in hope I suppose. It's strictly business Mate but Mads wouldn't understand that. She'd naturally assume exactly what you just did. Just keep it in mind if you ever get asked please."

"No trouble, Rob, you'll owe me one though."

Chapter Twenty-Five

Katherine decided to take her Ducati to Devon for the weekend. She finished at the shop just before ten o'clock, it was a beautiful June morning, hot and sunny with no chance of any rain. She left home at eleven, had lunch and filled up with fuel at Honiton on the way down and arrived at just after three o'clock. She put the bike away, had a shower and walked to the beach until the early evening.

Robin messaged later to say goodnight and told her that he'd try to get there well before lunch-time on Saturday, he said he'd flown in from Italy that day, was tired but had some exciting news for Katherine. She'd had a meal in Honiton and didn't really want to cook so she just made herself some sandwiches for supper and went to bed with a book at ten o'clock.

She looked longingly at her Ducati on Saturday morning, it was a beautiful sunny day and she was up by seven o'clock. She was still feeling a little stiff and saddle-sore after the ride down and wanted to be there when Robin arrived so she just walked to the shop for a newspaper and some food and then had a morning indoors. She prepared some food for the evening meal and had a shower before lunch. Robin messaged her that he'd be there by one o'clock so she got them some food ready and was waiting outside when he arrived.

He saw Katherine waiting in the drive, she waved and pointed to a spot where he could park the car. He was driving a black Mercedes saloon, similar to the one he'd driven to Burley the first time they'd met.

As soon as he stopped, he got out of the car and held his arms open, Katherine fell into his embrace; he held her tightly and kissed her hungrily.

When they disentangled themselves, he looked directly at her face and smiled. "Good to see you, Katherine," he said.

"I thought you were pleased to see me, Rob," she said, she was trying to sound sexy but it came across as if she had a sore throat. "Unless that's a tube of smarties in your pocket."

Robin half closed his eyes and said in a very deep voice, "I don't eat sweets."

Katherine giggled a little and kissed him again. "Where did you park your jeep?" he asked.

"I didn't use it for this trip," she answered with a smile. She led him round to the back of the cottage where her Ducati was parked in a lean to.

"Wow," he yelled. "That's a limited edition nine-sixteen, how long have you had that. I didn't know you rode bikes."

"There's plenty you don't know about me Rob. I bought it new about eighteen years ago. Mark wanted a limited edition Honda and it only had a single seat so we bought this for me to ride."

"Have you get a set of leathers? I bet you look very sexy in them."

"I do look very sexy in them," she agreed. "I could wear them to bed tonight if you like."

"Maybe not actually in bed, you'd be very hot wearing them."

Katherine led him indoors, she'd laid out snack food and drink on the kitchen table.

"Tea or coffee?"

"Tea would be nice, the food looks good enough to eat, as do you by the way."

"We'll do the food first and then you can have a little sample of what you can expect tonight, Rob."

The next half an hour was spent eating and drinking with the conversation mostly small talk about their weeks and Katherine's motor biking.

When they'd finished eating they sat on the settee holding hands and kissing.

"Let's go for a walk to the beach for an hour," Katherine suggested. "A nice walk will do us good after the food."

Robin agreed and they walked through the village and to the beach, it was only about a mile along a level road with a pavement.

"It's a lovely village Katherine, is that your cottage or do you rent it when you come here."

"It's mine, Rob, I've had it a few years but I couldn't really use it while Mark was ill. I rented it out until earlier this year. Now I want to get some use out of it."

"You're certainly full of surprises."

They spent an hour by the sea, a few people were swimming. "I wish I'd brought a costume," Katherine said. "I'd love a swim."

Robin wanted to get back to the cottage and try to turn the conversation around to Tuscany and the sale of the vineyard but didn't want to seem obvious. Eventually Katherine looked at her watch and suggested that they made their way back.

"I'll put some dinner in the oven and then we can find something to do for a couple of hours."

After Katherine seasoned some chicken fillets and put them in the oven on a slow heat she took Robin by the hand and led him through into the bedroom.

"This is a nice room," he commented. "That big bed looks comfortable."

"I expect you're tired, Rob, why don't you lay on the bed and try it out."

Robin sat on the edge of the bed, Katherine lifted his legs and stretched him out.

"Don't do anything or say anything please, try not to fall asleep."

Robin laid back and relaxed, Katherine undid his trousers and pulled then gently off him, she undid his shirt and pushed it away from him. Then she pulled his pants down slowly.

The first time she'd given him oral sex she was a little nervous but this time she was a lot more confident. She licked and kissed him until he was hard enough and then took him in her mouth.

As soon as she started sliding up and down him Robin put his hands on her head and held her tightly. Once or twice she nearly gagged when he pushed himself right into her mouth.

He didn't suggest taking it out this time, she felt him slow down her movement with his hands, eventually he stopped her movement, cried out and almost straight away Katherine felt the warm liquid almost fill her mouth. She swallowed it greedily and kept her mouth there until she was sure he'd finished.

Robin wasn't quite sure what to say so he lay there quietly for a moment. Katherine smiled at him and told him it was his turn to return the compliment. She climbed over him, crawled up until she was above his head and then lowered herself onto him.

Robin didn't seem quite as enthusiastic this time, Katherine had to encourage him to keep going, she put her hands underneath his head and pushed him closer to her. As the sensations built up she rocked backwards, she had to hold Robin in place, eventually she screamed out and stopped moving.

They laid side by side in silence for a while, eventually she decided to go and get them a drink. She had a bottle of wine in the fridge so she poured two glasses and took them back into the bedroom. Robin was sat on the edge of the bed putting his trousers on.

"You did say I looked good enough to eat," she said cheekily. "You tasted lovely as well."

They took their drinks back into the living room and sat close together on the sofa, Katherine still wanted to tell Robin that she loved him but he still seemed to be holding back so she decided to wait until they were in bed later.

"When did you take your pants off?" he asked. "I was looking forward to doing it."

"I haven't been wearing any today, I was a little concerned at the beach that the wind didn't blow my skirt too high and give them all an eyeful."

They had an early dinner, Robin produced a bottle of wine from his overnight bag.

"Let's have this with our dinner Katherine," he suggested. "I brought it back from Tuscany with me."

That wasn't his first lie of the day and certainly wouldn't be his last. He'd managed to find a very expensive bottle of wine produced at a vineyard just outside Florence. He'd taken it home and carefully steamed the labels off.

He poured Katherine a glass and encouraged her to sample it and give him an opinion.

"It's from the yard that's causing me all the problems," he lied. "The wine is excellent, if only they had some good management there."

Katherine sipped the wine and swilled it round in her mouth, Robin almost expected her to spit it out but was relieved when she swallowed it.

"It's really good, Rob," she agreed.

"So's this food, Katherine, this chicken tastes amazing."

They ate in silence, Robin kept topping their wine glasses up throughout the meal. When they'd finished eating, Katherine put a disc in the player and they sat on the settee.

"What did you think of the wine?"

"Really nice; quite the best I've tried for ages."

"I'd really like to put a proposal to you before I go to any other potential investors, Katherine," he began. "The owner of the vineyard has agreed that I can buy it for a million pounds. The sale needs to go through within the next few months or his creditors will take possession and the opportunity will be gone."

"Is it a wise move to be buying investments in Europe at the moment, Rob? No one really knows how leaving The EU will affect things."

"It actually makes perfect sense, Katherine, you see I know that given proper management the yard alone will be worth half as much again inside two years. As you've said the wine from that area is excellent, there's serious money to be made out there."

Katherine interrupted, "It hasn't done the current owner a lot of good, Rob. You said he's likely to be going bankrupt shortly."

"Bad management, Katherine, the trouble at the moment is that I've a lot of capital tied up there. If he goes under, he may well take me with him."

"You've been having meetings with investors, Rob, if it's that good surely they'll back you."

"I think I've got the money in place when I need it," Robin lied. "I was hoping that you'd want to come in with me on it."

Katherine didn't say anything straight away, she went through to the kitchen and put the kettle on while she was thinking.

"I don't think it's for me, Rob, much as I'd love to be involved in wine production in Tuscany, why don't you try and put a syndicate together. Maybe if you did that, I could come in for a small share in it."

Robin took Katherine through his presentation, the projected value of the yard, the yield on short and long-term investment, the probable development of some of the land as holiday cottages, he took her through the technicalities of wine production and the marketing of the final product.

When he'd finished, Katherine was impressed with his knowledge and salesmanship but if anything she was less inclined to invest in the vineyard.

"I'm really sorry if you're disappointed in me, Rob, but I think it's best for me to stay away from it. You really need something like one of those hedge funds to back you. As I said, if it was a syndicate, I might come in for a share but only a small one."

Robin thought briefly. "How much would you be willing to invest?"

"I could possibly raise fifty-thousand but certainly no more, Rob. Even then I'd have to cash in some pensions and sell some stocks."

"I thought you said you were selling the factory and business, Katherine, surely you can raise more than that."

"I'm kind of selling up, Rob, but it's a management buy-out. They've got to take on all the staff contracts and then re-locate the whole factory. I certainly won't get any money out of it, the re-location costs are astronomical. If the expenses of the re-location are a lot less than the buying costs anything left over will be divided up between the staff."

"Surely, you deserve something after forty years work." Robin knew exactly what Katherine was getting but had to be a little careful in case Katherine noticed.

"I may have to keep a small percentage if the moving costs are less than the value, otherwise they'll think it's some sort of tax fraud. I'll only get a small annuity from it though."

"If they have to move the factory surely you'll own the original site, won't you be selling that?"

Katherine didn't answer straight away, she was getting a little suspicious because Robin was trying to raise a million pounds and seemed to think that she could raise that kind of an investment.

"It's being developed as affordable housing for local people Rob. We're hoping to put forty flats for sheltered housing and maybe sixty-one, two- and three-bedroom houses."

"Even as affordable or even social housing that's still a hundred properties Katherine, you'll get quite a sum for that." As he spoke, Robin was frantically trying to work out how much money Katherine could expect to sell the site for now.

"I'd never sell it, Rob, Mark and I discussed it before he died. I'm leasing it to the housing trust, I'll collect a little ground rent for each property. It provides a good income for ever."

Robin had to try and think of something to say while he hid his disappointment, Katherine made it easy when she leant in and kissed him very passionately.

"Shall we go for a walk before bed, Rob? We could either go to the beach again or take the car up to Doone Valley for an hour."

"Do you mind if we don't, Katherine, how about a drink in the pub?"

"That'll be nice, let's not just go to the local though. If we walk to the one at the beach, they usually have a group on a Saturday night."

Katherine was ready in less than fifteen minutes, even when she was just going to the pub she liked to look good. She wore a pair of black trousers matched with a smart leather bomber jacket. A quick hair brushing session and a little light make-up completed the look.

When they walked into the pub Katherine felt several sets of eyes looking at them, she knew one or two of the locals and was proud to be seen with her handsome man. The landlord recognised her and came over to serve them. They managed to find a table just before the music was about to start. The group played a selection of classic rock songs from the sixties and seventies, although Katherine preferred classical and opera music she found herself singing along with the group.

They walked back to the cottage at eleven o'clock, although the group had finished the pub was still crowded and they'd keep serving until the early hours if enough people stayed.

Katherine made coffee when they got in, she'd been watching Robin closely through the evening and had noticed that he looked tired and drawn, she put it down to his hectic week of travel. They sat on the settee with their coffee and had the late night television on for an hour.

Robin didn't seem as enthusiastic to go to bed as Katherine, eventually she took him by the hand and led him through to the bedroom. He seemed a bit keener when Katherine started kissing him, they undressed each other and got into bed.

Robin seemed distracted, he stroked Katherine with his fingers; she kissed him hungrily and felt him getting harder. She climbed on top of him with her head pointing to his feet.

"Let's try it at the same time," she suggested. She wrapped her legs round his head, leant forward and took him in her mouth.

Robin seemed a little keener now, he put his hands round her waist from behind and pulled her in closer. Katherine felt herself starting to climax so she disentangled herself and turned round to face Robin. She sat astride him and lowered herself carefully onto him.

"Do you like me being on top?"

"I like it with you anywhere Katherine."

Robin laid still on his back and let Katherine do the work, she stopped every time she felt herself starting to climax to make sure she could keep going long enough to satisfy Robin. He seemed different this time, Katherine finally let herself go, a moment later she heard Robin moan quietly so she stopped moving. He still didn't seem as enthusiastic, she climbed off him and laid next to him.

"Is everything all right Rob? You seem distracted."

"I'm just a little tired, it's been a long week."

"Get a good night's sleep, I'll bring you a cup of tea in the morning."

Robin turned onto his side, Katherine snuggled up beside him and they fell asleep almost straight away. Katherine woke once or twice in the night feeling content that her man was sleeping peacefully next to her.

The sun was shining through the window when she woke in the morning, she slipped her dressing gown on and went through to the kitchen. Five minutes later she put Robin's cup of tea on the nightstand and climbed back into bed with hers.

Robin woke up when she got back into bed, Katherine put her tea down and put her arm across him.

"Good morning, sleepyhead, I've brought you a nice cup of tea."

"What time is it, Katherine?"

"Almost eight o'clock, you slept like a log."

Robin sat up and leant on one elbow. "I have to leave quite soon, Katherine, I have to make sure my father is seen to and I'm flying out tomorrow."

Katherine was disappointed, she'd planned on spending at least the morning with Robin. "When are you back?" she asked. "Don't forget I'm going to London with my friend Liz next Friday for the weekend."

"I'm not really sure yet, if it all goes wrong in Tuscany, I may have to go there as well. I'll keep you up to date each day."

Katherine didn't want Robin to see that she was upset so she sipped her tea and didn't look directly at him.

"Are you upset with me because I can't invest in your venture, Rob? I can be part of a syndicate if you like."

"I was hoping that we could go into it together, Katherine, I don't think a syndicate is the answer." Robin knew that forming a syndicate would now be his only hope but even if Katherine raised a hundred thousand he'd still need several more members.

"If you're in real trouble, Rob, I could back you for a few months until it's sorted out. I could get twenty or maybe as much as thirty thousand straight away for you."

Robin was disappointed that Katherine hadn't offered to buy the vineyard, he assumed that if she'd had the funds available that he'd have been able to sell her the idea. Now he was feeling guilty because the way she was behaving towards him was with total trust. Had he been a confidence trickster, he would probably have taken thirty thousand off her and ran.

"I really appreciate the offer, Katherine," he said quietly. "But if I don't raise the million to buy the yard myself, I think my days in the wine business will be short-lived now."

Katherine made them both some breakfast when they went through to the kitchen. Robin still seemed different to her, he had his food and another drink and barely said a word. Almost as soon as they'd finished eating he announced that he should be leaving soon.

Katherine walked round to his car, after he'd put his overnight bag they hugged and kissed for a few minutes, she still got the impression that he was distracted and almost in a hurry to leave.

She whispered the words in his ear. "I'm falling in love with you, Rob. I know you've got some problems with your business and I'll try and help if I can."

"Thank you so much, Katherine, I'm so sorry I've been a little distracted."

Katherine was a little upset that he hadn't responded to her feelings. They kissed again before Robin got in the car, he promised to message her and apologised again before driving off. Katherine went back indoors almost in tears.

She had a quick clean and tidy through before packing her things and getting ready to leave. It was a four hour journey including a stop for fuel and lunch so she left at eleven-thirty.

She wasn't really in the mood for the ride, it was a hot sunny day with heavy traffic so by the time she got home it was well after four o'clock. She stripped her leathers off and gratefully stretched out in a hot bath for half an hour. Dinner didn't appeal to her so she put a pizza in the oven and sat in front of the television for an hour before going to bed at just after nine o'clock.

Chapter Twenty-Six

Robin arrived home in time to take his father a late lunch and calm him down.

"You need to get some control over that wife of yours Rob, I didn't get any dinner last night, when I asked her what was going on she yelled like some fucking banshee at me, told me to send out for a takeaway."

"I expect her sciatica was playing up again Dad, take it easy on her. You can call her Madelaine; that might help."

Robin went back to his house, Madelaine was still in her dressing gown and had been drinking.

"For Christ's sake, Mads, just try and keep the peace will you. He's blowing his top next door."

"I had a call from Cheralyn yesterday, she's finishing at the end of July. She said she told him on Friday, his answer was: 'Fucking good job too, that lazy bitch next door will have to pull herself together,' it's not happening Rob, I'm not going to be at his beck and call till he croaks."

Robin tried to lighten things by joking about his father but Madelaine was fuming, she poured herself the last of the wine and stormed out of the kitchen. Claire came downstairs a few minutes later.

"She was on the booze all day yesterday Dad, I had to get Jon some food before I went out. Where the fuck were you all night?"

"Mum knew I was off to the cricket with Darren, all she had to do was cook Dad a meal and take it round."

"He came round here, Dad, told her off and dumped a load of dirty washing here. As soon as he'd gone she started drinking. What's going on Dad? She's on about leaving in September."

"Where's Jonathon?"

"He went round to his mate's house; he said he'll be back tonight. He doesn't know what's going on Dad, at least I'm away at uni soon."

Robin poured himself a glass of whisky and sat in the chair taking stock of his life. In his fifties with a job that looked good on the surface but something that his secretary could do easily, living in a house owned by his father and hoping eventually that the old man would leave them something when he died.

When he'd put the syndicate together to buy the vineyard it seemed that they'd been offered a way out; trying to get Katherine to invest kept the dream going for a little longer but now he realised that this was as good as his life would get for the foreseeable future.

"What the fuck was I thinking about," he said out loud to himself. Even if Katherine had agreed to finance the project, she'd probably have pulled the plug as soon as she'd realised she'd been lied to. He knew that he'd crossed the line by having sex with her, the weekend before at her house had been the first time he'd ever been unfaithful; he'd had plenty of opportunities on his travels with his wine business but had always stayed loyal.

He hadn't had sex with Madelaine for what seemed like several months and when Katherine had thrown herself at him he couldn't resist, he knew that he shouldn't have gone to Devon but had thought he had a final chance to talk Katherine into the investment. Now he had to choose how to finish things with her, should he let her down gradually or just stop any contact. He knew that he'd covered his tracks and that for Katherine to trace him would be virtually impossible.

As he left, she'd told him she was falling in love with him and offered to give him up to thirty-thousand pounds to shore up his business. He went over to the cabinet and poured himself another whisky. He was feeling guilty at the way he'd treated Katherine and knew that whatever he did she'd be devastated. He decided to keep messaging her for a while and let her down gradually, maybe he could tell her that he'd been made bankrupt or that he'd bought the yard and was moving to Tuscany. He smiled to himself, maybe if she had invested the money he'd have left Madelaine and settled down out in Italy with her. When she'd told him that she was falling in love with him it had tugged at his heartstrings, if Madelaine and the children hadn't been his priority he'd have said very much the same to her and meant every word.

"You were quiet tonight Kath; everything all right with your hunky guy?"

Katherine had been worried since her ride back at the weekend. Robin had messaged her apologising for leaving so hastily on Sunday, he said that he'd had to see to his father and catch a flight to Portugal to sort out an issue with a grower out there. His messages had seemed more polite than anything without a hint of passion. She'd been thinking that maybe she'd jumped the gun by telling him that she was falling in love with him. What else was she supposed to do? She'd never have slept with him if she hadn't had those feelings for him; surely he knew that much about her?

"I'm okay Liz, looking forward to our trip at the weekend."

"So am I, Kath, you were lucky with Rob, the guys I've been messaging and meeting are fucking useless. No wonder they're all divorced, I did meet one widower; I'd say his wife committed suicide through boredom."

"I told him I was falling in love with him, I think I might have scared him off Liz. His messages have been different this week. He told me he's got all sorts of business worries as well."

"When are you seeing him again?"

"We haven't arranged anything, he's busy with his travels; he knows we're going to London on Friday so I suppose it'll be whenever he decides."

"Not good enough Kath. You should be calling the shots."

"There's something wrong Liz, I can feel it; I just don't know what it is. He was different at the weekend."

"Was the sex as good?"

Katherine didn't comment. They'd been for their swim and meal at the country club and she'd driven Liz home. She'd gone in for a coffee but as it was nearly ten o'clock she stood up and said she'd better be getting home.

"We'll pick you up here on Friday Liz, Jen said she'll pick me up, collect you and drop us at the coach stop. It'll be lovely to get to a London theatre again."

"Don't worry about Rob, as soon as he gets back he'll be chasing you like a rat up a fucking drainpipe."

Katherine hugged her friend. "You've certainly got a way with words Liz. I'll see you Friday."

She drove home and put her Jaguar in the garage, she'd been looking forward to surprising Robin with it soon but now was a little concerned that he'd be more interested in its value. Her house was worth at least three-quarters of a million pounds, the motorbikes would fetch another fifty or so, with the pension plans she had she thought that even without the factory sale or the development land that she could probably have raised enough to buy the vineyard.

Although she was tired she poured herself a glass of wine and got her phone out. She'd kept all the e-mails and texts that he'd sent since she'd been sent the original profile from the agency. She spent an hour reading all the messages, some made her smile but the ones that he'd sent since the weekend seemed totally different.

When she got to the message that had arrived that afternoon she seemed to know that the relationship was coming to a premature end. The message was polite enough and he'd said that he was looking forward to seeing her but it was written in the style of a business meeting rather than a lovers tryst.

Jennifer noticed that something was wrong with her mother but didn't ask too many questions. Most mornings they could get on with their work without having to discuss it so conversation was usually about family matters and general gossip. This week her mother had only really chatted about the shop and what was happening at the factory.

Jennifer was relieved when Friday came round, they'd baked extra on Thursday and Elaine had covered for Katherine to give her the day off. Jennifer collected her from home at one o'clock as they'd arranged. Katherine had been to the hairdresser and had a trim and restyle, Jennifer thought that her mother looked exceptional but also a little tired and drawn.

"I like your hair, Mum, did Samantha do it?"

"I'm too old to wear it quite as long, Jen, I'll have a little bit extra cut off each time for a couple of years."

"Nonsense, Mum, it looks lovely long. How long are you going for again?"

Katherine had put several different outfits in her large case, Jennifer lifted it into the car laughing at the amount her mother was taking for a weekend. They went to the flat to collect Liz, Jennifer waited in the car while Katherine went in, they were out in less than three minutes; Liz had brought a far smaller bag with just one change of clothes and her toiletries.

"I think Mum's staying on, Liz," Jennifer joked. "She brought most of her wardrobe."

Jennifer dropped them at the coach stop and waited with them. "Make sure my mother behaves herself please, Liz, don't let her near too many men; make sure she doesn't drink or smoke too much as well please."

Liz looked at them in turn, Katherine explained that Jennifer was taking revenge for them being strict when she was living with them at home.

As soon as the coach arrived, Jennifer hugged Katherine and Liz, they got on the coach and waved through the window as Jennifer got into her car.

"We did try our best with her Liz but she was a nightmare when she was a teenager. I don't think she took drugs but there were so many boyfriends and I know she used to smoke and drink a lot. She seemed to calm down when she went to catering college."

"She turned out all right, Kath. And she'll know how best to keep the twins on track."

They settled into the hotel and went out for a meal at a small bistro a short walk away. Katherine was determined to enjoy the weekend but was still concerned about any future with Robin. His messages on Thursday and Friday were even shorter. He told her that he'd flown from Portugal to Italy and was still trying to put a package together to rescue his business. He seemed to have forgotten that she was going to London with her friend for the weekend and didn't give her any idea of when they'd see each other again.

She checked her phone when they went up to the room after a drink at the hotel bar, he hadn't messaged since the morning. Liz fell asleep almost straight away but Katherine lay there until nearly two o'clock in the morning thinking about Robin and how she could have done things differently.

They spent Saturday seeing as many of the sights of London as they could fit in, the coach company took them on a tour of the main sites with a commentary from the courier.

After lunch they had a trip on The London Eye, they'd promised themselves a visit to an art gallery so they visited The Tate and spent two hours there before going back to the hotel to get ready for the theatre.

"That might be the nicest day I've had for years Kath, all the tourist stuff, a bit of culture and a west-end show. Please can we do it again, maybe we'll be able to bring men next time as well."

Katherine had enjoyed the experience as well, she'd been to several shows with Mark over the years; she knew that he didn't really enjoy the bright lights of London but had tolerated it to please her. Liz had come alive as the day went on and hadn't stopped smiling since they'd got back to the hotel after the show.

"It'd be lovely, Liz," Katherine agreed. Privately she was thinking that it was very unlikely that she'd be involved with a man anytime soon. As soon as they'd got back to the hotel she'd checked the inbox on her telephone but there'd been no message from Robin.

Liz saw Katherine check her telephone and knew that she was upset. "No word from him, don't worry. He most likely thinks you're too busy enjoying yourself to worry about him."

Katherine was near to tears. "I haven't heard from him since yesterday morning Liz, I've got a horrible feeling I'm getting dumped."

"He came all the way to Devon to spend the weekend with you, Kath. He'd hardly do that if he was dumping you."

"He spent more time talking about his business problems than on our relationship Liz, he wanted me to invest in a vineyard in Tuscany."

"Did he actually ask for money, Kath?"

"He seemed to think I could raise a million pounds to buy the place."

"Phillip used to keep on about how loaded you were, what did you tell Rob? You're not planning on going in with him are you?"

"I couldn't raise that sort of money, he seemed to think it'd be easy for me to get hold of it."

"How would he have thought that? Did you tell him about the land?"

"I expect I mentioned I was selling the business to Pete and Gav. Maybe he thought it was worth millions. When I explained the situation he seemed to go quiet on me, as if I'd let him down. Then I told him that I wouldn't sell the land, I'm developing it and just taking a small income from it. That ended the conversation, he hasn't been the same since."

"You know what Phillip was like, he's a fucking bean counter Kath. He worked out one night that if you'd sold the business to one of the national engineering outfits and sold the land to a developer you'd get between ten and fifteen million. Then there was the shop and flats you gave Jen, your house and the cottages, Phillip reckoned you might be worth twenty million."

"What did you tell him?"

"To mind his own fucking business. You're my best friend and the finest person I know. If you were homeless and broke you'd still be my best friend."

Katherine hugged Liz. "I'll never go hungry but I wouldn't be able to raise a million for a risky venture. It just seemed as if Rob thought much the same as

Phillip. How the fuck do you meet someone and within a couple of months ask them for that sort of funding?"

"Do you think it was some kind of scam, you hear about all these wealthy women handing their savings over to con-men they meet on the net."

"It can't have been a scam, Liz, I certainly wouldn't have just given him the money without all the legal searches and a lot of advice. I think the deal was probably genuine. Please don't tell anyone but I offered him some money to prop up his business."

"How much did you offer him?" Liz asked anxiously.

"I said I could raise twenty or thirty thousand if it'd help. He more or less sniffed at it."

"It doesn't sound like he's some sort of scam artist then, that's one good thing. He's probably just busy travelling, Kath. Message him in the morning and it'll all be fine again."

Katherine hugged her friend. "I hope so, Liz."

Robin was having one of the worst weeks of his life. His father had insisted that when his housekeeper had left that Madelaine take her place, Robin hadn't passed that bit of news to his wife. Her car had finally given up on Wednesday.

"They've got a deal at the Vauxhall garage, no deposit and five years free finance on year old cars," she told him. "It's only a hundred and forty a month Rob, it'll be cheaper than trying to get that shit-heap back on the road."

Robin relented and went to the garage on his own, he was going to try and get a better deal as he considered himself to be in the motor trade. The salesman managed to persuade him that they'd cut the price and finance deal to the bare bones and couldn't go any lower. That was all academic, when the credit check came back the finance company had said that Robin had to provide a guarantor to be allowed to borrow the money. His father was the only person that would be able to guarantee the money so Robin thanked the salesman for his trouble and left the dealership.

Once again he tried to talk Madelaine into not having a new car, she was having to rely on public transport and was getting angrier each day.

"What progress have you made with this rich widow Rob, is she going to finance you or not?"

"I put the whole package to her Mads, I don't think she'll go for it."

"Some fucking salesman you turned out to be, you said she'd be putty in your hands."

"I think it was you that said that, Mads, I'll message her this week but I think it's a non-starter."

Robin hated lying to his wife, it had been her idea to try and talk Katherine into making the investment, perhaps he should have said no straight away but secretly he thought that the challenge would be something that could boost his self-esteem if he managed to pull it off. He'd messaged Katherine up to Friday, he knew that she was away with her friend all weekend, he thought that he'd send a message on Monday saying that he was being made bankrupt and that he thought the relationship wouldn't be able to survive. She'd either finish with him or possibly come up with enough money to buy the vineyard.

"I've got to have a car Rob, ask his fucking lordship for the money to get one."

Reluctantly Robin asked his father for a two-thousand pound advance on his salary, he pointed out that if Madelaine had to look after him she'd need a car.

The next day he found a dealer who'd taken in a hatchback as a trade in on a luxury car and bought it off him at trade price.

"It's a hundred a month, Mads, we'll have to tighten up on the wine and whisky."

"Why don't you get yourself a proper job? You still know more about wine than most people have forgotten. You could easily get something better paid than you've got now."

"This house goes with the job, Mads, do you know what it'd cost us to rent somewhere? We're stuck here, make the fucking most of it."

Madelaine poured herself a large glass of wine. "You fucking make the most of it if you want Rob, I'm going to live with Mum and I'm taking Jonathon with me. You just make fucking sure to send me enough money every month to pay for him. I'll get a job part-time to earn what I need. I'll have the car as a parting present."

Chapter Twenty-Seven

Katherine messaged Robin as soon as she got home on Sunday afternoon. She gave him a run-down of her weekend and asked him what he'd been doing. She was tempted to put an 'I Love You', at the end of the message but decided against it. He hadn't messaged her since Friday morning and she was getting increasingly concerned.

Her phone bleeped with an incoming e-mail alert just as she was getting ready to go to bed. Robin apologised for not sending a message on Saturday but said he'd had to fly back to England for a couple of days and then leave for Italy. She rested a little easier when she went to bed but his tone was still business-like in his messages.

His message on Monday was the one that she'd feared most. He told her that the banks had withdrawn their support and that unless he could come up with the promise of a million pounds finance straight away he'd be facing ruin. He didn't ask Katherine for the money directly but hinted that if she did want to support him he could still put a rescue package in place. Katherine sent a reply straight away saying that she didn't have access to that sort of funding but offering him a short-term emergency loan of up to thirty-thousand pounds.

She didn't hear from him on Tuesday, on Wednesday she went out for her swim with Liz but her heart wasn't in it so after a few lengths she dressed and went to the bar for a drink. Liz joined her soon afterwards. She sensed that her friend was upset and tried to cheer her up.

"No word yet today, Kath?"

"Not since Monday, I already told him that I couldn't raise that sort of money. I don't think I'll hear from him again Liz. I think I've been taken for a ride."

"You haven't actually given him any money have you, girl?"

Liz noticed Katherine start to well up with tears and put her arm round her to console her.

"He promised to give me the money for the tickets I got for the Tivoli and never did. Apart from that he's spent more money than I have, he bought me presents and paid whenever we went out."

"Did you message him this morning?"

"I wouldn't really know what to say, Liz, I'll wait a day or two and see what happens. I'll either get a message finishing things or he won't get in touch again."

"Let's not eat here tonight, Kath, come back with me and I'll knock us up something. You can have a drink as well, I'll take you home or you can stay over if you like."

They went back to the flat, Liz cooked them a simple meal and they watched a DVD in almost total silence. At ten o'clock when Katherine checked her telephone no new messages had arrived. Liz took Katherine home and went indoors with her.

"Do you want me to stay over Kath? I will if you like."

Katherine managed a weak smile. "Don't worry, Liz, I'm getting up at four o'clock. I'll be fine."

Fine was far from now Katherine felt but she didn't want to appear foolish to her friend.

"If you're sure, call me if you need me and I'll be here."

Katherine let Liz out and locked up behind her. She watched her friend drive away before bursting into floods of tears. In her heart she knew that even if Robin messaged her again it would only be to say goodbye.

Robin was feeling guilty about how he'd treated Katherine, when Madelaine had suggested that he joined the agency and made contact with Katherine it had all seemed simple. Gain her confidence, build the friendship and sell her the investment. He knew that he'd crossed the line by sleeping with her and that he shouldn't have gone to Devon to stay at the cottage with her. Before they'd met he'd imagined her as a wealthy woman who'd see Tuscany as an opportunity to get even richer. He hadn't foreseen that she'd use her wealth for the good of her workforce and to develop low-cost housing for local people.

He believed that he'd covered his tracks and that Katherine wouldn't be able to trace him. Even if she did there was very little that she could do to hurt him.

Madelaine was determined to leave anyway so the knowledge that he'd been unfaithful to her wouldn't make a great deal of difference.

Even if she tried to trace him through the dating agency he doubted that they'd release his details without a court order. He didn't think she'd be savvy enough to have noted the registration number of either the cars that he'd used but even if she had they'd only lead her to a leasing company. Unless she actually visited the office when he was there she wouldn't be able to get his details. He'd called himself Rob Jones instead of Robin Pargeter-Jones so he didn't think that would leave her any clues to his true identity.

He was going to send her a final message on Thursday calling a halt to their relationship but decided to just switch off the telephone that he'd been using and leave it at that.

"Are you all right, Mum? You've been sad all week. Do you want to talk about it?"

"I'm not all right, Jen, but I really don't want to talk about it too much. I thought I'd met the man of my dreams and it didn't work out."

"I'm feeling guilty now, I shouldn't have bought you the subscription for your birthday present."

Katherine managed a weak smile. "Don't be silly, Jen, you weren't to know how it would work out."

"You'll meet a nice man one day, Mum, you're too good to be on your own for the rest of your life."

"Maybe I will Jen but I don't think I'll be using the internet. Liz has had a few disasters and Aunty Doreen hasn't done much better."

Just after she got home from the factory Liz telephoned to see if she was all right and if she'd heard from Robin.

"I'm feeling very hurt and more than a little foolish Liz. No word from him so I think that's probably it."

"I know we spent last weekend away, Kath, but how about a weekend at your cottage? I don't mind driving. It's an inset day on Monday so I don't have to work."

They travelled down to the cottage on Friday.

"Tell me to mind my own business if you like. Do you think he targeted you as a rich widow right from the start or did he genuinely find you by chance?"

"I've been thinking exactly the same thing, it'd be a hell of a co-incidence for him to be going bust and in need of a million pound investment and find what he thinks is a multi-millionaire at a dating agency."

"Have you completely given up on him, Kath? Have you messaged him again?"

"I messaged him this morning, Liz. I kept it quite formal and polite. I told him that I was sorry that I couldn't support his business but if it was just about the money that he should get in touch with me and we'd talk things through."

"And no answer yet?"

"I checked when we arrived, no reply and I don't think there will be."

"Can you do anything about it Kath?"

"I don't really see that I can do anything, I suppose I could get hold of the agency and complain but it wouldn't do any good."

They put a DVD on, just a light comedy that Katherine liked but she wasn't really in the mood so they went to bed soon after midnight. They shared the bedroom again, Katherine was glad to have someone in the room with her, they chatted for a few minutes before saying goodnight. Liz seemed to go to sleep almost straight away, Katherine was tired after her long day but couldn't sleep, after an hour she crept out of the bedroom and made herself a hot chocolate. When she went back to bed the tiredness finally caught up with her and she drifted off to sleep almost straight away.

Liz was up first on Saturday morning, she let Katherine sleep in until eight-thirty.

"Good morning, girlfriend, I've bought you a cup of tea."

Katherine sat up in bed and drank her tea, after they'd both had a light breakfast they went for a walk to the beach. It was a beautiful summer morning, both of them were only wearing light tops and shorts, they sat on the beach for nearly two hours, Katherine was wearing her bikini under her clothes but didn't feel up to going for a swim. They went to the shop on the way back to the cottage for some food for lunch. They'd decided to eat out in the evening and had booked a table at the pub. After lunch they drove to Barnstable and spent the afternoon shopping.

After the meal they went to the pub next door to the cottage, both of them were tired after their busy day so after two drinks and exchanging pleasantries with the landlord and some locals they went back to the cottage. Katherine made them hot chocolate and they sat in the lounge with the television on low.

"It's lovely here, Kath, when I meet a man I'll rent it off you if that's all right and I'll bring him here for a weekend."

"Use it any time you like, Liz, that's what it's for."

As soon as they'd got back to the cottage Katherine had checked her telephone but there was still no message from Robin. She'd said to herself that Sunday was the finishing point, if she hadn't heard by then she'd assume that was the end of things. Liz saw her check her inbox.

"No word yet Kath?"

"Not a peep," Katherine admitted. "I'm quite sure that I won't hear from him Liz, I've given it up to tomorrow night and then that's it."

They both slept through the night, Katherine was up first, made the tea and woke her friend. As it was warm and sunny they decided to walk to the beach and have a swim in the sea.

Neither of them wanted just to lay on the beach for too long so after they'd had a drink in the café they walked back.

"I'll make an early lunch and we'll go out Liz, maybe Minehead for the afternoon."

Katherine cooked them a roast when they got back; later in the evening Liz saw her check her inbox for a message.

"Nothing?"

"That's it, Liz, I don't know whether to be angry or sad. He fucking took me for a ride and I fell for it."

"Be angry, it wasn't your fault, Kath."

Katherine almost collapsed into the arms of her friend. "I'm sorry to put this on you Liz, I'm fifty-nine; surely I should have realised it was too good to be true. If I hadn't been silly enough to sleep with him I wouldn't have minded so much. I thought we'd be growing old together."

"What are you going to do about it, Kath?"

"What can I do, Liz? I got over losing my husband, I suppose it'll be like doing that all over again. It'll get easier but I'm going to have trust issues for a long time."

"I wonder if he's fucking married, Kath. You could get hold of his wife and drop him in the shit."

"If he is then she's quite likely to be in on it. He deserves to be punished somehow though. The first issue is at all I really know about him is his e-mail address and his name. Jen said that all you need to get a new e-mail address is a SIM card. He might not even be Rob Jones. For all I know the whole thing was a pack of fucking lies."

"Can't you report him to the agency, surely to God they've got some sort of responsibility,"

"There's all sorts of small print when you join. They give you plenty of advice about safety before you actually meet anyone. I bet they've got themselves well covered."

"I doubt they'd want to do anything then."

"He must be Rob Jones I reckon, Liz. Don't you remember; I saw him park that Jaguar with the private plate that had his initials on it. No wonder he didn't want me to see it and never told me about it."

"Do you remember the number Kath? You could find his name and address from that. There must be a way to do it on the internet."

Katherine told Liz the number of the Mark Two Jaguar that she'd seen him park when they'd met in Bournemouth.

"How much would that be worth? As much as the E-Type?"

"I'm out of touch and I didn't have a really good look at it Liz. I don't think they're worth anything like that, maybe twenty or thirty thousand depending on the condition. That number plate is worth a few thousand on its own."

"When we get back to your place tomorrow, we'll go on the internet and see if we can trace his name and address."

"Let's get fucking drunk, Liz. I just want to forget about him now."

Katherine opened a bottle of wine and poured them a large glass each, she also produced a packet of cigarettes that she'd bought while they were out.

They sat together on the settee, Liz was careful not to drink too much, she had to drive back the next day. By the time they went through to the bedroom Katherine had drunk nearly the whole bottle of wine and smoked four cigarettes.

Liz helped her undress and get into bed, she put a jug of water by the bed and made sure her friend was all right before she undressed and got in the second bed.

"I feel like I've been eating gravel Liz," Katherine complained the next morning. Three strong cups of coffee helped and by ten o'clock she seemed to be back amongst the living.

"You did get through some wine last night, girl."

"Sorry, Liz, I haven't done that since Mark died. I had a couple of sessions back then, I'll be all right. Thanks for looking after me."

They had a quiet morning cleaning the cottage and packing up. Katherine made them some lunch and they left at two o'clock. Liz drove and Katherine sat alongside her hardly speaking. They arrived back at just after six o'clock.

"Let me make you some food Liz. Thanks for everything this weekend."

Katherine made them some ham, egg and chips but her heart wasn't really in it. "Sorry, Liz, not my best effort."

"Your rejects are still better than my good stuff," Liz said as she tucked into her food. "Will you be okay or shall I stay over?"

"I'll be fine," Katherine lied. She was feeling if anything worse than when she'd come back to the house after the funeral. Mark had struggled with his illness but Katherine knew that he'd never have let her down deliberately.

Liz went back to her flat at nine o'clock, Katherine decided against drinking and smoking so she went straight to bed. She was crying until she eventually drifted off to sleep at well after midnight.

Chapter Twenty-Eight

If anything the next two weeks were the worst that Katherine could remember. She excused herself from going to the factory several times. Jacqui rang to make sure she was all right, Katherine told her that she'd been feeling a little run-down but was on the mend and would be back soon. She tried to get to the shop most mornings but Jennifer knew that her mother was struggling so she organised Elaine and Becky to provide cover.

Liz spent every evening with Katherine, she stayed over most nights so that she could make sure her friend didn't drink too much. All Katherine seemed to be thinking about was how Robin had tricked her into believing that he wanted a relationship.

They'd tried tracing the car on the internet but hadn't had any success, Katherine didn't seem very interested in finding out the truth about who Robin was and how much he'd lied to her. They went away for a few days in July, Liz suggested that they fly to Amsterdam, they left Southampton airport on Tuesday and came back Sunday afternoon.

The trip seemed to work wonders for Katherine, they did all the usual tourist visits and she didn't mention Robin for most of the trip. When they got back to her house Katherine told Liz that she thought she could cope now.

"Thank you so much for being my friend Liz, I honestly don't know what I'd have done without you. I'm determined to pull myself together now."

"You're doing great, Kath, I still think he should be fucking punished for what he did to you."

"I still don't know what to think, Liz. I've got to get back on track otherwise I'll land up some sort of a wreck. I haven't ridden the Ducati or been swimming and I've hardly worked for two weeks."

"We still haven't got his real name and address, do you still want to find out about him?"

"I think I might have gone past the sadness, Liz, I'm just angry now. I've been thinking, we can't seem to find out too much, I'm going to try and get hold of a private detective tomorrow. I went online and there's some agencies in Southampton."

"What happens if you find out about him?"

"I'm making this up as I go Liz, if he is some kind of a fucking conman maybe there's some way of making him pay. I could go and burn his house down."

Liz laughed, she was pleased to see that her friend was a little more like her old self. She hadn't drank or smoked while they were in Holland, Liz noticed that Katherine was swearing a lot more than she ever had and hadn't been to church for some time. Maybe getting angry would help the healing procedure.

"I don't think burning his house down would help. Are you going to work tomorrow?"

"I am, Liz, and when I get back, I'm calling in the cavalry."

Katherine was at the shop before five o'clock the next morning. Jennifer was pleased to see her mother looking better.

"How was Holland, Mum? You look better for the trip."

"I'm going to be all right now I think Jen. Liz and I might get a week away again, maybe the last week of the summer holidays or half-term."

Katherine went to the factory for a few hours after the shop, Jacqui was relieved that she was looking so much better. Pete and Gav came into the office and went through their progress with the new factory. She went home at one o'clock, had lunch, showered and telephoned a detective agency in Southampton.

After going through an automated answering system she eventually spoke to a receptionist. She explained that she was trying to trace the name and address of someone from the registration number of the car.

"It's something we can do of course Mrs Reynolds. We do have a minimum charge that is non-negotiable. It'll cost you one thousand pounds for us to get the information you require."

"That seems a little extortionate for a few minutes work," Katherine commented.

"There's a major problem with insurance fraud at the moment," the receptionist explained. "The insurance companies can't afford to investigate small claims. So a clever criminal gets agencies like us to trace the owners of expensive cars and then put in a bogus claim. They say for example that a Range-

Rover or similar bumped them in a car park, claim seven or eight hundred pounds and mostly either the owner or their insurance company pays up. So we charge a thousand pounds for the service, that way we only get genuine enquiries. We can do extra work of course to warrant charging what we do."

"What would a thousand pounds get me?"

"The name and address of the registered keeper and as much information as we can gather until the fee is justified."

"Then go ahead please."

The receptionist e-mailed Katherine a contract and took her card details to charge her the thousand pounds. She promised that Katherine would get a full report in a few days' time.

Katherine rode her Ducati to Devon on Friday for the weekend. It was a lovely hot sunny day and she gave the Ducati its head on the twisty Devon roads. On Saturday she cleaned the cottage right through and went swimming in the sea. She had a meal in the local on Saturday evening, the couple that had rented the cottage joined her, they stayed until well after midnight chatting and listening to the live group.

Sunday was warm and sunny again, Katherine was up at just after five o'clock and set off for the return ride before seven. The roads were nearly deserted, she rode her Ducati as it was designed to be used and was back home at just after ten o'clock. She spent the rest of the day relaxing and preparing for a busy week at work.

Everybody was pleased that Katherine seemed to be back to her old self, she'd told Jennifer a short version of what had happened but apart from Liz no one else knew all the details.

The detective agency e-mailed her on Tuesday afternoon, they'd traced the registered owner of the Jaguar and included a report on him and his immediate family. Katherine texted Liz and invited her round for an early tea when she finished work.

When Liz arrived Katherine made them a tray of soft drinks, they sat out on the patio and she read the report to her friend.

"The registered keeper of the car is a seventy-nine year old man called Richard Pargeter-Jones Liz. He lives on his own in a large house just outside Southampton and is a partner with his brother in a car-leasing business."

"He did lie about his age then Kath," Liz said with a smile. "Is that it?"

"Just the beginning; be patient. Richard Pargeter-Jones also has another car that he obviously uses as his day-to-day transport. A financial check shows him to have an excellent credit rating. He also owns the smaller house next door which is occupied by his fifty-two year old son Robin and his family, wife Madelaine, daughter Claire and a son Jonathon. Robin Pargeter-Jones has no credit rating as he was made bankrupt. He works for his father and uncle at the car-leasing business."

"It's the son then, Kath, Robin Pargeter-Jones aka Rob Jones."

"He also lied about his age, most people take a few years off; he added some. That means he joined the agency just to get in touch with me, Liz. No one would join a dating agency and make out they're older than they were."

"How the fuck did he know about you then? All your ad on the agency site gives is your first name and your age; even your profile doesn't say you're loaded."

"I think I worked it out. When I saw him park the Jaguar I thought he was trying to hide it because he didn't want me to know he had an expensive car, I thought it was great because we'd have something in common. Now I think he must have seen me at one of the Jaguar club meetings when I used to go with Mark."

"It's a bit thin Kath, surely you'd have seen him there as well and recognised him."

"I only went to support Mark, he'd stand by his car all day polishing it. I used to go to the craft tents and stalls. It's true, Liz, I got the Jaguar club magazine for eight years ago when Mark won best-in-show with the E-Type. He told me some old fool thought he should have been disqualified for fitting a CD player in it. A Mark Two with that number came third. Rob must have been at the show and seen me with Mark. Then he saw my photo on the agency site and recognised me."

"Do you think his father was on the site looking for someone? Does that detective agency say if he's married?"

"I told you Liz, he lives on his own."

"So the old guy joins up and shows his son the available women, he recognises the lady with the E-Type owning husband. How does he figure out you've all those millions to spare?"

"If he saw me on a dating agency site he'd know I'd either been divorced or widowed. I suppose if he was smart enough on a computer he could have found out Mark had died. Maybe his father knew about the factory, he could have got my address from the phone book and looked at the house on Google Earth. There was a write-up in the paper about the factory site going for housing, all most people would see is fucking pound notes, Liz."

"I told you about Phillip reckoning you could be worth twenty million, I suppose Rob could have worked out something similar."

"A lot of women in my position might have chased the money. Do you know what Liz; I'd rather have got conned out of a million pounds than sleep with a married man."

"Do you think it was a con? You said you offered him thirty thousand and he didn't want it. Maybe the vineyard in Tuscany is for sale at a bargain price."

"I think it is Liz. He sounded as if he knew all about the wine business, he had loads of pictures of the place and all the figures for production and how much profit it was going to make. There's no way even the dizziest woman would just hand over a million pounds without checking up on it."

"If he thought you were that wealthy why didn't he just find out your e-mail address and ask if you were interested in going into business with him?"

"Maybe he thought he could charm me out of it. I can't tell you whether or not I'd have gone in with him if I'd had the funding. It's a lovely place and he certainly seemed to think it'd be profitable. If I'd just got an e-mail from a stranger I'd have dismissed the idea straight away."

"Have you decided what to do then? No ideas about burning the house down I hope."

"I'm angry enough, Liz, I don't want to go to prison for the fucking man. I don't know what to do, in some ways I'm relieved, I didn't get cheated out of any money I suppose and I know it was all a set-up. I feel dirty, I fucking slept with a married man for Christ's sake. One thing I always had was my pride, I was proud that I'd only slept with one man and he's taken that away from me."

Katherine took the tray indoors and got them both a meal ready. Liz helped and an hour later they sat at the table with a meal of grilled lamb cutlets, new potatoes and salad. Katherine opened a bottle of low alcohol wine to drink with the food.

"I just don't see what you can do about the shithouse Kath. It's not as if he actually conned you out of anything. I know you want to do something but don't get yourself in trouble, he's not worth it."

"I can't believe how gullible I was Liz, he got me doing stuff I'd never have thought of. I asked him to tie me up and then sucked him off. I let him come in my mouth for fuck's sake."

"I thought you were on the up and getting over him. Don't let this get you down again, Kath. You're too good a person."

"I'm not sad anymore, Liz, I'm fucking furious, he's even got me swearing now. You know the cliché 'Hell hath no fury like a woman scorned'; he's going to find out what that means."

Chapter Twenty-Nine

Detective Chief-Inspector Linda Hislop was having another one of her bad days at work. She thought that being promoted six months before would be an advancement but now she seemed to spend more time on committees and doing paperwork than ever before in her police career. She'd been to a local station in Bournemouth to try and sort out an internal dispute and now she was back in her office trying to get to grips with a month's overtime figures. Her civilian secretary Joan Clark brought her a coffee soon after she got back to her desk.

"Coffee, ma'am; an Inspector Docherty called earlier wanting to speak to you. He said he'll ring back."

"I've asked you before Joan; please don't call me that, it makes me sound like some old dragon. It's Lin when we're on our own or Mrs Hislop if we have company."

"Sorry, Lin, shall I put him through when he calls?"

"Tell him to put his head down between his legs and kiss his arse please Joan."

Five minutes later the telephone buzzed, "Inspector Docherty for you Lin," Joan said and put the call through.

"Your new secretary isn't very good Lin, she put me straight through."

"It's your charm, Tommy, which I'm immune to by the way. What do you want?"

"Perhaps I just called to see how you are and how the job's going."

"Perhaps I'm going to stop smoking, drinking and swearing Tommy and then join a fucking monastery but it's highly unlikely. What do you want?"

"A bit touchy today, wrong time of the month is it. All I'd really like Lin is half an hour of your time, maybe a drink after work?"

"I've been out all day, I've got hours of paperwork and all I really want to do is sit in front of the telly with a pizza Tommy, is it urgent?"

"Doesn't the lovely new husband have a dinner ready when you get in?"

"The lovely new husband is away on business for a few days. Buy me dinner and I'll give you an hour, what's it about?"

"Just an odd case they've given me. It's one of those that no one else wants."

"Meet me at The Fish Inn at half-six Tommy. If you're not there don't bother ringing again."

Linda left her office at six o'clock with a pile of paperwork on the desk, as soon as she drove into the car park, she saw her old sparring partner get out of his car and walk across. Despite the occasional animosity between them she thought the world of him, he held his arms out for a hug as soon as she got near him.

"Good to see you, Lin, how's the new job? Wearing a hole in the seat of your trousers."

"I'm a DCI Tommy, I get all the top jobs. Today I had to sort out a dispute at a local nick, they've got a pre-op transsexual on the civilian staff; he or she wants his or her own toilet."

"Tough at the top."

They went into the bar, bought their drinks and ordered the food. As soon as they sat down Linda asked Tommy what it was about, he took a long sip of his beer before he spoke.

"It's one of those no-win cases I reckon, that's why they gave it to me. I'm getting all the shit because I'm retiring next year. It's about a fifty-nine-year-old lady who met a guy on the internet."

"How it's done these days, Tommy."

"So they tell me. This lady's a bit special, Lin, she looks twenty years younger than she is. I only spent half an hour with her this afternoon and I think I'm in love."

"Tell me about the case please Tommy, not about your fantasies."

"This lady has everything Lin, except her husband died last year. She'd been with him forty years. Her daughter bought her a subscription for a dating agency for her birthday. She e-mailed a few guys, met up with one and didn't get on with him and then she got contacted by some handsome guy. She said he looked like Pierce Brosnan; he's the Irishman that played James Bond."

Lin interrupted his explanation. "You don't have to explain to any woman in her fifties who Pierce Brosnan is Tommy."

"She met him for afternoon tea, she followed all the advice of the agency. She said he was charming, brought her flowers and generally made a good impression. They met twice more, she thought he was the bee's knees. The fourth date was a meal and a show in Wimborne and then back to her place."

He paused for a moment when the waitress put their meals on the table. Linda tucked in hungrily.

"I had a cup of coffee and a cigarette for breakfast and the same for lunch Tommy, this is heaven sent. You paying for it makes it even better."

They ate in silence for a few moments, after they'd finished Tommy went to the bar and got two more drinks and carried on with the story when he came back.

"They went back to her house and it got a bit steamy. He laid on the floor downstairs, got her to kneel over him and he gave her a seeing to with his tongue. Then they went upstairs, had full sex and spent the night together. Sunday morning she gave him a blow-job in the bedroom."

"Is all this relevant Tommy or are you trying to wind me up?"

"You'll have to be the judge of that in a minute. He went off abroad again, he'd told her he had a wine importing business. The next weekend they met at her holiday cottage in Devon. She said he was different this time, they had the same amount of sex but in a different order. He kept saying his business was in trouble, eventually he offered her the chance to invest a million pounds in his business."

"Has she got that kind of money?"

"She owns a business and land that potentially is worth ten million plus, she won't sell them though. She turned down the chance, said she'd go in if he put a syndicate together. Then she offered to shore up his finances short term. She offered him up to thirty thousand straight away which he turned his nose up at."

"He's not just a conman then."

"She thinks not. The e-mails and texts were a bit less lovey-dovey after that. Eventually she got an e-mail saying that unless he got backing of a million he was going bust. Once again she said he could have thirty thousand and that was all. The e-mails and texts stopped, she assumed he'd just dumped her. Anyway she'd got the number of a car he'd used and got a Southampton P.I. to trace him. Turns out he's married with two kids and a bankrupt. Works for his dad and uncle."

"I suppose this fucking saga has a point, Tommy. What happened when she traced him?"

Tommy leaned across the table and lowered his voice. "She e-mailed him and said he could have the million. They met in a hotel, she gave him a cheque and opened a bottle of champagne. Maybe it had something in it, he blacked out. Next thing he knew he woke up strapped in a wheelchair. She had one of those portable barbecues, he smelt meat frying as he came round. She started feeding him sausages, they were tough as old boots. Turned out she'd cut his todger off and was cooking it up for them."

He sat back in his chair and had a drink, Lin saw a smile appear on his face.

"Bollocks, Tommy, you had me going. What happened?"

"Sorry, couldn't resist it. She had a couple of weeks moping round, drinking and crying. Then her and her friend went to Amsterdam for a few days. That seemed to do the trick, she came back and started getting angry; she traced him and then reported him to the good old police to sort him out."

"Apart from being an asshole Tommy I can't see what he can be charged with. He didn't get the million and he even turned down the thirty thousand. Maybe if he'd had that we'd have a shot at him."

"She knows he can't be done for fraud. She wants him charged with six counts of rape."

Linda didn't say anything straight away, she thought for a few seconds.

"Because he lied to her I suppose. It's too thin Tommy, you'd never get it to a courtroom. I assume the sex was with her full consent."

"A bit more than that if anything Lin. She dressed up in sexy gear the first time, she was gagging for it as they say."

"Tell her to forget it, when did all this happen?"

"Just over a month ago."

"Christ, Tommy, remember that joke about the whore who reported a guy for rape. She said it happened two weeks before but she didn't report it until the cheque bounced."

"I had much the same thought. Her point is that if he'd told her the truth she'd never have slept with him in a million years."

"It'd be a nightmare trying to get The CPS to even look at it. They go through all the evidence, you haven't got any of that. Then they check all the witness statements, I don't suppose there's any witnesses either."

"I'm not daft Lin, I told her very much the same thing. There is evidence of a sort, she's got all his texts and e-mails on her phone. That'll prove the lies and some of them refer to the sex they had."

"I'd have to have some advice on that, I don't think it'd be admissible Tommy. Get hold of her and tell her it's a non-starter."

Tommy finished his drink, they both decided not to risk any more, they went outside so Linda could have a cigarette.

"Now tell me the proper reason you called me Tommy."

"I thought you could run it past that friend of yours at The CPS Lin. I'm pretty sure what the answer is but an official no would help. There's another small problem; she said if we don't prosecute him, she'll start a private prosecution."

"I know what she'll say, Tommy. Did you tell this woman how much a private prosecution would cost her?"

"She's well aware it'd cost a fortune, I said it could cost a few hundred thousand and she didn't seem too bothered."

"Have you only spoken to her, Tommy? Maybe you should have a word with this James Bond lookalike."

"I wanted to see if The CPS would take it on Lin. Your friend is pretty high up and I know if she gets something in her head she'll never let it go."

"If she says no make very sure you advise this woman against taking it any further. You said she's wealthy, has she got friends in high places? If she's pally with The Chief Constable or something it could come back and bite you Tommy."

"She reported it at her local nick, they gave her a specialist rape officer who didn't take it seriously and maybe upset her a bit; eventually it got put on my desk to sort out. Like I said I think I got it because I'm so close to retirement; they think it won't matter too much if I mess up."

They chatted about things for a few minutes, Linda had another cigarette before she left to drive home.

"Are you not smoking these days, Tommy?"

"The odd one but I'm trying to stop. Micky keeps on at me about it."

"What's he doing these days?"

"Still lecturing at the university. I keep telling him to get a proper job, what about your little ones?"

Linda Hislop had two sons, one of twenty-eight and one two years younger. Both of them were in the army and had been to most of the trouble spots in the world.

"I worry all the time about them but they're doing what they want to do. Every day I think I'll get the call that one of them has been blown up or shot."

"And the lovely new husband?"

"He's a good man, Tommy. I'll speak to Gill Hopkins and ring you tomorrow."

Chapter Thirty

Katherine and Liz had been swimming on Wednesday, Liz took Katherine home and went in for a coffee. Katherine told her friend what she'd done.

"Jesus Christ, Kath; why the fuck didn't you talk it over with someone first. What did the police say?"

"They sent me to a specialist rape suite with a very sympathetic lady officer. Basically she told me to forget about it. She said I should get some counselling and try to move forward."

"Obviously that went down like a lead balloon."

"Eventually I got to see an Inspector Docherty, he listened and told me he didn't think I had a great deal of hope. I told him if the police didn't pursue it that I'd take out a private prosecution."

"Are you serious?"

"Probably not but they don't have to know that. Inspector Docherty said it'd cost a few hundred thousand. Anyway he took me seriously after that. He's going to try and get The CPS to take a look at it, he said he'll get back to me in a day or two."

"I still can't believe you actually reported him for rape Kath. Did you have to give this Inspector all the gory details?"

"Most of them," Katherine admitted. "He didn't seem to be too concerned and didn't judge me."

"What's he doing about Rob? They'll surely have to get his side of the story before they take any action."

"Inspector Docherty said he won't talk to him until he gets some sort of decision from The CPS. He said he knows a female Chief Inspector who knows a senior prosecutor there. He's going to get his friend to run it past her and get some sort of a decision whether they can proceed."

"Fucking hell, Kath. If they prosecute him, you'll have to stand up in court and get grilled about it. They'll be writing a fucking book about it afterwards. Give me an honest answer, do you think it'll get to court?"

"I doubt it, Liz. I got hold of a lady at the dating agency first. She was quite sympathetic but said that they advise all their clients to be absolutely certain before even meeting up with anyone. I said if I went ahead with a prosecution that there'd be negative publicity but it didn't seem to worry her."

Linda Hislop kept her word and spoke to Gill Hopkins, a senior prosecutor with The Crown Prosecution Service. They spoke for half an hour and Linda more or less agreed with what her old friend had to say. She telephoned Tommy Docherty, he was driving so he let the call go to answerphone and called her back when he stopped.

"What did she have to say then Lin?"

"When she eventually stopped laughing, she agreed with my thoughts Tommy, make it disappear. The only evidence is on her phone and any decent defence brief would get it ruled inadmissible in about thirty seconds."

"No hope at all?"

"Fair play to her, Tommy, she listened to the full story and she has a certain amount of sympathy for your victim. You know what she's like, if she thinks she'll get a guilty verdict she's like a fucking Rottweiler."

"Is there anything we can do, Lin?"

"Basically you need some sort of proof that he actually sent those messages. She said a defence brief would say it's simple to setup an e-mail address and send the messages to yourself. You need proof that he sent them Tommy. You'd have to interview this guy, he'd deny everything and then make sure he lost the phone he used. He's probably already got rid of it. What she did say is that if you can get him to hand over the phone, she'll go with it."

"And as soon as he realises he's under suspicion, he'll get rid of it, if he already hasn't. Do you think I'd get a search warrant based on what I've got?"

"Gill says not, you'd have to have a warrant for his house, office and car to look for a phone or possibly a SIM card the size of a fingernail. She said a magistrate wouldn't give you a warrant anyway."

"You know we go back a lot of years Lin and I think the world of you. How about another little favour?"

"I'm not telling her, Tommy, no fucking way."

"I promised I'd call her as soon as I knew anything. What I was thinking about was popping in on the way home tonight. Is there any chance you could meet me there? I'll text you the postcode."

"I don't want to get involved Tommy, surely you can explain things to her,"

"Come on, Lin, it'll give you a chance to see how the other half live. I looked at her house on Google Earth; it's beautiful."

"When are you planning this home visit? Most people would be lucky to get a phone call or letter."

"She finishes quite early on a Friday apparently, I'll give her a ring and see if we can go there tonight. Will you meet me there please Lin. I'll text you the postcode and time if she says it's all right."

"If it's tonight, John isn't back till at least nine o'clock, if it's not tonight Tommy then forget about me coming to hold your hand."

Tommy telephoned Katherine just after lunch-time on Friday and arranged to meet her at her house at six o'clock. He said he'd be bringing a female colleague with him if that was all right. Katherine said that she'd be at home and would be pleased to meet his colleague.

Tommy sent Linda Hislop the address, postcode and time of the meeting. He said he'd wait in the road so that they could go in together. Linda left her office at five-thirty which gave her plenty of time to arrive and hopefully smoke a cigarette before she went in.

The sat-nav guided her to the road and she saw Tommy's car parked in the road, when he saw her park he got out of the car and stood by her door. She lit a cigarette as she got out of the car.

"Give me a minute to smoke this before we go in Tommy, did you say anything when you rang her?"

"Not really, I said you'd spoken to a senior prosecutor at The CPS and would explain when we got here."

"Thanks Tommy, give me the fucking job of letting her down."

When Linda had finished smoking, they walked up the drive, Tommy rang the doorbell and Katherine answered almost straight away.

Linda was amazed at the lady that answered the door. Tommy introduced Linda Hislop to Katherine. He'd told her that she was fifty-nine but if Linda hadn't known she'd have guessed that she was maybe in her early forties at the oldest. She politely shook hands with Linda and invited them in.

"It's a lovely house, Mrs Reynolds," Linda said truthfully. "How long have you been here?"

"Please call me Katherine. We bought it just over twenty years ago. Shall we sit out on the patio with some cold drinks, it's too nice to be indoors."

Katherine led them through the conservatory and out onto the patio, she invited them to sit down while she fetched a tray of cold drinks and some snacks.

"I see what you mean, Tommy, she's stunning," Linda said quietly.

"She might also be the nicest lady I've ever met," Tommy answered. "She cares about others like you wouldn't believe."

Katherine came back and put the tray on the table, she poured them all a glass of what looked like lemonade and put some ice in each glass. There were also three plates of snack food on the tray that she invited them to help themselves to.

"If we're to call you Katherine, then you must call us Tommy and Lin," Linda said politely, "Tommy has given me the basics of your complaint, I spoke to a senior prosecutor from The Crown Prosecution Service about it this morning."

Linda took Katherine through her conversation with Gill Hopkins and how any potential prosecution would progress. She outlined the lack of evidence as crucial.

"Without any actual physical evidence or witnesses Katherine it wouldn't even get to Crown Court I'm afraid. Gill also said that any prosecution would be for two counts of rape and two of sexual assault. The two instances of him giving you oral sex would have to be dropped. But without evidence I'm afraid it's hypothetical."

"This business of you chasing a private prosecution is very risky, Katherine," Tommy added. "You'd have no better chance than The CPS and something like that could cost you hundreds of thousands."

Katherine didn't say anything straight away, she excused herself and went into the conservatory. She was back a few seconds later with a packet of cigarettes and an ashtray.

"I've been smoking a little since all this happened," Katherine admitted. "It's very similar to when I lost my husband. I'm through the sadness a lot quicker though and I'm in the angry stage. After I lost Mark, there was nothing I could do but I thought this time I could try to make him face the consequences."

As Katherine had decided to smoke, Linda and Tommy both lit up as well. No one said anything for a few moments.

"Don't go ahead with a private prosecution, Katherine," Tommy suggested. "It'd be an unmitigated disaster."

"I doubt you'd be able to remain anonymous as well, Katherine," Linda added.

"Isn't there any way of getting his telephone?" Katherine asked. "If you had it that the lady at The CPS said she'd try and pursue it."

"I can't see how," Tommy answered. "As soon as we spoke to him, he'd get rid of it. He'd know it's the only thing that could convict him."

"Don't forget he's not really a criminal Tommy," Linda offered. "He might just be stupid enough to have kept it."

"Maybe so but as soon as he got a visit from us he'd destroy it, Lin."

"At the moment he thinks he's free and clear I suppose," Linda said. "You haven't contacted him at all since you found out who he is have you Katherine?"

"Not since a few days after his messages stopped. I feel so stupid, for a woman of my age to be taken in by someone like him is ridiculous."

"How about some sort of sting Tommy," Linda suggested. "We get someone to join the agency and ask for his profile. Then we e-mail him pretending to be a wealthy divorcee or widow. If he replied we could see if he was using the same e-mail address. Then all we'd have to do is arrange a meeting and nick him with the phone when he arrived."

"Isn't that illegal?" Katherine asked, "Entrapment or something."

"It's only entrapment if you encourage someone to commit a crime," Linda explained. "The crime's already been committed. The defence might still be able to make something of it I suppose."

"My friend Liz joined after she and her husband split up, she could ask for his profile and e-mail him. Or I could re-join under a fake name with a different e-mail address."

"You'd need a fake photograph, Katherine. I thought you only joined in April. You said you'd re-join."

"My daughter Jen got me a three-month subscription."

"Then I doubt Mr Rob Jones is a member now," Linda said.

"If he joined just to meet, Katherine, he'd only have stumped up for three months."

"That blows your idea of a sting then, Lin," Tommy said, "It was a long-shot at the very best."

"I'll make some drinks," Katherine said, "Tea or coffee?"

Both of them asked for tea, Katherine went indoors and made a pot. She came back with another tray five minutes later. She poured them all a cup.

"That's it then I suppose. As you said if The CPS don't think it would work I'd hardly get a private prosecution through to a guilty verdict."

"He deserves to be punished Katherine," Linda said. "It was a horrible trick. Even if he didn't cheat you out of any money."

"I was worried you'd think I was just a spoilt rich bitch," Katherine said, "I'd actually have felt better if some stranger had dragged me off the street and assaulted me."

Tommy hadn't said anything for a few minutes, he'd been sat at the table thinking. He lit a cigarette and sat there smoking.

"How about The Doc and The Whizz Kid paying Mr Rob Jones a visit Lin?" he suggested. "We could spin him some of the old bullshit, I miss those days."

"The criminal world and the complaints department don't miss them Tommy. Do you reckon this guy deserves you two?"

"Who or what are The Doc and The Whizz Kid?" Katherine asked, "They sound like a pantomime double act."

Linda spluttered on her tea. "That's almost a perfect description of them Katherine. The Doc is this old fossil and The Whizz Kid is William Whitcher. Have you heard of a television series called The Sweeney?"

"Mark used to love it."

"Billy Whitcher was a Detective Constable who took more notice of The Sweeney than the training manual Katherine. He was on the verge of getting thrown out of the force. They put him with Tommy and they rubbed off on each other. Tommy got his head out of his arse and Billy calmed down a bit. He's a D.I. in Southampton now."

"They nicknamed him The Whizz Kid because he's well into computers and technology, Katherine," Tommy added. "He heads up a computer crime unit now. He'd welcome a break I expect."

"Would he be all right with the complaint that followed Tommy?" Linda asked.

"I haven't spoken to him for a couple of months but Billy Whizz still looks about sixteen and he's got the old sparkle in his eyes Lin. He'll be well up for putting one over a guy like our Mr fucking Pargeter-Jones."

Linda glared at Tommy, he realised he'd slipped up and sworn. "Sorry, Katherine," he said. "I forget sometimes."

Katherine patted the top of Tommy's hand across the table. "I've been using some pretty ripe language myself lately Tommy, don't worry. Do you really think you can get him to hand over the phone?"

"If those two are anything like they used to be he'll be begging to be arrested to get some peace, Katherine," Linda answered, "I just hope they don't appoint me to the complaints committee."

"We were never that bad," Tommy moaned. "At least we never got violent with anybody. Can I use your toilet please, Katherine?"

"Use the downstairs one, Tommy, go through the kitchen and it's the first door on the left."

Linda didn't quite know what to make of Katherine, she'd come expecting to find a spoilt, wealthy lady just out for revenge on a man that had spurned her. Within a few minutes of arriving she'd realised that Katherine was a charming woman who did the right thing by everybody and just expected to be treated the same.

"Tommy's a nice man, Lin; have you know him long?"

"Twenty very long years, Katherine. He is a nice man but he's a bit of an enigma. He hates any discrimination and he hates being lied to. But he's not one of those guys who just fight for the underdog. If he thought you were lying to him or on some sort of revenge mission, he'd very soon tell you."

"Is he married with a family?"

"He's divorced, there's one son who's a university lecturer in Manchester."

Katherine was about to ask another question but Tommy came back and joined them at the table.

"It's beautiful here, Katherine, is that the garage on the side? It's bigger than most people's houses."

"Mark wanted somewhere to work on his cars and bikes Tommy. They were his passion. Would you like to see inside?"

Linda and Tommy were glad of the distraction so they said they'd like to see the garage. Katherine led them round to the side door and keyed some numbers and letters into a keyboard on the wall. They heard the locks click open; Katherine led them through the door.

The first thing they saw was the E-Type Jaguar, Katherine had left the roof down the last time she'd used it.

"That might be the most amazing car I've ever seen Katherine," Linda enthused. "It's beautiful."

"My father-in-law bought it new in nineteen-seventy-two. He hardly used it and Mark inherited it when he died. Mark would always rather take it to shows and clean it than actually drive it. I've done more miles in it this year than it did in the last ten."

Tommy had wandered over to the other side of the garage and was looking at Katherine's Ducati.

"I know you said you rode, Katherine, you didn't say you had a Nine-Sixteen Senna."

"I love riding, Tommy. When Mark got his single-seater, I treated myself to it."

Katherine took a cover of a second bike to reveal a limited edition Honda RC45. "He didn't really like riding it too much, it's only done a few thousand miles."

"Are you going to sell it?" Tommy asked.

"I'm going to donate it to a museum Tommy, they'll display it and keep it up together."

The third bike was a Triumph Bonneville. "That belonged to Marks dad as well," Katherine explained. "I'll never sell it but I don't really like riding it."

"It's a sixty-eight model," Tommy commented. "Most people reckon they were the best ones."

Linda wasn't all that interested in the motor-bikes, Tommy was examining the Triumph from all angles. She was looking at the photographs on the wall in the corner of the garage.

"That's what Mark called his study," Katherine said with a smile. "I'll have to sort it all out one day I suppose."

"Is that you next to the lorry?" Linda asked.

"We had two at one point," Katherine explained. "Mark, Pete and Gavin all took their tests and we did our own collection and deliveries for a few years. Transport was costing us a fortune and we were always being let down."

"You look like you were getting in the driver's seat in the picture Katherine," Tommy said. "You didn't drive an artic, did you?"

"I took my test the same day as Mark," Katherine said proudly. "Mark failed and I passed, I did remind him now and then, he passed the second time. I only drove now and again if we were really busy."

By now it was almost seven o'clock, Linda and Tommy had done all they could for Katherine. She seemed to have accepted that it was very unlikely that Robin would hand the telephone over and that any prosecution would succeed.

"We'd better get going, Katherine," Tommy said. "Thanks for making us so welcome. We'll leave you in peace."

"Quite the opposite, Tommy," Katherine said. "It's been nice having some company. Usually on a Friday night I'm here by myself watching television and missing Mark."

Katherine walked down to the gate with them, Linda smoked a cigarette before she got in the car. She felt sorry for Katherine, she'd lived alone for a while after her divorce and when her boys had left home. The evenings were always the worst for her, going back to an empty house after a busy day at work.

Tommy lived alone as well, he knew exactly how Katherine was feeling. He'd had the nicest Friday evening that he could remember for a long time. When Katherine said goodbye to them, she hugged them both and thanked them for doing their best. She diplomatically went back to the house before they drove off, she obviously realised that they wanted a few moments on their own to discuss the situation.

"What do you think, Lin?" Tommy asked.

"She's lovely, Tommy, and she certainly didn't deserve an asshole like that trying to rip her off."

"She's almost crosser with herself for being taken in. The stupid thing is Lin is that if he'd taken any money off her we'd be after him like a fucking shot."

"That's the way of things. Be careful Tommy, I can see exactly how you feel about her. Jesus; if she ever gets in front of a jury, they'd convict him like a shot."

"She has that effect," Tommy agreed. "Can I get Gill Hopkins' number off you please, Lin? Now you've got her in the loop I'll need to keep her up to speed. If he hands that phone over, I want him charged straight away. She'll have to get all the paperwork and a court slot ready."

"Do you think you can con him out of it?"

"We'll give it a shot but unless he's a complete idiot he'll have got rid of it. I've got a throw down phone; I put a new SIM card in every time I buy some credit."

Chapter Thirty-One

"Detective Inspector Docherty and Detective Whitcher Miss, we'd like to see Mr Robin Pargeter-Jones please."

"Do you have an appointment?" Sandra Rodgers asked.

Tommy looked at Billy and sighed loudly, he turned back to face Robin's secretary and receptionist.

"As you appear to be his receptionist, Miss Rodgers, I'd like to think you'd know if we were expected. Will you please tell him we'd like a few moments of his time."

Sandra didn't use the intercom, she got up from her desk, asked them to wait and went through into the next office without knocking.

"She's a cracker, Tommy; reckon she'd do a turn?"

"Not for the likes of you and me Billy. Behave yourself for fucks sake. Just remember your lines."

"It's like the old days, Tommy, it's good to be out from behind that desk."

Sandra came back into the outer office and invited the two policemen to follow her through. She introduced them to Robin Pargeter-Jones. Tommy saw the resemblance to Pierce Brosnan straight away. The man who offered his hand was over six feet tall with short dark hair and a ready smile. Even on a hot day he looked relaxed in a smart white shirt and tie.

"What can I do for you gentlemen?" he asked after the introductions were completed.

"Firstly, sir, I must tell you that this is an informal visit, I'm not going to caution you so anything you say remains behind the door your receptionist just slammed. You could tell me that you were planning on killing the queen and I couldn't do anything about it."

"I understand that, Inspector Docherty, you still haven't told you why you're here."

"I'm here because I'm a senior detective that's seen most things in his life and doesn't get surprised any more. Detective Whitcher may not be as cynical as I am but they call him The Whizz Kid because he's an expert on computers and modern technology. Before we start, sir, I'm going to give you a little advice; don't lie to me. I'll ask you questions, some of which I already know the answer to. Basically if you lie to me, I'll make this an official interview, arrest you and interview you under caution at the local station. Is all that clear, sir?"

"Quite clear, Inspector," Robin said cautiously.

Billy Whitcher hadn't spoken while Tommy was giving Robin his prepared speech. He looked bored, checked his watch and shuffled his feet. Tommy gave him a dirty look and started the interview.

"I haven't got the records of the dating agency that you joined and I'm sure they value their client's privacy, I'm sure that if I got a warrant I could get the relevant information. I believe that you joined in April using the name Rob Jones. Is that correct, sir?"

Robin knew better than to answer immediately or try and lie his way through the interview.

"True Inspector, everybody calls me Rob and I rarely use my full surname. My father is a bit of a snob I'm afraid, when he married my mother he added her family name to ours. So as far as I'm aware most people know me as Rob Jones."

"I've seen the profile from the agency, sir, not strictly true is it?"

"On the contrary Inspector, everything I wrote is true."

Tommy gave Billy another look. "This is going to be harder than I thought Billy," he commented.

"I'll try again, sir, what you wrote may well be true but you seem to have left a lot of information out, your current wife and children for example."

"There may have been some omissions," Robin admitted.

"Some fairly important ones I'd say," Tommy commented.

"You then e-mailed another client of the agency; Katherine Reynolds, several e-mails were sent until you arranged a meeting at Burley tea rooms. Correct so far, sir?"

"That would be a short version of it Inspector. Is this going somewhere?"

"Eventually, sir," Tommy looked at Billy as he was talking. "All right Billy, not boring you am I?"

"Sorry, Guv," Billy said as he stifled a yawn. "Long day."

"Bear with me, sir," Tommy said politely. "I'll get to the point shortly. This relationship developed quickly, a few more dates and it became intimate; correct?"

Robin thought about lying but decided it wasn't worth it so he just nodded in agreement.

"One weekend at her house and the following weekend at her holiday cottage; correct?"

Robin nodded again.

"After Mrs Reynolds turned down your invitation to invest heavily in your non-existent business you ended the relationship; correct?"

"It was a genuine opportunity Inspector, not some scam as you appear to think."

"I'm sure you believe that to be true Sir and I've no reason to doubt you. So would it be fair to say that you joined the agency with the specific aim of getting into contact with Mrs Reynolds?"

Robin didn't answer straight away, Tommy noticed that he was getting twitchy, Billy shuffled his feet; Tommy glared at him again.

"Yes, Inspector, I think it would be fair to say that."

"And would you say that's ethical, sir?"

"Probably not ethical but not illegal Inspector. I've known salesman with plenty worse pitches than that."

"I'm glad you didn't try to sell me anything, sir," Tommy commented. "As you said; nothing illegal in what you did. There would have been however if you'd accepted any money from her, it would have constituted a fraud."

Robin seemed a little relieved that Tommy agreed he hadn't tried to defraud Katherine.

"Is that the reason that you're here, Inspector? As you say no fraud took place."

"Are you still with us Billy?" Tommy snapped. "I'm sorry, sir," he said to Robin. "Detective Whitcher doesn't seem to be with us today."

"Sorry, Guv," Billy said. "I was hoping to be home by now, or at least in the pub getting a pint after work."

"You and me both Billy, we won't be much longer here. Is there a pub near here, sir, that we could get a drink at when we've finished?"

"There's a bar a short walk away," Robin answered.

"As I said, sir, this is an informal chat. I'd gladly buy you a pint and continue in a quiet corner of the bar. What time do you lock up here?"

"Sandra locks up when I'm not here, I could use a drink as well Inspector Docherty."

"We'd better get Billy down there before he falls asleep on us. If we're going to be drinking pals it's Tommy and Billy. Can I call you Robin? Or would you prefer Rob?"

"Rob please. I'll tell Sandra to finish up here. Give me a minute please, guys."

Five minutes later they were sitting in an almost deserted bar, Tommy brought three pints back to the table. Billy didn't have to drive home so he greedily drank half of his in one gulp.

"The reason we're chatting is a bit touchy Rob," Tommy began. "That's why I had to drag Billy out of his comfortable office. You're aware I assume of revenge porn?"

"I've heard of it. A couple in a relationship take intimate pictures of each other, then when it goes wrong one of them puts them on the internet. Quite popular amongst celebrities I believe."

"Also now a criminal offence," Billy commented. He seemed a little livelier now he'd got a drink.

"Mrs Reynolds contacted us Rob. She's very concerned that you have images of her that she wouldn't want made public."

"Not with you I'm afraid," Robin said truthfully.

"Mrs Reynolds is standing for the local council next year, Rob. Imagine if a picture of her in a compromising position was made public. For example a picture of her in very skimpy underwear, her hands tied behind her with what appears to be a black stocking and knelt on the floor of her spare bedroom. She appears to be giving an anonymous man oral sex. This image would be familiar to you I believe, Rob?"

Robin took a gentle sip of his drink while he thought, He'd been warned not to try lying and the policeman seemed quite sure of his information.

"I'm quite aware of the position you describe Tommy but I don't see how there was a photograph taken of it."

"It sure as fuck wasn't a selfie," Billy joked. "Not with her hands tied like that."

"The only person that could have taken such a picture would be the man standing who was benefitting from her actions," Tommy said.

"I can assure you I took no such picture," Robin insisted. Tommy seemed to ignore Robin and continued.

"Or images of Mrs Reynolds in another compromising position Rob. She seems to be laying on top of a man facing his feet. She's got his member in her mouth this time as well. Or asleep on the bed with her legs spread open. She's terrified of any images like those being made public."

"I'm sure she is, Tommy, but I didn't take any pictures of her either time I stayed overnight."

"I'm a little confused, Rob, I can't see any way you could gain an advantage by publishing any images; if you have any. I assume that your wife doesn't know about the relationship."

"She knows I met her once or twice, she obviously doesn't know we slept together."

"That's what I thought, Rob. And Mrs Reynolds told me she offered you a considerable amount of money which you didn't accept so it's not for financial gain. Young Billy Whizz has an idea of what's going on."

"Since the police have been involved with this revenge porn, we've had a few cases of what's been dubbed reverse revenge porn. In this case for example Mrs Reynolds sends the images to herself and blames you. She reports you to the police in the hope of having you arrested."

"Surely you'd be able to see that she's sent them to herself?"

"Actually, it's not that simple to spot. Did you send any photographs to her phone?"

"I sent her some pictures of the vineyard in Tuscany."

"So all she'd have to do is replace those images with the dirty ones," Billy said. "It'd look genuine to the untrained eye."

"So what you're saying is that she can replace my pictures with those, report me and get me prosecuted?" Robin asked.

"We're ahead of that game, Rob," Billy said. "All we'd have to do is take her phone to the lab and we'd be able to download the records. They'd show that the original image had been replaced."

"Do you intend to do that, Billy?"

"Too fucking right he will, Rob," Tommy said. "She reported a crime to the police, we're duty bound to investigate. If no crime was committed, she'll be prosecuted."

Robin looked alarmed. "What would you charge her with? Would the whole saga have to be made public?"

"Attempted malicious prosecution or wasting police time I expect, Rob. If she pleaded not guilty there'd be a trial. I expect you'd be called as a witness so the answer is probably yes; I'm afraid it would be made public."

"Isn't there any way to make this go away quietly Tommy?" Robin asked. "I'm not exactly proud of what I did, surely she doesn't need to suffer a court case."

"We'll obviously be talking to her again shortly Rob, if she still insists that any pictures on her phone were sent by you we'd have to take it for forensic tests. After that it'd have to go to The CPS for prosecution."

Robin looked as if he was getting a little desperate, he certainly didn't want to be called as a witness when the whole sorry story would be told. Billy went for more drinks.

"How did you trace me, Tommy? I thought I'd covered my tracks."

"I'd like to say it was good old-fashioned police work Rob," Tommy answered. "I'd be lying if I did though. It's very hard to do anything these days without leaving a trail, there's CCTV just about everywhere, ANPR cameras, mobile telephone tri-angulation and card payments."

He didn't tell Robin that the reason they'd traced him was the fact that Katherine had spotted him parking his dad's car.

"It wouldn't do any good if I contacted her I suppose?"

"Keep very clear of it, Rob, you'd do more harm than good."

Billy came back from the bar with a pint for himself and a half for the other two.

"I could try and talk her out of it I suppose, Rob," Tommy said. "If I say I've spoken to you and you insist that you didn't send any pictures she might see sense. What phone did you use? You didn't use your everyday phone I assume?"

"I got a new contract one so all I had to do was replace the SIM card in my old one. Easy to set up a second e-mail address on it."

"If you've still got that phone with the SIM in it we could take it with us when we go to see her. We'll tell her that you handed it over voluntarily and we need hers to test them both at the lab. Maybe if she sees we've got the phone that she alleges the messages were sent from she'll back down. I don't want to see her prosecuted if we can help it. No one would come out of it with any credit."

"I've still got the phone, it's at home."

"Is the SIM that you used still in it, Rob?"

"Yes; I haven't used it since."

"I assume the images of Tuscany are still on it, Rob. I reckon as soon as she sees it she'll admit what she did. If she does, I'll make it go away quietly; just give her a warning perhaps."

"What's the procedure? Will you call in and collect it?"

"We need to do this officially, Rob. Can you drop it into the station near your office tomorrow afternoon? Maybe get the lovely Sandra to lock up again and bring it in around four o'clock. I'll make sure I'm there to take it off you."

"That'll be fine, do you think you can persuade her?"

"I may not have your charm with the ladies Rob," Tommy said with a smile. "But if I have that phone I think we'll have all we need."

"I won't be there Guv," Billy announced. "You'll have to seal it in an evidence bag."

"The Whizz Kid thinks I should be put out to grass Rob, maybe he's right at that. There'll be a few procedures when you bring it in. Don't worry though, I'll lead you through them first, then we'll go into an interview room, I'll caution you and warn you that if there is any information relevant to our enquiries we can use it. You'll be offered the services of a solicitor which you'll obviously decline, I'll take the phone and seal it in an evidence bag and it'll all be over."

Robin looked relieved. "I'll be there at four o'clock."

"Thanks for your time, Rob. One more thing please, can you make sure the phone is charged."

Chapter Thirty-Two

"What do you mean, Sandra, arrested? What's he been arrested for and where is he?"

Robin had taken the telephone to the police station, followed the instructions that Tommy had advised and promptly been arrested on two rape charges and two of sexual assault.

"He didn't tell me the reason Madelaine. He tried to call you but didn't get an answer so he called me. I'm just locking up, is there anything I can do?"

"What did he say to you, Sandra?"

"He said I had to tell you not to worry, he's apparently been charged, they've got him in court in the morning and he'll probably be bailed straight away. He asked for a solicitor and they've found one to go to court with him in the morning."

"Where's he being held, Sandra?"

"He rang me from the police station that's quite near the office but they've not got any custody facilities there so he'll be sent somewhere else until the morning."

Madelaine tried to keep calm but she didn't know what to do. She'd been drinking so she couldn't drive anywhere, Richard was at the golf club and wouldn't have taken his mobile phone out of the car while he was playing.

Eventually, after several frantic telephone calls she tracked down a sergeant who knew what was happening. He explained that Robin had been taken to the main police station in Southampton because they had a custody suite. Madelaine asked if she'd be allowed to see Robin but was firmly told that she wouldn't. The sergeant told her that the first court appearance would be the following morning at the magistrate's court. He also told her that Robin had been charged with two counts of rape and two of sexual assault.

As soon as she saw that Richard had arrived home from the golf course, she went round and told him what had happened.

"Rape and sexual assault, not true. It must be some sort of mistake. I'll get hold of a barrister straight away, we'll soon get this sorted out."

"I don't think we'll be allowed access to him until the morning. If he's already been charged and got a court date, I don't think there's anything we can do."

"You said Sandra told you that he's confident of getting bail in the morning but if the charges are that serious I find that very hard to believe."

"Can we please both go to the court in the morning to find out what the fuck is going on?"

"What time is the hearing, did they tell you?"

"The first case is at ten o'clock, they don't know when his committal will happen. We'll have to be there by ten."

"Don't you dare drink any more tonight young lady. Get up early, have some food and a shower, take your son to school and pick me up at nine-thirty in the morning."

Madelaine nodded her agreement and went home in tears.

"You got him to bring the phone in, cautioned him and he handed it over voluntarily. How the fuck did you do that Tommy?"

"I'll explain it when we get inside Lin. Even better; he charged it up for me. That Hopkins woman is a dragon, is she a lesbian?"

"She says she's between men, I don't think she's gay but I wouldn't be surprised. We'd better go and see your fantasy woman."

Tommy had texted Linda Hislop to tell her that he'd arrested Robin and arranged a committal hearing for the following morning. He was going to see Katherine on his way home and persuaded Linda to meet him there again. They had a cigarette and then walked to the house.

Katherine came to the door straight away and invited them in. An attractive lady in her fifties was sitting at the table in the conservatory, Katherine introduced her to the two officers.

"This is my best friend Liz Powell, Liz; this is Inspector Docherty and Chief Inspector Hislop. They don't mind me calling them Tommy and Lin. Tommy has some news for me about Rob Jones."

"Mr Robin Pargeter-Jones brought the mobile telephone that we need as evidence into the station this afternoon. He was under caution at the time. As soon as the phone was sealed in an evidence bag, I arrested him and charged him with two counts of rape and two counts of sexual assault. He's in custody overnight, has a court appearance in the morning, the police will not oppose bail."

"Christ, Tommy; you made it sound like a press statement," Linda commented.

"How the hell did you manage to get him just to hand it over?" Katherine asked.

"After a few minutes with Tommy and Billy Whizz it was probably a relief to get arrested Katherine. They're like some kind of double act when they get together. Who do you think they'll get to play the pair of you in the film Tommy?" Linda joked.

"Simple, Lin. The guy who played Jack Regan in The Sweeney can play Billy Whizz and the one who played Inspector Morse can play my part."

"Don't worry, Katherine, he's been spending too much time with his sidekick; it'll wear off in a few days."

"It might have been one of our better performances," Tommy said proudly. "Billy looked like a delinquent teenager and then dazzled us with technology. We told him you'd faked up some photos on your phone and accused him of sending them. We threatened to arrest you for wasting police time, he actually seemed worried about you. Then we said if we had the phone, he used to send genuine messages we could prove he didn't send them."

"It sounds like some sort of flim-flam," Liz commented. "Won't his defence bring all that up in court?"

"I was thinking much the same," Katherine said.

"If he got a decent barrister, they'd make an application to have it thrown out as inadmissible," Tommy answered. "I'd bet good money any half-decent judge would keep it though. I've got footage of him handing it over under caution. He'd already been warned if the contents were evidence of a crime that they could be used against him."

"What about all the nonsense you gave him about me having faked photos Tommy?"

"He wasn't under caution then Katherine. We were just three guys shooting the shit in the pub. Billy and I will just deny it all and there's nothing he can do."

"I'm going to open a bottle of wine, back in a minute."

Katherine went into the kitchen for a bottle of chilled white wine, as soon as she was out of earshot Liz asked the two officers what they thought of the case.

"I think she's got a strong case and I think she'll get a result," Linda answered.

"So do I, Liz," Tommy agreed. "The only problem is that she's going to have to tell it all in court. If he gets a smart-arse brief it'll be hard on her to say the least."

"Perhaps he'll plead guilty and save the trouble of a trial," Linda said hopefully.

Katherine came back out as they were discussing it and overheard the last comment from Linda.

"I doubt if he'll plead guilty, it'd be nice to think he had the decency to do so," she said.

Tommy stood up. "I'll just have one small glass please Katherine, can I use your toilet."

"You know where it is, Tom," she said pleasantly. She poured them all a glass of wine. When he was out of earshot, she turned to Linda. "I still can't believe he got Rob to just hand the phone in."

"You can smile now," Linda warned. "Soon you'll have to deal with Gill Hopkins from The CPS and have to face a trial. They'll try pretty much anything to get him off Katherine."

"That's in the future and I'll tell you this Lin, if he gets found not guilty at least I'll have made him aware that he can't just do that to people and get away scot-free."

Tommy came back and sat down, he sipped his wine. "This is nice Katherine."

"It's only a cheap one, very low alcohol as well. I'm cooking for Liz and myself, you two are welcome to stay and join us if you like."

"Not for me Katherine, I'll have to be going soon," Linda answered.

Tommy seemed to be dithering, Linda answered for him. "Tommy would love to stay, Katherine; he doesn't eat properly. You know what men are like on their own."

"I'm actually a very good cook," Tommy said indignantly. "It's difficult cooking for one."

Katherine got a pen and paper and wrote some numbers and letters down. "Let us three have a girly chat Tom, that's the code for the garage door, go and play with the Bonneville for ten minutes please."

"Tell me a bit about him then, Lin," Katherine said. "All I know is he's a bit of an enigma."

Linda was curious as to why Katherine wanted to know about Tommy but didn't say anything about that.

"He's that all right Katherine. I've known him for more years than I care to remember and I don't know that much. He's retiring next year, I guess he's nearly sixty. He's divorced with one son."

"You said he won't discriminate against anybody."

"It's probably held him back, I was a constable when I first knew him; he was a sergeant. He won't kow-tow to anyone or join the masons to get on. He treats everyone the same."

"He just seems so sad sometimes when you look at him, Lin."

"He has his moments Katherine but I know what you mean. His son Michael is gay, it's what caused the divorce, he stuck by his son and his wife couldn't get her head round it."

"It's normally the other way round," Liz commented.

"I'd better start some food," Katherine said. "Are you sure you won't join us, Lin?"

"I may well be a minority in this day and age but I've a husband coming in from work who'll hopefully have some food on the go when I get home. Thanks anyway Katherine. I hope all this goes well for you."

Linda handed Katherine a card with her mobile number and e-mail address on it. "Call me if you need anything Katherine, I'd better be going. I'll tell Tommy he can come back now."

Katherine showed Linda to the door, gave her a hug and promised to keep in touch. They heard her shout goodbye to Tommy as she went past the garage. He came back indoors five minutes later.

"Do you need any help with the food, Katherine? I'm a dab hand with a potato peeler."

"I'll let you into a little secret Tom but keep it to yourself. We're having a salad which I can knock up in five minutes and a lasagne that I made when I got in from work and will be ready in fifteen minutes. So we'll have another glass of wine and then I'll make the salad and then we'll eat."

"Sounds good to me, Katherine."

"She went to catering college Tommy and her daughter runs the finest bakery in Hampshire, that should tell you that you're about to experience the best meal you're ever likely to eat."

Katherine blushed a little, she lit her first cigarette of the evening. "I'm going to have to give this up soon," she said. "I've been having two or three a day since all this started."

Fifteen minutes later, the three of them were sitting in the conservatory eating lasagne and salad, Tommy couldn't recall eating a nicer meal for a long time.

"This is wonderful, Katherine, no wonder your daughter's doing so well with her shop."

"You ought to try her chips, Tommy," Liz told him.

"I like cooking but I find it difficult catering for just myself," Tommy said. "It's easier to just throw a ready meal in the oven."

"That's why Liz and I get together a couple of times a week, since we both live on our own now it's good to have someone else to cook for."

"I've just broken up with my husband," Liz explained. "He decided to start screwing someone else and buy a Harley."

She served them a trifle for dessert and then made them coffee. "Thanks for that, Katherine," Tommy said. "That's the nicest meal I've eaten for a long time."

"Mr Rob fucking Jones will be eating prison food Kath," Liz commented.

"I thought I'd dislike the man," Tommy said. "But he actually surprised me, unless he's a really good actor and I got taken in as well. He seemed as if he was upset at what he did to you. When I gave him the nonsense about you being arrested, he was quite concerned about you."

"So he fucking should be," Liz said.

"I rang Billy to tell him I'd nicked Robin, he said much the same thing."

"This Billy Whizz sounds a bit of an article Tommy," Katherine said trying to change the subject.

"He is that," Tommy smiled "They put him with me when he was waiting for a disciplinary hearing. He'd been on a drugs raid. A constable beat the door in, Billy was first in; he stormed into the bedroom, whipped the covers off to reveal a naked couple and yelled the iconic line 'Get yer trousers on, yer nicked'. Turned out they'd got the wrong house."

"Did he get in trouble?" Katherine said with a smile.

"A slap on the wrist, luckily it wasn't his fault they'd gone to the wrong house. We were together for nearly three years after that. Lin reckons they use some of it in the training manuals but I think she made that up."

"What's the procedure now Tom?" Katherine asked.

"No doubt Gill Hopkins will be in touch Katherine. She'll take you through the options. If he pleads guilty it'll be over with nice and quick, I doubt if he will though. She'll take you through the likely course of a Crown Court trial."

"When do you think it'll be?" Liz asked.

"Late autumn at a guess, certainly before Christmas. There'll be a few committals along the way until they set a date."

"You said he'll be out on bail tomorrow Tommy. What do I do if he gets in touch with me?"

"Call the police straight away. One of his bail conditions will be that he doesn't contact you in any way, shape or form. If he does, they'll revoke his bail immediately."

Tommy and Katherine stood in the garden after dinner and enjoyed a cigarette.

"Thanks for everything, Tommy. I didn't think anyone was going to take me seriously until you came along."

"It's been my pleasure, Katherine." He handed her a card with all his contact details on it. "Call me anytime, day or night."

Chapter Thirty-Three

Robin spent a very uncomfortable night in the cells. He was offered food and drink but apart from asking for some water he didn't want anything. As soon as the Inspector had arrested him, he'd asked for a solicitor to be called. They kept him waiting in the interview room and a solicitor was there within half an hour. Robin assumed that they must have had one on standby. A thirty-something lady called Nicola Hill arrived.

"They've got it all in order I'm afraid Mr Pargeter-Jones. The CPS have done all the paperwork, apparently you came here voluntarily, you were given all the proper cautions, gave them the evidence they needed and were arrested. They just showed me the footage of you declining a solicitor. Now they've actually charged you there's really nothing I can do until the committal in the morning."

"Call me Rob please, it's a lot easier. They say I'm in custody overnight but will be bailed in the morning. That may be an issue Ms Hill, I doubt we can raise the funds to bail me out."

"Don't worry, Rob, you don't actually need funds, they'll set certain conditions and release you on what they call your own recognisance. Basically if you break any of the conditions you'll be arrested and they'll revoke the bail."

"What's the procedure now and in the morning?"

"They'll have to take you to a station with a custody suite, make sure you're comfortable and settled, feed you if necessary and keep you overnight. Then there'll be the first of the committal hearings which is scheduled for tomorrow morning. You'll have to confirm your name and address and that you understand the charges. I'll apply for bail and you should be released within around half an hour."

"Won't I have to plead guilty or not guilty?"

"That's way down the line and it'll be in Crown Court, probably Winchester. One strange thing Rob; they had all the paperwork in place to charge you straight away. Normally there's all sorts of interviews before any charges are laid."

"Will you be representing me right through?"

"I'm the duty solicitor, Rob, all I've got to do at the moment is explain the situation to you. I'll get your bail organised in the morning I expect. Then it'll be up to you whether you appoint your own defence or use legal-aid. Either way it won't be me in charge of it. That's more or less all I can do now. Do you want me to call anyone for you and explain things?"

Robin thought briefly, the sergeant had told him that he'd spoken to Madelaine and explained the situation to her. He hoped that she'd be at the magistrates in the morning but if she wasn't he'd have to wait till he got home to explain things to her and his father. Sandra was perfectly capable of running the office for the day, as soon as he was released he'd collect his car and go straight home.

"It looks like there's nothing I can do tonight thank you. I'll see you in court in the morning."

They put him in a van soon after Nicola Hill had left and took him to a much larger station. The custody sergeant booked him in, took his tie, belt and shoes and put him in a cell with a small single bed, a toilet and hand-basin. He showed him the button to push that summoned an officer but asked him only to use it in an emergency. Robin was dreading the moment they locked the door on him but strangely felt relaxed when the door slammed.

He didn't think he'd sleep at all, the thoughts of a prison sentence were going through his mind. Two rapes and two sexual assaults were serious charges and if he was found guilty he knew that he could be sentenced to a long stretch in prison. After he'd charged him Inspector Docherty had told him that the police wouldn't be opposing bail the following day. He was almost more nervous of facing Madelaine and his father than making his court appearance in the morning.

He drifted off to a disturbed sleep in the early hours of Friday morning. By six o'clock he was pacing his cell, the duty officer bought him a cup of tea at seven o'clock and advised him of the schedule. A van would take him to the court at nine-thirty and all being well he'd be out on bail well before lunch-time.

Everything went by in a blur after they collected him from the station and took him to the courthouse. Nicola Hill was already there, she made sure that he knew what to say and not to make any comment apart from confirming his details and that he understood what was happening. His case was second on the schedule and by ten-thirty the five-minute procedure was over. Nicola Hill applied for bail, The CPS and police had no objections and the magistrate released him on his own recognisance. He was told that he had to report to the police on a weekly basis, surrender his passport and under no circumstances to have any contact with Katherine Reynolds or any of her family.

His father and Madelaine were waiting outside the door of the court. As soon as he came out he gave them a weak smile and waited for Madelaine to explode. To her credit she managed to contain herself until they got to her car. He'd walked from his office to the station so the first thing to do was take him to collect his car.

"You'd better have some very good fucking explanation Rob," she yelled "All Sandra said was that you'd been arrested, I spent fucking hours trying to find out why and when I did they told me it was for two rapes and two sexual assaults."

Robin started to try and explain but before he spoke his father started talking. "How come they gave you bail so easily, are they some sort of bullshit charges from years ago?"

"If you two shut up for a minute, I'll tell you. Madelaine knows that I joined a dating agency to get contact with a wealthy lady in the hope that she'd invest heavily in the Tuscany venture. Unfortunately I took the relationship further than I should have and we spent two nights together."

"You fucking slept with her. That's it, Rob, we're done. As soon as school breaks up, Jonathon and me are leaving. We'll go and live with Mum."

"How the fuck was it rape?" Richard asked. "You said you spent two nights with her, surely if you raped the stupid woman, she wouldn't let you come back for more?"

"It doesn't matter to me," Madelaine yelled. "He cheated on me, that's all that matters at the moment."

"It wasn't what you'd call traditional rape," Robin tried to explain. "She's claiming that if I hadn't lied to her she'd never have slept with me."

They arrived back at the leasing company offices. Robin gratefully got out of the car and told them that he'd be home by lunch time. Madelaine drove off without saying goodbye.

He spent an hour in the office explaining to Sandra what had happened. She'd worked there for two years and was a very attractive girl in her late twenties. They'd obviously got close since she'd worked there but to his credit Robin had never even suggested anything more than a friendly hug.

She made a tray of coffee and listened to his explanation. She listened without comment for most of the time, she was confused at the charges, he explained that it was just down to the lies he'd told.

"The sex was consensual, Sandy; if anything, she was the aggressive one. We went out for dinner, the theatre and back to her house. She was wearing a short dress, black stockings with sexy underwear and she really came on to me. Madelaine and I haven't been very active in that department lately and I couldn't resist."

"I understand, Rob, but it's four charges, isn't it?"

"I went to her holiday cottage the next weekend Sandy. Both times we had full sex and she also gave me a blow job."

"If you weren't married to Madelaine, maybe I'd be feeling sorry for you Rob but to be honest right now my sympathy is for your wife and this other woman."

"Yours and mine both, Sandy, I know I crossed the line. What's making me feel even worse is that I thought I'd got away with it all. I still don't know how they traced me. The phone I used isn't registered and if she'd given them the number of the car, I used they'd have had to apply here for the name of who'd hired the car."

"Are you going to plead guilty at the trial?"

"I haven't given that too much thought yet, Sandy. Madelaine is leaving me, I actually thought if I got the investment we'd move to Tuscany and rebuild things."

"The way you've told me how it happened Rob makes me think you'll be found guilty at trial. You might be better off admitting you were wrong and that you were prepared to face the consequences."

"I'm finished if I go to prison for rape, Sandy. If I plead guilty, I'll get three or four years I think. So I'll probably try and plead not guilty, it'll be a longer sentence if I get convicted but at least I'll have tried."

Sandra made them another tray of coffee, Robin knew that he had to go home soon and face a furious Madelaine but he was putting it off as long as he dared. Eventually he plucked up the courage to leave. He asked Sandra to hold the fort for the day and told her that all being well he'd be in as usual on Monday morning. He had enough cash on him to buy a litre bottle of whisky on his way home.

Liz stayed overnight with Katherine, they'd got into the habit of her staying there when she had a meal with her friend and Katherine staying there when Liz cooked for her. She got up at her normal time and left Liz a note on the fridge when she went to the shop. She hadn't told Jennifer what she'd done but she'd decided to give her all the facts today. The only other person she trusted enough to tell was her sister Doreen.

Friday was a busy morning for baking so they worked tirelessly for nearly four hours before they sat down for a break. Becky arrived as usual at seven o'clock and got the shop ready to open. At nine o'clock the baking was finished and they sat down for a well-earned break.

Katherine told Jennifer that she'd felt Robin was trust-worthy and that at the time she'd genuinely thought that she was falling in love with him and that they were heading for a loving relationship and possibly marriage. She explained that he'd targeted her as a possible investor when he'd recognised her photograph on the internet dating site. Once she'd told him that the sort of funds that he needed weren't available he'd stopped any contact with her.

"I knew he must have done something bad Mum but that's fucking evil. I'm feeling guilty now for buying you that subscription for your birthday."

"Don't be silly, Jen. You couldn't possibly have foreseen anything like that happening."

Katherine then told her daughter that he'd managed to trace Robin because she'd seen him in the distinctive Jaguar with the personal number plate. When she'd found out that he was married with children she'd decided to report him to the police. She told her that Inspector Docherty had been given the case and had arrested and charged Robin.

"You've muddled me up, Mum. You told him that you didn't have a million pounds or anywhere near, you said he turned down thirty thousand. How the hell have they managed to charge him?"

"It's nothing to do with the money he asked for Jen. He's been charged with two counts of rape and two of sexual assault."

Jennifer was confused, as far as she was concerned rape constituted forced intercourse. Katherine quietly explained that as far as she was concerned, she'd never have even met him for tea in Burley if she'd known he was married.

"Jesus Christ, Mum; how the hell did you ever think of that? I know how upset you were before you went off to Holland with Liz but I didn't think you were that angry with him."

"It's almost like when your father died, Jen. After the sorrow the anger arrived. I couldn't do anything about your father being ill but I sure as hell wasn't going to let anyone get away with doing that to me."

Becky called for some help in the shop, Jennifer went out and served, Katherine started the cleaning routine that they diligently carried out every day. When Jennifer came back, she sensed that her mother was finished talking for now and helped finish the cleaning.

They were finished by ten o'clock, Jennifer and Katherine covered the shop while Becky took her break. As soon as she was back in the shop Katherine got her things together and got ready to leave.

"Becky's doing well, Jen, the shop looks great and the customers seem to like her."

"She's going to be something special, Mum. When you were in Holland, she came in early a few days and helped me with the baking. I'm going to get her a day release course at college."

"She'll do you proud, Jen. Pete and Gavin both started out as apprentices. Mark had faith in them and look how they turned out."

"She said that she and her mum don't get on very well. She asks me things and tells me stuff that she says she could never tell her mum."

"We had to put Gavin in the caravan in the garden for a few months when he fell out with his dad. He always said he thought more of Mark than he did his father."

"Am I allowed to tell Danny about all this, Mum?"

"Of course you are but please tell him to keep it to himself. I don't want my love life all-round the local comprehensive."

"He won't tell anyone. Christ, Mum, have you thought this through. If he gets found guilty it'll make the national news. They'll be making a film about it next year."

"The lady from the police said that last night. She asked Tommy who'd play him and his mate. They set up some sort of sting to get the phone off Rob that he used to message me. He said a young John Thaw could play his mate and an old John Thaw could play him. I suppose he knows he's dead."

"Who's Tommy?"

"Inspector Docherty, He stayed for dinner last night with me and Liz."

Robin arrived home at a few minutes before two o'clock. The first thing he did was pour himself a large glass of whisky. Madelaine came downstairs when she heard him come in.

She poured herself a large glass of wine. "Don't fucking look at me like that. I've arranged for Jonathon to go to his friends after school so I'm not driving again today. You're sleeping down here, Rob, no fucking way do you come in that room. I've put your things on the landing."

"Jesus Christ, Mads; I can't sleep on that settee every night. Be reasonable, will you. I'll get the little bed from next door and put it under the window in our room."

"It's my fucking room, you're not going in there any fucking more. Here's a better idea, sleep on that single bed but leave it where it is."

"Move in with him, no fucking way, Mads."

"It's not long till the end of term. We'll be gone straight away and you can come back here."

"What about Claire?"

"She's going to university soon and she's old enough to make up her own mind. Move next door, it'll be easier all round."

Robin poured himself another drink and went into the kitchen to get some food. Eventually he found a pizza in the freezer and put it in the oven. Madelaine was drinking another glass of wine when he came back through.

"You win, Mads, I'll take some things next door. I don't want you to go, I thought if we moved to Tuscany, everything would be all right. It was your idea to contact her through the agency."

Madelaine threw her half full glass of wine at him, it missed and shattered against the wall.

Robin picked up the shards of glass and cut his finger on one. When he came back from the kitchen with a plaster on it Madelaine had got another glass and was drinking again.

"You haven't taken any tablets have you Mads?"

"Like you fucking care. Did you tell the police it was all my fault? Am I likely to get arrested and locked up for the night?"

"I didn't mean it to sound like that. I know I crossed the line and all I can do is keep apologising."

"And all I can do is keep telling you that I'll never forgive you. When did all this happen?"

"The weekend you went to visit your mother and the next weekend."

"You fucking lied to me then. You told me you were going to the cricket with Darren. Did he know? I bet you both had a good laugh about it all."

"He didn't know, Mads. I'm not exactly going to brag about it to anyone."

"Start moving your stuff next door please. I want the keys to this house. If you need anything you can ask Cheralyn to call round for it."

Katherine arrived home at eleven-thirty on Friday, she'd been shopping on her way home. Liz had left her a note on the fridge thanking her for dinner and a bed. She said to call her anytime if she needed anything. Katherine put the shopping away and made some lunch. Just after she'd finished eating the telephone rang. It was Gill Hopkins from The CPS.

She introduced herself and asked Katherine a few basic questions. Katherine had the feeling she was being questioned so that Gill could find out what sort of woman she was dealing with but she answered the questions honestly and patiently.

"I'll be handling the prosecution myself, Katherine," she said pleasantly. "It's obviously going to be slightly unusual to say the least. Inspector Docherty told me all the circumstances. I firmly believe we'll get a successful prosecution. If Mr Pargeter-Jones has any sense he'll plead guilty and throw himself at the mercy of the court."

"Do you think he will, Ms Hopkins?"

"I doubt that he will, it depends whether or not he or his family can afford to pay for a decent defence counsel. If he has to go down the legal aid route he'll have to take what he's given and he may decide to plead guilty."

"What will I have to do Ms Hopkins?"

"Until we have an idea of his intentions there's very little that you need to do Katherine. Two things for you to think about. Firstly as a rape victim you'll get anonymity, you can decline that privilege if you wish. Sometimes people think that it gets them more sympathy. Secondly if he is found guilty you'll be given an opportunity to address the court with a victim's impact statement. It'll be a good idea for you to write your thoughts down as soon as you can."

"The anonymity stays in place for the foreseeable future and I don't think I'll change my mind. I'll start writing down my feelings but I may decide to waive the right to address the court."

Chapter Thirty-Four

Madelaine finished a bottle of wine by the early evening on Friday and went upstairs. Robin drank far more than he'd intended and fell asleep in front of the television. He woke up at four o'clock in the morning, went to the toilet and tried to sleep on the settee. He was still awake at six o'clock so he got up and made some strong coffee. He assumed that Madelaine was asleep so he showered quickly, she'd left all his clothes on the landing; he carried them downstairs and put them by the back door. He'd decided to move in with his father until Madelaine left.

At seven o'clock he went next door to face his father. He'd finished his breakfast and was dressed ready to go to the golf club.

"Madelaine thinks it would be better if I moved in here for a while, Dad, do you mind if I use one of your spare rooms for a while?"

"Would it make a difference if I did mind, Rob? Of course you can stay here, will she leave you?"

"She seems determined to, she was on about it anyway. I thought getting an investment from Katherine Reynolds was our last chance of buying the vineyard and moving to Tuscany."

"By the sound of things you didn't do too much thinking or you'd have realised what a fucking hare-brained scheme it was. Do you think she'd have coughed up that sort of money without checking up on you?"

"I thought I could get her to invest and then quietly fall out with her. As long as she was getting a good return on her money, she may have left it in place. We'd have made enough in a few years to repay the whole lot."

Richard looked old and tired suddenly, he sat at the kitchen table. Robin made a pot of tea and poured them both a cup.

"Have you given any thought to your defence Rob? From the little I know you're certainly guilty of something. How are you going to get it sorted out?"

"I don't know," Robin admitted. "If I plead guilty, I'll go to prison. At least if I plead not guilty people can see I'm not some sort of monster."

"Maybe not a monster, certainly a fucking con-man who didn't mind what he did to raise money. Did you tell her you loved her?"

"No, Dad, I didn't. I'm feeling bad for what I did to her, even before they came for me, I was feeling like a proper shit."

"So you should. I'm not on the course till ten o'clock, take me through the whole sorry fucking saga."

Robin spent the next half an hour telling his father the whole story, from seeing her photograph and recognising her through to spending the weekend with her in Devon. He didn't leave anything out apart from the fact that Katherine had said she was falling in love with him.

"So the first time was at her house after you'd been to Wimborne, you shouldn't even have gone indoors."

"I know that now for fuck's sake, Dad."

"I'm trying to make some sense of things, don't get fucking snotty with me, boy, or you can go back to your house and beg your wife to let you stay there."

"I'm sorry, Dad. We were on the settee, she pushed my hand up her dress. I said I didn't want to offend her and she said she'd be offended if I didn't. She had black stockings and slutty underwear on, I'm only fucking human. Mads and me haven't been very active in the bedroom lately."

"Please spare me all the details, tell me how they've got four counts against you."

"We gave each other oral sex twice and had full sex twice. I assume they're not charging me for going down on her."

"You said she came on to you, won't that be some sort of defence?"

"I don't think so, the idea is that by lying to her I got her to do things she wouldn't have done if she'd known the truth."

"So the only actual evidence is the messages you sent her, why the fuck did you keep the phone? Even worse you handed the thing over, talk about a lamb to the slaughter."

"I didn't think it would come back on me. I still don't know how they traced me, I thought I'd covered my tracks. Then like I told you, those two coppers conned me into taking it to the station."

"I'm no legal expert but as far as I can see, if some smart defence lawyer got that ruled inadmissible, it'd be your word against hers and you could deny everything."

"I don't know, Dad, I'd be lying again. I'd have to stand up in court and say I didn't have sex with her."

"If they lose the evidence, I reckon they'd have to drop the whole thing. They wouldn't stand a fucking chance with no evidence at all. If they even thought you'd get off, they wouldn't proceed."

"Maybe we can try. I've got to get hold of a solicitor, the trouble is that I can't afford to pay one so it'll be a public defender. I can't think they'd go all out for me, Dad."

"You can kiss goodbye to Tuscany anyway, I'll get hold of Clive Weatherly at the golf club today. He's a barrister, I'll have to pay the fee; I can't see you going with some fucking trainee who'll get you sent down for ten years."

"It's going to cost a fortune to mount a defence, Dad. If they don't get the phone thrown out I'll probably still get found guilty."

"We've got to try, Rob."

Katherine wanted her life to be as normal as possible so on Saturday she collected the twins from their house and took them swimming. Danny got them strapped in the back of the Jeep and then spoke to her.

"You're very brave to do what you're doing, Katherine, it's going to be tough if he pleads not guilty. They rip the shit out of rape victims in court."

"I've thought it through, Danny. Even if he gets found not guilty, the whole story will be made public. Guys like him will know they can't get away scot-free."

Katherine didn't usually swim on a Saturday but as she hadn't been in the pool as much recently, she changed into her costume and swam several lengths while the twins had their lesson. After they'd all showered and changed she took them to McDonalds for lunch. When she took them home Jennifer had arrived home from the shop.

"Hi, Mum, did they behave?"

"They were both very good, we had lunch out so don't feed them until next week please."

"Danny is going to take them to the play park later, Mum. What are you doing tonight?"

"Watching *Midsomer Murders* unless you have a better plan. Liz is on a date with a guy she met through the agency."

"Stay over here, Mum, I'll get us some food and we can go somewhere tomorrow. Even if we just take Snowy for a long walk in the forest."

"I've got to try and get things back to normal Jen, it'll be lovely to stay over here."

Katherine had intended to go to church on Sunday morning, she hadn't been for several weeks. She thought spending time with her grandchildren was more important.

After his father had left for the golf club Robin ventured home and got his things ready to take next door. Madelaine had thrown his clothes in black refuse sacks, he carried them through and unpacked them in his father's spare room. Madelaine eventually came downstairs at ten o'clock, she looked like she hadn't slept very much.

"Do you want me to make you a cup of tea, Mads?"

"What I want you to do is fuck off next door with all your things and leave me alone Rob. Put the key through the letterbox when you've got the rest of your things out."

While Robin got everything that he thought he'd need ready Madelaine made herself a hot drink and went back upstairs. He put all his washing and shaving things from the bathroom and the half-drunk bottle of whisky in a shopping bag and as soon as he found his passport, he decided that what he hadn't packed he'd have to do without.

He locked the door on his way out and put the keys through the letterbox. After he'd unpacked everything at his father's house he went to the local police station and signed in. He had to report weekly and he'd decided that Saturday would be the easiest day. The desk sergeant gave him a receipt for his passport when he reluctantly handed it over. He'd briefly considered getting on a cross-channel ferry and trying to disappear. Maybe if he had some funds, he would have been brave enough to have given it a try; or possibly cowardly enough he thought.

"Twenty-five thousand pounds. You're kidding me, Clive."

"I'll tell you this Richard and I won't even charge you for telling you. If it goes to Crown Court and it's a drawn-out saga it could cost you six or seven times that. Twenty-five is just to get things rolling. If I was charging you the going rate for that bit of advice it would have been about thirty quid."

"Let me buy you another drink, Clive. Tell me what the procedure is?"

"A large brandy will get you a short consultation Richard, I'll get that quiet table in the corner."

Richard had driven himself to the golf club so he bought himself a soft drink and a brandy for Clive Weatherly. He took them to the table and sat down opposite the semi-retired barrister. He told him as much as he knew of the case.

"I won't be taking it myself Richard, I haven't done court work for years. An associate of mine would have to handle it. I doubt we could apply to have the telephone evidence ruled inadmissible until they've set a date for Crown Court and appointed a judge. We'd of course investigate the alleged victim; do you know anything about her?"

"That might be a waste of time, Clive. According to Rob, she's a cross between Mother Theresa and fucking Cinderella."

"It would have to be done. Talk it through with Robin over the weekend and get back to me on Monday. Another route we can take is to try and get the charges reduced in return for a guilty plea. They might go for that, it depends who The CPS appoint to prosecute. It could make the national headlines you know, Richard. If he got found guilty of rape and assault when it was all consensual, it'd set a precedent."

"Thanks for your time, Clive. I'll talk it through with Rob and get hold of you on Monday with our decision."

Richard was grateful he hadn't drunk anything at the golf club, he was stopped by the police on his way home. They said that he'd been driving erratically and asked him to take a roadside breath test. He was told to concentrate on his driving and the constable advised him that maybe it was time that he stopped driving himself to and from the golf club.

"Fascist bastards," he said to Robin when he got home. "Fucking good job I hadn't drunk anything."

"What did Weatherly have to say Dad?"

"Firstly, he wants twenty-five thousand for a starter fee, he said it'd be six or seven times that if it goes to trial. He doesn't seem to think he can apply to have the phone evidence thrown out till it goes to trial. He says they'll investigate this Reynolds woman. I've got to let him know on Monday."

"Ring him now, Dad, and tell him to write all that down, roll it up and ram it up his arse."

Richard actually smiled at the idea. "He also said depending on who prosecutes the case it may be best if you agreed to plead guilty to a lesser charge."

"If they dropped the two rape charges, I suppose that'd be worth thinking about, Dad. Are you prepared to back me with that amount of money?"

"I was prepared to back you with the vineyard but I'd hoped you'd be making a success of that and I'd be actually making some money. If your wife leaves, I suppose I could sell next door to pay for it."

"Thanks, Dad. I know I've been a disappointment but maybe if I get through this, we can make a bit more effort to get on."

"You'll likely be living with me till I die, Rob, we'll have plenty of time to mend fences. I'll get that fucking shyster his twenty-five thousand on Monday and get the ball rolling."

Chapter Thirty-Five

"That's the whole story Doreen. What do you think of your big sister now?"

"You're the sensible one, Kathy, and I'm the waster. Mum and Dad always said you'd get on better than me and they weren't wrong, were they?"

"I've been lucky, Doreen, Mark turned out just as everyone thought. That idiot you married messed things up from the start for you."

"I can't get my head round it, I'm amazed the police even followed it up."

Doreen had come down to stay with Katherine for a week, Jennifer had asked Elaine and Becky to cover for her and they'd gone to Devon to spend a week in the cottage. Doreen had met another man online but so far it hadn't developed into a serious relationship.

"I don't think they would have a few years ago. With all these famous people being accused of historical sex offences I suppose they thought they had to be seen to be doing something. I got lucky as well Doreen. They put an Inspector on the case who agrees with me."

"I think everybody would agree that the guy treated you like shit; that goes without saying. Fucking rape charges though Kathy; I don't know about that."

"I've calmed down a little and I think maybe I went a bit too far Doreen. I can't undo it, I've got to see it through now."

"Do you know when the trial is?"

"The Rottweiler from The CPS reckons sometime in early November. She says all the paperwork is in; it's just a question of getting a slot in Crown Court."

"The Rottweiler?"

"Her name's Gill Hopkins. Tommy nicknamed her that, he says now she's got her teeth in she'll never let up. He said she looks like one as well but she's not that bad."

"Who's Tommy?"

"Inspector Docherty, the one I told you conned the evidence out of Rob."

"First name terms with the investigating officer then; what's he like?"

"He's very nice and no Doreen; I'm not going to introduce you to him. You've got this Alistair on the go."

"Hardly on the go. We've only met twice. I'm going to be a bit wary after what you told me."

"I've been telling you that for ages. Then I'm the one who got caught. What do you think about a week away at the end of August then?"

"I don't know Kathy. I really like Liz but I don't want to spend a week with the two of you. Go with her in August while the school's broken up. We can get a trip anytime, maybe after the court case."

Katherine and Liz had decided to go away for at least a week during the school holiday, Katherine didn't like leaving her sister out of the plan but she was quite relieved that she wasn't going with them. They'd narrowed down the options to Italy or Portugal but then Katherine had seen a cruise that looked inviting. Now she knew that her sister wasn't coming they'd be able to pick one.

"Right then, Doreen. As soon as the trial's over we're going away. It doesn't matter how you and Alistair are doing, we're going; all right?"

"Make me another gin and tonic and you've got a deal."

They hadn't got on very well as young children and teenagers. Doreen thought her elder sister was stuffy and strait-laced. From the age of fourteen she'd been boy-mad, she had posters of all the latest pop sensations on her bedroom wall. She started smoking and Katherine was fairly sure she'd tried cannabis.

Katherine had never taken to Doreen's first husband and had warned her that the marriage wouldn't last. Doreen saw that as a challenge and they hardly spoke for the three years that the marriage lasted. Sadly her judgement of men hadn't improved over the years, she'd met several men online and had been let down by most of them.

Doreen lived in Shropshire so they didn't get to spend a lot of time together. Every time she got let-down by a new man she'd be on the telephone to her elder sister. Katherine had been patient and tried her best but sometimes despaired of her sister's lifestyle. Several times they'd had to pay her debts to save her house being re-possessed, at least she seemed to be more sensible with her finances recently.

"I can't believe you turned down five million for that land, Kathy."

"We discussed it before Mark died Doreen. This way there's an income for ever and we do something good. It's the right thing for everyone."

"If you had the money, would you have gone in on that vineyard he tried to sell you?"

"Probably, I'd have checked it out thoroughly first and I expect I'd have found out about Rob at some point. I don't want to talk about him all week Doreen; what do you want to do while you're here?"

"Relax, drink, eat, swim and maybe a few walks on Exmoor please. I wish you'd driven the Jaguar down, you're not getting me on the back of that bike."

Jennifer, Danny and the twins had been to the cottage the weekend before and brought some things down for Katherine so she'd ridden her Ducati down on Sunday morning. Doreen had arrived by coach soon afterwards.

"That's easy then, you've been relaxing, you've got a drink and dinner is in the oven. We'll have to swim and walk tomorrow, too late now."

Life for Robin was getting worse. Madelaine had carried out her threat and moved out with Jonathon as soon as school had broken up. Claire was still living there so Robin moved back, his daughter rarely spoke to him; she was leaving to go to university in September and had taken a summer job to earn some money. Clive Weatherly had summoned him for a case conference on Monday afternoon.

"I've stumped up twenty-five thousand, that means I get to sit in on this conference and see what my money's getting, Rob."

"I don't mind you sitting in Dad, I just don't know if it's allowed," Robin answered patiently.

"I'll meet you there at two o'clock, if I'm not allowed in they can tell me so. I can't see why I shouldn't be allowed to discuss what I'm paying for."

Robin had been trying to live as normal a life as possible, he'd been to work every day, signed in weekly at the police station and gone straight home from work most nights. Sandra had been distant from him since the arrest, she'd been efficient but a lot cooler towards him. He had lunch in his office and then drove to the meeting. His father was waiting in the reception when he arrived.

"Cutting it fine, Rob, I rang just now to see where you'd got to."

"I was just parking, Dad, it's only five to."

Clive Weatherly didn't get back from lunch until quarter past two, his receptionist showed them through to the conference room at just before half-past.

"Sorry to keep you both waiting. This is my associate Melanie Watkinson, if this goes to court, she's going to be handling things."

"Is it all right if my father sits in Mr Weatherly?"

"I don't see why he shouldn't, it's only a case conference."

They sat at the huge table; Clive Weatherly invited his associate to bring Robin and his father up to date.

"The first line of defence would be to get the telephone evidence ruled as inadmissible," Melanie began. Robin noticed a slightly foreign accent as she spoke. "I've been through the police report and it all seems to be in order; therefore I'd consider the application to be frivolous to say the least."

"They told me a pack of lies to get me to hand it in," Robin protested.

Richard thought that someone lying to his son was quite appropriate but didn't say anything.

"They very well may have but all we can use is what you said while you were under police caution. The records are clear, the detective gave you the proper caution; you declined a solicitor and handed the telephone over. He clearly told you that it could be used as evidence and you agreed. Whatever else you were told prior to being cautioned is meaningless I'm afraid."

"What's the best course of action Ms Watkinson?" Robin asked.

"We did some investigation on Katherine Reynolds. All we can find out shows her to be an honest and ethical woman. She's lived a blameless life, has a better credit rating than I have and owns a business that employs more than forty people. If any defence counsel tried to pass the blame to her they'd lose the jury straight away. I contacted the prosecutor at The CPS and we had a brief meeting yesterday."

"What was the outcome of that?" Robin asked.

"Just bad news I'm afraid Mr Pargeter-Jones, the case is being taken by a senior prosecutor called Gill Hopkins, She rarely gets into court and seems to be relishing prosecuting this case."

"Can you call me Mr Jones or Rob please. I'm dropping the double-barrelled name from now on. I'll do it officially when all this is over with."

"Well Mr Jones," she continued. "I put forward a proposal that you'd plead guilty to the two sexual assaults if they dropped the rape allegations. I'm afraid the only concession they would consider would be the opposite. That means if you plead guilty to the two rape charges, they'll drop the charges on the two lesser offences."

Robin looked at his father hoping for some guidance but was met with a wall of silence.

"I don't believe I'm guilty of rape, Ms Watkinson."

"I'll quote what Ms Hopkins told me, Mr Jones, this is not my language you understand. She said that if you plead guilty not only will they drop the lesser charges they'll waive the right for the victim to give an impact statement and they'll allow us quite a lot of freedom to try and mitigate the offences so the judge may give you a shorter sentence. She then said and I'll quote her exact words, 'Tell that arsehole that if he pleads not guilty and takes Mrs Reynolds through a trial, I'll nail his hide to the fucking wall. By the time I've finished ripping the shit out of him, he'll be begging the judge to lock him up.' She's quite vocal is our Ms Hopkins."

"What's your best advice, Ms Watkinson?" Richard asked.

Clive Weatherly had been quiet, he put a hand in the air and motioned his colleague to let him speak.

"As far as we're concerned, Richard, there's only one course of action. Robin pleads guilty to the two rape charges, we'll put all the mitigating circumstances to the court and hope he gives you a short sentence."

"What do you think, Rob?" Richard asked Robin.

"I'm not going to prison for rape, Dad. Even if I plead guilty, I'll get at least three years. I accept I'm guilty of being an idiot and telling some lies but not rape."

"That's our answer then, Clive. He'll plead not guilty and hope the jury uses their common sense."

"You misunderstood what I just said, Richard," Clive Weatherly said. "If he pleads not guilty, our belief is that he'll be convicted. It's not just our advice that he pleads guilty; it's the only way we're prepared to represent him."

"So basically for my twenty-five thousand you've told us that this woman is some kind of an angel which we already knew, that The CPS won't budge and that he should plead guilty and hope the judge didn't argue with his wife or have a headache."

"Don't be hasty, go home and talk it through. As soon as you've decided what to do let me know. You can either plead guilty and we'll represent you or not guilty and find someone else. I'll give you a list of barristers or you could go with the public defender. If you decide that you don't require our services, I'll pass on our preliminary work to whoever you appoint to represent you. We'll prepare an account, there may be a small refund from the retainer."

Clive Weatherly and his associate stood up to signal that the meeting was over. Usually Richard would have shook hands but he stormed out of the conference room with Robin close behind him. He said he was going straight home, Robin was going to the office for the rest of the day and had arranged to meet Darren for a quick drink afterwards.

"You're fucking having me on, Rob. Two rapes would get you five years at least. How come you're out on bail?"

"I'm hardly some fucking lunatic rapist who grabs women off the streets, Daz. They took my passport, where would I run off to anyway?"

"Fair enough, mate. Fucking hell, Rob, you're the one who's been giving me advice on my love life."

"How is it anyway?"

"It was great at first but she seems a bit off now. Maybe it's me, Rob; I always thought I was normal and the rest of the world was weird, maybe it's the other way round."

"You might be right at that Mate, let's go and sit down for a bit. I've got to be away soon."

"You're not under curfew or tagged, are you?"

"No curfew or tag, mate, I have to sign in at the local nick every Saturday. We had a meeting with the lawyers earlier; they said I should plead guilty."

"You can't do that, Mate."

"I'm not going to, Daz. I'll get locked up either way, at least I can give it a shot. I'll have to find a new lawyer now."

Robin went home after one drink, he showered and went next door to see his father.

"I've made my mind up, Dad. We'll tell Weatherly to shove it where the sun doesn't shine and I'll go down the legal-aid route."

"He said he'd recommend another lawyer."

"They'd charge you a fortune and probably come up with much the same result Dad. All those fancy folders with ribbons round them and I could have told them all that before they started. I'll qualify for legal-aid, I haven't got a pot to piss in. They'll be all right Dad. I just hope Weatherly gives you a refund."

"I'll call him tomorrow, he said he'll pass over all the preliminary work to whoever takes it on. Okay, Rob; we'll do it your way."

While he'd been married to Madelaine, Robin and his father hadn't been close but since she'd left, he'd been spending most evenings drinking and chatting to his father. He poured them both a glass of whisky and they sat down in the lounge.

"If you get sent down, Rob, I'll have to change things round. I'm not as fit as I was, I'll have to get a full-time housekeeper. Next door will be empty again so I may get someone there to keep things up together, maybe a husband and wife team who'll do the work in lieu of rent."

"I understand, Dad. You'll have to sort out the office as well. Sandra can run things for you, it'll be a lot easier to hire a new receptionist."

"Of course you might be found not guilty."

Chapter Thirty-Six

"I missed you, Kath, how did your week go?"

Katherine had ridden back on Saturday because the weather forecast was for heavy rain all day on Sunday. She rang Liz and invited her for over for dinner. Because they stayed at the others house so often they'd both left spare clothes and wash bags there.

"It was all right, Liz. Doreen can be hard work but she seems to be getting things together now. She doesn't drink as much now as she used to. She doesn't want to come with us this time. Have you had any ideas about the holiday?"

"The cruise if you don't mind, Kath. There'll be so much to do and we'll go to loads of different places."

"I'll book it tomorrow then if you're sure. I was hoping you'd say that."

"Any word on the trial yet? What about Tommy, any police liaison going on?"

"The Rottweiler e-mailed me last week to keep me up to date. His lawyer offered a guilty plea to the assaults if they dropped the rapes, she said if they pleaded guilty to the rapes, they'd drop the assaults."

"It'd be handy if he did plead guilty, Kath, save a lot of bother."

"She wants me to waive my right to anonymity."

"And are you going to?"

"Not at the moment but possibly if he pleads not guilty I might. She said if I did, I'd get more sympathy from the public."

"Do you want the world to know? That's not why you reported him Kath."

"She's getting me a bit muddled, says I can strike a blow for women. Tommy said he thought she was a lesbian but I think she just hates men."

"He has contacted you then?"

"Not since he stayed for dinner when you were here. I don't think they're allowed to have contact with crime victims."

"He's retiring soon, after it's all over you could invite him round again."

"I might be a little embarrassed Liz. Don't forget I had to tell him what Rob and I got up to."

Liz looked at Katherine and they both burst out laughing. "It's good to have my old friend back, I was worried about you Kath."

"You got me through the worst of it, Liz, and the Dutch trip did the rest. Thanks for being there for me. The other thing she told me was that Rob sacked his lawyer and he's going with the public defender, I just want it all to be over."

"I'll be in court with you every day, Kath."

"Doreen said she'll stay with me through the trial as well."

"What's Jen saying about it all?"

"She says she'll support me whatever happens, I doubt she'll be able to get to court with the twins and the shop to look after. I think she blames herself a little because they bought me the subscription to the agency for my birthday."

Katherine had put a chicken casserole in the slow cooker for dinner so they didn't need to do much cooking. They watched a film on television until the food was ready and sat down to eat at just after six o'clock.

"Thanks, Kath, that was lovely. When I cook for us I feel guilty that it doesn't come up to your cooking."

"Nonsense, Liz. There's nothing wrong with your cooking. Are you staying over?"

"If you don't mind, Kath, it's weird now I'm off work for the summer and don't have to get up."

"It'll be like that next year, I'm determined to retire, Liz. I've got a meeting with the housing society this week about the development at the factory site."

"That'll keep you busy, I think I'll have to work until I'm sixty-six."

"Any word on the house being sold?"

"It's on the market, if it sells, I'll look round for a bungalow, I like the flat but I need a garden."

There was nothing on the television that they wanted to see so Katherine put a disc in the player and they spent the evening chatting about their plans for the future. Katherine still wanted to stand for the local council at the next election.

Liz was seeing a man that she'd met through the agency but wasn't holding out too much hope. At ten o'clock Katherine announced that she was going to bed.

"Do you mind if I go up later, Kath? I want a good look at that holiday brochure. I'll try not to disturb you when I come up."

"Of course not. If I don't see you before, I'll pick you up at the usual time on Wednesday evening."

"There's a Mrs Gina Anderson on the phone for you Rob," Sandra said, "She's a bit rude, I asked her what she wanted and she told me to mind my own business."

"Put her through, Sandra, please."

When he heard the familiar click of the call being put through Robin answered politely and asked what he could do.

"I'm Mrs Gina Anderson and I assume you're Mr Robin Pargeter-Jones. I'm your best hope of staying out of prison, I'll be handling your defence at the trial."

"Thank you for calling Mrs Anderson," Robin said, "Please call me Rob or Mr Jones."

"We'll pretend we're old pals then and be Rob and Gina. I need some of your time this week, Rob. Tomorrow afternoon is best for me, would two-thirty be convenient for you to come to my office?"

"That'll be all right with me. Did Clive Weatherly send you the preliminary work they'd done?"

"For what use it is. Yes; I've read most of it."

Gina told Robin where her office was and asked him not to be late, after the call he poured a coffee and felt a little better. Her comment about Clive Weatherly had confirmed that he'd made the right decision, at least if he was sent to prison his father wouldn't have to pay a huge legal bill.

When he got home he went straight round to see his father and tell him. Richard hadn't eaten so Robin made them a snack and ate with him.

"She sounds all right, Dad, I've got to go and see her after lunch tomorrow. She wasn't very complimentary about your golfing buddy."

"He didn't speak to me at the club this morning Rob. I might give up golf."

"Don't do that, Dad, join another club."

Robin stayed with his father for the evening. They had a few drinks, chatted and played two games of chess.

"Do you want me there tomorrow, Rob?"

"I don't need you there, Dad, you can come if you like."

"See her on your own tomorrow then, make sure you tell me all the details when you get in."

The next day Robin took an early lunch, had a pint at the sports bar and was at the given address five minutes early. The very attractive receptionist asked him to wait and showed him into a small room off the main reception. Ten minutes later she came for him and showed him into an upstairs office.

The first thing he noticed was how untidy the office was, paper covered the entire surface of the huge desk. The room seemed to be empty but straight after he came in a middle-aged woman appeared from behind a thick curtain. She offered her hand and introduced herself.

"They say I have to go outside for a smoke but I get away with opening the big window. I smoke, drink and speak my mind Rob. If my knickers go up the crack of my arse you'll see me pulling at them. I might be vulgar and swear a lot but believe me I'll fight like fuck to get you off."

"I assume you've read up on the details Gina. Do you think I'm guilty or innocent?"

"What I think doesn't matter, for the record I think you're guilty of being a fucking idiot. Trying to con someone into that sort of investment by screwing them isn't the mark of a genius is it?"

"Can you get me off the charges?"

"I'll try but to be honest, Rob, I doubt it. I spoke to the evil bitch that's prosecuting you yesterday, one piece of news; they're dropping the two sexual assaults."

"That's good news, Gina. Clive Weatherly did some good then."

"Did he bollocks, they'd always have dropped those, it gives the jury an option you see. They wouldn't want that."

"I'm not with you."

"Let me try and explain. Say you disliked someone, you went and got a machete and hacked him to death in front of witnesses. What are you guilty of?"

"Murder I assume."

"Correct. Now say you just hit him hard, he fell over, hit his head and died, what are you guilty of now?"

"Maybe manslaughter?"

"Exactly, you've got the same outcome. A guy you detest is dead but you're looking at ten years instead of life. Now say you got charged with murder for the time you hit him. The jury would find you not guilty of murder but guilty of manslaughter, are you with me?"

"I think so."

"So with your case they haven't got that option. You can't say you had sex with her by accident. But the jury might think rape is a bit strong, so they could clear you on the rape charges but find you guilty of sexual assault. You'd get six months tops; they'd see you'd been punished but not too much. By taking the lesser charges off the agenda she's taken that option away from them. They'll probably have to find you guilty of rape. She'll spin Katherine Reynolds some bullshit no doubt."

"You don't sound confident you can get me off, Gina."

"The case came to chambers through the legal-aid folk, Rob. As soon as I saw that evil bitch was in charge of prosecuting you, I asked for the case. I'll fight like fuck for you and that's a promise."

"Have you got a history with her, Gina?"

"She hardly gets to court now, she's doing this to make a name for herself. It'll set a hell of a precedent if you get done for it. Tell me one straight guy who hasn't lied to get in a girl's pants and I'll say he's a fucking saint."

"What do you mean by setting a precedent, Gina?"

"Just imagine if every time a guy lied to get a bit of nooky he got done for rape. They'd have to build a prison about the size of Scotland to put them all in."

Robin laughed for the first time in several weeks, he spent just over an hour in the office with Gina. She agreed with Melanie Watkinson that it would be pointless trying to get the telephone evidence ruled as inadmissible. She asked Robin to take her through the whole story right from when he'd seen the photograph of Katherine and recognised her.

After he'd told her the whole story, she excused herself and went behind the curtain for a cigarette, Robin found it a little unnerving because she was talking to him but he couldn't see her.

"Would you say your wife came up with the idea of the sting then, Rob?"

"Between us I'd say. I told her that Katherine may be worth as much as twenty million, I'm not really sure who came up with the idea of joining the agency, I think it may well have been Madelaine."

"That's something we might be able to use."

"I'd rather not, I don't see it'd do any good to start with and we'd surely have to call her as a witness. She left me and she's living with her mother."

"Keep it in mind."

Robin noticed that he'd been making notes while he was talking, she'd added to the pile of paperwork on her desk but he didn't see that they'd made any progress. She announced at three-thirty that she had another meeting and thanked Robin for coming.

"We've done good work today Rob," she said as she shook hands with him. "Keep believing you're innocent."

Robin went back to the office and let Sandra go early, after the meeting he felt a little more confident, at least Gina seemed to believe that while his actions had been foolish they hadn't constituted a major crime punishable by several years in prison. He believed that if she could make him feel that way then she had a better than even chance of talking some sense into a jury.

He went next door after his shower and explained the situation to his father, after their experience with Clive Weatherly and his associate they'd almost believed that a guilty plea was the best option, now Gina Anderson was taking his defence he thought he had a chance.

Gill Hopkins telephoned Katherine with the news that they'd decided to drop the sexual assault charges and just prosecute Robin on the two charges of rape.

"I'm surprised Ms. Hopkins," Katherine said, "My original complaint was six rapes, they knocked it down to two and the two assaults and now just two rapes; what next?"

"Imagine he'd beat you up badly and killed you Katherine. He'd hardly be charged with GBH and murder would he. We just take the most serious and go with that. Don't forget when the judge gives the sentence for each charge they're served concurrently, so if he was convicted of four charges he wouldn't serve any more time than for two. The whole case should be simpler this way."

"You're the expert Ms Hopkins, I'll bow to your knowledge. Have you any idea when the trial will be and where of course."

"Almost certainly Winchester Crown Court and probably late autumn, early November looks likely. Unless they have a long trial that collapses and a slot becomes vacant. We're scheduling five days for this case but it ought to be as short as three."

"I'm booking a holiday for late August."

"I'd advise against it but it's up to you if you want to take the risk. If you have to cancel your trip I doubt the insurance would be paid."

"I'll take that risk. Is there anything else I need to know?"

"Keep thinking about waiving your anonymity Katherine. You can do a lot of good here for a lot of women don't forget."

"I'll keep it in mind but at the moment the answer is still no I'm afraid."

Chapter Thirty-Seven

Nothing was done through August on the case, Robin signed in at the police station every Saturday and had the occasional conversation with Gina Anderson. Claire went off to University in early September and Madelaine told him that she wanted a divorce as soon as possible.

Katherine worked full-time at the shop for a week while Jennifer and her family went to the cottage for a well-earned holiday. Elaine and Becky both worked extra hours and the week went by with no major mishaps.

Liz and Katherine went on the cruise for the last two weeks in August. They flew to Rome, spent a day there and then were taken to the ship by coach. The cruise visited Croatia and Malta and finished up in Venice. They arrived home late on Saturday afternoon tired but full of happy memories. Jennifer had stocked the fridge with fresh food; Katherine insisted that her friend stayed for the weekend.

Daphne had been in every day and sorted out the mail, there was a letter from The CPS saying that the trial date had been fixed for the second week in October.

"I'm relieved, Liz, it'll be good to get it over with."

"Are you nervous? You'll have to face Rob across the court. Don't forget what happened the last time you saw him."

"I hardly need reminding, Liz. I'm at the acceptance stage now, there's nothing I can do about it. If he's cleared at least I'll have got my point across. No one fucks with me."

"You're swearing rather a lot these days, Kath."

"Drinking and smoking as well but I can soon stop. I'll put this year behind me, Liz. We're almost certainly getting planning permission for what we want on the factory site. Pete and Gav have signed the lease on the new site and are well on schedule with the plans for the new building and the trial will be over. Onwards and upwards now."

"I see the trial starts on the Monday, Kath. I'm booking a week off work so I can be there every day to support you."

"Only if you're comfortable with it, Liz. Doreen said that she'll come down for the week."

"Then you'll have two of us on your side, girl."

"I've got to write a victim's impact statement, if he gets convicted, I can read it out in court if I wish before the judge sentences him."

"Are you going to stand up in court and read it out? I'd be shitting myself."

"I'll write it anyway, if I decide I want to have the last word I can, if not I can just tear it up."

"Or keep it for the book. Who do you want to play you in the film?"

"I just want to fade into the background. Bad enough the Rottweiler wanting me to strike a blow for femininity."

They spent the evening sorting out the digital photographs they'd taken on the cruise. Kathrine had a photo printer at home so all they had to do was take the memory card out of the camera, slot it into the printer and choose which ones they wanted to print off. By the time they'd finished they'd used up two full ink cartridges.

Liz went back to her flat after lunch on Sunday. They went to church in the morning and walked back. As soon as her friend had left Katherine drove across to Jennifer's with their presents and the photographs they'd printed.

As soon as they saw her Jeep stop in the drive the twins rushed out to meet Katherine. She walked inside with one each side of her and an excitable dog following close behind.

"Hi, Mum, you look like you enjoyed yourself."

"I think cruising might be on the cards again one day Jen. Maybe fly to America and cruise The Caribbean. Here's your presents."

"Are you staying for tea Nanny? We missed you."

"If Mummy says it's all right, then I'd love to stay."

After they'd put the twins to bed Jennifer and Katherine joined Danny in the lounge.

"We've been given a date for the trial Jen. It's at Winchester Crown Court the second week in October. It starts on the Monday so I doubt I'll be at work for the week."

"It's good practise for when you retire, Mum. I'll get the troops organised for the week. We coped okay for the last two weeks so we should be all right."

"Of course you'll be all right," Katherine said. Then she realised Jennifer was being a little sarcastic. "How was Becky last week?"

"Amazing, she came in most mornings by six o'clock, I didn't ask her to. Elaine was here with me at four o'clock so it was fine. I still missed having my mum looking after me though."

Katherine suddenly blinked back a few tears. She found herself doing that occasionally, at first she'd put it down to the experience with Robin and the forthcoming trial but possibly it was the beginnings of the menopause or maybe that she was still missing Mark.

"Stay over, Mum," Jennifer suggested "We can go in to the shop together in the morning."

Robin came home from work on Monday to find an e-mail from his old friend Giovanni in Tuscany. He'd told him that there was no chance of him buying the vineyard now and advised him to put it on the open market. A consortium of Italian businessmen had bought it for just over a million and a half Euro. He went next door and told his father the news.

"No use worrying about it now, Rob, all in the past."

"I know that, Dad, it just makes me feel a bit spiteful. If they'd had a bit more faith in me Madelaine and I would be moving to Tuscany and making good money and all your buddies at the golf club would have made the best investment of their lives."

"Make sure that Gina woman knows, Rob. At least it'll look a bit better in court. They'll see that you weren't trying to scam her out of the money."

"Maybe it'll help but I doubt it Dad. I've resigned myself to getting sent down for a few years. Even Gina seems to think I'll be found guilty. I'm thinking about changing my plea to save Katherine having to testify."

Richard looked alarmed. "Don't even think about it, boy, a guilty plea will get you prison for fucking certain. Maybe you'll get a sympathetic judge. Gina Anderson seems to believe in you."

"She said I can change my plea if the case seems to be going badly but I reckon it'll be too late by then."

As the trial neared Katherine got more nervous, she thought about asking that the charges against Robin be dropped but was worried about suggesting it to Gill Hopkins. She hadn't heard from Tommy since the evening he'd eaten with her and Liz so she decided to message him and ask for some advice. He telephoned her in the evening.

"Hello, Katherine, nice to hear from you. I hope you're ready for a week on Monday."

"To be truthful Tommy I'm nervous as hell. I've been thinking about withdrawing the complaint, any comment or advice."

"I don't think you can now that The CPS have filed all the paperwork Katherine. Why the change of heart?"

"I don't want all the sordid details read out in court Tommy. Gill Hopkins has asked me several times to waive my rights of anonymity."

"Would you like me to pop in and see you tomorrow after work? I could be there by six o'clock."

"Are you allowed to? I didn't think you could consort with victims of crime."

"First I've heard of that, Katherine."

"Come round for a bite to eat then Tommy. I make a mean sweet and sour chicken."

"I'm looking forward to it already Katherine. I'll be there by six o'clock."

Tommy was as good as his word and arrived at just before six o'clock the following evening. He brought a bottle of low alcohol wine that he knew Katherine liked. As soon as he arrived, she put it in the fridge to cool down.

"It's nice to see you Katherine," he said, "You're looking well."

"Do you remember my friend Liz? We went on a cruise for two weeks. Italy, Malta and Croatia. I'll show you the photographs later. Have a coffee, food will be half an hour."

They sat in the kitchen with their coffees, normally Katherine would have suggested they sat in the family room but she thought Tommy might have the image of Robin laying on the floor with her kneeling over him in his mind. She proudly showed him the photos they'd taken on the cruise.

"It looks amazing, Katherine, I went to Italy several years ago."

"What do you do for your holiday now Tommy?"

"I bought an old house in Ireland a few years ago. I try and get there twice a year, the plan was to get it all up together for when I retire but it's far from that."

"In the North or the Republic?"

"The Republic but it's not that far from the border. I can make a run for it if the natives turn nasty."

"I don't think that'll happen, we do a lot of business with the Irish at the factory; they must be the friendliest people in the world. You're not of Irish descent, are you?"

"Not as far as I know, would you like to see some pictures of the house? I've got some in the car. I can have a smoke while I'm getting them."

"I smoke occasionally as well Tom, I'll walk down with you."

They sat at the table with a photograph album showing the house and village. Tommy had taken pictures of the house before he'd started working on it and charted the progress as he completed each job.

"It's beautiful, Tommy, how far is your nearest neighbour."

"A five-minute walk I suppose. They keep an eye on the place while I'm away."

Katherine served the food, she'd made the sweet and sour sauce from scratch added chicken fillets and left it in the oven for nearly three hours simmering. She served it with new potatoes and a salad.

"That's two perfect meals I've had this year Katherine. I ought to start cooking again. Too easy to put a pizza in the oven or microwave a ready meal I'm afraid."

"Tell me about it, Tommy. There's an elephant in the room as the saying goes. We're avoiding what I wanted to talk to you about."

"Just stand up in court and tell the truth. You've nothing to be ashamed of and it'll soon be over. I just hope his defence counsel doesn't have delusions of grandeur."

"There's no way of pulling out is there Tommy?"

"I suppose if you didn't show up at court there'd be a mistrial. Just get through it, Katherine, have you got someone going with you?"

"Liz is taking a week off work and my younger sister is coming down from Shropshire for the week. I didn't ask, will you have to give evidence?"

"I'll be first up for the prosecution I think, you'll be second and I think that'll be it for our side. Mind you that's twice as many as the defence has."

"Are you going to get in any bother for the stroke you pulled to get the phone off Rob?"

"The defence might try and make something of it. They wouldn't have a chance because everything I did officially is quite legal, the bullshit we gave him in the pub won't count."

Tommy stayed till ten, Katherine walked to his car, gave him a hug and said she was looking forward to seeing him at Winchester Crown Court in a little over a week.

Chapter Thirty-Eight

The second Monday in October was one of those gloomy autumn days. It was more a heavy mist than rain but they had to have the headlights and wipers going for the whole journey to Winchester. Doreen had arrived on Friday, she caught a coach to Southampton and Katherine collected her in the Jeep. Liz came on Sunday and stayed over so that they could leave together for the trip.

Gill Hopkins was waiting at the court to meet them, she showed Katherine into a small room to discuss the prosecution case. Liz and Doreen had time to go the cafeteria for fifteen minutes before taking their reserved seats in the public gallery.

"There's representatives from a women against rape group here Katherine. Have you thought about waiving your anonymity? You'll certainly get all the public sympathy."

"It's not about getting sympathy or revenge Ms Hopkins. It's about making him responsible for his actions. I'm not going to try and conduct a crusade for you. I have thought about waiving my right to privacy and I've decided that I want my anonymity upheld."

"That's your decision," Gill Hopkins replied; she looked a little disappointed at the answer. "Have you written your victims impact statement?"

"I haven't written it, I've made some notes, obviously a lot of what I'll say depends on how the case goes. He may be found not guilty of course."

"That's highly unlikely, Katherine. He may well change his plea; if his defence counsel has any sense, she'll advise him to. They've appointed Judge Tomlinson AKA the hanging judge. If a defendant pleads not guilty and is found guilty, he'll give him a longer stretch because he'll assume that he's been telling a pack of lies. Mostly the defence advises them to plead guilty."

"If he does change his plea, I won't have to give evidence then?"

"You'll still be invited to read your impact statement, it makes a big difference in the sentence."

"Will I be called today?"

"Almost certainly, Judge Tomlinson likes everything brief and concise so neither of us will spend long on our openings. Inspector Docherty is up first, and then you. It depends if she spends ages trying to put down everything he's done."

"Is what he did against the rules?"

"It may not have been totally according to PACE; that's the police and criminal evidence act. To be honest the more she digs into it the worse it'll look for her client. I'll have a little dig when I question him, that'll most likely put her nose out of joint. His first solicitor said he was going to apply to have the phone evidence ruled as inadmissible. Gina knows better than to even try that one."

"When you've both done with Inspector Docherty it'll be my turn then. How long will I be in the witness box do you think?"

"I won't be long with you Katherine. I'll take you quickly through the first meetings, we don't need to talk too much about the sex. It's enough for the jury to know that there were two instances and both times he spent the night with you. We'd better get into court, Judge Tomlinson will be there in a few minutes."

Robin was expecting to be remanded in custody for the duration of the trial but Gina managed to keep him on bail. He had to be tagged but at least he could stay at home. He was allowed to sit next to his counsel rather than in the dock as well which Gina had managed to persuade the court would be helpful. They had a brief meeting before going into the courtroom.

"The hanging judge, that's not giving me a lot of confidence, Gina."

"He's not too bad, I've been up before him before. I'll tell you this, Rob, and I mean it. Do not lie, he'll throw the fucking book at you."

"I'm not going to lie, Gina. Last time; would it be better to just plead guilty and let you try and make me look half-decent?"

"Forget it, Rob, you'll get five years if you're lucky."

"I'm worried about Katherine, you won't rip into her, will you?"

"The more I question her and Inspector Docherty, the worse it'll get for you. We'll try and get through their case without doing too much damage. Put out of your mind all the court cases you've read about or seen on telly. This is real and it's boring as fuck. You won't see me and Hopkins jumping up and yelling objection every few minutes. It'll all be very low key."

"Will you do me one small favour, Gina?"

"I'll do my best; depends what it is of course."

"If your knickers ride up the crack of your arse, will you please leave them there."

Before the judge arrived, everybody was in the correct place in court. The usher asked everyone to stand up and Judge Tomlinson strode confidently to the bench. After everyone had sat down Robin stood up and listened to the two charges against him. He was asked how he intended to plead and he answered clearly and confidently, "Not guilty."

Judge Tomlinson asked both the counsels for the prosecution and the defence to present an opening statement to explain the case for the jury. He warned them both that he liked the proceedings to be concise and that he disliked theatricals in his courtroom.

Gill Hopkins stood and faced the twelve members of the jury first. She gave a brief account of the facts, told the jury that she intended to prove Robins guilt beyond any doubt and that the proceedings should be dealt with quickly. Her speech took around ten minutes before she sat down with a confident smirk on her face. Robin was trying to look confident but was dreading that they'd already made their minds up.

If anything the speech that Gina Anderson gave made him feel worse. She said that her client wouldn't be denying the facts that made up the evidence that they were about to hear but would be disputing the interpretation that had been made of them. She sat down after spending even less time on the speech that the prosecution had taken.

Katherine watched as the prosecution called Tommy as their first witness. The first surprise of her day was when he confirmed his name as Alan Docherty. He took the oath, Gill Hopkins stood and addressed him. She invited him to take her through the complaint and investigation. She let him talk for nearly five minutes before she asked him any questions.

"Thank you for the clear account of your investigation, Inspector. Just a few questions to clarify some points. There seems to be rather a long gap between your initial interviews with Mrs Reynolds and the defendant."

"It was unusual that the alleged offences had taken place several weeks before the complaint was made, ma'am. I felt that if I'd approached the defendant for an initial interview, he would have had the chance to destroy vital evidence."

"The defendant obviously tried to cover his tracks Inspector. Would you like to explain to the court how you identified him as the chief suspect?"

Tommy thought for a moment before answering, "I'd rather not divulge the details at this time, ma'am. It involves police procedures, obviously I'd rather keep those confidential."

"I'll accept that for now, Inspector Docherty, but the defence may ask you the same question and insist on an answer. If so, the court may insist that you answer the question."

Gina whispered to Robin, "She knows full well we won't ask, she's just making sure that the jury knows you tried to cover your tracks."

"Inspector Docherty," Gill Hopkins continued, "After a police investigation you decided that the telephone used to message Mrs Reynolds would hold the key to the case. You'd already identified the defendant as the only suspect. Are you confident that the way you acquired the telephone to use as evidence was in accordance with the guidelines laid down by the police and criminal evidence act?"

"Yes, ma'am," Tommy replied confidently. "A colleague and myself had an informal chat with the defendant and the following day he handed the telephone in at the station nearest to his office."

"The defence may say the tactics that you used were unethical Inspector. Any comment?"

"Any informal interview is irrelevant, ma'am. Everything relevant was while the defendant was under caution."

"That's all I have to ask you for now Inspector, I may ask you a few more questions after my colleague has finished her cross-examination."

"It's only going to be a little damage limitation I'm afraid Rob," Gina said in a whisper. She stood up and addressed Tommy.

"Just a few questions, Inspector Docherty. How long have you been a detective?"

"I've been a policeman for thirty-five years, ma'am, and I've been in CID for more than twenty-five of them."

"Have you been subject to a lot of complaints or disciplinary proceedings?"

"Obviously a few complaints over the years, none upheld and no disciplinary charges, ma'am."

"During your informal chat to the defendant you commented that possibly it was a malicious complaint by Mrs Reynolds and that if it was you would have prosecuted her for misuse of police time. Was that a genuine threat?"

"Indeed it was. Both handsets were examined by technicians. They concurred that the telephone handed in by the defendant was the one used to send the messages."

"In all your years as a distinguished officer you must have dealt with hundreds of criminals Inspector. Murderers, rapists, burglars and muggers I assume."

"Yes, ma'am," Tommy said proudly. "I'd say I've dealt with hundreds of criminals over the years."

"No doubt most of them have come up with excuses, lies, and false alibis et cetera."

"Very few of them admit their crimes straight away, ma'am."

"Did the defendant lie to you at all Inspector? Try to hide evidence and cover up his crimes?"

"No, ma'am. As far as I'm aware every question that I asked was met with a truthful answer."

"Would you say Inspector that when you threatened to have Mrs Reynolds prosecuted if she'd wasted your time that he immediately agreed to give you the handset?"

"He agreed to co-operate immediately, ma'am."

"No more questions, Your Honour."

Gill Hopkins stood briefly. "I do not wish to re-direct, Your Honour."

The only other witness for the prosecution was Katherine, rather than split her testimony they decided to break for lunch. Katherine met Liz and Doreen and they walked to a small café round the corner for a coffee and snack.

"I'm scared," Katherine said to her sister and friend, "Gill Hopkins said she'd take it easy but Christ knows what his counsel will come up with."

"She took it easy on the policeman," Doreen said. "Is that the one you told me about, Kathy? I thought you said he was called Tommy."

"He said call me Tommy, it's probably a nickname, I don't know whether I'd prefer that or Alan."

"Interested then, Kathy?" Doreen asked.

"He's been kind to me," Katherine commented. "He didn't judge me at all. The lady that I saw when I originally complained wasn't interested in even listening to me."

"That's the first time I've seen Rob for real, Kath," Liz remarked. "He is one good-looking guy."

"I don't see a wife supporting him in court, Kathy."

"Forget it you two," Katherine said half-jokingly. "He's off-limits I'm afraid."

"I'm only saying that I can see why you wanted him, Kathy, he is gorgeous."

They'd finished the food and coffee so Katherine stood up, she paid the bill and they walked back to the court.

Liz and Doreen made their way to the public gallery, Katherine took advantage of a minute of solitude to smoke a cigarette and gather her thoughts. Seeing Robin had been a shock to her, she'd wondered how she'd feel and still wasn't sure. She knew that she should feel angry towards him but the memory of the times they'd spent together almost out-weighed her feelings. If anything she felt sadness that a man she'd thought would complete her life was in court with a likely prison sentence in his near future.

Gina Anderson knew that Gill Hopkins had done a little bit of damage to their case when she'd questioned the police inspector but nothing too serious. She was concerned that her adversary was more concerned with getting a guilty verdict than on protecting Katherine Reynolds. Robin had insisted that she take things easy on Katherine, he'd said as they broke for lunch that he was still willing to change his plea rather than see Katherine being bullied. She had a quick snack and drink before going outside for a cigarette.

Gill Hopkins was stood outside talking to one of the junior prosecutors that was working in another court. As soon as she was by herself she spoke to Gina.

"I'm amazed you didn't tell him to plead guilty, Gina, Clive Weatherly wouldn't touch it with a not guilty plea. Now you've got the hanging judge; when he's convicted, they'll throw away the fucking key."

"What did you tell Mrs Reynolds when you dropped the two assault charges?"

"Just the truth. The original complaint was six rapes, Gina."

"Why don't you just admit you're a fucking dyke, Gill? It's so obvious that you took this case because you hate men."

"Always nice to see you across a court, Gina, how many times have we batted heads over the years? And how many times have you come away with a result?"

"Only because you only pick the ones you think you can win, Gill. Maybe I'll get a result this time."

Before she'd even finished speaking, Gina stubbed out her cigarette and walked back indoors. She was fully aware that she'd never beaten Gill Hopkins across a court and she was fairly certain that this case would continue the losing streak.

After the ritual of rising for the entrance of Justice Tomlinson and sitting down again Katherine was called to the witness box. She confidently read the oath and waited for Gill Hopkins to start her examination. This time the tall and confident prosecutor came from behind the table and walked out into the courtroom. As soon as she smiled at her Katherine was reminded that Tommy had likened her to an attack dog.

She started quietly asking questions about Katherine's life before she'd joined the dating agency, about her marriage and about her hopes for the future. Katherine answered every question with confidence but was getting more nervous as the examination continued. Finally she questioned her about her meetings with Robin and how things developed.

"After you'd arrived at Burley for your first meeting, did he give you any idea that the messages he'd been sending weren't entirely truthful Mrs Reynolds?"

"No, Ms Hopkins, he didn't. We chatted for quite a long time. He bought me food and drinks, gave me flowers and seemed to be enjoying my company."

"Surely at that point if he was only interested in meeting you as an investor it would have been the ideal opportunity for him to be honest with you."

Katherine sat there not quite sure whether or not to say anything in response to the statement. Gill Hopkins had warned her that Gina Anderson would make statements sometimes rather than ask direct questions. She decided to sit there and wait for Gill Hopkins to ask her a question.

"After that meeting, did he tell you that he was travelling abroad and would like to see you again on his return to England?"

"We were e-mailing each other every day then, he asked if we could have a meal when he came back to England."

"If you'd known that in fact he'd never left England would you have agreed to see him again?"

"If I'd known that he'd lied to me at all I'd never have agreed to meet him."

"Your second meeting was a meal out, once again he had the opportunity to come clean then?"

"He brought me a gift that he'd allegedly bought while he was abroad. I didn't suspect that he hadn't been where he said he had."

The questioning continued with more or less the same questions and answers. When she arrived at the Saturday when they'd been to Wimborne Gill Hopkins' voice changed slightly.

"You'd had an enjoyable evening out, a meal followed by the theatre and then he took you home. Did you invite him in when he stopped the car at your house?"

"I assumed that he'd come in, I got out of the car and he followed me in."

"There's no real need for too many details Mrs Reynolds. You went into the room that you call the family room and sat on the settee. Who would you say made the first move so to speak?"

"I think that may well have been me Ms Hopkins."

"Did the defendant resist your approach?"

"He said that he didn't want to offend me. My reply was that he'd offend me if he didn't respond to my advances."

"Then you allowed him to perform a sex act on you."

"I did, Ms Hopkins."

"Did you reach a climax at that time?"

Katherine felt herself blush slightly before answering that she had.

"After that you led the defendant upstairs to your bedroom where you undressed and got into bed. Is that correct, Mrs Reynolds?"

"We went into the spare room, I didn't want to use the room that I'd shared with my husband."

"You once again indulged in oral sex before having intercourse with the defendant, is that correct?"

"Yes."

"And the defendant stayed the night?"

"Yes."

"In the morning you asked the defendant to tie you up tightly, you knelt on the floor and performed oral sex on him. Did he ejaculate in your mouth?"

Katherine was almost squirming in the chair, she said yes in almost a whisper.

"He left on the Sunday once again telling you that he had to travel overseas didn't he, Mrs Reynolds?"

"Yes, if I remember correctly, he said he hoped that he'd be back fairly soon. I told him that I was going to my cottage in Devon the following weekend and that I hoped he could meet me there."

"He arrived the following Saturday. What was his mood?"

"He seemed worried, he told me that he had business problems in Italy."

"Did he ask you for investment in his business?"

"He may have mentioned it."

"Once again you indulged in several sex acts, you gave each other oral sex and then had full sex; did he at any point tell you that he was in fact a married man with no intention of a permanent relationship with you?"

"No."

"He asked you if you wished to invest a million pounds in a project that weekend did he not?"

"I thought that he'd assumed that as I was selling the factory that I had enough funds. I explained that there was no way that I could raise that sort of money."

"Did he accept that?"

"He seemed to have done so."

"And that was the last time that you saw him?"

"We messaged each other the following week. That was the last time I actually saw him."

"In the messages that followed did he give you any idea of his intentions or marital status?"

"No, Ms Hopkins. The messages were more business-like. He once again asked me if I wished to invest in his business."

"So from the time that you read his profile from the dating agency to the last time that you saw him you were convinced that he was a divorced man, several years older than his true age who was looking for a long-term relationship?"

"Yes, Ms Hopkins; I was."

"Had you known that he was married would you have had a sexual relationship with him?"

As she answered Katherine looked across at Robin "Had I know he was married Ms Hopkins I wouldn't have considered even meeting him the first time in Burley."

Gill Hopkins looked triumphant "No more questions at the moment your honour. Thank you, Mrs Reynolds, I may ask you some more questions after the defence has cross-examined you."

Katherine took a drink of water and braced herself for the questions. Gina Anderson paused briefly before standing up and smiling. Robin had whispered to her as Gill Hopkins sat down to be gentle on Katherine. She knew anyway that the jury would already have sided with the victim.

"I'll try not to detain you too long or upset you too much, Mrs Reynolds," Gina Anderson said pleasantly. Katherine was actually dreading this part of the trial more than anything. She'd been warned by Gill Hopkins that Gina would give her a very hard time and try to make her lose her temper in the witness box.

"When the defendants photograph appeared on the agency website were you immediately attracted to him Mrs Reynolds?"

"Yes, ma'am; he's very handsome. I assumed that the information he'd posted was true and that he'd been divorced for a long time."

"He admits that he joined the agency with the specific intent of getting in touch with you. Of course he realises now how foolish it was. Had he contacted you in a normal way to offer you the chance of an investment in the vineyard would you have made an appointment for him to see you?"

"Very doubtful. Especially if he'd told me that the outlay was a million pounds. I'm afraid that I don't have access to that sort of money."

"Were you attracted to the defendant when you met him for the first time in Burley?"

"As you said; he's very handsome. So yes, ma'am; I was attracted to him. But the attraction was also because I thought that he was interested in me for a relationship and not an investment."

"Had he told you straight away that he was married would you have arranged to see him again?"

"No."

"That's what he assumed, Mrs Reynolds. He's an excellent salesman, part of selling anything is to build up trust between the salesman and the client. He knew that if he'd come clean that he'd have lost any chance of your investment."

Katherine sat there quietly, she thought that if anything the defence counsel was making Robin look worse.

"Can we move forward to the first time the defendant came to your house. You had an enjoyable evening out, the theatre and a meal out. When you arrived home, you didn't give him a lot of choice but to follow you in did you?"

"No. I leant over and kissed him and got out of the car. I assumed that he'd follow me indoors."

"You were dressed very seductively I believe. A short dress and very skimpy underwear. Do you normally dress like that?"

"Not usually. It's the first time that I've tried to seduce a man."

"You'd already made up your mind that you wanted to have sex with the defendant, had you Mrs Reynolds?"

"Yes."

"Did he instigate the sex, did he make advances to you?"

"I would say that I made the running."

"Can you recall any of the conversation?"

"There was very little conversation, ma'am. I remember him saying that he didn't want to offend me. I said that I'd be more offended if he didn't carry on with what he was doing."

"There's no real need for us to actually talk about the sex acts, Mrs Reynolds, Ms Hopkins seemed to make a meal of them. Just one reference to them, you asked the defendant to tie your hands tightly behind your back, was this something that you'd done before?"

Katherine tried to think of a suitable answer that wouldn't make her feel any worse than she already was, after a few seconds thought she replied that it was the first time she'd experimented with bondage.

"They say that anything like that requires a great deal of trust. Obviously, you had a great deal of trust in the defendant."

"I had no reason to distrust him at that time."

"When he asked you if you were interested in investing money, did you consider doing so?"

"If it had been a lot less then perhaps I would have. I didn't have the kind of funds that he was looking for."

"Had you sold the development land for several million pounds would you have gone into business with him and bought the vineyard?"

"That's a hypothetical question that I can't really answer. I'd probably have given it careful consideration."

"The vineyard in question went on the open market recently and was sold for one and a half million Euro. That would have made a considerable profit for you Mrs Reynolds."

"I'm sure it would have been a good investment. Rob was never accused of any fraud or attempted fraud."

"Let's go back a little if you don't mind Mrs Reynolds. The defendant will freely admit that he told some lies to gain your confidence. Did he ever promise you a long-term relationship or tell you that he loved you?"

"I assumed that he wanted a long-term relationship or he wouldn't have responded to my profile. I made it clear what I was looking for."

"He didn't tell you that he loved you or promise any long-term future. Did you feel that by seducing him that you could persuade him to fall in love with you and make it more permanent?"

"Yes; I would say that's a fair comment. But it was based on the information that I had at the time; that Rob was single."

"He'll admit under oath that he told those lies to gain an introduction. Most of them were a version of the truth. Do you think he told more lies during the relationship?"

"Certainly that he was travelling abroad, I assume he told me those lies when he was with his wife and family."

"Did those lies draw him closer to you?"

"No; I wanted to see more of him."

"Just a little more background if you'd bear with me Mrs Reynolds. An often-used defence strategy in a rape case is to raise the subject of the victim's sexual history, possibly even their promiscuity. I don't think that would be a wise course of action in this case would it?"

"Hopefully not," Katherine said, she felt more relaxed now.

"The defendant originally engaged a law firm to represent him. They did a background check on you Mrs Reynolds. Quite a life you've led. Do you mind if I reveal the highlights to the court?"

"Not at all, ma'am. I've nothing to be ashamed of."

"Quite a privileged childhood, private school, you met and fell in love at nineteen to a boy with a similar background. Then you started the business which is a roaring success, married and had a daughter who is a successful business woman. Your factory flourished and now has a multi-million-pound turnover. How am I doing so far?"

"There's a lot missing, the days we worked fifteen or sixteen hours to keep the business going for example."

"On the deaths of both sets of parents you both inherited large sums of money and property. Some would say that you were fortunate."

"I inherited a great deal of money and property when my husband died. I don't think that makes me feel fortunate."

"You only ever had one relationship in your life before you met the defendant. Do you think that's unusual in this day and age?"

"It's usual for me. I can't speak for other people."

"You passed your driving test first time. I'm told that you ride a motor cycle. That's unusual for a middle-aged lady. You also passed a test to drive an articulated lorry I believe."

"I passed my motor cycle test because my husband wanted to buy a single-seat race bike. We took on our own deliveries at the factory for several years. I passed my lorry test so that I could take my share of the workload."

"Very impressive Mrs Reynolds. This year you've turned down an offer of five million pounds for your land. Most people would have been tempted to just sell it."

"I don't really need the money, it's important that we build houses for local people that they can afford."

"Think carefully, Mrs Reynolds. We're supposed to all be equal in the eyes of the law in the democracy that we live in. Do you honestly believe if you were a normal lady who worked in a shop, lived on a council estate and had been involved with several men that this case would have been followed up by the police and The CPS? Do you think that you'd have been visited at your home by a Detective Inspector and had the might of the legal system on your side?"

"I'd like to think that a person's lifestyle shouldn't affect the way they're treated, ma'am. So yes; I believe that the police and CPS would have followed up the case with due diligence."

"I'd like to think that as well, Mrs Reynolds, but somehow I doubt it. No more questions your honour."

Gill Hopkins stood straight away. "A short re-direct, Your Honour. Mrs Reynolds if you'd known the full truth about the defendant, would you have had a relationship with him?"

"No."

"Would you under any circumstances sleep with a married man?"

"No."

"No more questions, Your Honour. That completes the case for the prosecution."

Judge Tomlinson checked the time and decided that it was too late in the day for the defence to begin their case and called a halt to the proceedings for the day. Katherine gratefully met her sister and friend outside the court and they went for a coffee before the drive home.

"You did great, Kath. I'm so proud to be your friend. Most women would have been shitting themselves up there in the witness box but you came out looking like a saint."

"I was shitting myself, Liz, that lady that Rob got hold of to defend him certainly went easy on me. I thought she'd try to convince the jury that I raped him."

"From where I was sitting that wouldn't have been far from the truth, Kathy," Doreen added. "If anything, the one you call The Rottweiler was tougher on you."

"I'm starting to have some doubts, I wish I'd never reported it now. All I want to do is get on with my life."

"Don't think like that, Kath, he should be held responsible. It doesn't matter how sorry he is, he crossed the line. All he had to be was honest about things."

"His wife must have left, I suppose that elderly man was his father. He's eighty odd, hard for him to have a son in prison."

They set off for the drive home and got back a little after six o'clock. As they pulled up at Katherine's house, they saw Jennifer's car in the drive. Two children in onesies came rushing out as soon as Katherine got out of the car.

"We've been here since school Nanny," Jessica squealed. "Mummy's made your dinner. She let us use your bathroom."

The twins knew Liz but they were a little wary of Doreen, after she chatted with them they relaxed and told her some of the things they loved about their Nanny. Jennifer had come straight from the shop and prepared food for them all. Danny had collected the twins from school and brought them straight over to Katherine's.

"Dinner at seven, Mum, I took a slow cooker into work and knocked up a casserole. Have a shower first if you like."

"We're having a drink first Jen; where's Danny?"

"Taking Snowy for a walk, he'll be back soon, we didn't think you'd be home so early."

"There's only Rob to testify and the judge said it was too late to start tonight."

Katherine opened a bottle of red wine and the three weary ladies gratefully had a drink. They all showered quickly and put some comfortable clothes on. When they came downstairs Jennifer had the table laid ready for dinner.

"That was unbelievable Jen. How the hell do you get food to taste this good?" Liz commented after they'd eaten.

Jennifer took hold of Katherine's hand. "I had the best teacher, Liz."

"If this is how the other half live, I may well be moving in with my big sister," Doreen said. Katherine threw her a look that didn't need explaining.

"Wait till you have dessert, if you think that was good you'll love this."

Jennifer served them fresh fruit coated in dark chocolate with fresh cream. All of them wanted a second helping.

"Let me die now," Liz announced. "When I go home, I'm going to be eating beans on toast. That was amazing, Jen."

"Becky made it," Jennifer said. "All I had to do was serve it and whip the cream. That girl is going to be a superstar one day. She's sixteen and most days she gets there at six o'clock. Her mum doesn't seem to care about her which is sad."

Danny loaded the twins and dog into the car while Katherine related the events of the day to Jennifer. They waved them off at half past eight promising them a meal when they got back every night.

"Have a drink if you want, Kath. I'll drive up to court in the morning. You deserve it after today. All over with now, girl."

"If you're sure you don't mind, Liz. A gin and tonic will help."

Katherine made drinks for Doreen and herself and a coffee for Liz. None of them really wanted to talk about the day in court so Katherine put a disc on as background music and then showed her sister and friend the outline plans for the development on the factory site.

"We've the first public meeting next week Doreen. The hope is that we can put forty flats for sheltered housing where the factory is and around sixty flats and houses on the rest of it."

"I'd have taken the money, Kathy, five million pounds, think what you could have done with that."

"It's better this way, Doreen; it's worth much more than that anyway but I don't want fifty or sixty houses for Southampton overspill. Mark and I talked it over and this is what we came up with."

They were all in bed by eleven o'clock, Katherine had drunk two more glasses of gin and tonic which sent her almost straight to sleep. Apart from a trip to the toilet in the night she had a full eight hours sleep. Liz had the better day to drive to court, it was dry and fairly bright all the way. They had time for a coffee in the cafeteria before taking their places in the court.

Chapter Thirty-Nine

Robin and Gina had a short meeting before taking their places in the court.

"Firstly whatever I ask you give me a truthful answer, Hopkins will be watching you like a fucking hawk. If she spots anything you can guarantee she'll bring it up when she starts on you."

"I'm not trying to lie my way out of anything, Gina, don't worry about that."

"They kind of won yesterday Rob, we knew that but today we've got to try and repair the damage. You don't want to appear too sad and down-hearted but neither do you want to be fucking arrogant. Sell yourself as a nice guy who's just mis-judged a situation."

They made their way to the court just after Katherine and Gill Hopkins had sat down. Robin tried not to look directly at Katherine but at one point their eyes met, he was pleased to see the beginnings of a smile on her face.

"The press is here in force today Rob," Gina whispered. "They've even got an artist so the telly news will be reporting it later. You're going to be a celebrity by tonight."

"Maybe I'll get a part in the prison panto for Christmas Gina," Robin commented.

They went through the ritual of the usher announcing the judge and inviting them to sit down after he'd taken his place on the bench. He invited Gina Anderson to present the case for the defence. Robin was called to the witness box and swore the oath. Gina stayed at her table at first.

"Mr Jones," she began. "You've been charged with two counts of rape which is obviously a very serious crime. Although you've entered a plea of not guilty the prosecution evidence says quite the opposite. You don't deny that you told several lies in your approach to Mrs Reynolds, do you?"

"I can't deny it, ma'am," Robin replied. Gina was pleased to hear him answer in a clear and confident voice. "Most of the lies were ones of omission but I put my age down stating than I was older than I actually am."

"Most people that lie about their age knock a few years off," Gina commented. "Why add some on?"

"I recognised the photograph of Mrs Reynolds, a friend of mine was a member of the agency. He'd applied for Mrs Reynolds' details and not been sent them. I tried to reason out what sort of a person she wanted to meet so that I'd be sent her full profile."

"Do you think that's an ethical thing to do? For a salesman to get to know a potential client that way."

"No, ma'am; I wouldn't say it's ethical. I've known salesmen that would do similar to get an introduction. All I can say is that it seemed like a good idea at the time."

"Didn't you discuss it with anybody, surely you're not too self-centred to take advice?"

"I discussed it with my wife. She seemed to agree that it was the only way to get in contact with Mrs Reynolds and put the proposal to her."

"I'm surprised that your wife was in on the scheme."

"I'm not trying to pass the blame, ma'am."

"You had ample opportunity to tell Mrs Reynolds the truth yet you continued the charade, even when you met her. Did you tell her any additional lies after you'd met?"

"Only that I was travelling abroad to pursue my wine buying business."

"You actually have a wine buying business registered to you, don't you?"

"In name only, ma'am. I'm having difficulty raising finance at the moment."

"Due to your former circumstances of being made bankrupt. You ran a successful company for many years I believe?"

"It was extremely successful, had the banks not lost confidence I believe it would still be thriving."

"You made contact with Mrs Reynolds with the sole aim of raising the investment then?"

"Yes, ma'am."

"You wrongly assumed that she had a worth of several million pounds."

"Most people in her position would have sold the business and the land. Mrs Reynolds is a better person than that. She wants to use her inheritance to build a future for other people."

"Do you admire her for that?"

"Very much so. Had I known the circumstances I'd never have made contact with her."

"You met three times before Mrs Reynolds agreed that you could collect her from her house. Surely you had ample opportunity to tell her the truth?"

"By then, ma'am, I was confident that she trusted me. If I'd admitted lying to her any chance of me getting an investment would have gone."

"You had a meal in Wimborne, an enjoyable evening at the theatre and took Mrs Reynolds home. Did she invite you in?"

"She leant over to my side of the car and kissed me. Then she got out and went indoors."

"And you followed her in?"

"Yes, ma'am."

"Did you instigate any sexual activity?"

"I didn't resist her advances, I wouldn't say I instigated anything."

"Did you make any promises to Mrs Reynolds or tell her that you loved her?"

"No, ma'am."

"So as far as Mrs Reynolds knew you were just a man that she'd met briefly three times. She obviously wanted the relationship to move to the next stage?"

Robin stayed silent, Gina pushed him for a response. "I assume so, ma'am. It's really not for me to say."

"We don't need to cause Mrs Reynolds any more embarrassment by discussing the sexual activity. You arranged to meet her the following weekend at her holiday cottage in Devon."

"Yes, ma'am. I'd decided that I'd continue trying to get the investment to buy the vineyard."

"Once again; did you tell her any more lies or promise her a long-term relationship?"

"No, ma'am."

"I realise that it's not relevant to the complaint but you were convinced that this was a sound investment, were you?"

"Absolutely. The vineyard went on the market when I told the owner that I couldn't raise the investment. It sold for one and a half million Euro."

"So it would have been a sound investment?"

"In my opinion it would have been even better as a long-term investment. Had anyone invested the capital I knew that a ten per cent return would have been achievable."

"You put the proposal to Mrs Reynolds and she told you that she didn't have the assets. Did you tell her any more lies to try and persuade her to invest?"

"I was disappointed, I'd told her that I was trying to raise funds, she offered me up to thirty thousand pounds straight away."

"So you could have taken that money?"

"It would have been a fraud had I taken that. I may have used the wrong tactics but I wasn't trying to cheat Mrs Reynolds."

"Once you knew that your crude attempt had failed you stopped messaging Mrs Reynolds I believe?"

"I thought it best. I know several people that have started a relationship through the internet. I thought it the best way to call a halt to things."

"How many women have you had a sexual relationship with?"

"Four, ma'am. I was engaged but we broke up, then both my wives and then Mrs Reynolds."

"I think that's about all Mr Jones. Just to recap; you only lied to Mrs Reynolds with the aim of getting an investment for a legitimate business opportunity and not with the intention of getting into a sexual relationship."

"Correct, ma'am."

"No further questions at this point Your Honour. I may come back to you after my colleague has asked you some questions Mr Jones."

Judge Tomlinson decided that lunch could be taken a little early and Gill Hopkins would cross-examine Robin straight after the break.

Gill Hopkins leant in closer to Katherine before they left the court for lunch. "My cross may be a record short one Katherine. She's pretty much conceded that he's guilty and she's trying to limit the damage. I only need to ask him about three questions. If Justice Tomlinson sends the jury out early enough, we may get done tonight. Have you done your impact speech?"

"It's not written down but I know exactly what I'm going to say Ms Hopkins."

Katherine and her sisters went to the same cafeteria and sat at the same table.

"I don't think much of his defence lawyer," Liz said, "I reckon she made him look worse if anything."

"I think I can see where she's going," Katherine said "He can't really dispute any of the facts and if he tries to then he's obviously lying and they'll all know. So she puts him on the stand to tell it exactly how it happened."

"Not much of a defence," Doreen commented. "He might as well have pleaded guilty."

"She's doing her best for him," Katherine continued. "I bet when she does her closing speech, she'll have the jury eating out of her hand. If anything The Rottweiler made me look worse than she did."

After lunch Robin took his place in the witness box, was reminded that he was still under oath and Gill Hopkins stood.

"I won't take up too much of the courts time Mr Jones. You admit that your application to join the dating agency contained some lies and was full of glaring omissions. In fact the whole thing was a pack of lies designed just to attract Mrs Reynolds."

"I've already admitted that, ma'am," Robin said confidently.

"You had ample opportunity to admit to Mrs Reynolds that you'd told a pack of lies but you continued to pretend that you wanted a relationship with her, is that an accurate description?"

"It may be splitting hairs, ma'am, but I didn't actually ever tell her that I wanted a long-term relationship."

"Mrs Reynolds would have assumed that you wanted a relationship surely, otherwise why join the agency."

Robin felt that a question hadn't been asked so he sat there quietly and waited for Gill Hopkins to continue.

"On the night you went to the theatre and went back to the house you had ample opportunity to explain the situation. Yet you claim Mrs Reynolds seduced you almost as soon as you followed her in?"

"I didn't claim that, ma'am. Mrs Reynolds admitted it during her testimony."

Gina Anderson covered her mouth so no one could see her smile at Robin's confident answer.

Gill Hopkins continued unabated. "You went to her cottage the following weekend knowing that another sexual encounter was likely didn't you Mr Jones?"

"I went there with the intention of offering Mrs Reynolds a chance of an investment, ma'am."

"Yet you still didn't tell her that you were a married man."

Robin sat there in silence, Gill Hopkins put the statement again in the form of a question.

"No, ma'am."

"Even after you knew that there was no chance of Mrs Reynolds investing you still let her believe that you wanted a relationship didn't you Mr Jones?"

"I thought it better to perhaps let her down gently, ma'am. Had she thought I was having business difficulties then maybe she'd have just thought that I'd decided against pursuing a relationship?"

"Why didn't you save us all the trouble of a trial Mr Jones? You've admitted that you told a pack of lies to get close to Mrs Reynold and you've admitted the two sexual encounters with her."

For the first time in the proceedings Gina Anderson stood and objected to the question of why Robin had entered a plea of not guilty. Judge Tomlinson agreed that he didn't need to answer the question. Gill Hopkins announced that she had no further questions. Gina Anderson didn't want to re-direct so she closed the case for the defence. Judge Tomkinson ordered a twenty-minute recess before the closing speeches.

Katherine took the opportunity to step outside for a cigarette, when she went back Gill Hopkins was shuffling her papers in preparation for addressing the jury. After Judge Tomlinson had taken his place on the bench she stood and began her short speech.

"Ladies and gentlemen of the jury," she began. "This may be the shortest deliberation in this jury room in the history of the court. The defendant has entered a plea of not guilty yet he stood in the witness box and admitted that he told a pack of lies to gain access to Mrs Reynolds. In The CPS office there's very often something known as 'Gallows Humour'; it's common in hospitals and police stations as well because it helps lessen the stress of emotional situations. Several years ago, I prosecuted a young man for raping a woman in her seventies. You can imagine the comedy that accompanied that. I was asked if the victim had stood bail for the young man, was he pleading insanity, the victim should have been grateful etcetera. I suppose in this case there's a few similarities, Mrs Reynolds had nursed her husband for several years before his sad death, obviously she hadn't had a sexual relationship during that time or since his death, should she have just been grateful that the defendant showed an interest in having sex with her? Then of course there's the instances of younger women going out wearing skimpy clothes and getting drunk. You'll hear the comment that they were 'Asking for it', well, Mrs Reynolds wore very skimpy clothes and had a few drinks during the evening. She admitted seducing the defendant, did she deserve it? Of course she didn't, she deserves the protection of the law. As I said at the beginning, the case is cut and dried because the defendant has admitted what he did. Their main defence seems to be that he actually only lied to get close to Mrs Reynolds and not to have sex with her. That's about as ridiculous as when the railways spent fortunes on engineering works and yet still cancelled the trains when we had a bit of snow. They claimed it was 'The wrong kind of snow'. The defence is that Mr Jones told 'The wrong kind of lies'. You'll have to make your own minds up on that excuse. Thank you for your time."

Gina Anderson leant in close to Robin. "This is why they pay me the big bucks, Rob, watch this and learn. And don't worry about me adjusting my knickers, I put a thong on so they're already up there."

Robin managed to keep a straight face, Gina stood up and addressed the jury.

She looked across them before she started speaking, "Ladies and gents, I was raped when I was eighteen; believe it or not this cynical old lady was a goody-two-shoes before she went away to study law at university. I didn't smoke or drink and apart from a few sneaky kisses, I hadn't been near a boy. I actually didn't start smoking till I hit forty. There was one boy there that I really fancied, he asked me out but it only lasted for one date because he smoked all evening. His clothes smelled of smoke, when we kissed goodnight it made me feel quite ill. Then a few weeks later he asked me out again, he told me he'd stopped smoking so I agreed to go out with him. After a few dates, I snuck him into my room and we went to bed together. After a few fumbling minutes when I was wondering what all the fuss was about my boyfriend lit a cigarette and told me that he hadn't or wouldn't stop smoking. I was upset for a few weeks but got over it. According to what we've heard, I should have called the police, perhaps with all the historic cases at the moment I still can."

Gina paused to take a drink, it was a deliberate pause to let her story sink in.

"I suppose my current partner raped me three nights ago as well," she continued. "He wanted an early night but I had a lot of work and plenty to do round the house. He promised me that if we went to bed early and had sex that he'd do the work round the house in the morning. He didn't do it of course, maybe I should have called the police and reported him for rape."

Gina paused for effect again and carried on addressing the jury, "I dated a hospital doctor briefly many years ago, he told me that the cliché of the quickest way to a man's heart being through his stomach was wrong in two ways. Firstly, when they inserted small balloons into arteries round the heart, the entry point was near the groin. Secondly, if you asked any man if he'd rather his new girlfriend had sex with him or cooked him dinner, he'd pick the sex every time and grab a takeaway on his way home. So my doctor friend insisted that the quickest way to a man's heart was through his groin rather than his stomach. Mrs Reynolds knew this to be true, the defendant hadn't promised her a relationship or told her that he loved her, he hadn't led her on. She decided to sleep with him to encourage him to want to be in a long-term relationship. If the defendant is guilty of anything, it's a lack of judgement and being a man. I heard another story a few years ago, I think it's a myth but it certainly makes sense. That when a man gets up close and personal with a woman and gets an erection, the blood needed to form the erection comes directly from his brain. I don't actually believe that one by the way. If you find the defendant guilty, then I suspect most men over sixteen or so and plenty of women will feel that they've had a lucky escape from prosecution."

Gina went back to her table and poured herself a glass of water, she apologised to the jury and said that she had a sore throat.

"The prosecution counsel referred to some so-called 'gallows humour'. There's a very old joke that I'll remind you of. It's about a known prostitute that goes into a police station and reports a rape that happened two weeks previously. When the desk sergeant asks why she didn't report it at the time, she said that she was waiting to see if the cheque cleared.

Inspector Docherty said he hoped that any woman would have the full protection of the law but we know that's probably not true, don't we. If an ordinary woman who'd slept with several men during her life had reported this case, the CPS would have almost certainly refused to prosecute. Maybe after this case is over, I'll contact Ms Hopkins and ask her if she's willing to prosecute my first boyfriend. I doubt you'll be reading press reports of that case. They only took this case because they had a perfect victim. The original defence counsel did a brief background check on Mrs Reynolds. She's the type of person that we'd all want to be in an ideal world. She's very wealthy in her own right but is willing to use that wealth for the good of others. She's in the process of selling her family business but won't actually realise any funds for herself because of the factory having to re-locate. The development land is worth in excess of five million pounds yet she refuses to sell it and is developing it for the good of the locals. I'm in awe of this lady, she's a shining example to all of us. But she shouldn't get any better treatment from the law because of it. When I first met the defendant, I said I thought he was guilty; but not of rape. He's certainly guilty of being a normal red-blooded man with a very poor sense of judgement and he knows he crossed a line that he shouldn't have. But he's not guilty of rape.

Just two short things left to say and I'll be done. There's been several high-profile transsexuals in the news recently. Every time they tell their story they say they've known all their lives that they're in the wrong body and that they had to have the operation to correct the mistake. Yet earlier on in their lives they've married and had children. Usually when they admit things their marriage ends in divorce. I've not heard any of the ex-wives calling for rape charges because their former husbands didn't tell them about their situation. In fact if they did, they'd be accused of all sorts of discrimination, quite rightly in my opinion. Yet the circumstances are very similar.

"My last point is something that the defendant hasn't told me but I think it may have a bearing on things. He's not some sort of love them and leave them man, he's only slept with four women including Mrs Reynolds. The other three were wives and fiancées. It's probable that although he didn't tell her so that he'd developed a strong attraction to her. I think I speak for every person in this court when I say this; I think we've all developed feelings for her, she's an exceptional woman, she's doing everything in her power to use her wealth and status to enhance other people's lives and she should be applauded for doing so. The defendant treated her badly, he admits to doing so and is ashamed of himself, yet none of us in court have heard her say a bad thing about him. As I said she's an exceptional woman.

"Thank you for your time ladies and gentlemen."

Robin didn't like to say anything when Gina sat down, the gratitude showed in his expression. Judge Tomlinson seemed to think briefly before speaking.

"This is a high-profile case that will surely be reported nationally. I don't want the jury to retire tonight because I doubt that they'd be able to reach a verdict. If their deliberations had to go into a second day, I'd have to send them to a hotel for the night. So I'll sum up first thing in the morning and they can have all day to deliberate."

The court usher ordered everyone to stand while Judge Tomlinson left the bench.

"That was amazing, Gina," Robin said, "You almost had me believing I was innocent."

"Damage limitation, Rob," Gina replied. "I told you I was good, I don't think it was good enough, Hopkins cherry-picks the top cases these days and she won't pick one that she's likely to lose. I can only do so much."

Robin met his father outside the court and they walked back to the car together. Very little was said until they got out of the city centre and started heading home.

"She did one amazing speech for you Rob. Fucking Clive Weatherly couldn't have come up with half of that."

"She still thinks I'll be found guilty, Dad, I agree with you; that was one hell of a speech."

"If I was on the jury, I don't really know which way I'd go."

"You did jury service, Dad, what's the procedure after they've retired?"

"Don't forget Judge Tomlinson has to sum-up first. He seems all right, I'd put a bet on that he's an ex-military man Rob. He's got to be neutral when he speaks so it won't damage you anymore. Then they'll go to the jury room and elect a foreman first. I expect it'll be the bald guy with glasses sitting in the front row. He looks the type who'd put himself forward. They'll go round the table to see how the vote is, maybe they'll have a unanimous decision straight away but I very much doubt it."

"If they find me guilty, I'll get at least three years Dad. I'm so sorry, I've let you down."

"Too late to worry about that now, Rob, you'll only do half of it, they'll give you full parole if you keep your nose clean and knuckle down."

"I wish they'd pushed that policeman to tell them how they traced me, Dad. This'll sound a bit weird but I'm almost relieved it's nearly over. I was feeling bad about the way I'd treated Katherine but by the look of things she's not holding grudges."

"She's a fine woman, Rob, if the jury find you guilty, she'll be able to read out a victim's impact speech, that'll be interesting to hear."

Katherine, Doreen and Liz were home by just after five o'clock. The twins were playing on the lawn with Danny and Snowy when they saw Liz drive her car in and park. They ran across and opened the door for Katherine.

"Nanny," Joshua yelled. "We've been helping Mummy with dinner."

"You've got chips, Nanny," Jessica added. "Mummy let us peel the potatoes."

They went indoors, Jennifer made a pot of tea and they sat in the kitchen trying to wind down. Jennifer sent the twins back outside while Katherine told her the events of the day.

The twins had eaten earlier with Jennifer and Danny so it was just the three of them at the table. They all showered and changed while Jennifer finished cooking and served the food.

"How can chips taste like this Jen?" Liz asked jealously. "Mine come out greasy and stuck together. I buy oven chips now."

Jennifer tapped the side of her nose and smiled. "You'll have to ask Mum, she showed me how to do them."

Danny drove them home at seven o'clock, Katherine, Liz and Doreen sat chatting in the lounge.

"Have you written an impact statement Kath?" Doreen asked.

"I don't need to write it down, if he's found guilty, I know exactly what I'll say."

"They'll have to find him guilty, Kathy," Doreen commented. "He as good as admitted it."

"The funny thing is I don't mind if they clear him," Katherine told her sister and her friend. "He's been held accountable for his actions, that's what I wanted."

Doreen made drinks for them, Liz only had one because she was driving them to court again. They didn't want to watch anything too heavy on television so they found a documentary on The Travel Channel to watch. Liz and Doreen had been getting on really well and the thought was that they could all go on a holiday together the following year.

Katherine didn't want to drink too much, she was tired and emotional after the day in court so she was in bed soon after ten o'clock. She hadn't been exactly truthful when she'd told them that she knew what she'd say to the court. She'd been going through it in her head for days but couldn't seem to find the right words. Maybe the jury would see things from the viewpoint of Gina Anderson and find him not guilty.

Robin decided that he wanted to drink a lot, it was probably the last drink that he'd get for the foreseeable future. Gina had tried her best, she'd surprised him with the passion she'd used in her speech. His father seemed to believe that he'd be free in as little as eighteen months but Robin was looking on the gloomy side of things. He believed that if the jury found him guilty and Katherine gave a negative side of things in her impact speech that he could be facing a five year sentence.

After he'd showered, he went round to his father's house for the evening. They chatted about almost anything except the trial. Richard opened a new bottle of expensive malt whisky for the evening. They got the chess set out straight away, Robin commented that they'd better get the game finished that evening.

They actually finished two games, Richard was a high standard club player and Robin wasn't concentrating. By eleven o'clock both of them were slightly tipsy, Robin called a stop to the drinking and said that he should go home.

"If I'm not at court on time, Dad, they'll have an arrest warrant out for me. That won't look good when he hands down the fucking prison sentence."

When they got to the back-door Richard opened his arms and hugged his son. Robin thought that he saw a tear run down his father's face but didn't say anything. As he walked back to his house, he tried to remember the last time his father had hugged him.

Chapter Forty

They had a dry day again for the drive to Winchester. Doreen and Liz took their seats in the public gallery, Katherine took the opportunity to smoke a cigarette before making her way in. Gill Hopkins looked confident and told Katherine that the jury should reach a guilty verdict by lunchtime at the latest.

"Judge Tomlinson won't hang about with his summing-up, Katherine. He likes things short and concise. They'll be in the jury room inside fifteen minutes."

When the usher announced that Judge Tomlinson was entering the court, they all stood until they were instructed to sit down. He began summing-up straight away and was finished fourteen minutes later.

He quickly went through the basics of the case and instructed the jury to stick to the facts and try to keep their emotions in check. He instructed them on jury procedures and asked them to retire and elect a foreman. Even Gill Hopkins and Gina Anderson were surprised at the speed of his speech.

The jury went out to their room to begin the procedure and the court emptied slowly.

"What do we do now?" Katherine asked Gill Hopkins.

"We wait Katherine. Somehow, I don't think they'll be very long. I wouldn't leave the building if I were you. Go to the cafeteria if you wish but keep yourself available."

Katherine, Liz and Doreen went to the cafeteria for a coffee, none of them were hungry so they sat there chatting about their holiday plans. Katherine was dreading the recall to the courtroom, Gill Hopkins had once again pressed her on her impact statement. Katherine knew what she had to say but was terrified of saying it.

The jurors sat round the table in no particular order, there were notepads and pens at each place and several trays with jugs of water and glasses. Their first task was to elect a foreman, as Richard had suggested the bald gentleman put himself forward. No one else seemed to take the initiative so he was unanimously elected as foreman. He moved to the head of the table replacing a man in his thirties who looked bored with the whole affair.

"My name's Perry," he announced. "I think we need to go clockwise round the table, each one of you can say guilty or not guilty and give a very brief reason. I'll be juror number twelve so the gentleman on my right will be juror one and the first to speak."

"My name's James and my verdict is guilty. He lied to her, she'd never have even met him if she'd known the truth."

Juror number two spoke, "My name's Allison and at the moment I'm undecided. I feel we need to discuss it before I decide."

"My name's Peter and my decision is a firm not guilty. I can't believe that any amount of discussion will make me change my mind."

Juror number four was a lady in her seventies. "Sadly I'll have to say he's guilty," she began. "The judge said stick to the facts and the facts point to his guilt. I'm Ruth by the way."

Juror number five told them that his name was Simon and at the moment he was leaning towards a guilty verdict but was still undecided.

"I'm Lorraine," juror number six announced. "The judge said stick to facts. He's admitted he told her a pack of lies which led to the sex. He's guilty, no question."

Juror number seven was a Polish man who'd settled in England several years before. "My name's Kamil," he told them. "I find myself feeling sympathy for the defendant but I have to say guilty I'm afraid."

"I'm Patrick," number eight said in a soft voice. "I'm undecided at the moment. I feel we need to discuss things a lot further before I decide."

Juror number nine was a tall attractive woman in her forties. "Leona; my decision at the moment is not guilty but it's not set in stone. The victim should have known better than to trust a man she knew so little about."

"Shane; and I believe him to be guilty," number ten said. "Stick to the facts, he lied to get the introduction."

Number eleven was a girl who looked about thirteen but was probably in her early twenties. "I'm Tiffany," she said in a quiet voice. "I suppose we have to find him guilty because of what he did but I wish it was something less than rape charges."

They looked expectantly at Perry for his verdict. "My decision is guilty as well I'm afraid. I agree with Tiffany, it's a shame that we can't find him guilty of a lesser charge. The count at the moment is seven guilty, three undecided and two not guilty. Peter at seat number three seems to have settled on a not guilty vote. Leona is undecided but leaning towards not guilty at the moment."

Katherine, Liz and Doreen were waiting in the cafeteria, they seemed to think that the jury would return quickly with a verdict but after an hour they were still sat there. After the second coffee Katherine went outside for a cigarette. Gill Hopkins must have seen her go outside, she followed her out and stood beside her.

"They'll be back soon, Katherine, they've no alternative but to find for us. You heard what his honour said, he told them to stick to the facts and the fact is he's guilty as charged. Get your speech ready, you'll be on soon."

"I hope they clear him," Katherine said. She'd seen another side to Gill Hopkins, she thought that she was being used as a test case and that the prosecutor was using the case to further her career. "I thought his defence counsel gave an excellent closing speech yesterday. If I was a juror, I'd vote not guilty."

Katherine stubbed her cigarette out in the ashtray and went back inside. She'd brought a book with her but was finding it hard to concentrate. They carried on the conversation from the evening before about holiday plans but Katherine's heart wasn't really in it.

They'd left early to miss the traffic and find a parking spot so when there was no sign of the jury returning an early verdict they ordered a light lunch and tucked into their food. The cafeteria was buzzing with an assortment of lawyers, court officials and witnesses circulating. Katherine was having very mixed feelings about the whole thing and alternated her opinion on Robin. Her head was telling her that he was guilty as charged but deep down she knew that she'd recover quickly and Robin would have to live with the consequences for the rest of his life. The case had made the national news the evening before and the national newspapers were featuring the case prominently.

Robin had been relegated to the cells while the twelve jurors deliberated and decided where he would be spending his immediate future. Madelaine had telephoned the evening before wishing him good luck. After the short conversation he was almost in tears, he didn't blame Madelaine for the way things had turned out but she'd been the motivation behind the whole charade with Katherine.

Seeing Katherine again had upset him almost as much, he knew that he'd wronged her and he knew that there was nothing that he could do to repair the damage. At least both the lawyers had taken it easy on her, in fact he thought that the closing speech given by his own counsel summed her up.

One of the guards brought him a lunch on a tray at just after twelve o'clock, although he wasn't really hungry he managed to eat all of it and drink the bottle of water. After he'd finished eating, he decided to try and go to sleep for an hour. He laid on the small single bed and closed his eyes but sleep wouldn't come. All he could think about was what a mess he'd made of things.

He wasn't trying to put the blame on any one person in particular, he thought that the investors that had pulled out of the original syndicate could certainly be held responsible. If they'd shown faith in him, they'd all be making good money and he'd never have met Katherine.

Gina Anderson got him a trip out of the cell in the early afternoon, she'd told the guard in charge that she needed to consult her client; he escorted Robin up to the interview room and stood outside.

"I thought you could do with some distraction, Rob," Gina told him. "There's not too much we can do until they come in with their verdict. They must be having some sort of discussion anyway, that's a good sign."

"What if they can't agree, Gina? Will a majority verdict convict me?"

"A ten two usually does the job, a judge always wants a unanimous verdict because anything less tends to leave things hanging. If it comes back with a ten two majority, we can launch an appeal almost straight away."

"I'm not going to appeal, Gina, I've made my mind up on that. You said it yourself; I'm guilty. Thank you so much for what you said, when Weatherly said I should plead guilty I didn't know what to do for the best, you've given me some hope at least."

"Maybe if the hanging judge gives you a really long sentence, we can appeal that Rob."

"Maybe, Gina, perhaps I should have just pleaded guilty and let them get on with locking me up. We'll soon find out."

The jury deliberated long and hard, they had sandwiches and water brought in at twelve-thirty. The first time they took a vote they'd had seven definite guilty votes, the juror at number two was still undecided but number eight had decided that the correct vote was for a guilty verdict.

"I'm extremely unhappy with the decision," Patrick Delaney announced. "But as you've said the judge told us we must concentrate on the facts and they speak for themselves. If he'd been truthful, Mrs Reynolds wouldn't have let him get anywhere near her. I just wish we could convict him for something less serious. He's likely to get a long prison term for what amounts to a lack of judgement."

Juror number three was still adamant that Robin was not guilty. "If he's guilty of rape for telling lies, then most men and a good percentage of women are guilty of the crime," Peter Groves told his fellow jurors. "In fact the week before last I lied to a girl and the lie culminated in us having sex that night. I told her that I'd broken up with my current girlfriend when in fact we were just on a short break. I was back with my girlfriend two days later. If we find him guilty here, then I'm just as guilty as him. I don't feel that I deserve to go to prison for several years for a white lie."

After another hour and a half of deliberation juror number two who'd up to then been undecided made her mind up and said that she was now in favour of a guilty verdict. At that point the count was nine votes for a guilty verdict, two were not guilty and one was still undecided.

Shortly after that vote was taken the juror at seat number five who up until then was undecided came down in favour of a guilty verdict. "I'm not really happy about it," Simon McGovern told the other eleven. "But the facts aren't being disputed are they. He lied to her which led directly to the sex taking place. I wish we could convict him of something less serious but as there's only one option I'm afraid I'll have to come down on the side of a guilty verdict."

The count was now ten in favour of a guilty verdict and two not guilty. The foreman decided to keep the deliberations going for another hour before seeing if the judge would accept a ten two majority.

Katherine, her sister and her friend waited in the cafeteria, Gill Hopkins joined them for a coffee after lunch.

"I'm surprised, Katherine," she said. "I thought they'd be back with a unanimous verdict in about twenty minutes. I hope they reach a verdict today."

"I'm sure they'll take as much time as they need to make the correct decision, Ms Hopkins," Katherine replied.

"If he's guilty, what sort of sentence will he get?" Doreen asked.

"The worst rape cases can get twelve years," Gill Hopkins answered. "I doubt he'll get anything near that, if he did, they'd be appealing the sentence. I just hope they don't appeal the verdict. The press seem to be split in their opinion but most of them are on your side, Katherine."

At three-thirty juror number nine changed her mind. Her not guilty vote at the beginning had been based on emotion rather than fact she told the others. This gave the jury a count of eleven in favour of a guilty verdict and one for not guilty. Peter Groves, the number three juror wouldn't be swayed from his not guilty verdict so at four o'clock they petitioned the judge and asked if he would accept a majority verdict. He said that as they had an eleven one majority he would find it acceptable.

By four-fifteen everyone was back in court, after the formalities Perry Armstrong announced a guilty verdict on both counts. The judge thanked them for their time and dismissed them.

"I assume Mrs Reynolds wishes to address the court," he began. "I also need some time to consider the sentence. The court will re-convene at eleven o'clock tomorrow morning. Mrs Reynolds will be invited to speak and then I will be ready to pass sentence. As is the case under these circumstances the defendant will be held in custody overnight."

Katherine and the others went straight back to the car and drove home. As before Jennifer had arrived and had the food ready for them. Katherine told her that the jury had found Robin guilty on both counts.

"Where's Danny and the twins?" Doreen asked.

"They go for their trampoline lessons straight from school so Danny's taken them. He'll take them straight home and get their tea. I'll make a pot of tea, food will be half an hour or so. How long did he get then, Mum?"

"We've got to go back tomorrow, I have to give my impact speech and then the judge will sentence him. The jury seemed to take ages to make up their minds, The Rottweiler said it'd only take them a few minutes."

"Don't slip up and call her that in court, Mum. Have you written your speech?"

"I know exactly what I'm going to say, Jen."

Robin thought that he'd be carted off to prison and was terrified of spending his first night there. Gina asked for him to be brought to the interview room.

"Sorry about the verdict, Rob. I did my best for you."

"I know that and I thank you for it, Gina. What do you reckon he'll give me?"

"The jury took a lot longer than I thought they would so they must have had some doubts; maybe Judge Tomlinson has some as well. At least you haven't been caught lying in his court. I've had a word with the custody guy here, they're going to keep you here overnight; it's a bit less traumatic than Winchester nick."

"Thanks, Gina, I appreciate that."

"I had a chat with your father, he's very upset, Rob. He's coming at ten o'clock with some shaving gear and a clean shirt."

Chapter Forty-One

Katherine didn't drink any alcohol so that she was clear headed to make her speech. Liz and Doreen had both drunk several glasses of wine after dinner but at least they had a later start to get into court by just before eleven o'clock. Her first surprise was seeing Jennifer's car in the car park. She was waiting for them when they arrived at the front entrance of the court.

"I should have been here right through to support you, Mum, I'm sorry but at least I'm here today."

"Did you leave little Becky on her own?"

"Elaine is with her all day, I left as soon as I'd finished the baking and had a quick shower. It's getting busy, we'd better get in the public gallery."

Doreen, Liz and Jennifer hugged Katherine and made their way to the public gallery, Katherine took the opportunity to have a cigarette before she went in. Gill Hopkins was waiting for her, Gina Anderson was at her table and Robin was in the dock next to a very tall uniformed policeman. Katherine noticed that the jury box was empty but the rest of the room was packed. She recognised one of the men in the public gallery as one of the jurors.

After the usual rituals Katherine was invited to stand and give her victims impact speech.

"Thank you for giving me the time to speak Your Honour," she began. She was trying to come across as a confident woman but wasn't sure she was succeeding. "I'm not sure how much influence my speech will have on your decision but at least you'll know my feelings. I started writing this speech several weeks ago and all I have to show for it is a blank sheet of paper, so what I'm about to say will come straight from my heart."

She paused for a drink and then continued speaking, "I've often wondered how victims felt and what I'd do in their position. A year or two ago, I listened on the radio to a news story about a driver that had been convicted of causing death by dangerous driving, the judge gave him a three-year prison sentence. The family of the victims were interviewed on the radio and were quite stunned at how short the sentence was, one of them was insisting that for the death of his relative the errant driver should have been jailed for a minimum of ten years. I felt sadness as I listened to the story, sadness for the family that had lost a relative but also a little sadness for the culprit, it wasn't a deliberate act after all and a long sentence wouldn't have brought the victims back or done any good.

"When the jury foreman delivered the guilty verdict yesterday, I felt a similar sadness, in some ways I was hoping they'd find Mr Jones not guilty. It would have saved me having to stand here quaking at least. I've got the same feelings now Your Honour; that a long prison sentence will do no good to anyone, I was never out for some sort of revenge, I asked for this action to be brought so that Mr Jones would be made to face his responsibilities, I believe that the guilty verdict has vindicated my decision. As the defence counsel so eloquently said I may have been the perfect victim for The CPS to use. I've no doubt that if I were someone that had been involved with several different men over the years they wouldn't have considered prosecution. Mr Jones isn't some sort of monster, he's a very good salesman, he sold himself to me and I think that if I'd had the assets I'd have considered the vineyard. He's not some sort of con-man either; I offered him money and he didn't even consider accepting it.

"It was a foolish thing to do but from what I've heard Mr Jones cared a great deal about his family and he thought that buying the vineyard would be the best thing for all of them, I haven't seen a wife here to support him so I presume he now has family difficulties as well. He has an elderly father that I believe he lives next door to, a long prison sentence for Rob would be a huge punishment for him as well.

"I may have been partly at fault for pushing him into a sexual relationship too quickly, as Mrs Anderson said I wanted him to fall in love with me and perhaps I saw that as the quickest way to achieve it.

"If anyone thought that I was going to stand here and demand a long prison sentence for Rob they'll be disappointed I'm afraid, it would be of no use to anyone. Rob has been brought to justice and convicted by a jury, that's quite enough for me Your Honour. Thank you for the court's time."

The judge called for a fifteen-minute recess before he passed his sentence, Katherine had calmed down a little; she slipped out for another cigarette. Gina Anderson came out with her and lit up as well.

"That may be one of the bravest things I've heard Mrs Reynolds. I meant what I said the other day, you are one very remarkable woman."

"He'll still do some prison time won't he Mrs Anderson?"

"A lot less than he may have been facing thanks to you. Hopkins looked like she'd swallowed something nasty, I was watching her face as you were speaking."

"I call her The Rottweiler," Katherine said with a smile. "I think it was Inspector Docherty that suggested she looked like an attack dog."

Gina shook hands with Katherine again before they went inside and sat down. Gill Hopkins didn't acknowledge Katherine as she sat down next to her.

A few minutes later, Judge Tomlinson came back into the court, once everyone had settled down he looked directly at Katherine and smiled, as soon as he started speaking the room fell into total silence.

"I know my nickname is 'The Hanging Judge'," he began, "I don't like obviously guilty people pleading not guilty and telling a pack of lies. I don't think Mr Jones lied in this court, I also don't believe that this case should have come before a court. I only hope that the guilty verdict doesn't start a landslide of similar cases. Mr Jones crossed a line that he should never have even been close to. I said that the case shouldn't have been brought but I agree with the verdict, all the facts are obvious and can't be disputed.

"Before I pass sentence, I'd like to offer two short pieces of advice. Firstly, that the defence shouldn't mount an appeal against the verdict, it would involve hundreds of hours legal work and I firmly believe the appeal court would uphold the verdict.

"My second piece of advice is that the prosecution don't mount an appeal against the sentence I'm about to pass. I can't enforce either of those pearls of wisdom but I hope both of you heed my advice. And so to the sentence, largely due to the statement given so eloquently by Mrs Reynolds I'm going to pass the minimum realistic sentence that I can. That sentence is one of two years in prison."

Judge Tomlinson paused and poured himself a glass of water. One or two people thought that he'd finished speaking but as soon as he glared at them they sat down again.

"Two years in prison as everyone knows is seven hundred and thirty days, I'm ordering that seven hundred and twenty-eight days of that sentence be suspended for two years. I believe that the defendant has already served the necessary two days in custody. Do you understand the sentence, Mr Jones?"

Robin understood the sentence very well, he knew that it meant he was free to go home straight away. "Yes, Your Honour," he said, "I understand, thank you."

"Make absolutely sure that you do understand, Mr Jones, you'll still be serving the sentence; just not in one of Her Majesty's prisons. But break the law and the sentence will be activated. You've Mrs Reynolds to be grateful to, I'd settled on two years, it was her speech that persuaded me to suspend most of it. Your name will also be added to the sex offenders register for an indeterminate period. Learn your lesson, Mr Jones, do not break any laws please."

The judge tapped his gavel on the bench, everyone stood and he strode into the judge's chamber.

"I'm not guaranteeing there'll be no appeal, Katherine."

"If you appeal the sentence, Ms Hopkins, I'll gladly waive my rights of anonymity and go public with the fact that I'm extremely satisfied with the punishment. I'm sure you were right, I'll get the sympathy of the public."

Katherine walked round to meet the others as they came out of the public gallery.

"I'm so proud of you, Mum," Jennifer said. "You're the best."

"You're a good woman," Liz Powell said as she hugged Katherine. "That was some speech."

"Can we please get a drink somewhere," Doreen suggested. "I'm very proud of you too, Kathy."

As they left the court, Katherine saw Robin walk out with his father. He looked across at her and mouthed a silent 'Thank You' to her. She smiled at him and walked away with her family and best friend.

They only had one drink to celebrate the end of the court case. Liz proposed a toast to her best friend, the other two joined in and they all raised their glasses in tribute.

"Onwards and upwards now," Katherine said. "The first public meeting is next week for a discussion on the plans for the factory site. Next year will be very busy and very fulfilling."

"Don't forget to leave time for our holiday," Liz said. "Your sister and I are looking forward to that already."

"I'll still need you at the shop, Mum, when I go away with Danny and the twins."

Katherine smiled at the prospects.

Chapter Forty-Two

The following Friday a public meeting was held in the village hall to discuss the plans for the factory site. The housing society had a provisional plan for forty flats where the factory was and sixty-four flats and houses on the rest of the site.

Katherine helped Jennifer until nine o'clock and then went to the village hall. She wasn't expecting too many people to call in on the Friday but the representative from the housing society was spending all day answering questions and she felt she needed to be there with her.

The plans would be on display all day Friday and until three o'clock on Saturday. A steady trickle of people came in on Friday, as far as Katherine could tell virtually all of them were in favour of the development. One or two questioned the wisdom of building sheltered housing on a site with housing that was designed mostly for younger people.

That was a question that Katherine found easy to answer, had they used the entire site for low-cost housing there wouldn't be a mix of people, the way the development had been planned was to house at least forty people of sixty or older that were currently in larger homes. This would free up between thirty and forty properties to house families. The low-cost housing would mostly be privately owned, one- bedroom flats for starter homes up to three-bedroom houses for families. The housing society would consider renting the properties, shared ownership or selling the property with a subsidised mortgage. All the properties would be on a leasehold basis giving Katherine a small income from every property.

The property agent that had offered Katherine five million pounds for the site called in.

"Just a social visit, Mrs Reynolds," Jack Collier said, "I'm very jealous but I applaud you for doing this in the village."

Katherine had brought pastries from the shop and had a coffee machine to provide drinks for the visitors, she made him a coffee and sat with him for a few minutes.

After he'd left, she went back to the shop for some more cakes, she went into the kitchen with Jennifer for a coffee.

"How's it going, Mum?"

"A lot of them are just being nosey I think, some are worried that their houses might be worth less with flats and houses on the site, only one actual objection so far, that was from an old couple that were concerned about just that. I advised them to sell up and move away before we started."

"They'll love you if you get elected to the council at the next local elections."

"Do you mean when I get elected?"

"Sorry. At least you're used to public speaking now, Mum."

"Can I take some sandwiches as well please Jen? If you've a few spare packs. Just in case people come in on their lunch hour,"

"You're getting very good at changing the subject Mum. Who did the housing society send; a handsome guy?"

"No, Jen, a very attractive lady in her sixties."

"You haven't given up on meeting someone have you, Mum?"

"Not at all," Katherine smiled. "My way and in my own time Jen."

Katherine spent a few minutes chatting to Becky and asked her how she was getting on at college.

"I love it, Mrs Reynolds, and I love being here. I'm going to learn to do all the baking soon as well so I can relieve Jen now and again."

Jennifer helped Katherine carry the cakes and sandwiches to her car. She hugged her mother, Katherine felt a tear coming and wiped it away.

"This is so silly," she said out loud to herself on the way back to the village hall. "Fucking menopause."

The afternoon was almost a complete success, most people that came in were in favour of the plans and just wanted to see what was going to be built on the site. Katherine said goodbye to the lady from the housing society at five o'clock when the hall closed.

"Here's my mobile number, Katherine," Lesley Jarvis said. "If you need anything tomorrow just call me. I can't get here but I can answer questions over the phone."

Katherine was tired when she got in, dinner was a frozen pizza, they'd become quite regular since the court case. She was still having her meal out on a Wednesday evening at the club and if either she or Liz was feeling lonely they'd organise a meal and sleepover.

Liz had been seeing a man she'd met through the agency but didn't think it was likely to lead to anything permanent so Katherine faced a weekend on her own. She watched a little television and was in bed by ten o'clock.

She went to the hall at just before nine o'clock on Saturday morning. The caretaker opened up and left her alone. A few people drifted in and looked at the plans but no one really had any constructive comments or criticisms. Katherine was in the kitchenette making fresh coffee when a voice called through the door.

"Can I come and help at all, Katherine?"

She turned to the door and saw Linda Hislop, the Chief Inspector that Tommy had introduced her to in the summer.

"Hello, Lin, nice to see you. Did you came to look at the plans?"

"I work with the housing society sometimes Katherine. I like what you're planning here. Sometimes local authorities just build two- and three-bedroom houses on these developments, they don't realise that by putting a lot of families with small children in the same place they'll be creating a ghetto in fifteen years' time."

"I like what we've planned Lin. I may as well get this over with. You heard about the court case I assume, any opinions on the outcome?"

"I did get rather a snotty call from Gill Hopkins last week. I don't know what she was complaining about Katherine; she won."

"I don't know if anyone won Lin," Katherine said in a sad voice. "I felt vindicated at the court but it's maybe a bit of a hollow victory don't you think."

"Not at all, he wronged you and he faced the consequences. Apparently that speech you gave for your impact statement is the talk of the town round the legal system. You actually got the hanging judge to show some leniency. You are one amazing woman and I'm proud to have met you."

"Have you spoken to Tommy lately; or should I call him Alan?"

"I wouldn't, he's been Tommy ever since I've known him."

"Where did Tommy come from then?"

"There were two or three guys called Alan when he joined, there was a famous footballer called Tommy Docherty, so everyone called him Tommy and it stuck. He didn't lie to you by the way; he just said call me Tommy."

Katherine had never even thought that he'd lied to her, for a moment she didn't realise that Linda was pulling her leg.

"He adores you, Katherine, you must have realised that surely?"

"I really like him, Lin; do you think we've a chance?"

"He's a bit of an enigma is our Tommy. I don't think he's been in a relationship since his divorce. I know Billy Whizz thinks the world of him, he once told me he'd die for Tommy. He was a sort of father figure to him I think."

"He's due to retire soon, isn't he?"

"At the end of the year I think. If he calls you and asks you out would you accept?"

"Did he put you up to this?"

Linda smiled at Katherine. "What gave you that idea?"

"I'd love to spend some time with him Lin, I've got his mobile number; I'll get hold of him in the week and we'll sort something out. No promises, we'll take it very slowly and see how it goes."

The caretaker locked the hall at two o'clock, Katherine went home to find Jennifer, Danny and the twins had arrived.

"Mummy came swimming with us Nanny," Joshua yelled. "They're better swimmers than I am, Mum," Jennifer said.

"Any chance of having them for the night, we've been invited to a party?"

"I'm not sure," Katherine said with a frown. "Will they behave themselves?"

"We will, Nanny," Jessica said. "We brought our onesies with us and Mummy said you'll take us to church in the morning."

After a very hectic afternoon and bath-time Katherine finally sat down at nine o'clock with a gin and tonic. Inspector Morse was on the television but she'd lost interest in police drama. She put her disc of show music on and listened to it for an hour. Before she went to bed she went out to the garage and got one of the guide books. She spent an hour looking through guides to Ireland. Maybe next year after she'd retired a trip there with a retired policeman would be nice.
